100 OBJECTS of DR WHO

PHILIP BATES

CANDY JAR BOOKS · CARDIFF
2021

The right of Philip Bates to be identified as the Author of the Work has been asserted by him in accordance with the Copyright, Designs and Patents Act 1988.

An unofficial *Doctor Who* Publication

Doctor Who is © British Broadcasting Corporation, 1963, 2021

Editor: Shaun Russell
Editorial: Will Rees
Cover and illustrations by Martin Baines

ISBN: 978-1-913637-48-4

Printed and bound in the UK by
Severn, Bristol Road, Gloucester, GL2 5EU

Published by
Candy Jar Books
Mackintosh House
136 Newport Road, Cardiff, CF24 1DJ
www.candyjarbooks.co.uk

This book is dedicated to Mum and Dad, who are always the first to read everything I do. Their editing fees are eye-watering, however.

WELCOME TO THE SS SHAWCRAFT.

SPECIAL EVENT, THIS MILLENNIUM ONLY: THE MUSEUM OF *DOCTOR WHO*, THE SUCCESSFUL BBC FRANCHISE AND ITS TIME LORD PROTAGONIST/ANTAGONIST/ONCOMING STORM/JELLY BABY ENTHUSIAST (delete according to racial, religious, and individual beliefs).

BOOK TICKETS IN ADVANCE/AFTER EVENT (ACCORDING TO LOCALISED FOURTH DIMENSIONAL LIMITATIONS).

- Please declare cybernetic implants to members of staff.
- Surrender any sonic probes at security.
- Anyone found to be harbouring tributes to deities will face judgement on Varos and up to ten months watching repeats of *Don't Scare the Hare*.
- Anyone in possession of Vraxoin will be sentenced to life imprisonment at the Stormcage Facility.
- Please keep all Polyphase Avatrons on metaphysical leashes.
- Respect the personal access codes of your fellow visitors.
- Follow the arrows on the floor or risk being sucked into another dimension.

Our award-winning on-site café is open all day, every day (except bank holidays, during the transit of Venus, and whenever there's a full moon on the third Sunday of a month). Fish fingers and custard available at advanced request.

Here you are at last. The SS Shawcraft, hosting a collection about a Time Lord you want to know more about. Who is (s)he? Doctor *who*? Perhaps if we knew his name, we might have a clue to all this…

Time works differently here. Impossibly in orbit around a black hole, while this exhibition covers the history of *Doctor Who*, it does so in fluctuations; the fabric of space-time warps, melding eras together with unexpected results.

You enter the main hall and look up to witness this stunning astronomical event yourself through an exoglass roof. The black hole sucks in time, space, and your breath. You gasp for air as the sheer immensity of this extraordinary sight – fizzing with red, orange, yellow, blue, and puce – overwhelms your senses.

Members of staff wander the hall, advising visitors not to stare for too long, lest they go mad. It's the same advice they give to anyone watching *The Tsuranga Conundrum*.

You know the basics, of course: that the show began in 1963, ran for seven Doctors, plus an eighth in a 1996 TV movie, before a revival by Russell T Davies in 2005. Steven Moffat took over as showrunner in 2010 then Chris Chibnall in 2018. That's without mentioning all the spin-off media, the way this universe has been enhanced by audio company Big Finish, for instance, which makes original full-cast dramas. You have to do a lot more than just scratch the surface, however…

The collection is made up of thousands of items. Maybe millions, even. But you've only got time for a select few because you're on a mission to decipher a message sent from within the exhibit.

This isn't just a museum either. There's a research department, though the public aren't admitted. One lab is trying to work out exactly how many e's are in Leee John's name. Another is working on releasing the potential energy contained in the Sixth Doctor's costume. And one research team has worked thirty-eight years to try to get a sonic screwdriver to work on wood.

After a few minutes staring at the black hole, you decide to begin your journey…

How to Read This Book

Turn Left: great story, inaccurate title.

The story is about what happens when Donna Noble turns right, yet the episode is called *Turn Left*. Doesn't that bother anyone else? No? You in the back? Really? Fine, okay, but in this book, I intend to set the record straight.

Let's rewind.

100 Objects of Doctor Who is all about *Doctor Who* because if it weren't, there'd be rioting in the streets. *Doctor Who*, you might have noticed, is about time (and space, but I can't go into that right now because I've a limited word count). This book needs to reflect that. And that's why this tome is designed to be read in three different ways.

100 Objects takes you on a tour of the *Doctor Who* universe: a biography of the franchise as highlighted by (you guessed it!) 100 objects, encompassing the series itself, wider tie-in material, and behind-the-scenes details, while also going on frivolous sojourns questioning how many companions have met the Daleks, how many planets the Doctor's made a return trip to, and which serials have the longest and shortest titles.

Your first option is the **Boring Old-Fashioned Way**: chronologically. Start at page 1 and finish on page 4,236 (or thereabouts). I'm not teaching you how to suck eggs here – that's in the sequel.

There's also the **Coffee Table Way**, which either involves you using this volume to prop up your furniture or dipping in and out at random. I always like the books you can start reading anywhere, put down, forget where you left off, and start again somewhere else.

Finally, there's the ***Turn Left* Way**, which restores balance to the universe.

At the end of each section, you'll essentially get to Choose Your Own Adventure (someone should really make a book series called that). You can carry on chronologically, or you can Turn Left, following directions to another object somewhere else in the book. You'll skip all over the place, without knowing quite how many objects you've got left to read. You could find yourself on the penultimate object but have eighty chapters still to read.

Don't worry, you'll read every section and it'll all make sense (loosely speaking), but this timey-wimey manner will keep you on your toes. You'll be living on the edge, exactly like the Doctor. Well, the Doctor would probably save the universe at the same time, but don't feel obliged to go above and beyond.

If you're going for the *Turn Left* Way, start with Object #1, go onto #2, then follow the instruction at the end of that chapter. If there's no "left" option at the end of a section, carry on chronologically until you reach the next left turn.

Personally, I'd go with the Boring Old-Fashioned Way, but Peter Davison read it the *Turn Left* Way* and said it reminded him of filming *All Creatures Great and Small*, specifically the days he'd have to shovel sh—wait, that wasn't a compliment at all! If I could afford a lawyer, I'd be furious.

(*This is not true in the slightest.)

1. St John's Ambulance Sign.

The staff usher you past all the queues. Clearly someone has told them it's your birthday. Well it was back where you came from, but you're in another time zone now, so should you tell them you'll wait with all the others? You check out the queue. There's the Keeper of Traken. Ashildr. Dorian Gray. Captain Wrack. All tutting, looking at their watches, moaning about immortality being a curse.

Nah, let them think it's your birthday. In fairness, you did open presents this morning: a toy Yeti, a handmade scarf, a Dalek playsuit... And now you're here, the ultimate present – learning about that wanderer in all time and space known as the Doctor.

This first room is meant to be experienced alone. Fog hangs in the air. It's dark, gloomy. You can't see anything apart from exposed brickwork and a sign directing you forwards: Totter's Lane Yard, This Way. You go on cautiously. Where's the first exhibit? There's nothing at the end of the lane. Except...

A spotlight focuses on a blue square, suspended impossibly ahead, in the mist, a few metres away. The corridor feels more intimate as you get closer.

Right at its centre is a circular logo: the St John's Ambulance sign, as seen on the first TARDIS.

Doctor Who debuted on BBC1 on 23rd November 1963 at 5:16pm. Though it only attracted a modest audience of 4.4 million viewers, the following week the BBC repeated this first episode, named *An Unearthly Child*, before the second (*The Cave of Skulls*) due to concerns its initial transmission had been overshadowed by the assassination of President John F. Kennedy on 22nd November. It proved a canny move: around six million tuned in for the repeat and its second episode, and the four-part serial, which concluded on 14th December 1963, averaged six million viewers.

By the end of the second serial, better known as *The Daleks* (or *The Mutants* to some), *Doctor Who* had crossed the ten million viewers milestone.

But this success belied troubles behind the scenes.

Likely due to the difficulties of realising extreme locations and characters on limited budgets, sci-fi was relatively rare on

TV: the first was an adaptation of a Karel Čapek play, *R.U.R.* (*Rossum's Universal Robots*), which also coined the term "robots", and aired on 11th February 1938, followed by a live transmission of *The Time Machine*. Other sci-fi dramas included *Quatermass and the Pit*, *Nineteen Eighty-Four*, and *Out of this World*, a 1962 spin-off of ITV's *Armchair Theatre*.

Nonetheless, a BBC Survey Group cautioned that "SF is not itself a wildly popular branch of fiction – nothing like, for example, detective and thriller fiction. It doesn't appeal much to women and largely finds its public in the technically minded younger groups. SF is a most fruitful and exciting area of exploration – but so far has not shown itself capable of supporting a large population."

And yet *Out of This World* had debuted to some eleven million viewers. Sydney Newman had commissioned it when working at ITV and was adamant that sci-fi was the answer to a gap opened in the BBC's Saturday evening schedule between *Grandstand* and *Juke Box Jury*. Donald Baverstock, BBC1's controller of programmes, instructed Newman (who'd joined as head of drama in December 1962) to find a family-friendly programme to fill it.

He, in turn, told Donald Wilson, head of the script department, to work on a sci-fi format which could run throughout much of a year. Wilson, with his colleague C.E. Webber and two members of the Survey Group, Alice Frick and John Braydon, came up with a show about a group of intrepid scientists, featuring "The Handsome Young Man Hero", "The Handsome Well-Dressed Heroine", and "The Maturer Man" – which Newman subsequently denounced as "corny". Instead, he focused on "The Maturer Man" with a "Character Twist", giving him an enigmatic name: the Doctor.

He approached very few to produce the then-unnamed show: Don Taylor, whose feathers had been ruffled by Newman's restructuring of the drama department, and Shaun Sutton, whose experience in the BBC children's department meant he could handle such an extensive production. (Sutton would eventually prove pivotal to *Doctor Who*, talking Newman into casting Patrick Troughton as the Second Doctor.) Both turned the position down.

Sydney then recalled a gutsy young production assistant who'd impressed him at ITV: Verity Lambert, who he put in charge of *Doctor Who*. On Friday 24th June 1963, she arrived at BBC Television Centre as its first female drama producer. Newman later described her appointment as "the best thing I ever did on *Doctor Who*".

That same month, just five weeks before expected airdate, Assistant Controller (Planning) Television Joanna Spicer raised concerns that no one had been cast in any lead roles. Even more troubling was the lack of scripts! *Doctor Who*'s transmission was subsequently delayed a further eight weeks.

C.E. Webber's *The Giants* was deemed unsuitable for the programme's first serial, too, meaning Anthony Coburn's *An Unearthly Child* would need rewriting to accommodate character and format introductions.

Worse still was the limited room at the allocated Lime Grove Studio D, as well as the old equipment it used. The TARDIS interior set would take up around half the studio space; in the other half, the production team would have to craft all of time and space.

The show's success is testament to the incredible achievements and dedication of Lambert; directors Waris Hussein, Christopher Barry, and Richard Martin; associate producer Mervyn Pinfield; and script editor David Whitaker; among many others.

Of course, Donald Baverstock had a vested interest in *Doctor Who* too; he was, after all, the person who approached Sydney Newman to develop a TV show for Saturday teatimes. Still, he kept a keen eye on finances. Each episode had a budget of £2,300, with a further £500 allocated to create the TARDIS interior, and when Baverstock rechecked the numbers, he became concerned that each episode of the first serial would cost over £4,000. He nixed the show, ordering the 13-episode commission down to just four. Fortunately, Lambert and Wilson convinced Baverstock that they could make *Doctor Who* more cost-effective.

Even its pilot episode, recorded a month before full filming for the rest of the serial began, ran into troubles. The practice of making pilot episodes didn't exist in the UK at that time, owing to cost and tight filming schedules.

There were dialogue mistakes. A camera ran into scenery at Totter's Lane. The Doctor was too bad-tempered and was described as being from the forty-ninth century. One of the biggest issues, however, was a technical fault resulting in the TARDIS doors opening and closing at random.

Newman instructed the team to remake the episode, meaning it would miss its expected 16th November 1963 transmission. This pilot wasn't aired publicly until 1991.

Famously, extensive news coverage of the assassination of John F. Kennedy held *Doctor Who* up too, though only by a few seconds, not the hours or days often quoted. After the disappointing viewing figures of this "delayed" broadcast, thankfully the BBC's considerable guile in replaying *An Unearthly Child* immediately before *The Cave of Skulls* secured the viewers it deserved.

You don't normally like to touch any exhibits, but this one actively encourages you to. You reach out a hand, palm stretching across the St John's Ambulance Sign. Somehow it's humming. It's... It's alive.

Vworp! Vworp!

The materialisation noise to your left beckons you towards a door, through which lies the rest of the *Doctor Who* Museum.

2. Asteroid 3325.

From small beginnings...

You enter a vast chamber, surprisingly dark despite the spotlights focusing on the massive object at the room's heart. You strain your eyes, not quite believing what you're seeing. But there it is: an immense rock, suspended in this monumental space by deep gravity well generators in the walls, ceiling, floor – everywhere. And you can see why. You're struggling to comprehend the enormity of it. Your neck aches when you look up, trying to see how far it extends. But the edges are lost in shadow. You check one of the plaques, interspersed on the smooth metal floor, and learn that this minor planet is around eighteen miles in diameter. Visitors have started to disperse around the room, though there's a high concentration near you, near the entrance: that's because it would take some seven hours to walk from one end to the other.

This is 3325 TARDIS, a carbonaceous asteroid discovered in May 1984 by Brian Skiff at Lowell's Anderson Mesa Station, Arizona, and named after the Doctor's space-time ship.

Doctor Who's influence extends far beyond the asteroid belt between Mars and Jupiter that the 3325 TARDIS normally calls home. One of 3325's neighbours is Asteroid 8347 Lallaward, discovered in April 1987 by C. S. and E. M. Shoemaker.

Closer to home, *Doctor Who* permeates the televisual landscape: it's easy to lose track of how often a property on *Homes Under the Hammer* has been described as "TARDIS-like". Less obvious is the Lomax family in *Hollyoaks*, whose eclectic number include Peri, Leela, Rose, and Tegan! Writer Eddie Robson jokingly recalled on Twitter his attempt to give *Hollyoaks'* Leela the line "I will cut out your heart", echoing the threat made by the Fourth Doctor's companion in *Horror of Fang Rock*. "But the script editor told me it was a bit OTT and I should take it out," he noted. "Which was fair."

Elsewhere, *Life on Mars'* (2006-07) protagonist, played by John Simm, was originally called Sam Williams, but production company Kudos requested an alternative. Writer Matthew Graham (*Fear Her*) asked his daughter for suggestions, and she came up with Sam Tyler – named after *Doctor Who*'s Tyler family.

The US remake later changed the name of Sam's mum from Ruth to Rose.

The extinct marine trilobite *Gravicalymene bakeri* was discovered in 1997 in Gunns Plains, Tasmania, but was only found to be a different species from previous arthropods in 2020. Dr Patrick M. Smith and Dr Malte C. Ebach had been inspired by *Doctor Who* to pursue careers in science, so named their find after Tom Baker. "Will I be allowed to tack 'Fossil' on official correspondence?" joked Baker.

It's hard thinking about small-scale matters when you're staring at this floating colossus. You've spent a while in here now, but as you move to leave, you notice an interactive display, similarly suspended in nothingness. It's a 3D approximation of a sector of space, a paint-splatter of shifting blue and black with specks of stars glowing in the gloom. This forms a series of unofficial constellations, named in 2018 to commemorate the tenth anniversary of Sol 3's Fermi Gamma-ray Space Telescope. These include the Hulk constellation, the Eiffel Tower, Mount Fuji, the Little Prince, and yes, the TARDIS. The last is primarily made up of six pulsars and probable blazars (supermassive black holes with luminous accretion disks of incredibly hot gas), with baffling names like AP Librae and PKS 1622-29. It's mind-numbing to consider the immensity of the universe you're currently in.

< 13. Tyrannosaurus Rex.

3. The TARDIS Fault Locator.

This object is actually comprised of numerous computer banks, originally taking up an entire wall in the TARDIS control room. It whirrs and purrs, an echocardiogram of the museum's vitals.

It first took prominence in *The Daleks*, then lit up in *The Edge of Destruction* to highlight there was a major problem with the Old Girl. (It's the first of only two stories to take place entirely on the TARDIS, the other being *Amy's Choice* – which also shows Upper Leadworth, but that's a dreamscape.)

The TARDIS is the mainstay of *Doctor Who*, having appeared in all but eleven stories: *Mission to the Unknown, Doctor Who and the Silurians, The Mind of Evil, The Dæmons, The Sontaran Experiment, Genesis of the Daleks, Midnight, The Lie of the Land, The Woman Who Fell to Earth*, and *Ascension of the Cybermen*.

Subsequent TARDIS consoles made the fault locator smaller but kept its functionality, to show that even this incredible ship is fallible, as is its pilot.

The TARDIS is the most impressive spaceship in science-fiction. It can travel across all of time and space, cross the boundaries that divide one universe from another, and exists on transdimensional planes. But that doesn't mean the Doctor is all-powerful when using it. In fact, he can be pretty useless.

So which Doctor is best at steering the TARDIS? Let's confine ourselves to TV serials because discussing canonicity can be more complicated than *Warriors' Gate*. Down the rabbit hole…

The First Doctor had little to no control over the ship, a fact highlighted by his bafflement in *Twice Upon A Time* at the Twelfth Doctor's precision. Barbara and Ian were effectively kidnapped and the Doctor couldn't return them to their own time; when they landed on contemporary Earth, they'd been miniaturised. They only got back to London, 1965, thanks to the Daleks, whose time travel machine they commandeered. The Doctor at least helped them operate the machine, so while he has a good understanding of the technology required, he can't put that to good use by accurately piloting his own time machine.

Verdict: Rubbish. Sorry, William.

The Second Doctor is still a stranger to accuracy, but is willing to experiment with the controls. He makes its hull invisible in *The Invasion* and activates the HADS in *The Krotons*. In the former serial, despite the TARDIS' landing circuit being jammed, he does manage to dodge a missile in space then rematerialise in a field on Earth.

Verdict: Promising but ultimately lacking. Still, in *Fury from the Deep*, he shows skill (or perhaps considerable lack of) to land the TARDIS on the surface of the North Sea – not that it was intended!

Exiled to Earth, it would be understandable if **the Third Doctor** were terrible with the TARDIS. But he's not. Earlier adventures involve his ship being commandeered by the Time Lords and when he tests the TARDIS, he ends up in another dimension (*Inferno*).

However, once he gets his knowledge of time travel back, he successfully returns to Metebelis III (*The Green Death*) and Peladon (*The Monster of Peladon*), which surely wasn't a mistake. Admittedly, *Carnival of Monsters* and *The Curse of Peladon* leave him and Jo in precarious situations (respectively, inside a Miniscope and on the edge of a cliff) but he's more fastidious than the First and Second Doctors.

Verdict: Not bad at all, barring teething errors. Can we infer that the Time Lords implanted a level of expertise in his mind he didn't previously have?

The Fourth Doctor is more carefree at the controls. Separated from the TARDIS soon into his journeys, he trusts the vessel to drift in time to find him, Sarah, and Harry again. He has numerous hiccups (landing on a fake Earth in *The Android Invasion*; being at the mercy of the Helix in *The Masque of Mandragora*; and falling into a C.V.E in *Full Circle*) and leaves a lot to chance. To escape the Black Guardian, he installs the Randomiser in *The Armageddon Factor*, leaving his and Romana's destinations open to serendipity.

Yet he can steer admirably when he needs to. He overrides the Randomiser in *City of Death* and *The Creature from the Pit*, successfully gets to Gallifrey to carry out a convoluted plot in *The Invasion of Time*, and instructs Leela on how to get them to the nearest medical centre in *The Invisible Enemy*, despite him contracting a virus.

Verdict: His nonchalance belies decent skills. He's far from infallible, but shows notable improvement.

Ask Tegan and she'll tell you **the Fifth Doctor**'s useless with navigation. Certainly you'd believe as much when viewing Season 19, during which he repeatedly fails to get her to Heathrow. Similarly, Adric is sure he can do what the Doctor can't – return to E-Space – and the Doctor is either incapable or unwilling (interference in time still being outlawed by his own species) to save the young Alzarian from his final fate.

Can this description apply to all his travels? Peter Davison's Doctor plans a route for Concorde to get back to contemporary London in *Time-Flight*, and, after *Arc of Infinity*, he doesn't *need* to return Tegan to Earth as she clearly didn't want to stay. Otherwise, his TARDIS is frequently ensnared: trapped in a warp ellipse in *Mawdryn Undead*; affected by the Tractators' gravity meddlings in *Frontios*; and caught in a time corridor in *Resurrection of the Daleks*.

Verdict: He's not given a chance to redeem himself after numerous failings in the early days. But he seems happy enough to come and go like a summer cloud.

At the mercy of his own people in *The Trial of a Time Lord* and the Kontron Corridor in *Timelash*, **the Sixth Doctor** takes a similar attitude to Davison's, albeit he's more willing to experiment with the TARDIS. In scenes sure to haunt fans until the end of time, he even briefly repairs the Chameleon Circuit in *Attack of the Cybermen*, hinting that he's more adept at handling the Type 40 TT than otherwise seen.

Admittedly, his landings leave something to be desired: Peri complains about wading through the sea on Thoros Beta (*Mindwarp*) and there's often a fair bit of walking before they reach their destinations.

Verdict: His bombastic nature extends to his technical prowess.

You definitely won't hear him admit to being a poor pilot. Peri might point it out, though.

It is during **the Seventh Doctor**'s era that he comes into his own. Many adventures seem random, certainly in Season 24 (at odds with his guiding the Nostalgia Tours Bus in *Delta and the Bannermen*), but this master manipulator has greater intentions. His plans – solving problems caused by himself or the Time Lords in, for instance, *Remembrance of the Daleks* and *Silver Nemesis*; and testing Ace in *Ghost Light*, *The Curse of Fenric*, and *Survival* – mean he *must* have a solid grasp of piloting the TARDIS.

Verdict: He knows what he's doing.

The TARDIS behaves strangely in the 1996 movie, so it's difficult to judge **the Eighth Doctor**. It doesn't particularly go anywhere, but a large portion of the action takes place inside. The Doctor has a good knowledge of its systems, particularly the Eye of Harmony, but it's hard to tell how well he can steer.

Then again, he's incredibly on point in *The Night of the Doctor*, materialising on a *crashing ship* at the *correct end* to avoid premature destruction.

Verdict: It's Paul McGann, so let's just say he's a TARDIS expert.

Presumably, **the War Doctor** spent a great deal of time mastering the controls in the Time War, though we don't see this. We do see him powering his ship through some Daleks, entering Gallifrey's atmosphere at equidistant intervals alongside the Tenth and Eleventh Doctors, and parking in a row with the others in the Museum. He also doesn't want the TARDIS to see his transgression, so materialises far enough away from the barn in which he's going to activate the Moment.

Verdict: From the evidence on show, this incarnation is a great pilot.

Right from the get-go, **the Ninth Doctor** impresses: in *Rose*, we see the TARDIS in five different spaces in the same time period (opposite Henrik's; near the Powell Estate; behind the restaurant; opposite the London Eye; and down the alleyway), implying the Doctor's had to move it while dealing with the sole threat from the Autons. From there, he's showing off: proving to Rose he can travel to the year 5.5/apple/26 (*The End of the World*), following distress calls (*Dalek*), and materialising in Cardiff to soak up energy from the Rift (*Boom Town*), topped off with a visit to Raxacoricofallapatorius!

Most impressively, in *Father's Day*, he lands the TARDIS on exact dates, firstly to witness Jackie and Pete's wedding, then to 7th November 1987, the day Pete dies. In fact, he visits the latter *twice*, the second time presumably against the TARDIS' protests.

Verdict: There are always exceptions: here, the landing in Cardiff, 1869 (not London, 1860); being late when on the trail of the Chula ambulance; and that major error, taking Rose back twelve *months* late, not twelve hours in *Aliens of London*. Apart from these brief slip-ups, the Ninth Doctor is fantastic.

The Tenth Doctor continues this trend. He makes numerous deliberate decisions, taking Rose and Martha to the same place in *New Earth* and *Gridlock*; finds Elton easily in *Love & Monsters*; and showboats with a visit to 1930s New York at the base of the Statue of Liberty. In *Fear Her*, he not only aims to hit the 2012 Olympic opening ceremony but also repositions the TARDIS perfectly after a dodgy initial landing. His pinpoint accuracy even gets the ship to materialise inside Martha's living room (*The Lazarus Experiment*).

Verdict: It's fortunate Adelaide brought the Time Lord Victorious out of his reverie; the Tenth Doctor's mastery of the TARDIS could've meant disaster across the cosmos. His mistakes are few and far between; however, in *Tooth and Claw* and *The Idiot's Lantern*, he gets the wrong time and place, and this tendency has a tragic outcome in *The Fires of Pompeii*, leading him and Donna to set off Mount Vesuvius.

When **the Eleventh Doctor** really intends to go somewhere and somewhen, he can: he and Amy relocate to inside Starship UK after floating outside, travel to an exact date to meet Vincent van Gogh, and tracks George through his cry for help. Though the TARDIS is caught in a solar wave in *The Rebel Flesh*, he targets locations to learn more about Amy's predicament here and in *A Good Man Goes to War*.

But he gets it wrong time and time again. Amy's fragile mental state is a direct consequence of his being late in almost his first action, and he doesn't improve that much – he's late to see Churchill, gets "the timing a bit out" in *The Girl Who Waited*, and can't lock onto The Thrasymachus in *A Christmas Carol*.

His navigation is like his manner: all over the place but well-intentioned.

Hide exposes a commonality among most of the Doctors. If you want accuracy, ask the Doctor to move in time. Or space. Not both together. There are various examples of spatial relocations – in *The Runaway Bride*, the Tenth Doctor even pulls the TARDIS alongside a travelling taxi! – but in *Hide*, he and Clara go "always", staying at Caliburn House (or where it will be or was, depending on your viewpoint) but drifting forwards and backwards in time.

Verdict: He's a liability unless he puts in extra effort. He marginally improves when Clara's there, getting on the plane in *The Bells of Saint John*; keeping an eye on his companion through her youth then arriving during the Festival of Offerings in *The Rings of Akhaten*; and outmanoeuvring Clara, assembled aliens, and the Papal Mainframe in *The Time of the Doctor*.

We come to the incarnation who, in a post-regenerative stew, asked Clara if she knew how to fly the ship. We can chalk that up to his brain still cooking. Aside from this, **the Twelfth Doctor**'s impressive.

Don't doubt his precision. In *Kill the Moon*, for instance, he determines to get Courtney Woods named the first woman on the moon and manages it… despite overshooting and instead materialising on a spacecraft headed towards the moon. He then nips off and returns at the exact instant Clara decides not to trigger the nuclear bombs on the lunar surface. He demonstrates further prowess when saving Journey Blue (*Into the Dalek*), relocating the ship before the Thames thaws (*Thin Ice*), and acting as a moving service for Bill (*Knock Knock*).

Verdict: "There's a few false starts, but you get there in the end."

Immediately separated from the TARDIS, **the Thirteenth Doctor** has quite a classic relationship with her ship in that she's laidback about where she ends up, at least in Series 11. Most destinations are by chance, although she targets the organisation in *Kerblam!* after a call for help.

Things change in Series 12. She has the same effective grasp on space-time co-ordinates as Peter Capaldi's incarnation, materialising on Gallifrey after the Master encourages her return in *Spyfall*. Then, with problems arising across the world in episodes like *Nikola Tesla's Night of Terror*, *Praxeus*, and *Can You Hear Me?*, she directs her attentions to different locations. It means that, by *Praxeus*, she can be relied upon to save Jake in the microseconds before a ship's destruction, something she failed to do in her fifth incarnation when Adric faced the same fate (causing a great deal of commotion from fans).

Verdict: Something of a passive driver, the Thirteenth Doctor goes where she's needed, without specifically aiming for a particular destination. But when she needs to be somewhere specific, she's on the ball.

< 36. Fossils.

4. "I'm Gonna Spend My Christmas with a Dalek" LP.

There's a tune floating through the air. You would tap your foot, sing along, start dancing, maybe draw a fellow visitor into a little rhythmic tête-à-tête. Except then you could never show your face in public again.

You track down the source of this ditty. Someone has just selected "I'm Gonna Spend My Christmas with a Dalek" by The Go-Go's on the jukebox.

"And hug him underneath the mistletoe/ And if he's very nice I'll feed him sugar spice/ And hang a Christmas stocking from his big lead toe/ And when we both get up on Christmas morning/ I'll kiss him on his chromium-plated head."

It was released in December 1964, a parody to cash in on "Dalekmania". It's... actually not too bad. Still, you're sure you'll walk away before you find out what the Daleks think of plum pudding and custard.

It might be a cliché to say that the Daleks saved *Doctor Who*, but it doesn't make it any less true.

Only thirteen episodes were originally commissioned. *The Edge of Destruction* and *The Brink of Disaster* concluded this initial order. Donald Baverstock extended the programme's run on 31st December 1963, seemingly impressed with the Daleks, even if viewing figures for the show's second serial remained roughly in line with *An Unearthly Child*. The cliffhanger of *The Daleks'* first episode, *The Dead Planet*, only teased a sink plunger advancing on Barbara; nonetheless, the Daleks themselves were wheeled out for photo opportunities around Shepherd's Bush, making their official press debut with the 28th December 1963 edition of Dutch newspaper *Het Parool* – hours before 6.4 million UK viewers tuned in for *The Survivors*, the story's second part, which showed the aliens in all their glory. Presumably, until then, the amassed crowds were left to wonder what these curious creations actually were.

Across *The Daleks'* seven episodes, the ratings shot up from 6.9 million to 10.4 million viewers for the serial's final two.

Letters flooded in from viewers eager to see the Daleks again. It's no great stretch of the imagination to consider their success as having influenced Baverstock in further extending *Doctor Who*'s commission in February 1964, then again from April.

The Daleks probably made *Doctor Who* a hit. They certainly made Terry Nation a hit.

His agent, Beryl Vertue, negotiated a deal which meant Nation co-owned the Daleks with the BBC. It was a canny move; although it's rumoured that the corporation turned down a licensing opportunity during the transmission of *The Daleks*, Nation accepted an offer to write *The Dalek Book* in 1964.

In the eighteen months following *The Daleks*' transmission, Nation earned an astonishing £4.5 million.

The Daleks' return was inevitable. Abandoning their home on Skaro, the Daleks would next terrorise the streets of London in *The Dalek Invasion of Earth*, leading to publicity shots of them crossing Westminster Bridge. The story gave *Doctor Who* its second Radio Times cover (the first was dedicated to *Marco Polo*), one of only three during the First Doctor era, the third being for *The Web Planet*. When, in November 1966, *Doctor Who* was highlighted for a fourth time on the Radio Times cover, it wasn't to herald in the Second Doctor; it was to publicise the return of the titular baddies in *The Power of the Daleks*.

The Daleks and the TARDIS remain *Doctor Who's* biggest marketing successes. You'll see Daleks trundling around conventions; if you're near Cambridgeshire, you might even run into one owned by Frank Danes, author of *Six Decades of Adventure in Space and Time*. "There comes a point in every person's life, usually at middle age, when they think: what is it all about? What is it all for? What have I achieved?" said Frank. "These difficult questions might be answered by buying a red sports car or learning to parachute. For a Whovian like me, the questions are answered by buying a full-sized Dalek. I've always loved the Daleks and I suppose I could only afford one when I was fifty and near to paying off my mortgage."

But Frank is actually the proud owner of two Daleks, as he explained: "I bought the first Dalek off eBay and she was made by a freelance props builder in Birmingham. She was a screen-accurate model of a *Genesis of the Daleks* Dalek, so my wife and I called her Genevieve. I then mused that Daleks love company, someone to share the exciting business of extermination and causing planetary mayhem, so I bought a second Dalek (eBay again). This was actually a half-finished model of a new series Dalek which someone had started as a project and then abandoned. I finished her off in my garage using, in best *Blue Peter* tradition, ordinary household objects: plastic drinks bottles for the lights and two mop handles for the sucker stick. The circular surrounds of the base hemispheres proved a bit more of a challenge, so in the end I cut circles out of forty-eight cereal boxes, glued them together three-ply, painted them black and – sorted.

"Genevieve was gun metal grey when I bought her, but I gave her a makeover into Dalek Supreme livery (black and silver) after a couple of years. Her present paint job is as an Imperial Dalek, gold and white. She is a fully operational Dalek and taking her round to fetes and concerts and so on means that she does get a bit bashed about, and in the end, it's easier sometimes to repaint her completely than to just do a bit of touching up. And repainting can be more fun. With my new series Dalek, I thought that the bronze and copper of the show's livery was a bit dull and wouldn't hide the domestic origins of her trimmings. An all-black colour scheme, like Dalek Sec, was a bit boring. I'd always loved the red Daleks in the Peter Cushing movies so in the end I went for red. This also gave me her name – Clementine – a name which was nicely of the same vintage as Genevieve and also recalled one of my heroes, Clement Attlee, Labour prime minister from 1945-51. He was red as well!"

Frank doesn't make any money from these appearances; he does this for a better cause: "I've discovered that Daleks make people happy," he concluded. "They usually beam at Clementine and Genevieve and they are enormously popular when I trundle them out in public. Joggers interrupt their jogs to ask if they can take selfies with them. I take them to local fetes and concerts and so on. Most children love the Daleks. One exception was when a concerned parent sidled up to Genevieve at a fete, to say that his toddler was very frightened and would I be very kind and show my face to reassure her. Happy to oblige, I lifted Genevieve's lid and said hello. The toddler was reassured, no doubt by the notion that there was not really a hideous mutant inside the Dalek. (I know what you're thinking and it's not big and it's not funny.)"

"Merry Christmas/ I love you/ Happy Christmas/ You love me/ Merry Christmas…"

Oh. Uh, yes, you're still here. But you'll definitely go now, before someone puts Roberta Tovey's *Who's Who* on.

≤ 26. A Bomb!

5. A Framed Piece of Wall.

Art is subjective, but this is taking it too far.

It's a nice frame and all, but still, the plaque says there should be a poster of *Dr. Who and the Daleks* starring Peter Cushing here. You peer closer. Someone has written "Sorry, we can't afford the copyright" in thick marker.

AARU, Amicus, and BBC TV Productions adapted the first two Dalek serials into movies starring Cushing as Dr. Who in 1965 and 1966 – such was the popularity of the menaces from Skaro.

There were major differences: Cushing's Doctor was a kindly human inventor who had created a time machine in his back garden. His *Tardis* still looked like a police call box, but its interior resembled a laboratory, particularly messy in his debut movie then a little tidier for *Daleks' Invasion Earth 2150 A.D.* The Doctor travelled with his granddaughter, Susan, played by Roberta Tovey, while Jennie Linden and Roy Castle respectively appeared as Barbara and Ian. For the second film, Cushing and Tovey returned, with Jill Curzon as Louise and Bernard Cribbins as Tom Campbell.

The Daleks, too, were redesigned, fashioned in glorious technicolour, complete with considerable bumper-car bases and projecting CO_2 from their gun sticks. These were made by Shawcraft Models for *Dr. Who and the Daleks*, but they were actually first seen in *The Chase*, which borrowed three from the films for background shots; this meant that, despite not having permission to make action figures related to Cushing's movies, Character Options released a set of these Daleks in 2020, marketed as hailing from "The Jungles of Mechanus".

A third film based on *The Chase* would've finished off the trilogy but was ultimately never made. Most intriguing, though, is the planned radio series, which would've featured Peter's Dr. Who and Roberta's Susan in fifty-two audio episodes. A pilot, *Journey into Time*, written by future *Doctor Who* scribe Malcolm Hulke, was made, sending *Tardis* to the American Revolution. Sadly, the tape was lost and the rest were never recorded.

"It was no surprise to me to learn that the first *Doctor Who* film was in the top twenty box office hits of 1965, despite the panning the critics gave us," said Cushing. "That's why they made the sequel and why they spent [£286,000, compared to *Dr. Who and the Daleks'* £180,000]. Those films are among my favourites because they brought me popularity with younger children."

They remain cult classics, and *The Day of the Doctor* would've included posters in UNIT's Black Archive; however, the production team couldn't afford the copyright fee.

In his Target novelisation of the fiftieth anniversary special, Steven Moffat reinstated the posters, with Kate Stewart telling Clara that the films were made with the Doctor's consent – in fact, he was such good pals with Peter Cushing, he lent him his waistcoast!

< 69. Toclafane.

6. Time-Space Visualiser.

You approach a large circular device, which almost resembles an eye. Crowds passing behind you are reflected in one of the arches, but it feels personal, exclusive. That's not entirely because you're standing at this exhibit alone: this is the Time-Space Visualiser from *The Chase*, which allows you intimate access to any point in space and time. Any event that has ever happened is accessible using photon and tachyon particles trapped in the Time Vortex. It's particularly curious, then, that one of the Visualiser's arcs lists Mars, Jupiter, Uranus, and the other planets of the Sol 3 system, but no other places in the universe.

Don't question the magic!

You peer at the black TV screen, right at the Visualiser's heart. You check behind you again. People are still strolling past, unaware of this contraption's significance. Now the black screen has been replaced by a jigsaw of eccentric, dancing, ricocheting pixels.

This, the noise seems to say, *is playing just for you.*

Static gives way to black-and-white footage of the countryside. A figure walks up a tree-lined avenue. This is from *Guests of Madame Guillotine*, the second episode of *The Reign of Terror*, and the first instance of location filming in *Doctor Who*.

It looks like William Hartnell, dressed in his typical black jacket and checkered trousers, walking with his stick. But it's actually Brian Proudfoot, who had attended studio sessions to study Hartnell's gait for the brief scene. And while it's meant to be the trail to Paris, it was actually filmed at Denham and Gerrards Cross in Buckinghamshire.

William Hartnell is the definitive First Doctor and played the character regularly between *An Unearthly Child* and *The Tenth Planet*. He returned for *The Three Doctors* (1973), while clips featuring Hartnell further appeared in *Earthshock*, *The Five Doctors*, *Resurrection of the Daleks*, *The Eleventh Hour*, *The Lodger*, and, most extensively, *The Name of the Doctor*, in which we revisit him stealing the TARDIS. Although we see drawings of his first nine incarnations in The Journal of Impossible Things in *Human Nature*, the first time we see any actual clips of classic Doctors in twenty-first century *Doctor Who* comes in *The Next Doctor* – the infostamp showcases the First Doctor forty-two years after he regenerated.

William Hartnell is the Doctor: the original, you might say.

Except he's not the *only* original. It's likely that more actors have portrayed the First Doctor than have any other incarnation.

These include:

- **Brian Proudfoot**, the first actor to appear in location filming in *Doctor Who*, albeit solely seen from behind, for *The Reign of Terror*. He also doubled for the First Doctor in *The Space Museum*.

- **Edmund Warwick**, best-known for playing the robotic duplicate of the Doctor in *The Chase*. He'd previously covered for an injured Hartnell in *The Dalek Invasion of Earth*.

- **Albert Ward**, the Doctor's hand in the two middle episodes of *The Celestial Toymaker*, shot while Hartnell was on holiday (as well as in *The Romans* and *The Smugglers*).

- **Gordon Craig** similarly doubled for Hartnell in *The Smugglers*, then the third episode of the next storyline, *The Tenth Planet*, for which William was too ill to feature.

- **Richard Hurndall**, who appeared in *The Five Doctors* alongside Carole Ann Ford as Susan. Hurndall sadly died in April 1984, shortly after the broadcast of the twentieth anniversary special; many believe that he passed away before getting paid for *The Five Doctors*, but this is a fan myth.

- **David Coker**, the voice of the first two Doctors in the video game *Destiny of the Doctors*.

- **William Russell**, aka Ian Chesterton, who further voiced the Doctor for Big Finish's *The Early Adventures* and *The Lost Stories* ranges, plus the fiftieth anniversary set *The Light at the End*.

- **Peter Purves**, the Steven Taylor actor who similarly voiced the Time Lord for *The Early Adventures*.

- **Joe Bassett**, credited as "Child" in the audio *Master*.

- **John Guilor**, who voiced the Doctor in the reconstructed episodes three and four on the *Planet of Giants* DVD. He then voiced the character in *The Day of the Doctor*: "Calling the War Council of Gallifrey: this is

25

the Doctor." Hartnell never mentioned his home planet by name (it didn't have one until *The Time Warrior*), although Hurndall did.

- **Kevin Legg**, double for Hartnell's Doctor in *The Name of the Doctor* and *The Day of the Doctor*.
- **Michael Jones**, uncredited in his presumed role as the Doctor as a child in *Listen*.
- **David Bradley**, who played William Hartnell himself in *An Adventure in Space and Time*. He then played the First Doctor in *Twice upon a Time* (following a cameo for the cliffhanger of *The Doctor Falls*), before reprising the role for Big Finish and 2020's lockdown webcast *Doctors Assemble!*

Why is this list so extensive? Untapped potential is an important factor; Hartnell passed away soon after *The Three Doctors* (in 1975, at the age of just 67). And so too is nostalgia, the longing to revisit a much-loved era, made possible by the presence of a time-travelling alien, despite so many of the contemporary cast and crew no longer being with us.

But most of all it's because he's the Doctor. The definitive article.

The screen momentarily gives way once more to interference, before settling again, this time on the TARDIS control room.

Sound crackles in the air around you – the distinctive, homely hum of the Space-Time Ship. And a warm, friendly voice: "Come here, Jamie. Look at that." There they are. The Second Doctor and Jamie, both a little older, both still at home in the TARDIS. As Jamie walks around the console, the greyscale disperses, and their era is welcomed into glorious colour.

The Doctor's hair is grey, and Jamie noticeably more mature; their clothes slightly bigger, slightly baggier. Nonetheless, it's always good to see them.

Before *The Two Doctors*, the Second Doctor had appeared in colour in *The Three Doctors*; alas, *Doctor Who* didn't adopt this new palette until after Troughton's era – specifically from *Spearhead from Space* in 1970.

John Logie Baird had worked on bringing colour TV to the

masses for several years, publicly demonstrating the capability in July 1928, less than two years after his first demonstration of the medium he'd helped invent. But his company folded during World War II so his research was then self-funded, including through the cashing-in of his life insurance policy. After his untimely death in 1946, companies in the USA pioneered the technology instead, beginning with select cities in 1954. Initial results were understandably poor, but made an impression on the BBC, so much so that the corporation secretly invested in a lone 405-line colour receiver, installed at Lime Grove, and invited the Queen for a special screening of a live show recorded elsewhere in the studios. After this single performance in 1953, the set was never used again.

NBC obtained the American broadcast rights for *The Adventures of Sir Lancelot*, starring William Russell, and the show proved such a success stateside that the last fourteen episodes, starting with *The Lesser Breed* (1957), were shot in colour – making it the first British TV series to have entire episodes filmed this way. These versions were only broadcast in America, however, and the UK's first colour programme didn't debut until 1967.

The BBC had promised colour television in the mid-1960s, but the spread was comparatively slow. A report on 3rd March 1966 promised that "Britain will be the first country in Europe to offer regular programming in colour", albeit initially confined to BBC2, in a move that the corporation predicted would cost up to two million pounds a year, immediately accommodating four hours of television per week, then increasing to ten hours a week after a year.

And so, on Saturday 1st July 1967, 1500 homes with colour receivers saw Roger Taylor's fourth-round Wimbledon victory over Cliff Drysdale against the bright greens of Centre Court.

For the fifteen million households still with black-and-white sets, there was no difference, but this new technology wouldn't go away. Colour TV licenses were introduced in 1968 (at £10, double the price of a black-and-white licence), and David Attenborough, then-controller of BBC2, acknowledged that "When you first see colour television, it's intoxicating, whatever you put on it… Anybody who invested in a colour television set had the thing on all the time."

Colour came to BBC1 and ITV on 15th November 1969, with the former broadcasting a Petula Clark concert from the Royal Albert Hall at midnight, while the latter's chromatic schedule began at 9:30am with a *Road Report* from the Royal Auto Club, *The Growing Summer*, and *Thunderbirds*.

Considering *The War Games* ended on 21st June 1969, and *Spearhead from Space* aired from 3rd January 1970, *Doctor Who* was swift in adopting colour (especially as colour sets didn't outnumber traditional receivers in the UK until 1976).

Jamie stares at the TARDIS scanner, displaying an angular space station, like a glittering Giant's Causeway, hanging in space.

"Look at the size of that thing, Doctor!"

"Yes, Jamie, that is a big one."

Hmm, yes, perhaps you should move on. But wait. Static returns, invading the TARDIS, and another voice drifts in the air.

A transmission from 2013, shortly after the broadcast of *The Day of the Doctor*, when "one particular group of fans have been watching the special in Los Angeles. They're joining *Doctor Who* on this, the 23rd of November, to celebrate a special day of their very own, that they've called 1D Day. Hopefully, now, we can hook-up with them." Rather unexpectedly, the Time-Space Visualiser bursts into life. It shows two rather awkward chaps, stood on a non-descript stage, as Zoe Ball's voice echoes around them.

That's right: it's a live link-up with One Direction!

Matt Smith's disembodied voice now: "So where do we look?"

"Wherever you want," comes Zoe's slightly panicked reply.

The voices layer over each other, often the same voice over and over and over; a cacophony of despair, piqued by Jenna Coleman's nervous giggle and a wave of stunted applause. The atmosphere smells of anguish, failure, and a cheap perfume called "Our Moment".

Someone shoves into your shoulder. A middle-aged man, dressed in a smart suit with a lanyard dangling around his neck. Staff.

"This exhibit is closed," he says, pushing you on.

Yeah, as if you could've stood that torment for much longer anyway...

≤ 85. The Moment.

7. Cabinet of Souls.

Okay, so the *Doctor Who* spin-off *Class* was far from a huge hit, but the Cabinet of Souls is beautifully designed in its simplicity. This small box – mostly burnished black with a series of curious shapes outlined in sharp silver and gold lines – is bigger on the inside, and contains the Rhodian race's afterlife. It's also a weapon of mass destruction: opening it causes selective genocide as Rhodians sacrifice their own souls to burn out those of others.

Class was created by Patrick Ness, who also took sole writing credit. The eight-part 2016 show, set at Coal Hill School, followed five students and Physics tutor Miss Quill (Katherine Kelly) charged with protecting the school from the Shadow Kin, aliens who wanted the Cabinet. Peter Capaldi starred in its debut episode as the Twelfth Doctor, while Nigel Betts, who'd played Coal Hill's headteacher in *The Caretaker*, cameoed in the first two.

Three enjoyable tie-in novels were released, but publicity fizzled and *Class* ultimately ended with a cliffhanger, seemingly to be left unresolved. That is, until Big Finish carried on the story.

Doctor Who has a decidedly dodgy history of spin-offs, but they have frequently been on the cards.

Following *Doomsday*, Russell T Davies mulled over another show, *Rose Tyler: Earth Defence*, featuring Billie Piper's character on the parallel world she was stranded in. This would've included alternate versions of several recognisable faces and monsters like Adam Mitchell, Gwen Cooper, and the Slitheen. Though commissioned by the BBC, it never came to be, as the showrunner felt it lessened the impact of Rose's Series 2 departure.

Davies nonetheless delivered two successful spin-offs to the BBC: *The Sarah Jane Adventures*, with Elisabeth Sladen reprising her role, this time saving the world from her attic on Bannermen Road with a cadre of youngsters; and the adult-orientated *Torchwood*, recounting the adventures of Captain Jack Harkness and his band of alien-fighters in Cardiff.

At one stage, it seemed possible that we'd learn a lot more about the Doctor's past, as a proposed tie-in would've centred around the young Doctor's time at the Time Lord Academy. The BBC's idea, to be launched during the height of the Tenth Doctor era, broke the mystery at the heart of *Doctor Who* and was so vetoed by Davies.

Still, it's not the first time such a mythos-shattering notion had been pitched. William Hartnell's love of *Doctor Who* (or perhaps desire for double pay cheques) meant he pitched his own spin-off series in late 1964.

"At one time, I thought we might extend the series and I suggested giving the Doctor a son and calling the programme *The Son of Doctor Who*," the actor recalled. "The idea was for me to have a wicked son. We would both look alike, each have a TARDIS, and travel in outer space. In actual fact, it would have meant that I had to play a dual role when I 'met' my son. But the idea was not taken up by the BBC so I dropped it. I still think it would have worked and been exciting to children."

Hartnell's *Doctor Who* schedule alone, shooting around forty-eight weeks a year with few holidays, was incredibly punishing, and meant he couldn't even have time off to attend the funeral of his Aunt Bessie in 1965. Nonetheless, his ambition and adoration of his role seemingly overwhelmed practical limitations.

Hartnell would play the Abbot of Amboise, a duplicate of the Doctor, in *The Massacre of St Bartholomew's Eve*, but the pair never met, negating potential split-screen effects issues at a time the series was recorded "as live".

The Son of Doctor Who can be considered the first abandoned *Doctor Who* spin-off, but it wouldn't be long until another failed to get off the starting blocks. Inspired by the success of their early appearances, Terry Nation wrote *The Destroyers*, a pilot episode for the proposed spin-off *The Daleks*.

Nation intended the programme to focus on Sara Kingdom, who he'd introduced in *The Daleks' Master Plan*, and for it to be filmed in colour. At that point, BBC2 was the only colour channel, so while Nation pitched the spin-off during filming of *The Power of the Daleks*, it was rejected by BBC2 Controller David Attenborough, largely due to lack of schedule space.

In response, Nation requested that the BBC relinquish the Daleks' rights to him, for potential sale to either an American network (ABC having been approached in 1967, though it wasn't taken up) or ITV. *The Evil of the Daleks*, therefore, was intended to be the final showdown between the Doctor and his archenemies.

By the early 1970s, it was clear a spin-off wasn't going to materialise, and Nation was happy for his creations to return for *Day of the Daleks*.

K9 and Company at least got further, albeit very slightly: its pilot episode, *A Girl's Best Friend*, aired on 28th December 1981, and paired the robotic dog with Sarah Jane Smith – both Fourth Doctor companions who had never met on-screen before, with K9 gifted to Sarah by the Doctor. *K9 and Company* was actually a compromise: John Nathan-Turner wanted Sarah to return after Tom Baker handed the TARDIS key over to Peter Davison, but Sladen didn't want to merely take on the role as she had before, i.e. as a companion. Nathan-Turner instead pitched her the idea of Sarah returning in her own series, clear of the Doctor's shadow.

K9 and Company brought in a considerable 8.4 million viewers, more than enough to justify a full series; however, the pilot had been commissioned by BBC1's then-controller Bill Cotton, and when Alan Hart took over the role he didn't like the spin-off idea so never ordered a full run.

An adaptation of the pilot closed out Target's *The Companions of Doctor Who* range; a sole *K9 Annual 1983* hit shelves; and the theme tune was released on vinyl (bizarrely, with Phil Wells' disco "Shana the Star Dancer" as its B-side in the UK). The story is still considered canon, however, with Sarah and K9 seen together in *The Five Doctors* and *School Reunion*.

Nonetheless, it was the last *Doctor Who* spin-off until *Torchwood*.

< 74. Photo of Sarah Jane's Parents.

8. The Monk's Record Player.

It's ironic that this gramophone, considered a symbol of the future in its original setting – 1066 in *The Time Meddler* – now feels antiquated. It's a gorgeous object, nevertheless: mainly wooden, with plastic gauges to one side, an ornate back bracket, tone arm, and reproducer, and the large horn sticking out, waiting to burst out all sorts of extraordinary sounds.

In Dennis Spooner's script, it was supposed to be a tape recorder, but was replaced on set with this grander unit, more capable of blaring out monastic prayers.

The Time Meddler is a big step for the show. It was the first time we saw someone else with a TARDIS, i.e. Peter Butterworth's Meddling Monk, who viewers inferred was the same species as the Doctor and Susan. It also introduced a new type of story to *Doctor Who* – one that would change the fabric of the programme forever.

Under its original remit, *Doctor Who* needed to be educational, meaning its first four seasons were littered with serials set during periods of history that young generations would easily have recognised. *The Time Meddler* changed that, effectively signing the death warrant of pure historicals by introducing the "pseudo-historical"; while the former format had limited sci-fi elements to the Doctor, his companions, and the TARDIS, *The Time Meddler* added in the Monk, who brought his own Time-Space Ship, futuristic gadgets, and agenda to 1066. This threw the doors open for more opportunities to tell alien invasion stories set in bygone times.

The Chase had flirted with the idea of introducing sci-fi tropes to the past (Daleks on the *Mary Celeste*, for example), but *The Time Meddler* fully embraced it, and proved a hit.

The format took a little while to take effect – the next pseudo-historical was *The Evil of the Daleks*, around two years later, which splits its time between contemporary Earth and 1866 – but eventually supplanted pure historicals altogether.

Can we credit *The Time Meddler* completely? The pure historicals were typically met with mixed receptions and lower ratings. *The Aztecs*, *The Reign of Terror*, and *The Crusade* were decidedly dark, while *The Myth Makers* and *The Romans* dispensed with established fact. Even the comedic historicals had their grim moments: *The Gunfighters*, for instance, might feature the jaunty "Ballad of the Last Chance Saloon", but it also saw Steven Taylor's head in a noose.

The Smugglers had the lowest audience figures since *Doctor Who* began, averaging just 4.48 million viewers an episode. Perhaps it was inevitable that these stories were phased out.

The Highlanders was the last pure historical of the 1960s, though 1982's *Black Orchid* briefly revisited the format, set in 1925 and concerned with an entirely fictional affair devoid of aliens (apart from the Doctor, Adric, and Nyssa, plus the time-displaced Tegan). Two Thirteenth Doctor adventures came close to being pure historicals; alas, *Rosa* included Krasko, a murderer who'd escaped the Stormcage facility using a Vortex Manipulator, and *Demons of the Punjab* added in the Thijarians, former assassins who'd decided to instead honour the dying in their final moments.

You check out the catalogue of LPs ready to play. *Doctor in Distress*, *Jon Pertwee Sings Songs for Vulgar Boatmen*, *Doctorin' the TARDIS*… Maybe you'll leave it for now.

< 83. A Really Quite Astonishingly Heavy Door.

9. Berwick Dalek Playsuit.

Made in 1965, this flimsy dress-up kit meant children could terrorise family and friends while yelling "EX-TER-MIN-ATE" at the top of their voices. Add a sink plunger and whisk for the full effect.

Simon Danes works as a volunteer at the Bedford Foodbank and organises the annual Bedford *Who* Charity Con, which benefits them – but his day job is selling *Doctor Who* collectables online. "I'm very proud of my claim to fame as a footnote in the panoply of props-providing people for the making of *Doctor Who* – or, in my case, of people who supplied props to the making of a programme about the making of *Doctor Who*," he enthused. "I was approached by the BBC because I had a Berwick Dalek Playsuit listed as up for sale. It lacked an eye-stick but it was in pretty good condition (the eye-stick was mocked up later by the props department)."

The early days of *Doctor Who* were revisited in the fiftieth anniversary docudrama, *An Adventure in Space and Time*, with Jessica Raine as Verity Lambert, Sacha Dhawan as Waris Hussein, and Brian Cox as Sydney Newman.

The script loosely followed William Hartnell (David Bradley) being taken on as the First Doctor, his attachment to the role, *Doctor Who*'s almost immediate success, and the illness which, it's implied, led to the very first regeneration.

Obviously, the drama couldn't cover everything and tweaked chronology to form a taut narrative.

Nonetheless, it covered an admirable amount, including the events of 19th September 1963, the first day of filming: a shadow falls across a rocky landscape, as a figure watches the TARDIS materialise, *Doctor Who*'s first cliffhanger. That was shot a day before William Hartnell, Carole Ann Ford, Jacqueline Hill, and William Russell even met (while rehearsals began on 21st September, over two months before *An Unearthly Child* eventually aired).

"The Berwick Dalek Playsuit used in *An Adventure in Space and Time* came from me," said Simon. "It was worn by Cara Jenkins as Jessica Carney, William Hartnell's granddaughter."

It is a small reminder that the story is *based on* real events, as

Simon continued: "In fact, the real Jessica Carney didn't have a Berwick Dalek Playsuit; she was given a Scorpion Automotive one, I think as a gift by the manufacturers. The problem for the makers of the film was that the Scorpion ones are now incredibly rare. I don't have the figures, but there can't be more than a handful still in existence. In ten years of daily eBay watching, I've never seen one come up for sale; any that did so would go for thousands of pounds – literally.

"The Scorpion Dalek was produced in 1964. Some made it to the shops, but the majority were destroyed in a factory fire. Three hundred complete Daleks were incinerated; the company had the materials to make another four thousand and they went up in smoke, too. Jessica was one of the lucky few who ever had one. Even at the time, they were expensive: they sold for £8 each, which is the equivalent of £165 today (and the average salary in 1964 was around £1000, so you can see the parental income bracket the toys were aimed at).

"Fortunately for kids whose parents couldn't afford the Scorpion Dalek, there was a bargain basement alternative: the rather less authentic and rather more risible Berwick Dalek Playsuit. I haven't been able to find any details about its original price or how many were made; however, it looks pretty cheap and so it's fair to assume it must have been pretty cheap, too. It's a little under four feet tall. The skirt's made from PVC (and tears quite easily); there are holes in it for you to stick your arms through and grasp the gun and sucker sticks (pieces of dowelling, unpainted (cheapskates!), with a rubber suction cap on one and a very flimsy vacuum-formed ray gun on the other). There's a helmet which goes over your head; it rests on leather shoulder straps and it consists of a red plastic dome and heavy-duty cardboard neck, painted silver. No shoulder section for this Dalek. It's not very well designed. Actually, it looks like something a five-year-old would draw after they'd been shown a photo of a Dalek for five seconds and was told to do the best they could.

"Anyway, the Berwick version's much more common than the Scorpion one. They're still comparatively rare – a few come up for sale on eBay and they generally go for around £200; a bit more if they still have the box."

The docudrama would have greater effects on *Doctor Who*

beyond a simple celebration of its origins.

At a convention in New York, Steven Moffat conceded that bringing the First Doctor back for a multi-Doctor story would be the most interesting contrast, even though Hartnell had died. Peter Capaldi threw David Bradley's name into the mix…

< 22. The Second Doctor's Destructive Recorder.

10. A Cardboard Cut-Out of Patrick Troughton.

Oh no! Patrick Troughton's face is missing!

Fortunately, Hamish Wilson is on hand to help you with this tricky situation. "Sit down," he advises, lowering you into a seat in front of a conveyer belt, "because we're playing…"

A huge sign drops from the ceiling:

"THE (re)GENERATION GAME!"

Wilson is suddenly wearing a sparkly tartan jacket and muzak blares from above.

An unseen audience bursts into applause.

"Are y'ready? Whit's fur ye'll no go by ye!"

But before you can say, "Excuse me, Hamish, but what's going on, is this a fever dream, and where are my trousers?" the first object appears:

1. "The Trilogic game!"

This Tower of Hanoi puzzle is from *The Celestial Toymaker*, in which producer John Wiles originally intended to write William Hartnell out. The titular villain makes the Doctor invisible, and, in the story's original plan, he would've been restored played by someone else entirely.

This was fortunately contested by cast and crew members, ultimately leading Gerald Savory, the BBC head of serials, to veto it.

2. "Capt'n Avery's treasure."

During production on *The Smugglers*, Hartnell agreed with Innes Lloyd that he should leave *Doctor Who*.

His wife Heather once said that it was on 16th July 1966 that he decided to leave. He was suffering from arteriosclerosis, a hardening and thickening of the artery walls, so found it increasingly difficult to remember his lines and keep up with the punishing filming schedule.

3. "The Tenth Planet script."

It was made with great reluctance, however, and Kit Pedler and Gerry Davis' original script ended with the Doctor, Polly, and Ben going back to the TARDIS without his regenerating.

4. "Who's There? The Life and Career of Will'am Hartnell."

In her biography of her grandfather, Jessica Carney wrote that the decision broke his heart. "Having told the press that it was going to run for five years, he was determined to play it for five years. But he couldn't remember his lines, plus his legs were beginning to give way at times. Between the end of 1966 and when he made [tenth anniversary special] *The Three Doctors* in 1972, he got progressively weaker mentally and physically. That's the awful thing about arteriosclerosis, as the arteries close up the flow of blood is not only weakened to the limbs but to the brain as well."

5. "Finally, a decent name: Count Grendel of Gracht!" A disabled android duplicate rolls past.

Various names were mooted for the Second Doctor, including Peter Jeffrey (who'd go on to play the Grendel in *The Androids of Tara*), Brian Blessed (who controversially wanted to play it blackface), and Valentine Dyall, aka the Black Guardian.

Sydney Newman obviously wanted *Doctor Who* to continue beyond Hartnell's time. It was ultimately decided by Shaun Sutton, the newly-elected BBC head of serials, who also suggested Patrick Troughton.

William and Heather Hartnell both said that they, too, had thrown Troughton's name in the mix and were happy to see him take over.

6. "A cuddly toy!"

You half-expected that.

7. "The island of Ireland!"

How did that fit on the conveyer belt? Oh, it's just a keyring. What a rip.

Troughton was filming in Ireland when he was offered the role. After a week of negotiations, he agreed to the part, fashioning it as a "cosmic hobo", purposely different to how Hartnell had played the part. Patrick was a fan of *Doctor Who*, having habitually watched it with his family, but was nervous that the BBC wouldn't continue its commitment to it. (Indeed, it was reportedly nearly cancelled in 1969, owing to decreasing viewing figures, then again in 1970.)

He at least had Anneke Wills and Michael Craze as companions; their friendship and trust quickly grew, which meant their forced departure in *The Faceless Ones* was particularly difficult.

8. "Aaaaaand finally: A Dalek!"
Yeah right, it's probably another keyring.

On 22nd July 1966, Gerry Davis approved *The Destiny of Doctor Who*, written by David Whitaker. It featured the Daleks recognising their old enemy – which some say was a means of helping the audience accept a new Doctor. Innes Lloyd, conversely, claimed they were always due to appear in that serial regardless of whether Hartnell or another actor were the lead.

Whitaker didn't know the identity of the Second Doctor when writing it, so kept the character sketchy. Troughton was anxious about this, so after a meeting with Gerry Davies to re-establish this incarnation's personality, Dennis Spooner rewrote the renamed *The Power of the Daleks*.

Aargh! No, it's an actual Dalek, screaming "EX-TER-MIN-ATE!" at the top of its grating voice.

You launch yourself from the seat and run. Behind you, Hamish Wilson is telling another visitor to sit down to play the (re)generation game.

"But wasn't it called 'renewal' back then…?"

< 4. "I'm Gonna Spend My Christmas With A Dalek" LP.

11. Yeti.

This incredible hulking beast towers over you, actually covering one of the museum's spotlights with its shaggy coat, deepening the shadows stretched across the room. Vicious claws hang down from either side of the egg-shaped brute. You're relieved to see that its chest hangs open, empty. Once controlled by the Great Intelligence, the Yeti is harmless. For now.

Innes Lloyd trained as an actor and joined the BBC in the 1950s, quickly moving to produce outside broadcasts, including coverage of Winston Churchill's state funeral in 1965. *Doctor Who*, then, was his first shot at producing dramas, and he helmed the show for virtually two seasons (bar *The Tomb of the Cybermen*, for which Peter Bryant took charge), from *The Celestial Toymaker* to *The Enemy of the World*.

It was an important time for the show and is now known as the "Monster Era" – which might seem a curious denotation for a programme that has featured monsters throughout many of its eras. But it was a transitional period, in which the First Doctor left (Lloyd being a key ingredient in the development of regeneration as a concept), historicals were abandoned, and the Daleks were seemingly written out too. This meant more opportunities for new concepts and creatures, and in the space of seventy-seven episodes, Innes oversaw the creation of the Cybermen (plus their return in *The Moonbase*), *The Ice Warriors*, and the Great Intelligence and Yeti; all creatures which would become ingrained in the fabric of *Doctor Who*.

The Cybermen would plague the Second Doctor in particular, while the Ice Warriors would appear opposite the Second, Third, Eleventh, and Twelfth Doctors. It's curious that the Great Intelligence came back so soon (for *The Web of Fear*, an acclaimed serial which cemented the Yeti as an iconic foe) then waited so long to return once more, for the 2012-3 stories *The Snowmen*, *The Bells of St John*, and *The Name of the Doctor*.

(The Intelligence was at least further explored in the licensed *Lethbridge-Stewart* range, which expanded on Alistair Gordon Lethbridge-Stewart's life. Its opening gambit, *The Forgotten Son*, is set in the wake of *Web*, delving into the entwined timelines of the then-Colonel and the Intelligence. Stand-alone adventures

41

mingled with several authorised sequels, including follow-ups to *Horror of Fang Rock*, *Inferno*, *The Dominators*, and more. The Great Intelligence's fiftieth anniversary was celebrated with *Night of the Intelligence*, while the entity also manifested in *Times Squared*, *Fear of the Web*, and *An Ordinary Man* – as well as launching *The Lucy Wilson Mysteries*, a spin-off franchise about the Brigadier's granddaughter.)

Lloyd's penchant for base-under-siege stories (i.e. in which a restricted location is besieged by foes) was nicely balanced out by tales with grander vistas, like Tibet in *The Abominable Snowmen*, Australia in *The Enemy of the World*, and metropolitan London in *The War Machines*. Despite tight budgets, the show's ambition remained incredible: *The Smugglers* took us to Cornwall's sprawling locales, *The Tenth Planet* to the South Pole, and *The Faceless Ones* was partially filmed at Heathrow. One particular shot in *The Gunfighters* boasts a superb O.K. Corral set that took up the entire length of the studio.

< 8. The Monk's Record Player.

12. Toy Lungs.

In a bell jar hang two red balloons. It's a simple school demonstration of how lungs work. The balloons fill up as oxygen is pumped into them through plastic tubes. This is the family-friendly version because someone has stolen the Cyber-chest unit.

The true horror of the Cybermen is rarely touched upon, which is probably for the best. Because they are terrifying.

Cybermen are like us, except they've had their bodies upgraded. Lungs are replaced with chest units. Hearts aren't necessary. Weak joints and muscles are supplanted by machinery. Diseases don't have any effect. The fate of the Mondasians, "humanity's closest cousins", is the end-point of technological integration, body augmentation, and our fascination with mortality.

That alone is troubling, but the pain of cyber-conversion, and of existing as an echo of their true selves, proved so overwhelming that the Cybermen eliminated emotions. This concept may have come from the idea of bodies rejecting donated organs; here, converted subjects attempt to reject their new form of being.

The Cybermen's coldness was immediately obvious in their debut story, *The Tenth Planet*, in which they consider emotions "weaknesses"; Polly's revulsion is natural, especially as those designs still included human hands, eyes, and a sing-song voice not entirely detached from humanity.

The terror of conversion is highlighted by the body horror in *Attack of the Cybermen*, then implied in the whirling razors and machinery in *Rise of the Cybermen/The Age of Steel*.

Perhaps most unsettling are their "top-knot" variants from *World Enough and Time/The Doctor Falls*. This story told a version of their genesis on a colony ship, naturally beginning with proto-Cybermen still hooked to drips and begging to be put out of their miseries. A nurse seems to help them – but only by turning down their volumes so others can't hear their cries of "pain" and "kill me". It's noted that they're forever screaming in pain, but an eventual compromise is found: "This won't stop you feeling pain," the surgeon relents, holding up a handlebar-like headpiece, "but it will stop you caring about it." Pain isn't curable;

emotions are.

It seems that Mondasians are always doomed to make the same mistakes. It doesn't take much of a leap to correlate that with mankind, especially as Mondas is Earth's twin planet.

The Cybermen were created by Kit Pedler and Gerry Davis, who specialised in speculative science. Pacemakers were invented in 1941, and defibrillators in 1949, both by John Hopps; early pacemakers were too large to be fitted internally, but in 1958, Wilson Greatbatch created one small enough to be fitted inside the body, alongside pacemaker batteries. While heart transplants are relatively commonplace now, the first didn't take place until December 1967, a year after the Cybermen first appeared. It seemed a miracle, despite the fact the first patient only survived eighteen days. By that time, immunosuppressant drugs had also been developed to aid organ transplants.

The concepts that inspired Pedler and Davis ensured the Cybermen tapped into the zeitgeist.

Experiments with transplants had been taking place since the turn of the century but remained controversial. Alexis Carrel received the 1912 Nobel Prize in Physiology or Medicine for his work on connecting blood vessels, but his 1908 collaboration with Charles Claude Guthrie led to an abomination of science: a two-headed dog, using head transplantation. The dog didn't survive. Vladimir Demikhov did similar in the 1950s, managing to make one survive twenty-nine days. Comparisons with Dr Frankenstein were obvious.

Pedler and Davis clearly recognised the two sides of the coin: these were incredible events, but they were also abhorrent. And so, the Cybermen were born – and thrived. They returned numerous times opposite the Second Doctor, starting with *The Moonbase*, but were used more sparingly throughout the rest of twentieth century *Doctor Who*.

Parallel versions, this time created on Earth, were unveiled in 2006, and were the go-to designs for many series. The first time we see this universe's Cybermen – i.e. the same design without the Cybus Industries logo on their chests – is 2011's *A Good Man Goes to War* (apart from the inert Cyber-head in *Dalek*), over twenty years after their last appearance in *Silver Nemesis*.

From there, they became more prevalent, perhaps due to Matt

Smith watching *The Tomb of the Cybermen* when he got the part and being impressed with them. They were present in every Twelfth Doctor series finale before posing a threat to the Thirteenth for the Series 12 conclusion. A new model was introduced in *The Haunting of Villa Diodati*: Ashad, a makeshift Cyberman, still displaying emotions but seemingly uncaring about conversion. In a way, the patchwork man brought their story full-circle, apparently inspiring Mary Shelley to write *Frankenstein; Or, The Modern Prometheus*.

< 40. *Revenge of the Cybermen* VHS.

13. Tyrannosaurus Rex.

Quick! Run away! Run for your life!

Only kidding. It towers over you, blocking out the glow of the overhead lights, teeth bared. It's also very much not real. It has too many fingers. It's slow. And it looks to be made of foam.

It comes from *Invasion of the Dinosaurs*, a wonderful story let down by dodgy models. The Doctor and Sarah Jane Smith find London deserted, and are then surprised to see Mesozoic Era creatures roaming the planet. This surprise was intended for the audience too, hence the first part of the story having the contracted title *Invasion*. Sadly, the Radio Times ruined this revelation with an illustration of a Pterosaur attacking the Doctor, accompanied by the caption, "Great to be back? The Doctor and Sarah Jane return to London from medieval England. But swinging London has been invaded by something from even further back in time – prehistoric monsters!"

Invasion was also the name of the penultimate part of *The Web Planet*, and further features in *The Dalek Invasion of Earth*, *The Invasion*, *The Android Invasion*, and *The Invasion of Time*.

Doctor Who has a complicated history with titles. The chief problem is that early stories had numerous names, with the surplus coming from differences in production titles and on-screen captions. To some, *An Unearthly Child* is *100,000 BC* and *The Edge of Destruction* is *Inside the Spaceship*. The problem with opting to use production names is that the First Doctor tale *The Mutants*, aka *The Daleks*, can be confused with the Third Doctor story, uh, *The Mutants*. *The Daleks* could also be called *The Dead Planet* and by its working titles *The Survivors* and *Beyond the Sun*. See? Complicated.

Many were gloriously melodramatic and (often in the case of Terry Nation's episodes) unrelated to the events of the narrative, like *The Ordeal*, *The Velvet Web*, *The Waking Ally*, *Journey into Terror*, and *Devil's Planet*.

The last individually titled episode of twentieth-century *Doctor Who* was *The O.K. Corral*, the final instalment of *The Gunfighters*; from *The Savages*, every one is identified by a serial name and either "Episode" or (from *The Time Warrior*) "Part".

But for the purposes of this exercise, we're dispensing with individuals and opting to focus on umbrella names; that is, until twenty-first century *Doctor Who*, which introduced episodic monikers. Apart from *The End of Time* and *Spyfall*. Anyway…

The word "the" appears in every *Doctor Who* serial title of the Second Doctor era. In fact, *Fury from the Deep* is the only Second Doctor tale not to begin with "The". Every story from *Mission to the Unknown* to *The War Games* has "the" somewhere in the title, and from the First Doctor era only *An Unearthly Child*, *Marco Polo*, *Planet of Giants*, and *Galaxy 4* do not – at least in the widely accepted serial names of this era. "The" is the most-used word in all titles, appearing up to and including *Revolution of the Daleks* an astonishing two hundred and thirty-four times – or two hundred and thirty-seven times if we add in *The Mysterious Planet*, *Terror of the Vervoids*, and *The Ultimate Foe*. The prolificacy of "the" means "e" appears six hundred and fifty-eight times in serial titles – unsurprising, given "e" is the most common letter, appearing in around 11% of all English words. "U" is the rarest vowel found in *Doctor Who* titles, with just seventy-two instances.

Though it's difficult to quantify, roughly sixty-two serial names include nonsensical words made up specifically for the show.

Take, for example, *Journey to the Centre of the TARDIS* referencing the Doctor's Ship (the only example of the TARDIS being named in an episode title, in this instance as a reference to Jules Verne's 1871 novel *Journey to the Centre of the Earth*).

The Tsuranga Conundrum names a ship. *Spyfall* is a spoof of the popular James Bond film *Skyfall*, while *Praxeus* is a pathogen.

Most of the rest are the names of either aliens or planets: *The Daleks*, *The Keys of Marinus*, *The Sensorites*, *The Dalek Invasion of Earth*, *The Daleks' Master Plan*, *The Power of the Daleks*, *The Macra Terror*, *The Evil of the Daleks*, *The Tomb of the Cybermen*, *The Krotons*, *Terror of the Autons*, *The Claws of Axos*, *Day of the Daleks*, *The Curse of Peladon*, *Planet of the Daleks*, *Death to the Daleks*, *The Monster of Peladon*, *The Sontaran Experiment*, *Genesis of the Daleks*, *Revenge of the Cybermen*, *Terror of the Zygons*, *The Masque of Mandragora*, *Image of the Fendahl*, *The Ribos Operation*, *The Power of Kroll*, *Destiny of the Daleks*, *The Horns of Nimon*, *Meglos*, *The Keeper of Traken*, *Logopolis*, *Castrovalva*, *Mawdryn Undead*, *Frontios*, *Resurrection of the Daleks*, *The Caves of Androzani*, *Attack of the Cybermen*, *Vengeance on Varos*,

Timelash, *Revelation of the Daleks*, *Delta and the Bannermen*, *Remembrance of the Daleks*, *Dalek*, *Rise of the Cybermen*, *Daleks in Manhattan/Evolution of the Daleks*, *Planet of the Ood*, *The Sontaran Stratagem*, *Victory of the Daleks*, *The Pandorica Opens*, *Asylum of the Daleks*, *The Rings of Akhaten*, *Into the Dalek*, *The Zygon Invasion/The Zygon Inversion*, *The Battle of Ranskoor Av Kolos*, *Fugitive of the Judoon*, *Ascension of the Cybermen*, and *Revolution of the Daleks*.

Note that this doesn't include *The Ice Warriors*, *The Sea Devils*, *The Time of Angels, The Wedding of River Song*, and *The Husbands of River Song*. Their components are all actual words, even if they combine to make something "alien" – or, admittedly, terrestrial in the case of *The Sea Devils*, or in River's case, part-terrestrial, part-Time Lord. *The Androids of Tara* names a planet, but it's also an English forename. *The Lazarus Experiment* namechecks the human antagonist, and of course, "Lazarus" is a biblical name. *The Mark of the Rani* and *Time and the Rani* are excluded as "Rani", sometimes "Ranee", is a Hindu/Sanskrit name. *The Talons of Weng-Chiang*, meanwhile, hyphenates two Asian names.

Obviously, "Doctor" doesn't count, even though it refers to an alien.

Shada would count – if it were broadcast.

The Trial of a Time Lord doesn't count, but *Terror of the Vervoids* would (*Mindwarp* is arguable: its earliest found use was in *The Washington Post* in the 1980s, albeit hyphenated). As it's intended to be one connected story, albeit comprising of four distinct segments using the titular trial as a framing device, *The Trial of a Time Lord* is nonetheless one entity.

The Dæmons refers to aliens but uses the spelling of "demons" that originated in the mid-sixteenth century. *Dragonfire*, either as one or two words, is associated with mythology; as a single word, it was used for a 1982 video game and its 1985 sequel, as well as a novel by Andrew Kaplan in 1987 (the same year as its *Doctor Who* namesake). Though in *Doctor Who* it's an Amazon-like organisation, *Kerblam!* is otherwise an onomatopoeic word signalling an explosion. *Kinda* is also an informal way of writing "kind of".

The Curse of Fenric includes a variant spelling of the Fenrir wolf of Norse mythology, while the Time Lord of *The Brain of Morbius* is probably derived from the word "morbid" and is found as a noun in other franchises, including *Forbidden Planet* (1956) and Marvel Comics. It's one of only two titles to feature names of Spider-Man villains, the other being *The Return of Doctor Mysterio*. The 2021 Marvel film *Morbius* co-stars Matt Smith, while Claire Rushbrook (Ida Scott in *The Impossible Planet/The Satan Pit*) and Joseph Long (*Extremis*), appeared in *Spider-Man: Far From Home* (2019), which featured Mysterio. The Fenris Wolf appears in *Thor: Ragnarök* (2019), as well as the source material. The Fenris twins debuted in issues of *Uncanny X-Men* in 1985, then were introduced to the small screen in *The Gifted* (2017-19).

The Daleks are mentioned in twenty *Doctor Who* story titles, which includes three instances of a singular "Dalek": *Dalek*, *Into the Dalek*, and *The Dalek Invasion of Earth*, though the latter refers to the whole species.

The Cybermen are mentioned five times; the Zygons three times; the Sontarans twice (as singular collectives); and Autons a pitiful once.

The Weeping Angels aren't directly named, although "Angels" appears in *The Time of Angels* and *The Angels Take Manhattan*. The Master is mentioned… but not in a serial he stars in: *The Daleks' Master Plan*, aired before the villain was even introduced. The same is true of the Silence/Silents, who we first see in *The Impossible Astronaut*, a little under three years after *Silence in the Library*.

Of the Doctor's recurring antagonists, only the Rani appears in the title of every in-canon story she appears in (we're not counting *Dimensions in Time*).

Beginning with *The Three Doctors*, the Doctor is mentioned fifteen times in titles – only four times in twentieth-century *Doctor Who* (including *The TV Movie*), and eleven times between *The Doctor Dances* and *The Doctor Falls*. Appropriately, his name appears in three consecutive titles in 2013: *The Name of the Doctor*, *The Day of the Doctor*, and *The Time of the Doctor*. Seven serials written by Steven Moffat namecheck the Doctor in their titles – nine if we include *Vincent and the Doctor* and *The Doctor's Wife*, both made during his time as showrunner.

The Next Doctor is the only story written by Russell T Davies to mention the Doctor in its name, apart from *Death of the Doctor*, his two-part Eleventh Doctor adventure for *The Sarah Jane Adventures*.

The Doctor's family are only alluded to in *An Unearthly Child*, *The Doctor's Daughter*, and *The Doctor's Wife*, although the latter is actually about his TARDIS. His race are only namechecked in *The Trial of a Time Lord* and *Last of the Time Lords*.

Interestingly, aside from *Doctor Who and the Silurians*, the relative pronoun "who" only starts appearing in titles after *The TV Movie* (itself debatably known as *Doctor Who*) and all refer to women: *The Girl Who Waited*, *The Girl Who Died*, *The Woman Who Lived*, and *The Woman Who Fell to Earth*. Imperatives are similarly more abundant since the show's 2005 revival, and include *Blink*, *Turn Left*, *Hide*, *Listen*, *Sleep No More*, *Face the Raven*, and *Smile*.

There are various "meta" names which refer to the programme itself:

- *The Greatest Show in the Galaxy* includes a character ostensibly representing a fan.
- *Survival* came when *Doctor Who*'s future was uncertain.
- *The Next Doctor* was broadcast after David Tennant announced he was leaving, but before Matt Smith was revealed as the Eleventh Doctor.
- *The Day of the Doctor* fell on *Doctor Who*'s fiftieth anniversary.
- *The Return of Doctor Mysterio* features the name of the TV series as it's known in Mexico (largely due to Peter Capaldi's enthusiasm for it).
- *The Woman Who Fell to Earth* introduces the first female Doctor.
- *Resolution* landed on New Year's Day, 2019.

Only *The Eleventh Hour* references the incarnation number of the Doctor who appears. "I sort of gave in to the national consensus," conceded Steven Moffat in the episode commentary. "Obviously, he saves the world at the last minute, it's the first hour of his life, he's the Eleventh Doctor. I think it was originally called, fans of dull facts might like to know, *The Doctor Returns*."

Doctor Who and the Silurians is the only serial title to directly include the show's name too, although production documents from before 1970 typically included the *Doctor Who* prefix. It's unclear quite how this error occurred, but we may gather it was due to confused messages between the graphics department and director Timothy Combe.

If we look at individual episode titles, episode five of *The Chase* is called *The Death of Doctor Who*, and the "Next Week" caption at the end of *The Gunfighters* promises *Doctor Who and the Savages*.

Historical figures mentioned in titles include Marco Polo, Saint Bartholomew the Apostle, William Shakespeare (whose *Macbeth* is quoted for *Sleep No More*), Vincent Van Gogh, Adolf Hitler, Saint John the Apostle, Rosa Parks, and Nikola Tesla.

Only three companions have had their first names included in titles: Rose Tyler (*Rose*) Amy Pond (*Amy's Choice*), and River Song (*The Wedding of River Song, The Husbands of River Song*), although Martha gets her surname in *Smith and Jones*. *An Unearthly Child* alludes to Susan; *The Runaway Bride* and *Partners in Crime* to Donna; *The Girl Who Waited* also to Amy; *The Magician's Apprentice/The Witch's Familiar* to Clara; and *The Pilot*, debatably, to Bill (at least after she joins Heather in *The Doctor Falls*).

Okay, we can't forget *The Feast of Steven* in *The Daleks' Master Plan*!

Christmas makes its first outing with *The Christmas Invasion*, then again, under two subsequent Doctors, for *A Christmas Carol* (named after the Charles Dickens novel) and *Last Christmas*. Of course, several stories share their names with novels, but *A Christmas Carol* is the only intentional reference that we're aware of. *The Doctor, the Widow and the Wardrobe* tips a hat to C.S. Lewis' *The Lion, the Witch and the Wardrobe*, and *The Snowmen* owes a debt to Raymond Briggs. *In the Forest of the Night*, meanwhile, borrows from the second line of William Blake's "The Tyger" (1794), and *World Enough and Time* is taken from the opening of "His Coy Mistress", an Andrew Marvell poem published posthumously in 1681, which begins "Had we but World enough, and Time".

"Time", English's most common noun, is mentioned an impressive seventeen times: *The Time Meddler, The Time Monster, The Time Warrior, The Invasion of Time, Time-Flight, Timelash, The Trial of a Time Lord, Time and the Rani, Last of the Time Lords, The End of Time, The Time of Angels, Closing Time, The Time of the Doctor, Time Heist, World Enough and Time, Twice Upon A Time*, and *The*

Timeless Children.

"Space" is more used more conservatively, with eight instances – *The Space Museum, The Wheel in Space, The Space Pirates, Spearhead from Space, Colony in Space, Frontier in Space, The Ark in Space*, and, its sole entry in twenty-first century *Doctor Who, Dinosaurs on a Spaceship*.

"Planet" makes a decent effort, appearing in *Planet of Giants, The Web Planet, The Tenth Planet, Planet of the Daleks, Planet of the Spiders, Planet of Evil, The Pirate Planet, Planet of Fire, The Impossible Planet, Planet of the Ood*, and *Planet of the Dead*; twelve times if we further allow *The Mysterious Planet*.

Earth puts in six appearances – *The Dalek Invasion of Earth, Earthshock, New Earth, The Stolen Earth, The Hungry Earth*, and *The Woman Who Fell to Earth* (or seven if we include *An Unearthly Child*) – as does "World": *The Enemy of the World, Underworld, The End of the World, World War Three, The Pyramid at the End of the World*, and *World Enough and Time*.

Recognisable cities are fewer and far between: London only features in *Aliens of London*, and Manhattan twice (*Daleks in Manhattan; The Angels Take Manhattan*). There's also *The Fires of Pompeii, The Vampires of Venice*, and *Robot of Sherwood*. Meanwhile, Mars is the only other planet of our solar system to be mentioned – *Pyramids of Mars, The Waters of Mars*, and *Empress of Mars* – though our star gets a nod in *The Sun Makers*. Ours is the only moon to be listed, albeit only thrice (*The Moonbase, Day of the Moon*, and *Kill the Moon*).

The sole two-part story that references locations in space and time is *Under the Lake / Before the Flood*.

The Doctor, the Widow and the Wardrobe is the longest *Doctor Who* title, with thirty-one letters. The longest of twentieth century *Doctor Who* is debatable. It's either *The Massacre of St Bartholomew's Eve* (thirty letters), which some call *The Massacre*, or *The Greatest Show in the Galaxy* at twenty-six letters.

The shortest titles consisting of actual words are *Rose, Hide*, and *Rosa*.

Those are three of thirty-five serials to have one-word names, alongside *Inferno, Robot, Underworld, Meglos, Logopolis, Castrovalva, Kinda, Earthshock, Snakedance, Terminus, Enlightenment, Frontios, Timelash, Dragonfire, Battlefield, Survival, Rose, Dalek, Doomsday*,

Gridlock, *42*, *Blink*, *Utopia*, *Midnight*, *Listen*, *Flatline*, *Smile*, *Oxygen*, *Extremis*, *Kerblam!*, *Resolution*, *Spyfall*, and *Praxeus*.

42 is the shortest numerical name; numbers also appear in the titles of *Galaxy 4* and *Orphan 55* (not counting instances of numbers being spelt out, like *The Tenth Planet*, *Four to Doomsday*, and *The Power of Three*).

Love & Monsters is the only title to include an ampersand so far, *Kerblam!* has the sole exclamation mark, and *Can You Hear Me?* is the only instance of a question mark. In fact, punctuation is a rare thing: though you might think numerous titles have a comma, only *The Doctor, the Widow and the Wardrobe* does so (and omits an Oxford comma!). *Journey to the Centre of the TARDIS* and *Arachnids in the UK* include acronyms.

Of all punctuation, apostrophes appear most frequently, but still not particularly regularly, beginning with *The Daleks' Master Plan*, then only twice more in twentieth century *Doctor Who*: *Warriors' Gate* and *The King's Demons*. Apostrophes are found four times during Russell T Davies' tenure as showrunner (*Father's Day*, *The Idiot's Lantern*, *The Doctor's Daughter*, and *Journey's End*), five times under Steven Moffat – *Amy's Choice*, *The Doctor's Wife*, *Let's Kill Hitler*, and *The Magician's Apprentice/The Witch's Familiar* – and once under Chris Chibnall (*Nikola Tesla's Night of Terror*).

14. The Sonic Screwdriver.

It's the Doctor's trusty sonic screwdriver. The Doctor's had quite a few of them, beginning with a simple silver cylinder similar to a penlight. The Third Doctor used a larger model with yellow and black spring-like stripes, and a red band, but changed it for another silver cylinder, albeit more elaborate than his predecessor's.

This model was ultimately destroyed in *The Visitation*, with the Sixth Doctor briefly sporting a relatively underpowered sonic lance. However, the Eighth Doctor inherited a traditional screwdriver from his seventh incarnation, while the War Doctor's screwdriver appeared as an amalgamation of the Second and Third Doctors'. Sometime between *The Day of the Doctor* and *Rose* (from the Doctor's perspective), the Ninth Doctor gets an extendible screwdriver with a blue light on top, which is destroyed first in *Smith and Jones* then more permanently in *The Eleventh Hour*. Fortunately, the TARDIS supplied a new bronzed version with extendible "claws" and a green end which resembled the glass shape in the ship's Time Rotor. (It's eaten by a shark in *A Christmas Carol*, but is used again in the following episode, so presumably the TARDIS supplies spares.)

The Twelfth Doctor ditches this in favour of sonic sunglasses in *The Magician's Apprentice/The Witch's Familiar*, but the TARDIS makes him a new screwdriver – a cylindrical unit with blue flashing lights – in *Hell Bent*. This doesn't last long: the Thirteenth Doctor makes a new one, largely from metal spoons, in *The Woman Who Fell to Earth*.

We see some variations, including River Song's sonic trowel (replaced by the Doctor in *The Husbands of River Song* with a screwdriver resembling the one used by his ninth and tenth incarnations), the Master's laser screwdriver (*The Sound of Drums/Last of the Time Lords*; *The Doctor Falls*), and the Eleventh Doctor's sonic cane (*Let's Kill Hitler*).

You especially like the one they've included in this exhibition. It's the one you love the most; the one you sometimes imagine thwarting an alien invasion with.

Victor Pemberton recalled writing *Fury from the Deep*, in which the Second Doctor realised something sinister was lurking inside a pipeline: "That's when he gets out what the script says is: 'Some device of mine. Neat isn't it?' He takes this thing out – it was nothing more than a battery light – and he opens the valve with it. That seemed to be better than just getting a screwdriver – and that would've taken time anyway."

The importance of the sonic screwdriver quickly grew. What was designed simply as an easy way to open equipment soon became a way to escape locked rooms (except when inconvenient to the plot), boasting a range of useful functions, like:

- Exploding land mines (*The Sea Devils*).
- Breaking trances (*Death to the Daleks*).
- Taking medical scans, including checking for life signs (*The Night of the Doctor*; *The Vampires of Venice*; *A Good Man Goes to War*).
- Upgrading roaming capacities of phones (*The End of the World*; *42*).
- Charging batteries (*Father's Day*).
- Piloting the TARDIS remotely (*The Parting of the Ways*; *Last of the Time Lords*; *The Battle of Ranskoor Av Kolos*).
- Amplifying sonic sound waves (*The Runaway Bride*; *The Lazarus Experiment*).
- Locking the TARDIS (*Cold Blood*; *The Doctor's Wife*).
- Locating the TARDIS (*Cold War*).
- Disabling invisibility fields (*The Time of the Doctor*).
- Playing audio recordings (*Spyfall*).

Some uses are a little more curious:

- Blasting through a wall (*The Dominators*).
- Resonating concrete (*The Doctor Dances*).
- Reattaching barbed wire, using Setting 2,428D (*The Doctor Dances*).
- Lighting candles and flambeaux torches (*The Girl in the Fireplace*; *The Pandorica Opens*).
- Cutting rope (*The Age of Steel*).

- Creating a sonic cage (*Partners in Crime*).
- Tinting glasses (*Planet of the Dead*).
- Forcibly opening and closing cracks in space and time (*The Eleventh Hour*; *Class: For Tonight We Might Die*).
- Stimulating chemoreceptors (*The Beast Below*).
- Disintegrating a door, albeit after some four hundred years of calculations (*The Day of the Doctor*).
- Sending 2D creatures back to their own dimension (*Flatline*).
- Generating an acoustic corridor (*The Magician's Apprentice*).
- Relocating DNA bombs (*The Woman Who Fell to Earth*).
- Erasing marker-pen scribblings (*Rosa*).

How does the sonic actually work? It's got a psychic interface, which Clara describes as "point and think" in *Death in Heaven*. *Deep Breath* revealed it can also be voice activated, though we've never seen this.

< 82. A Spoonhead.

15. The Philips EL3548.

This was owned by Graham Strong, who used the reel-to-reel recorder to tape the soundtracks of *Doctor Who* episodes as they went out live. It's mainly silver at the front and sides, with large white clicking buttons similar to an early tape player. It's quite a chunky unit and seems rather fragile. Maybe that's just your reverence talking: this machine helped give fans a way to experience lost stories.

Ninety-seven episodes of 1960s *Doctor Who* are missing. Due to the BBC's policy of junking recordings – either literally destroying them, marking them for waste disposal, or recording over them, in a effort to save storage space and money at a time when commercial releases were impossible – large swathes of the First and Second Doctors' eras are lost. These include some complete serials (for example, *Marco Polo*, *The Smugglers*, and *The Highlanders*) and partially-missing stories where some episodes have been retained or subsequently found, like *The Celestial Toymaker*, *The Underwater Menace*, and *The Space Pirates*.

Initially, Strong made this archive by hanging a basic crystal microphone over his TV speakers, held in place by a plant pot. He upgraded his Sound Riviera A41 recorder to the Philips EL3548, and such was his love of the series that he managed to hook the tape directly into the TV.

It's recordings like Graham's – and similar ones made by dedicated fans in the 1960s and 1970s – that have meant audio versions of lost stories can be listened to on CD and downloaded, with accompanying narration from cast members. They've also been remastered and paired with animation on DVD, Blu-ray, and digital. These animated episodes began with *The Invasion* in 2006, but it wasn't until 2013 that more were made (*The Reign of Terror*, *The Tenth Planet*, and *The Ice Warriors*), filling in gaps in otherwise archived footage. Animated releases have continued at regular intervals, covering a mix of wholly-and partially-missing stories like *The Moonbase*, *The Faceless Ones*, and *Fury from the Deep*.

In 2018, Kaleidoscope, specialists in locating missing TV shows, also uncovered The Randolph Tapes, original off-air recordings, significantly ending with *The Moonbase* Episode 1, suggesting that more reels might still be recovered.

"[The] quality is the most consistent of any collection of these episodes we have found; many of the episodes here are now probably our best source for future remastering," reported composer Mark Ayres (owner of the Radiophonic Workshop's scores and sound effects). "They are particularly useful given that all cliffhangers and reprises are intact."

Missing episodes can pique interest in the series, with occasional media reminders that tapes of the programme are sought after. Some have been found, and there is ample reason to hope for more. The BBC shipped tapes to international stations, and not all were returned, meaning they might not have been destroyed.

A good example of this is Philip Morris' incredible find in Nigeria: *The Enemy of the World* and *The Web of Fear*, apparently in their entireties. But when the reels were shipped back to the UK, Episode 3 of *The Web of Fear* – crucially, the first appearance of the Brigadier – was missing. Morris suggested at a convention in 2015 that word got out of its significance and it was sold to a private collector.

Such a dearth in the archives seems to inspire fans too. Some serials were pieced together using telesnaps, off-screen photographs taken by John Cura to document TV, up to 1968's *The Mind Robber*; however, expense meant that not all episodes were catalogued, and, after Cura's death in 1969, the BBC refused his widow's invitation to buy his thousands of negatives. Nonetheless, information about missing episodes can be gleaned from these prints.

Behind-the-scenes information like character and set designs mean fans can fill in the blanks.

The University of Central Lancashire (UCLan) even remade the entire one-part *Mission to the Unknown* in 2019. Featuring Nicholas Briggs as the voice of the Daleks, it took advantage of the university's creative departments – acting, fashion, music, design, and dance – to accurately recreate the story, which was then released on YouTube by the BBC. "I'm incredibly impressed with what's been done with the whole production; it looks and sounds authentic," Peter Purves enthused. "I watched the first scenes being filmed and they're faultless."

Rick Lundeen, creator of *The Swede* and the *Mickey & Maj*

books, celebrated *Doctor Who*'s fiftieth anniversary by adapting *The Daleks' Master Plan* into a graphic novel.

"I think it was late 2011 and there was already some slight buzz about the fiftieth anniversary, even though it was still two years away. Somehow, I got it in my head to create a sort of anniversary present for the celebration. I'd always loved *The Daleks' Master Plan* and I thought transforming the epic story into one big, full-colour graphic novel would not only be a fitting celebration but a challenge as well," Rick recalled. "I also knew I had to start well in advance of the actual anniversary to get it done, as I was doing all the art and lettering.

"I also figured that with so many episodes missing in general, it was *probably* a fairly safe bet that those nine missing episodes weren't going to turn up anytime soon. So, I tracked down the scripts, and working on the side (from my regular storyboarding job), by spring 2013, I'd finished the 168-page project. Christian Cawley was good enough to run a chapter (i.e. episode) each week leading up to the fiftieth itself on [popular website] *Kasterborous*. Then, he had a limited run of the graphic novels printed up and all proceeds went to Children in Need. I was just happy to have some small part in the big celebration."

Yes, we've lost a lot, but the resultant outpouring of creativity is astounding. Maybe it's not all bad...

< 60. Peter's Painting of Pertwee.

16. Ballerina.

A frosted, opaque model of a ballerina pirouettes, arms describing an arc above a warm, smiling face. Somewhere nearby, music from *Carmen* plays.

This is from *Asylum of the Daleks*, an immediate focus after the title sequence, found in Oswin's make-believe room. Later on in the serial, Amy would see a ballerina spinning around, frizzy hair following in loose waves, in the place of a Dalek similarly spiralling on the spot – foreshadowing the revelation that Oswin had already been converted.

The shock appearance of Jenna-Louise Coleman made headlines, and she'd become one of the longest-running companions.

The Doctor forgetting Clara (for a while) recalls her Series 7 plea to "run, you clever boy, and remember", and neatly subverts an occasional way companions leave the TARDIS: through forgetting their travels with the Doctor. Most harrowingly, Donna Noble's mind was wiped to save her life, resulting in her reversion to her more ignorant self as seen in *The Runaway Bride*; the Doctor reinforces the idea that their adventures have changed the universe and saved lives but the true tragedy is that Donna will never know. (At least the Doctor is aware he travelled with Clara, just not what she looked like or seemingly how they parted – that is, until his memory is restored in *Twice Upon a Time*).

Fortunately, this is a rare occurrence for companions. Donna is one of only three to have forgotten their journeys, the others being Jamie McCrimmon and Zoe Heriot, whose memories were largely wiped by the Time Lords in *The War Games* before they were sent back to their own times. Their only recollections of the Doctor are the events of *The Highlanders* (for Jamie), and, for Zoe, *The Wheel in Space*. They leave with more understanding, patience, and acceptance than Donna – and indeed the Doctor doesn't exactly rage when they leave but rallies against the Time Lords' treatment of them all (and certainly at being forced to regenerate).

Many companions do find their way back to their own time – roughly speaking – the first of whom are Ian and Barbara, returning to London in 1965, a couple of years after they departed but concurrent with the programme's airdate. Dodo, too, gets back, albeit shuffled off-screen in a careless manner in *The War Machines*. Polly, Ben, Sarah, Harry, Tegan, Adam Mitchell, Mickey, and Martha all return to their own times. Rose too (though to a parallel version of Earth).

Some are harder to determine: Liz never really left her own time period (nor was afforded a proper send-off story); arguably neither did Jo, whose travels in the TARDIS regularly returned her to her present day; and Turlough was banished to Earth and got back to his home planet, Trion, only after political exiles were welcomed back. Then there are those instances where companions had to live in different eras, including Vicki, Steven, Victoria, Leela, Nyssa, Peri, Mel, Amy and Rory, and Nardole – although all are effectively self-imposed exiles after either falling in love or deciding to help peers fight disease (*Terminus*, for example) or strive for peace (*The Savages*). Susan is a grey area: she found love and clearly didn't want to leave David Campbell, but it takes the Doctor locking her out of the TARDIS to actively move her on.

Of those we see on screen, only two companions continue their adventures in space-time without the Doctor: Clara, living between heartbeats, dotting around in a stolen TARDIS with Ashildr/Me; and Bill Potts, converted into a Cyberman, saved by her crush, Heather, and leaving the Doctor after thinking him dead.

< 3. The TARDIS Fault Locator.

17. Airplane Remnants.

You'd heard about this in advance: an exhibit that won't last long. See it while you can. It's not even from *Doctor Who*; it's from *The Plastic-Eaters*, the debut episode of *Doomwatch*, created by Kit Pedler and Gerry Davis.

Broadcast on 9th February 1970, *The Plastic Eaters* observed plastic's prolificacy and questioned what would happen if a virus could dissolve it; sure enough, a plane made of the compound fizzles away in mid-air. The aircraft before you is a second example, made specially for this exhibition, to highlight the ongoing struggle against climate change.

A plaque by the disintegrating plane displays a quote from *How to Give Up Plastic*, a 2019 book by Will McCallum, head of oceans at Greenpeace UK: "Less than half of the thirteen billion plastic bottles that British people throw away every year are recycled. Coca-Cola, the world's largest producer of drinks sold in plastic bottles, estimates that it produces over one hundred and twenty billion per year – if you laid them down top to tail, that's enough bottles to warp around the circumference of the earth nearly seven hundred times. It is no wonder then that so many end up in our rivers, on our beaches, and, eventually, in the ocean."

You can't help thinking that maybe the Doctor had a point using Anti-Plastic to combat such a threat.

A long, gloomy corridor lined with shop-window mannequins. That's what greeted fans at the Earl's Court *Doctor Who* exhibition in 2008. Even without the allusion to *Rose*'s opening, dummies twitching as they came to life, this was enough to freak people out.

Have you ever wandered through a store, shortly before closing or after hours, when the lights are dim, and been concerned by the line of facsimile humanoid figures sporting an array of brightly-coloured clothes? Their purpose is to sell goods, yet they can elicit incredible anxiety. This is due to the uncanny valley.

"Uncanny Valley" describes the gulf on a graph charting how we feel towards robots that look like us; as an inhuman creature's likeness to humanity increases, so too does our affinity, until a hard-to-determine point (largely established on an individual basis) where the valley takes effect and we feel unease – or genuine terror – towards it.

We often associate the uncanny valley with robots, so creepy electronic faces scare us in numerous *Doctor Who* serials, like *The Robots of Death*, *The Android Invasion*, and *Voyage of the Damned*.

But the term finds its origins in mannequins.

"Since I was a child, I have never liked looking at wax figures," said Masahiro Mori, former-professor at the Tokyo Institute of Technology, who coined the term "uncanny valley". "They looked somewhat creepy to me. At that time, electronic prosthetic hands were being developed, and they triggered in me the same kind of sensation. These experiences had made me start thinking about robots in general, which led me to write that essay [in which graphs plotted likenesses to humans on horizontal axis and affinity on verticals, with industrial and toy robots, and classical bunraku puppets as immediate examples]. The uncanny valley was my intuition." His essay further considered movement, and lack thereof, further citing masks, prosthetics, and even corpses.

Mori's paper was, coincidentally, published in 1970, the same year the Autons debuted in *Doctor Who* (although they are frequently called "duplicates"; the name "Auton" isn't heard onscreen until *Under the Lake* in 2015). These life-sized plastic models were imbued with life by the Nestene Consciousness, which then widened its field to create replicas and caricatures, and manipulate toys, furniture, cables – anything made of plastic (including breast implants, as Rose pointed out).

Plastic had proved increasingly useful and familiar in commercial aspects from the 1950s onwards. Compare the ease of construction and realism of dummies from the turn of the twentieth century to those made in the 1960s: models created in the early 1900s were hand-made using iron, wood, and wax, and boasted false teeth, glass eyes, and real hair in an effort to resemble (loosely speaking) humans. *Spearhead from Space*, meanwhile, shows the alternative: widely-made to order, cheap, and uniform. By the 1970s, plastic was experiencing something of an image problem, associated with tacky products, but synthetic compounds were still commonplace.

"It was everywhere," recalled writer Robert Holmes. "As there was so much of the stuff around, I thought it would be effective to have an alien force that inhabited and used it. *Doomwatch* did a plastic scare story at exactly the same time, so it was a kind of current issue. The Nestene itself I thought of as a plasticky, swirling mass, a glob of pure instinct which spawns the Autons. The Autons come from the word 'autonomous', because although they were formed from the Nestene element, they weren't a part of the host form."

They proved a hit and returned to open Jon Pertwee's second season the following year; *Terror of the Autons* extended the Nestene's reach to accommodate the wider range of products made of plastic. Two instances in particular caused controversy: a troll doll coming to life and killing someone, and a plastic chair engulfing another unfortunate victim.

With *Doctor Who*'s penchant for scares, it's a surprise that the Autons didn't return again until 2005's *Rose* then, aside from a cameo in *Love & Monsters*, for 2010's *The Pandorica Opens/The Big Bang*, as Roman duplicates only. Admittedly they were also due to appear in *The Five Doctors*, only to be written out due to budgetary concerns, and a scrapped Season 23 story, *Yellow Fever and How to Cure It*.

Yet they're iconic monsters. That could be because they're so memorably horrifying, or it could be because they've enjoyed extended lives in tie-in media. There have been comics (*Business as Usual*; *Plastic Millennium*), short stories (*Tales of Trenzalore: Strangers in the Outland*; *The Target Storybook: Decoy*), and novels (*Synthespians™*; *Autonomy*). The mostly-silent killers have even ventured into audio, in tales like *Brave New Town* and *UNIT: Extinction*. The last title should particularly strike a chord: a warning in case we don't turn the plastic tide.

≤ 42. Celery.

18. Eyepatches.

These are borrowed from The Courtney Collection, a separate wing of the Museum of *Doctor Who*, which also included Bok's broken hand from *The Dæmons*, jelly babies, and a fake moustache.

Playing Lethbridge-Stewart in the parallel world of *Inferno*, Nicholas Courtney wore an eyepatch; in one scene, he swung a chair around to confront the Doctor, and Jon Pertwee attempted to throw him off his lines by arranging for the cast to all be wearing eyepatches too. But Courtney was unphased and carried on regardless!

It's an oft-quoted anecdote, but demonstrates how well the team got on behind the scenes. Katy Manning described Courtney as "just the loveliest person to work with in the world".

Earth became the Doctor's new home. Exiled to Sol 3, he set up a base of operations, a lab at UNIT HQ where he could work on fixing his TARDIS and fighting off alien incursions. The Brigadier was accommodating, even when he and the Doctor disagreed on what to do about threats, but it was clear the Doctor cared for his new-found "UNIT family".

However, Caroline John's contract wasn't renewed at the end of Season 7. Liz Shaw was too competent, it seemed; companions needed to have complicated things explained to them by the Doctor, but Liz was essentially the Time Lord's equal. She remained sceptical yet open-minded in *Spearhead from Space*; recreated and distributed the cure for the Silurians' plague; and proved a match for her kidnappers in *The Ambassadors of Death*.

It's unfair to call Jo Grant the opposite of this: she brought the same enthusiasm to the show, but was more doting of the Doctor. Nonetheless, she didn't always believe his tales, at first unconvinced he could really travel in time. Jo quickly proved a go-getter when she did venture into space-time, and if she didn't understand all the scientific jargon, then she was at least quick-witted and intuitive.

It made her growing apart from the Doctor in *The Green Death* all the more heart-breaking.

It wasn't long before there was another change at the heart of UNIT: Mike Yates (Richard Franklin), at first introduced as a love interest for Jo, had a breakdown and betrayed his friends, albeit for a good-intentioned, but ill-informed, cause: Operation Golden Age, which aimed to undo the ecological damage caused by humans. Still, he redeemed himself in *Planet of the Spiders*, and the Doctor was understanding of his motives, continuing to think of him as a friend.

But this clan had had its time. After the Third Doctor regenerated, Sergeant Benton (John Levene) made his last regular appearance in *The Android Invasion* and the Brigadier in *Terror of the Zygons*, both adventures also featuring journalist Sarah Jane Smith and UNIT doctor Harry Sullivan.

Still, for a time, the Doctor had a family here on Earth. He remained on UNIT's payroll too…

< 71. Bubble Shock!

19. Soup Dragon.

You may think that you've stumbled into the wrong exhibition, as this item is clearly aimed at fans of 1960s/70s children's programmes. Then you figure out the significance of this green soup-loving scaly creature.

"So this is your tribute to the Master?" you ask a staff member.

"Yep," they reply proudly. "Because the Master has a thing for children's TV. Remember *The Sea Devils*?"

You nod. "Yeah, he watches *Clangers*."

"That's right. Very clever, don't you think?"

"Mmm. I guess. Why didn't you just have the Tissue Compression Eliminator though? Or Missy's umbrella? Or his TARDIS column from *Logopolis*? Or—"

The first time we meet him, this troublesome Time Lord claims to be universally known as the Master – although you may also call him Colonel Masters, Professor Thascalos, Emil Keller, Mr Magister, the Portreeve, Kalid, Sir Gilles Estram, Bruce, Professor Yana, Harold Saxon, Mr Razor, and Agent O.

The idea for the Master came from a desire to meet the Doctor's equal, frequently described as the Moriarty to the Doctor's Sherlock Holmes. Barry Letts and Terrance Dicks mooted the possibility of having one narrative for a whole season, but rejected it after weighing up its pros and cons. The Master, however, provided a further linking character throughout Season 8, first appearing in *Terror of the Autons*, before swiftly returning for *The Mind of Evil*, then for every serial that year. He was arrested at the end of *The Dæmons*, and came back twice in Season 9, taking over the prison in *The Sea Devils*, and making a right TOMTIT of things in *The Time Monster*.

His appearances no longer came as a surprise, but the character nonetheless proved endlessly mesmerising. Actor Roger Delgado was a magnetic presence on screen, and the Master brought out different sides to the Doctor. Here were two childhood friends turned nemeses; *Colony in Space* writer Malcolm Hulke said, "One felt that the Master wouldn't really have liked to eliminate the Doctor... The Doctor was the only person like him at the time in the whole universe, a renegade Time Lord, and in a funny sort of way they were partners in crime."

Steven Moffat would revisit this idea in *World Enough and Time*, with the Doctor describing Missy, the Master in female form, as "the only person that I've ever met who's even remotely like me" and recalling a pact they'd made as kids to see every star in the universe.

Delgado's Master needed to be a match for the Third Doctor, but Roger was famously nervous about stunts. Jon Pertwee recalled Delgado's anxiety about all the action his character had to be involved in during *The Sea Devils*. "He was incredibly cowardly but therefore the bravest man I've ever known in my life," Pertwee warmly recounted at the Panopticon convention in 1993. "I would do these things joyfully because I'm a complete berk. I've been gadget-mad all my life. I fly, I've raced speedboats, I've raced motorcars, I've raced motorbikes in my lifetime, and so I loved all that. Roger hated it. His idea of a wonderful life was for us all to go out and have dinner, or eat at his house or mine, have a great dinner, drink several bottles of wine, put his carpet slippers on and then drink a bottle of port. That was a really dangerous evening and a good one."

Despite not being part of the on-screen taskforce, Delgado was instantly cemented in the "UNIT family". Sadly, his last appearance was in Season 10's *Frontier in Space*.

Roger passed away in a car crash, alongside two film technicians, while filming the Franco-German TV series *La Cloche tibétaine*, in Nevşehir, Turkey. Pertwee described Delgado as "one of my greatest friends". His shocking death was often cited as a reason Jon left *Doctor Who* at the end of Season 11.

The Master's journey was intended to end with the Third Doctor's. *The Final Game* would've revealed the Master as either an amalgamation of the Doctor's dark side, or his brother. He would've sacrificed himself to save his friend, nonetheless initiating the Doctor's regeneration.

As it was, the Master's story was left open, and the character would be played by a further fourteen actors:

- Peter Pratt (*The Deadly Assassin*).
- Geoffrey Beevers (*The Keeper of Traken*, plus various audio adventures, beginning with *Dust Breeding*).

- Anthony Ainley (*The Keeper of Traken – Survival*).
- Gordon Tipple (a brief cameo at the start of *The TV Movie*, showing his extermination at the hands/whisks of the Daleks).
- Eric Roberts (*The TV Movie*).
- Derek Jacobi (*Utopia*, plus audios like *The War Master* sets).
- John Simm (*Utopia*; *The Doctor Falls*; *Masterful* for Big Finish).
- William Hughes (a young Master seeing the Temporal Schism in *The Sound of Drums*).
- Michelle Gomez (the first female incarnation, *Deep Breath*; *The Doctor Falls*).
- Sacha Dhawan (from *Spyfall*, onwards).
- Mark Gatiss (an alternative universe's Master in audios from *Unbound: Sympathy for the Devil*).
- Alex Macqueen (on audio, from *UNIT: Dominion* onwards).
- James Dreyfus (the first incarnation of the Master, according to Big Finish PR, who debuted in *The Destination Wars*, starring David Bradley's version of the First Doctor, before transferring to the main range with *The Psychic Circus*).
- Milo Parker (*Masterful*, a young Master).

(We may also consider Norman Stanley as having played the Master, as he's the telephone mechanic in *Terror of the Autons* who turns out to have been the Time Lord in disguise.)

The Deadly Assassin reintroduced the character, bereft of regeneration energy, and teased another face-off between him and the Doctor. This waited some four years, until *The Keeper of Traken*, in which the Master demonstrates a new ability: stealing bodies.

Inhabiting the body of Tremas, Nyssa's father, played by Anthony Ainley, this Master would then appear throughout the Fifth and Sixth Doctors' eras, including the twentieth anniversary special. Dicks had initially wanted the Master to be its core villain, but was talked into making him something of an ally, sent into

Gallifrey's Death Zone by the High Council of the Time Lords to aid the Doctor.

Ainley's only appearance in the Seventh Doctor era was also his last on the show: *Survival*.

"He enjoyed being in the series," Karen Louise Hollis, author of *The Man Behind The Master: The Biography of Anthony Ainley*, wrote, "and later on he attended conventions, revelling in the appreciation he got from the fans, happy to quote lines from the series or re-enact his famous Master laugh. He not only replied to fan mail personally, composing witty letters in beautiful handwriting, but with some fans struck up a correspondence which lasted for years, even having long telephone conversations with a number of them."

The Time Lords granted him a new regenerative cycle in the Time War, but he was scared, fled the conflict, and used the Chameleon Arch to transform his Gallifreyan biology into that of the human Professor Yana. Martha Jones accidentally helped him realise his identity, and his next regeneration became the prime minister of the UK, massacred the population using the Toclafane, and named himself ruler of the Earth, intent on intergalactic war.

Things didn't go according to plan and instead he ended up greedily chomping down hotdogs, turkey, and people in *The End of Time*.

In the meantime, Geoffrey Beevers reprised his role as the decaying Master for Big Finish, first playing "Mr Seta" in *Dust Breeding*, then exploring the Time Lord's origin and relationship with the Doctor in *Master*. Various audio appearances led to his meeting another incarnation, played by Alex Macqueen, in *The Two Masters*, the first multi-Master story – but certainly not the last.

Simm returned for *World Enough and Time/The Doctor Falls*, opposite Michelle Gomez's Missy. The female incarnation was introduced in Series 8, making cameos throughout the run before revealing her plan – to give the Doctor an army of Cybermen, apparently to prove they're one and the same – in *Dark Water/Death in Heaven*.

Missy seemingly made an about-turn and allowed the Doctor to redeem her. For much of Series 10, she was locked in a quantum fold chamber with the Doctor as her gatekeeper, but she slowly convinced him she'd changed, leading to his trialling her by answering a distress signal on the Mondasian colony ship.

And it seems she really did intend to change her nature. Alas, she stabbed Simm's incarnation, forcing his regeneration, and he, in turn, shot her to stop their redemption.

And that was that. Until it wasn't.

Another incarnation of the Master, played by Sacha Dhawan, announced his arrival in Series 12 by ostensibly slaughtering the Time Lords and converting them into Cybermen.

"Oh, how about the robes from *The TV Movie*? Or the Temporal Schism? Actually, I've always liked the laser screwdriver. Or what about—"

You look around and realise the member of staff has gone.

≤ 18. Eyepatches.

20. Cyberman Head.

This head, described by the Ninth Doctor as "an old friend of mine. Well, enemy. The stuff of nightmares reduced to an exhibit", is from Van Statten's Museum, and was supposedly found in the London sewers, although it's the wrong design to have hailed from *The Invasion* or *Attack of the Cybermen*.

The Ninth, War, and Eighth Doctors are the only Doctors not to have met the Cybermen on screen. Still, that doesn't mean they appear anywhere near as often as the Daleks – in fact, apart from a brief cameo in *Carnival of Monsters*, the Cybermen were only in one serial throughout the 1970s. The Third Doctor didn't technically face them either, but witnessed their swift execution in Gallifrey's Death Zone in *The Five Doctors*.

The Second and Eleventh Doctors faced them most often, while the Fourth, Fifth, Sixth, and Seventh Doctors only met them once each. Curiously, they appeared in every Twelfth Doctor finale, thanks to a cameo in *Hell Bent*.

But likely due to their frequent returns opposite Troughton, they were used less frequently from then on. Tom Baker, despite serving seven years in the role, only met the Cybermen once, in *Revenge of the Cybermen*.

It means lots of companions have never battled them on TV either. It's actually quicker to list those who have: Polly, Ben, Jamie, Zoe, Sarah, Harry, Nyssa, Tegan, Adric, Peri, Ace, Rose, Mickey, Captain Jack (though in *Torchwood: Cyberwoman*), Amy, Rory, Clara, Bill, Nardole, Yaz, Graham, and Ryan. River has appeared in a story with the Cybermen (*The Pandorica Opens*), but doesn't come face-to-face with one – unless we count a deleted scene in which she picks up the Cyber-head lurking around Stonehenge and demonstrates knowledge of them by recognising their ships. That means she's met them elsewhere... as have several other companions.

That's because the above list doesn't include multimedia adventures; Liz met them in the audio, *Blue Tooth*, for instance, and Leela in *Return to Telos*.

< 65. Chalice.

21. A Terrifying Army of Three Daleks.

Everyone knows that even one Dalek can pose a serious threat to all life. Still, the attack on Auderly House in *Day of the Daleks* was a little underwhelming. Pertwee and Manning were especially unimpressed.

Still, you're a bit nervous about them being here – that is, until you notice a sign saying that these are emptied Daleks, found in the banana groves of Villengard.

Some might've taken issue with *Asylum*'s Parliament of the Daleks, but the tinpot despots have always had a hierarchy. It's hard to define, however, largely owing to the civil wars established in 1980s *Doctor Who*.

Right at the top *should* be Davros, creator of the Daleks, but some sects turned against him – after all, they consider Daleks the superior beings, so anything not-Dalek, including Davros, is inferior. These are generally split into two categories: Imperials and Renegades.

The head honcho, then, is the Dalek Emperor (who Davros pretends to be in *Remembrance of the Daleks*), debuting in *The Evil of the Daleks* and returning for *The Parting of the Ways*.

But what about the Cult of Skaro? The Tenth Doctor describes Dalek Sec, Caan, Jast, and Thay as "a secret order, above and beyond the Emperor himself". As for who ordered the Cult to think of new ways of killing… we just don't know. Was it the Emperor? Or an unseen higher-ranking model?

The Dalek Prime Minister in *Asylum* is in charge of the parliament, including the white Dalek Supreme of the Paradigm established in *Victory of the Daleks*. That Paradigm exterminated the "unpure" Ironside models of the Time War, so presumably they consider themselves a lower-rank than the Strategist (blue), Scientist (orange), Eternal (yellow), and likely red Drone Dalek. (We never found out what's so special about the Eternal; Steven Moffat said he and Mark Gatiss thought it was just a cool name. Gatiss later wrote, "Its exact function is a mystery, but it's probably something to do with the progenitor device and the continuation of their race.")

The Supreme Daleks of *The Dalek Invasion of Earth*; *The Chase*; *Planet of the Daleks*; *The Stolen Earth*; etc., are typically in charge of any Dalek ground units, so obviously hold authority. They're generally deployed in strategic matters during incursions or dilemmas.

Lesser seen are the tank-like Special Weapons Daleks, one of which appeared in *Remembrance* then cameoed in *Asylum* and *The Magician's Appentice/The Witch's Familiar*. The Reconnaissance Daleks are probably on a level with the Special Weapons Daleks.

Standard Daleks, whatever their colour schemes, come next, and on the bottom rung of the metaphorical ladder (DALEKS HAVE NO NEED FOR LADDERS) are the uncased Kaleds, left to rot in the Skaro sewers.

It is difficult to compare different Daleks, but that's okay – as far as they're concerned, any Dalek is superior to other races.

The Cybermen, on the other hand, have a more defined hierarchy. At the top are the Cyber-Controllers (*The Tomb of the Cybermen*; *Attack of the Cybermen*; *The Age of Steel*), with exposed brains as a common feature, and Cyber-Planners, notably "Mr Clever", aka the Doctor in *Nightmare in Silver*, although non-humanoid versions appeared in *The Wheel in Space* and *The Invasion*.

Next come the Cyber-Leaders, delineated with black "handles" on their heads, the first of which is seen in *Revenge of the Cybermen*. The standard Cybermen are next down, then the Cybermats (which debuted in *Tomb* then changed look in every subsequent appearance), Cyber-Shades (*The Next Doctor*), and Cybermites (*Nightmare in Silver*).

There are variants, of course, including an all-black Stealth Cyberman, only briefly spotted in *Attack of the Cybermen*; *The Time of the Doctor*'s wooden model; and the *Cyberwoman* in *Torchwood*.

≤ 43. Glass Dalek in Acid.

22. The Second Doctor's Destructive Recorder.

"Recovered from Black Hole JPPTWH10.73 (museum designation)," reads the plaque.

This recorder sits inside a metal cube, charred but stable. As a source of matter in an anti-matter world, this simple musical instrument is as terrifying to renowned Time Lord Omega as it is to children forced to learn about it in school.

By today's standards, *Doctor Who*'s tenth anniversary was a low-key affair, and not even celebrated on the relevant date.

In fact, nothing was released on 23rd November 1973. Season 10 had concluded with *The Green Death* on 23rd June, although *The Time Warrior* was on the horizon (starting on 15th December). Radio Times at least released a tenth anniversary special in November, consisting of interviews with cast and crew from throughout *Who* history, as well as *We Are The Daleks!*, Terry Nation's eccentric alternative origin story of his famous creations, which saw them evolving from humans on the planet Ameron. It was less than two years before *Genesis of the Daleks* revealed their true backstory.

Season 10 nevertheless celebrated a decade of *Doctor Who* – including a twelve-part epic space opera, spread across two stories (*Frontier in Space* and *Planet of the Daleks*) – and kicking off with an unprecedented multi-Doctor story, *The Three Doctors*.

Written by Bob Baker and Dave Martin, the four-part tale brought back Patrick Troughton's Second Doctor and, in a limited capacity due to illness, William Hartnell's First Doctor.

The serial itself concerned Omega, the stellar engineer who gave the Time Lords time travel by sacrificing himself to a black hole, albeit on the expectation that his fellow Gallifreyans would rescue him.

The story peaked with Part Four, watched by 11.9 million viewers, while all four episodes were repeated as part of 1981's *The Five Faces of Doctor Who* season.

Hartnell primarily appeared in a black void, communicating with his peers via the TARDIS screen and through mind-melds; he'd struggled to remember his lines, and this meant that he could read them from cue cards around Ealing Studios while still proving a presence throughout.

This was his last appearance as the Doctor, indeed his last TV credit at all. He died in his sleep from heart failure on 23rd April 1975 at the age of just 67. His name will always be best associated with *Doctor Who*, and it was a part that he seemed to genuinely love. He famously noted, "If I live to be ninety, a little of the magic of *Doctor Who* will still cling to me."

< 6. Time-Space Visualiser.

23. Automated Laser Monkey.

"Sontarans, perverting the course of human history!"

You realise you must've drifted off for a short time there. The effects of being this close to a black hole? Either way, you look up to discover the next exhibit, an Automated Laser Monkey.

The plaque reads: "Often used in conjunction with scalpel mines and acid. Borrowed from the armoury of Strax."

You don't imagine he's too pleased about that.

Though Strax is a superb character, it's a shame many younger viewers won't know about his war-mongering race, the Sontarans. Not seeing Strax the nurse/butler facing up to others of his species, who would no doubt hate what he's turned into, feels a missed opportunity.

Still, *A Good Man Goes to War* provided an interesting chance to take another look at the clone race.

It's actually comparatively rare to see numerous Sontarans together, which seems particularly odd given that they're clones who are hatched at astonishing rates. Strax appears without other members of his species in the aforementioned 2012 episode, plus *The Snowmen*; *The Crimson Horror*; *The Name of the Doctor*; and *Deep Breath*.

The Time Warrior introduced Linx, a sole member of the species stranded on thirteenth-century Earth during a reconnaissance mission. This was Sarah Jane Smith's first adventure, and she later misidentified Field Major Styre as Linx (both played by Kevin Lindsay) in *The Sontaran Experiment*. As clones, they are supposed to look the same, but there are some differences across episodes, most obviously in their next two stories, *The Invasion of Time* (Commander Stor has a very different complexion to other Sontarans) and *The Two Doctors*. The latter also featured two Sontarans, Stike and Varl, both noticeably taller than previous members of the race.

The Sontarans are generally short, owing to the intense gravity on their home planet, Sontar. While that leads to foes underestimating them, it also means an increased muscle density, making them stronger than you might presume.

As with *The Invasion of Time*, *The Sontaran Stratagem/The Poison Sky* showed an invasion force of the species. Their other efforts have been in advancement of war – specifically against their shape-shifting enemies, the Rutans – but for their twenty-first century *Doctor Who* debut, General Staal's fleet was tasked with repurposing Earth into Sontar Mk II by converting the air into a breathable atmosphere conducive to the warmongers.

(*The Sarah Jane Adventures: The Last Sontaran* came in the wake of *The Poison Sky* and once more featured a lone member of the species, Commander Kaagh.)

The Series 4 story mentioned that the Sontarans weren't allowed to get involved in the Time War, and hinted at their desire to be like the Time Lords. *The Invasion of Time* showed their invasion of Gallifrey (with the surprise help of the Doctor!), and *The Two Doctors* featured Sontarans keen to learn the secrets of time travel.

This is the genius of writer Robert Holmes: he created a war-loving race which risked being one-dimensional cannon-fodder or unfeeling nemeses, but which were instead fascinating, layered, and terrifying, with a thoughtful backstory, interesting complexes, and the ultimate short-man mindset.

< 76. Wilf's Service Revolver.

24. K1 Robot.

Shining under glittering lights stands the Robot. It's huge and cumbersome, clunky and antiquated in its idea of the future. And yet you can't help but be in utter awe. It's stunning. Iconic. The first foe the Fourth Doctor faced – but can you even call this gentle giant a "foe"?

Alongside Barry Letts, Terrance Dicks helped guide the ship through uncharted waters in the Third Doctor era: for the first (and, so far, only) time, the Doctor was exiled to Earth. Dicks wasn't content with the status quo, telling *Invasion of the Dinosaurs* scribe Malcolm Hulke that it limited *Who* to only two types of story: alien invasion or mad scientist. He sought to do something different with the set-up: *Inferno* switched the action to a parallel world; the Time Lords sent the Doctor to Uxarieus in *Colony in Space*, Solos in *The Mutants*, and the titular planet in *The Curse of Peladon*; and the show travelled to the future for *Day of the Daleks*. It's ironic, then, that Dicks' first serial for the Fourth Doctor is set on Earth, firmly in the "UNIT family" set-up, and features a mad, if compassionate, scientist.

Robot, produced by Letts, reportedly came about because Dicks convinced Robert Holmes that it was tradition for the outgoing script editor to pen a final tale before departing (although this tale might be slightly fabricated, as Holmes was an old hand at *Doctor Who* and might've been inclined to accommodate Terrance regardless). Either way, Dicks indulged freely in the traits of the previous era, meaning that this is the last regular story featuring Nicholas Courtney as the Brigadier and John Levene as Benton. Bessie also makes her final appearance until *The Five Doctors*.

Of course, this certainly wasn't the last time Dicks contributed to the show. He'd joined the production team for *The Invasion* in 1968, before co-writing *The War Games* with Hulke. He'd proceed to write three more Fourth Doctor serials: *The Brain of Morbius* (though with extensive rewrites by Holmes); *Horror of Fang Rock*, the only appearance of the Sontarans' nemeses, the Rutans; and *State of Decay*, a reworking of his *Vampire Mutations* script, which had been replaced by *Fang Rock* due to the BBC's wish to avoid comparisons with a new *Dracula* adaptation. He then returned to pen the twentieth anniversary special.

But arguably his biggest contribution to *Doctor Who*, and to children's lives, is in helping kids to read through his sixty-seven Target novelisations, starting with *Doctor Who and the Auton Invasion* and concluding with *The Space Pirates*. His prose contributions continued until his death in 2019. These include *Blood Harvest*; *Players*; *The Eight Doctors*; *Revenge of the Judoon*; *The Sarah Jane Adventures'* novelisation of *Invasion of the Bane*; *World Game*; and *Mean Streets*. His last *Doctor Who* work was *Save Yourself*, a short story set on Karn for *The Target Storybook* (2019), bringing him full circle by pitching the Second Doctor against the War Lord from *The War Games*.

Terrance is ingrained in *Doctor Who*'s DNA; he is missed but his influence will always be felt.

< 19. Soup Dragon.

25. Fourth Doctor Scarf.

This next item loops across the floor, tripping up men, women, children, and the occasional Kastrian. Unfurling around you, seemingly endless, a rainbow voyage through the doors of perception: the Fourth Doctor's multi-coloured scarf.

Tom Baker was working on a construction site when he was cast as the Doctor. BBC Head of Serials Bill Slater had directed Baker in a *Play for Today* adaptation of George Bernard Shaw's *The Millionairess*, and recommended him to Barry Letts, who was immediately impressed.

There are many iconic Doctor costumes. The bow tie. The beige cricketing number. A suit and converse combo. But the definitive outfit surely consists of a multi-coloured scarf.

It's an extraordinary look, perhaps resulting from a mistake. The legend goes that Begonia Pope was given a load of different wool and instructions to make the Fourth Doctor a scarf. She misunderstood and used all the material she was supplied with; the production team fell in love with it and used it from Baker's first serial, *Robot*. Subsequent seasons even lengthened the scarf, though shorter versions were often used during action sequences and when Tom was running. Romana, too, sported a similar outfit, with a shorter white silk scarf, in *Destiny of the Daleks*.

The Fourth Doctor's clothing was inspired by Henri de Toulouse-Lautrec's 1892 lithograph *Ambassadeurs*, which depicted French cabaret singer Aristide Bruant in a black cape and lavish red scarf.

There is, however, some question about whether Pope really did make a mistake. Designer James Acheson's sketch of the Fourth Doctor features an extra-long scarf – but it's up for debate whether it was drawn before or after Begonia gave him her creation.

Either way, the scarf has become iconic: a staple for cosplayers, as synonymous with the programme as the Daleks, Cybermen, and TARDIS.

In Season 18, it was replaced by a burgundy version, accompanying a darker jacket, which the Fifth Doctor unravelled in *Castrovalva* to help him navigate the labyrinthine TARDIS corridors while in a post-regenerative stew. Still, it's a look he's obviously fond of: the Seventh Doctor wears a paisley scarf, the Thirteenth a stripy one in *Resolution*, and the Eleventh and Kazran wear a couple of multi-coloured scarves in *A Christmas Carol*. The one seen in the TARDIS wardrobe in *The Christmas Invasion* was knitted for producer Phil Collinson when he was a kid.

Strangely, no replicas were commercially available in the UK until October 2012, when Lovarzi launched a bright replica which proved a bestseller.

Since then, the company has produced variants, like the Season 18 burgundy scarf, an 18ft version circa Seasons 16-17, and shorter versions of the main two, designed to be more manageable. Lovarzi has also released jumpers, umbrellas, phone cases, and laptop bags… plus a Fourth Doctor knitted tie, incorporating the iconic stripes! Heck, they've even made an anthology of original fiction, *Loose Threads*, available by subscribing to their newsletter. All four stories – *Four Percent*; *The Unravelling Incident of the Beach of Cantellios 12*; *Can You Wear Me?*; and *The Man With Seven Half-Scarves* – relay the unfolding importance of knitwear.

< 78. "Ooh, Ain't Modern Society Awful" Art Installation.

26. A Bomb!

This next exhibit takes some getting to. You have to climb down an elevator shaft. The cable is slippery but you inch downwards, slowly, getting ever closer. There's a gust of air, and your breath catches in your throat. A whooshing sound fills the tunnel, and the cable shakes. They really should've warned you about this interactive section.

Finally, you get to the bottom. If only you'd spotted the stairs and ramp before now.

You come to a jungle. You presume it's the ship's "oxygen factory", but no, this jungle is petrified. The wood is held in perpetual suspension, cold and hard, partly cracked, stone branches arching past walls and grey vines looping from airducts.

And right in the middle is... a bomb. Counting down. Set to release a biological weapon. Engineered by Nazi-like androids.

A bomb. It's a bomb. It's "A BOMB!" you yell, starting to back away. "Get away, there's a bomb!" Panic is etched over the faces of other visitors, who duck and run and scream. You dart back towards the entrance and dive to the floor, bracing for impact.

The tropes of a Terry Nation script are plain to see. There's a bomb (not always nuclear, but radiation surely plays some part in the story, if only through the Daleks' warped biology). Otherwise, the bomb will be a biological weapon: see *Genesis of the Daleks* and *Revelation of the Daleks*.

Characters often have to ascend or descend through some sort of shaft, the best examples of which are probably in *The Daleks* and *Planet of the Daleks*, both of which also include perilous journeys through a monstrous jungle and/or cave system. *Destiny of the Daleks* includes the android Movellans, robots also typical of Nation's *Doctor Who*.

Terry very nearly didn't write *Doctor Who* at all. Script editor David Whitaker had been impressed with his *Out of this World* episodes, so contacted Nation's agent (the now-legendary Beryl Vertue, founder of Hartsfood Films and mother-in-law of Steven Moffat) to ask about *Who*. Terry phoned his friend Tony Hancock for advice, who apparently said, "A writer of your calibre being asked to work for flippin' kids!" Nation was writing for *Hancock's Half-Hour*, so famously turned down the *Doctor Who* invitation.

Reportedly that very evening, he and Hancock had a heated argument and Nation was either fired or walked out. Suddenly, *Doctor Who* was very appealing.

He didn't rest on easy ideas: his scripts dealt with monumental problems, i.e. the nature of good versus evil, and crossing those boundaries. "I had a bad time with the first episodes of *Doctor Who*," Nation, a pacifist by nature, recalled in 1966. "The Doctor had to say to the Thals: 'If you are worth keeping – if you have anything to contribute, it is worth fighting for, it is worth laying down your life for.' It was against all my beliefs – but I made him say it. There were lots of 'turn the other cheek' letters from viewers, but it is a problem that we all have to face."

Initially contracted only for seven episodes – which he reportedly completed within a week – Nation's popularity skyrocketed hand-in-plunger with that of the Daleks.

As much as we poke fun, Nation's stories brought in the viewers and were generally delivered on time and to budget – two sought-after traits in writers. [You're telling me. – Ed.]

You cover your head, preparing for the explosion. You wait for immense heat, the ceiling collapsing, an all-consuming ringing in your ears…

And wait. And wait. And—

You look again at the bomb. 00:00. Ah, now it's reset. It's counting down again. Huh. Other visitors glance warily at it too, having heeded your warning. Then all eyes on you. "Uh, sorry, I thought…" But there's no point in explaining. People are already leaving, grumbling about "that idiot", "the one who said we were all gonna die."

You search around, desperate for an explanation. You're glad to be alive, of course, but you're still irked. You look quizzically at the nearest member of staff, who says, "Faulty fuse."

"Why didn't you–?"

The man points to the CCTV in the corner of the room. "£200 on *You've Been Framed*, mate."

< 51. Unlimited Rice Pudding.

27. A Regenerating Hand.

A fractured stone hand lies inert in the middle of a Tupperware box. The lid is at a slight angle. Curious...

"Eldrad must live," mutters a nearby visitor.

"What?"

"Nothing," she says cheerily, rubbing a bright ring on her finger and skipping off. Nice dungarees.

Our fear of radiation is understandable: it is, for all intents and purposes, an invisible enemy. Yet we're surrounded by it – radio waves, infrared, wi-fi, microwave, ultraviolet... But what we're actually concerned about is ionizing radiation, because this can damage DNA. It has its uses, however, and can be managed in harmless ways, i.e. x-rays. Nevertheless, news coverage of disasters like Chernobyl has resulted in "radiophobia", so anyone living near a nuclear power plant will probably feel a little troubled, at least when it's initially opened.

Entertainment media naturally reflects our fears, and in *Doctor Who*, stories about radiation are, paradoxically, both comparatively rare and common.

1960s anxieties in America resulted in many stories where people were infused with the transformative power of radiation – Bruce Banner's exposure to gamma rays turned him into the Hulk; Peter Parker became Spider-Man after being bitten by a radioactive spider – and by 1976, *Doctor Who* was intrigued enough to explore these concepts itself, in *The Hand of Fear*.

Here, exposure to a nuclear reactor regenerated Eldrad, the Kastrian's rocky limb absorbing all the rays, inadvertently saving Sarah.

A few years later, *City of Death* detailed how Scaroth's exploding ship unleashed a wave of energy and radiation that kick-started life on primordial Earth.

Terminus embraced the idea of radiotherapy too, with a dose capable of holding back the advance of Lazar's Disease. However, it did also see Bor suffering from radiation sickness, indicating the treatment to be a poisoned chalice.

Radiation, it is frequently underlined, is something to be wary of. The Cybermen in *The Tenth Planet* are damaged by it – as they're augmented humans from Earth's twin planet, the warning to the viewer is clear – and to varying degrees it afflicts multiple planets, including Dulkis (*The Dominators*), Solos (*The Mutants*), Oseidon (*The Android Invasion*), Atrios (*The Armageddon Factor*), Argolis (*The Leisure Hive*), Messaline (*The Doctor's Daughter*), and, in one timeline, a future Earth (*Orphan 55*).

But it is the show's most famous antagonists that serve as its starkest reminder of the threat of radiation.

Doctor Who showed the effects of a nuclear war in just its second story. Skaro is a world scarred by radiation, and natives took two approaches to living in the fallout: Thals managed the danger using drugs; Kaleds retreated into protective shells. For them, it was too late: they'd devolved into irradiated monsters, fuelled by hatred. *Doctor Who* doubled down on the idea in *Genesis of the Daleks*, allusions to World War II heightened by audiences' memories of Hiroshima and Nagasaki.

Even Time Lords aren't exempt. While *Smith and Jones* establishes that the Doctor can survive some types of radiation, he can't deal with Sted radiation in *Utopia* later that series, and in *The End of Time*, it would trigger his regeneration – as it had before. But it is just one of many causes of the Doctor's changes of face:

First Doctor: Seemingly old age, although Mondas' energy-draining effects might've exacerbated the issue.

Second Doctor: Forcibly by the Time Lords in *The War Games*, being exiled on Earth as punishment for interfering in time.

Third Doctor: Radiation from the caves of Metebelis III.

Fourth Doctor: Falling from the Pharos Project's satellite dish.

Fifth Doctor: Contracted spectrox toxaemia.

Sixth Doctor: Accounts differ; *Time and the Rani* says it's the Rani's attack on the TARDIS, while Big Finish's *The Last Adventure: The Brink of Death* suggests radiation is involved.

Seventh Doctor: Caught in the crossfire between gangs, and further complicated by invasive surgery.

Eighth Doctor: Crash-lands in a spaceship on Karn.

War Doctor: Likely old age, echoing the First Doctor's feeling that his body is "wearing a bit thin".

Ninth Doctor: Absorbs the Time Vortex.

Tenth Doctor: A high dose of radiation.

Eleventh Doctor: Probably old age, and being granted a new regenerative cycle by the Time Lords.

Twelfth Doctor: Attacked by Cybermen.

≤ 86. Victorian Mirror.

28. Talking Cabbage.

Not many Doctors can get away with a decorative vegetable. Peter Davison manages it with ~~Kamelion~~ celery. This cabbage would've been an earlier attempt.

Here it is, muttering away to itself. It's rare to see any sort of talking plant, but you're not surprised, exactly. After all, this is all about *Doctor Who*, a show where aliens fart, the lead breaks the fourth wall to wish viewers a Happy Christmas, and a mysterious Doctor rips a rhinoceros' horn clean off its head.

You get closer, trying to hear what the cabbage is saying. Then leap back, repulsed. No wonder they couldn't let that be part of a series screened before the watershed.

Legend has it that Tom Baker wanted a talking cabbage as his companion after Louise Jameson departed the series. His idea was apparently that it would sit on his shoulder and ask all the pertinent questions. It's *Doctor Who*, so not an entirely unreasonable notion; fortunately, however, the production team vetoed it, and we instead enjoyed Mary Tamm as fellow Time Lord/Lady Romanadvoratrelundar for a season before she regenerated, apparently at will, into Lalla Ward.

Baker had frustrations with his companions. After Elisabeth Sladen left, he'd wanted the Doctor to travel solo. Philip Hinchcliffe and Robert Holmes reportedly gave him *The Deadly Assassin* to demonstrate that it couldn't work – only seemingly to prove the opposite. Tom wasn't keen on Leela either, figuring that the Doctor wouldn't take on a companion whose natural instincts were to kill.

Baker's feelings seem like something of an injustice, however, considering how iconic and much-loved many of his companions remain.

Consider, firstly, Sarah Jane Smith, one of the longest-running companions, arguably just behind Jamie McCrimmon. While he was in one hundred and sixteen episodes (including *The Five Doctors* and *The Two Doctors*), Sarah starred in eighty-two, from *The Time Warrior* to *The Hand of Fear*, plus *The Five Doctors* and *K9 and Company*. However, this jumps to eighty-six if we add in her 2006-10 appearances in *Doctor Who*, then to a massive one hundred and forty if we further count the fifty-four episodes of

Romana was, of course played by two people: Tamm and Ward, the latter of whom also played Astra in *The Armageddon Factor* – which we're not counting, as Tamm was Romana there. Mary was also Princess Strella in *The Androids of Tara*. Therefore, Tamm's Romana was in twenty-six episodes, and Ward's in forty, bringing her episode count to sixty-six.

K9 was in sixty-six episodes, discounting John Leeson's voicing the Nucleus of the Swarm in *The Invisible Enemy* and the computer in *Remembrance of the Daleks*. (Not including *The Power of Kroll* either, as K9 doesn't appear, even if Leeson himself does.) Twelve of these episodes featured David Brierly as K9's voice.

It's perhaps unfair to count Nyssa and Tegan Jovanka, seeing as they respectively joined in *The Keeper of Traken* and *Logopolis*, Baker's last two stories. Still, Tegan was in sixty-five episodes, and Nyssa in forty-nine, both accounting for fleeting cameos in *The Caves of Androzani*.

Adric's in forty-five, primarily between *Full Circle* and *Earthshock*, then adding in brief scenes in *Time-Flight* and for the Fifth Doctor's regeneration.

Next is Leela, with forty-one, from *The Face of Evil* to *The Invasion of Time*. And Harry Sullivan's in twenty-seven, mostly in Season 12 then for seven episodes in Season 13. We're not counting Ian Marter in *Carnival of Monsters* as he was John Andrews there.

Baker found particular resonance with the Season 12 team, but nevertheless warmed to all his co-stars, eventually starring in Big Finish audios with many of them.

"I admired her wit and style and warmth," Tom wrote in a tribute to Mary Tamm after she passed away in 2012. "We used to meet at different *Who* conventions and sometimes had time for a little chat. I remember meeting her at Heathrow in the first class section: her section, of course. She was flicking through a magazine and sipping a beer: the epitome of cool style."

< 27. A Regenerating Hand.

29. Memory Weave.

"A man is the sum of his memories", a wise Time Lord once said. That makes this object particularly important. The Memory Weave featured in *The Sarah Jane Adventures*: *The Death of the Doctor*; it has the power to make physical objects materialise, prompted by memories of anyone hooked into the device.

The Weave is connected to a museum computer running a set program, which begins with an 8mm film of the final day of rehearsals for *The Dalek Invasion of the Earth*. This was recorded by Carole Ann Ford as a memento of her time on *Doctor Who*. However, it was double-exposed, meaning Daleks, William Hartnell, and Robomen are spliced with footage of her family playing in the park.

The Dalek Invasion of the Earth was the first time a companion left the TARDIS, although Ford never thought of Susan as a companion; she was the Doctor's peer.

This was part of the problem: the character had been pitched as a go-getter, but Ford felt that every story instead saw her as the damsel in distress, twisting an ankle and needing to be rescued. Carole envisioned her to be more like Emma Peel in *The Avengers* – intelligent and heroic. Ford's prompting led to Susan's telepathic abilities being touched upon in *The Sensorites*, although they were never alluded to again.

Carole had turned down plenty of work offers due to her commitment to *Doctor Who*, but it was no great surprise that she didn't want her contract renewed. This seemed to come as a great blow to Hartnell in particular, as the two got on well.

David Whitaker wrote Susan's final scenes, not Terry Nation. It was his last act as script editor; he'd return to script several other serials, concluding with *The Ambassadors of Death*. The Doctor's farewell speech was immediately iconic, replayed for *The Five Doctors* and *An Adventure in Space and Time*.

The Doctor and Susan's relationship was warm and engaging; it's no shock that attempts have been made to recreate this dynamic. Vicki was introduced in the next story, *The Rescue*; her patter and fervour with the Doctor nicely facsimiled what he had had with Susan. It's less true of Dodo, although it could be argued that she was in the TARDIS so briefly, that their partnership didn't have chance to grow grow.

The Second Doctor is certainly protective of Victoria similarly to his way with Susan – his advice on dealing with grief in *The Tomb of the Cybermen* is a highlight – and the same is true of the Third Doctor with Jo. Reaching a crescendo in *The Green Death*, in which Jo effectively outgrows him and the Doctor must admit defeat, the grandparental figure is arguably abandoned for much of *Doctor Who* (saving something of a resurgence in the Seventh Doctor's warmth to Ace), until the Twelfth Doctor's final season. Bill Potts treats him with reverence, largely as she's his student at university, and in *Knock Knock* tells her housemates that he's her grandad.

The footage is too difficult for the Weave to process, the air in front of you fizzling with an innate magic and nostalgia, unsettled between visions of work and leisure in 1964. It moves onto the next memory.

< Going to Turn Left? But the Memory Weave has more to show you! Stay with it until Page 101. >

30. Our Moon.

Materialising out of thin air is… the Moon!

The Memory Weave strains as it tries to accommodate such a massive, impressive object, which is bending gravity around it. You can hear equipment struggling, then a rasping, whispering voice: "You should kill us all on sight."

The live transmission of the Apollo 11 landing has long been a source of fascination and frustration. Neil Armstrong and Buzz Aldrin's moonwalk lasted just over two hours thirty-one minutes, while Michael Collins stayed in *Columbia* command module. "That's one small step for man, one giant leap for mankind," Armstrong said as he stepped onto the lunar surface. However, he was sure he'd said "*a* man". But maybe we can blame the Doctor for our questionable recollections: according to *Day of the Moon*, he inserted a segment of a Silent into the footage, in which the "memory-proof" aliens instruct us to massacre them. Who knew such a monumental event could be so grim?

Yuri Gagarin was the first human in space, orbiting the Earth for one hundred and eight minutes in April 1961. It took until July 1969 for us to reach our nearest neighbour – which is also the furthest celestial body that a member of humanity has explored.

Doctor Who got to the moon before then, of course. In 1967, *The Moonbase* envisioned a settlement formed around the Gravitron, a machine installed in the 2050s, capable of manipulating Earth's gravity to control the weather. In 2070, the Cybermen deemed this a strategic weakness and infected the crew of the Moonbase with an epidemic.

The Ice Warriors thought similarly, attacking another base on the Moon in *The Seeds of Death*. This was part of the T-Mat control centre, a method of instantaneous travel using transmat signals, i.e. teleporting citizens around the world using the Moon as a relay. T-Mat had utterly supplanted space travel. With this story, airing in early 1969, writer Brian Hayles foresaw perhaps the most unlikely consequence of our finally reaching the heavens: that we'd lose interest.

In a 2019 YouGov survey of 2,061 people, which asked how many would take a trip to the Moon if a safe return were guaranteed. 48% said they wouldn't go. 43% actively would, and the remaining 9% were undecided. 11% said there's "not enough to see or do" there, while 9% said there was "no point".

These contrasting attitudes are best summed up in *Smith and Jones*, in which the Judoon use a H20 scoop to transport the Royal Hope Hospital to the lunar surface. While many patients and professionals panic about the situation, Martha's enthusiasm, awe, and wonder – not just at the Moon itself, but the new world she metaphorically finds herself in – marks her down as companion material. Mr Stoker's awe, meanwhile, translates into bafflement and hopelessness; his appreciation of what's happening soon leads him to the natural conclusion that he won't see his family again. Martha similarly thinks of her family, of what plans she had before her life changed, but nonetheless remains optimistic, fuelled by adrenaline.

Both sides of the coin are acknowledged in *Kill the Moon* as well: the Doctor recognises that mankind has lost its wayfinding spirit, but it is revived when looking at the Moon. With this mysterious unexplored land seemingly on our doorstep, how could we not venture into the darkness?

(Also, the Moon turns out to be an egg.)

But the dark side of the Moon is always lurking. It's where the Daleks hide in *Victory of the Daleks* and the Cybermen in *The Invasion* and *Silver Nemesis*. It can bring out the worst in people: we dump our excess political prisoners on a moon prison in *Frontier in Space*; it has a literally transformative effect in *Tooth and Claw*; and in the Ninth Doctor *DWM* comic *The Love Invasion*, an invader plans to destroy the Moon so that humanity doesn't have an easy first foothold into space (mankind having played a crucial and brutal role in a future space-war against the invader's native species).

The Moon was the first step into space for Jamie and for Martha. It was humanity's first step into space too.

It is vital to life on Earth yet drifts away at a rate of around 4cm a year; let's never not be amazed by it.

31. Destiny of the Doctors.

"Hehehehahhh!"

You'd recognise that laugh anywhere. It's the Master. He's trying to invade the Museum via the Memory Weave. A shrewd plan... except instead of the big bad himself, a copy of *Destiny of the Doctors* is materialising. The 1997 PC game featured filmed inserts and was Anthony Ainley's final Masterly performance.

How do you capture all of time and space in 8-Bit?

Inadequately, if *Doctor Who* is anything to go by.

In 1983, the first official *Doctor Who* game launched: made for the BBC Micro, *The First Adventure*'s swirling packaging promised excitement with the Fifth Doctor! Instead, the title simply added a TARDIS to versions of perennial favourites *Pac-Man, Frogger, Space Invaders*, and *Battleships*. It wasn't exactly a hit, but in its way it was an important step for the franchise (and the Doctor would surely appreciate the ease with which he could regenerate – just tap the space bar!). Plus, its labyrinth resembles the caves of Androzani, which is a neat, if unintentional, touch.

This was followed up with *Doctor Who and the Warlord* (designed by former producer Graham Williams) and *Doctor Who and the Mines of Terror*, Sixth Doctor puzzle games released in 1985. You can play those three on the BBC Micro website, while 1992's *Dalek Attack* (which let players fight Daleks as either the Second, Fourth, or Seventh Doctors, or as Ace or the Brigadier) – developed for the Amiga, Atari ST, Commodore 64, PC, and ZX Spectrum – is on the Internet Archive.

Destiny of the Doctors is a more significant entry, and not solely for Ainley's segments: it was written by Terrance Dicks, and featured audio from Davison, McCoy, both Bakers, and Nicholas Courtney.

It got a mixed reception; it's unsurprising, then, that the next video game in the franchise wasn't until 2008. However, it's interesting that *Top Trumps Doctor Who* is the only Tenth Doctor title, and that a Ninth Doctor and Rose game was planned to tie into the show's return, but never materialised.

In this time, *Doctor Who* found commercial success away from video games – in board games, jigsaws, and roleplaying efforts.

"I've always been a fan of *Doctor Who*, always will be, and stuck with the series through thick and thin. I'm also one of those people who collects everything to do with the series. From figures to videos, from money boxes to inflatable Daleks, I wanted the lot, so getting to be part of the *Doctor Who: Adventures in Time and Space* roleplaying game from Cubicle 7 was a bit of a dream come true," said James Whittington. "I had already been reviewing *Doctor Who* books and audios for places such as regional press, *DarkSide Magazine*, and Ottakar's books stores' magazine but this was a chance to be part of actual merch!"

His job on the RPG was "to write a few character profiles and a couple of story scenarios to inspire players. Okay, not exactly making me Terry Nation, Robert Holmes, or Malcolm Hulke but what it felt like was just amazing. Here I was, contributing to something which was official, something for fans by a fan.

"Released in 2009-10 (where did that time go?), I wrote most of my additions whilst on a family holiday in Keswick. Instead of taking in the natural beauty of the area, my mind was filled with strange, strange creatures and planets a lifetime away. Well, why not? The area had inspired so many creatives in its time so why shouldn't it help inspire me?

"When I saw the finished product on a trip to London, the sense of pride was overwhelming. I didn't care about how little my input had been: here it was, an official piece of *Doctor Who* merchandise with my name somewhere in the contributors' section. I wanted people to walk past and pick it up and see my name – shallow, I know, but tell me someone who hasn't gotten a buzz when they see their name in print!"

Cubicle 7 continues to release RPG instalments and sourcebooks.

During the Eleventh Doctor era there came a slew of video games, starting with the linked titles *Evacuation: Earth* and *Return to Earth* (2010), which boasted Sam Kent-Smith, Sylvester McCoy's son, as a 3D artist.

Sadly, neither they, *The Mazes of Time* (on iOS and Android), nor *The Eternity Clock* (for Steam and PlayStation) were well-received.

Most successful were *The Adventure Games*, a free-to-download PC series which ran to five episodes: *City of the Daleks, Blood of the*

Cybermen, TARDIS, Shadows of the Vashta Nerada, and *The Gunpowder Plot* (starring Sontarans, Rutans, and Silents). These new narratives included voice acting from Matt Smith, Karen Gillan, and, for *The Gunpowder Plot,* Arthur Darvill, alongside impressive cast members like Ralf Little, Emilia Fox, Sarah Douglas, Nick Briggs, and Alexander Vlahos.

Too good to last, *The Adventure Games* were cancelled in 2011.

More niche but with positive reviews was the Massively Multiplayer Online (MMO) *Worlds in Time* (2012-14). In the game, time is shattered, and to put it back together, players had to complete puzzles and unlock customisations, across numerous locations like Skaro, Starship UK, and The Library.

"We really wanted to fulfil the fantasy of having the Doctor choose the player to take them on adventures through space and time. I think that's a huge part of the appeal of the companions, and part of staying true to the show," said Ben Badgett, then-creative director of BBC Worldwide Digital Entertainment & Games. "Throughout the development process, we stayed aligned with the *Doctor Who* team in the UK. For instance, in December [2012] we released an update that allows players to specialise in one of three gameplay based categories, or be a generalist. It's a system fairly analogous to the class system in most MMOs, but in crafting the classes, we lined them up with the common traits of the Doctor's companions. We feel that even though it is a subtle touch, it's the kind of thing that kept the game tied into the larger brand."

Villains were inserted from across the show's history, while staying current too; the Great Intelligence's Snowmen were added shortly after the 2012 Christmas special. "Of course, we're telling stories through word balloons in the midst of multiplayer gameplay, rather than an hour-long drama format, so dialogue and narrative have to be considerably compressed," Ben continued. "Even with those limitations, the game writers have tried to capture the voice of the current Doctor and the show as a whole. It also doesn't hurt that both the BBC Games team and the team at [co-developers] Three Rings are full of long-time *Doctor Who* fans; I've personally been watching the show since the Jon Pertwee years!"

Despite the amount of thought that went into it, *Worlds in*

Time closed in 2014, and the only Twelfth Doctor game came as an extension pack for *LEGO: Dimensions*.

Fortunes seemed to have changed with the Thirteenth Doctor. *The Runaway*, a virtual reality title allowing players to travel in the TARDIS, received a warm welcome, as did *The Edge of Time*, a longer VR experience with an effective use of Weeping Angels, also available in some arcades. Maze Theory builds on that success with the Tenth and Thirteenth Doctor adventure, *The Edge of Reality*, and returns to Wester Drumlins – the spooky house from *Blink* – for *The Lonely Assassins*, available on smartphones as well as the Nintendo Switch, PlayStation, Xbox, and PC.

Arguably most popular of all is *Thirteen*, a simple tile game available for free on the BBC website, which went down a storm on social media by being infuriatingly difficult.

32. The Immoveable Sofa.

The Memory Weave moves on and a large comfy shape begins to form at an odd angle in the air.

It's the immoveable sofa from *Dirk Gently's Holistic Detective Agency*. Elements of that book were reused from Douglas Adams' *Doctor Who* magnum opus *City of Death*, as well as the unfinished *Shada*. Adams had also submitted a script entitled *Doctor Who and the Krikkitmen* (though it was never used), and would rework it into *Life, the Universe and Everything*, the third book in Adams' *The Hitchhiker's Guide to the Galaxy* "trilogy of five".

Douglas Adams' commitment to work was fantastic – in both senses of the word. "I love deadlines," he famously noted. "I like the whooshing sound they make as they fly by."

He was passionate about his ideas, just not necessarily the ones he needed to be working on. And though that description may apply to many writers, Adams took it to another level. He admitted to writing three essays in three years while studying English literature at Cambridge. According to some accounts, his editor, Sonny Mehta, locked Douglas in a hotel suite to finish the late manuscript for *So Long, and Thanks for All the Fish*; in any event, Mehta at least moved in with him to ensure it was finished. Procrastination and a wealth of ideas meant *The Hitchhiker's Guide to the Galaxy* became an ever-evolving text, spread across multiple mediums.

Like many in the creative industries, Adams found breaking into his chosen career difficult. After writing and starring in sketches for *Monty Python*, Adams' TV and radio pitches were generally rejected. He took on other jobs to pay his way – hospital porter, chicken shed cleaner, bodyguard – before *Hitchhiker's* finally propelled him to stardom.

The radio pilot script for *Hitchhiker's* impressed the *Doctor Who* production team so much that he was invited to write *The Pirate Planet*, a zany story with Adams' characteristic mix of joyous humour, larger-than-life antagonists, and dark ideas.

He then became script editor for Season 17 – not an ideal position for someone who struggled with confidence and organisation.

On the other hand, when presented with a problem, he

worked solidly to resolve it. The best example is *City of Death*, which he wrote when a script fell through; it was his job to fill that gap. He recalled that producer Graham Williams "took me back to his place, locked me in his study, and hosed me down with whisky and black coffee for a few days, and there was the script."

He rewrote *City of Death*, now considered a cult classic, over a weekend.

His time as script editor came to an underwhelming end when filming for *Shada* was interrupted by industrial action. The tale never made it to air, but audio, animation, and novel adaptations subsequently filled the gap.

Adams' time on *Doctor Who* was short but sweet, and earned him new legions of devotees, all with towels in tow.

Ah. It really is immoveable. The settee is now fully formed at the Memory Weave's centre and is jamming it up. Smoke erupts from the device. An unnerving whirring stirs the chamber. It's knackered (technical term).

You move on before someone blames you.

< 58. Encyclopaedia of the Worlds of Doctor Who: Volume 4 – S to Z.

33. Three Nimon.

Odd. Three upright bulls in platform shoes wander around a big pen. The plaque says there's only a single Nimon in there. You alert a member of staff who informs you that, no, there's only one in the museum.

"How many Nimons have you seen today?" you ask.

"The Museum will—"

"How many Nimons?"

The staff member checks the pen. Then digs her fingers into her cheeks, eyes popping, face etched with pain. "Three! I have seen three!" And she runs off.

Doctor Who tells us that myths are based on fact. The show frequently draws on the legends of Ancient Greece, arguably the most well-known of which is the Minotaur. This part-man, part-bull was the result of a tryst between the Queen of Crete, Pasiphaë (wife of Minos) and a bull, after Minos backed out of sacrificing a bull to honour Poseidon, god of the sea and the storm. This hybrid had no natural sustenance, so grew up to devour humans. To protect his people, Minos trapped him in a maze.

The closest comparison to this story within *Doctor Who* is *The God Complex*: its Minotaur is close in design and motive to that of Greek myth. It's ferocious and imposing, stalking the halls of the twisting hotel. This creature is sympathetic, though, prompting the viewer to wonder what life would've been like had Theseus not killed the mythic Minotaur and the creature had been forced to live out his prolonged days in a cage.

The episode mulls over the nature of faith, the symbiotic nature of deities and their worshippers.

More ferocious, if less grandly realised, are the previous two instances of Minotaurs: in *The Horns of Nimon* and *The Time Monster*. The latter's half-bull creation was played by The Green Cross Code Man, Dave Prowse, although he claimed not to remember the role at all (and insisted upon autographing DVD covers as "Darth Vader"). Set on the islands of Thera, once the home of Atlantis, the serial introduces the mythology-derived Kronos. Where *Doctor Who*'s Kronos is an agent of chaos, Greek myth shows Cronos as presiding over a time of prosperity.

Cronos, god of the harvest, is often mixed up, understandably, with Chronos, the father of time; it's not just the names – confusingly, both of them also carry a scythe or sickle. (The Greeks wouldn't have been so confused, as in their alphabet, the two begin with different letters.)

Both the Greek Cronos and *Doctor Who*'s Kronos undergo seeming changes of personality: after destroying Atlantis, Kronos turns out to be fair in her judgement of the Doctor and the Master; while Cronos starts out eating his own children – including Poseidon – later he is found presiding over the bounties of the harvest. Time is a fickle mistress.

Linguists will identify further allusions within *The Horns of Nimon*, set on Skonnos and Crinoth (from the principality of Corinth), referring to the planet Aneth (Athens) and featuring a character, Seth, reminiscent of the latter's founder, Theseus.

Meanwhile, *Underworld* is a loose distillation of the tale of Jason and the Argonauts' quest for the Golden Fleece, an instruction given to Bob Baker and Dave Martin by incoming script editor Anthony Read. Jason becomes Jackson; Heracles or Hercules becomes Herrick; Orpheus contracts into Orfe; the Minoans are Minyans; and Persephone is Jackson's ship, the P7E.

The snake-haired Medusa is briefly seen in *The Mind Robber* – though, thankfully for the Doctor, Jamie and Zoe, not her stony gaze. However, the Gorgons are only given centre stage in *The Sarah Jane Adventures*. Embracing the notion that these creatures of mythology were aliens, it's interesting to consider the Weeping Angels as the opposite of the Gorgons: whereas Medusa and her kin could turn humans to stone with one look, humans make the Angels revert to statues in the same way.

< 87. Christ the Redeemer.

34. A Brighton Bus.

This bright yellow bus is the 937 John Nathan-Turner from Brighton and Hove. It's named after *Doctor Who*'s longest-running producer. JN-T, who lived in the seaside city, won the public vote in March 2015.

There's a well-worn argument that John Nathan-Turner stayed too long as producer on *Doctor Who* – in fact, he would probably have agreed with that assessment – and made some curious decisions, like introducing the question mark motif on the Doctors' outfits.

He knew *Doctor Who* though. He'd worked as a floor assistant from *The Space Pirates* then sporadically throughout the Third Doctor era. Following a stint on *All Creatures Great and Small* (in which he cast his own pet, Pepsi, as Pepper, one of Sigfried Farnon's dogs), he joined *Doctor Who* from *The Leisure Hive* and remained producer until *Survival*.

"What he's done for the programme," argued Colin Baker, "is ten times what anyone else has done for it." So what *did* JN-T do for *Doctor Who*? Stay tuned…

- He was its greatest proponent. He was vibrant and enthusiastic in interviews, showing great passion and knowledge.

- He was responsible for casting Peter Davison (who he'd met on *All Creatures*), Colin Baker, and Sylvester McCoy.

- He was a fantastic publicist. Through interviews and tongue-in-cheek comments, he baited the media, grabbing headlines by threatening to do away with classic elements like the sonic screwdriver and the TARDIS exterior.

- In contrast, he also knew when to keep his cards close to his chest. Revealing the return of the Cybermen in *Earthshock* could've got them column inches in advance, but would've ruined the cliffhanger surprise.

- He was accommodating to fans. He built the fanbase by granting fanzine interviews, appearing on shows like *Blue Peter* to communicate directly with viewers, and appearing at conventions.

- He saved *Doctor Who* by staying on as producer. He reportedly knew that it was, to some extent, a poisoned chalice, and that, if he left the series, no one else wanted to take it on. Faced with the choice between career progression and keeping *Doctor Who* alive, he chose the latter.

- He made smart production decisions that kept the ship sailing. Andrew Cartmel, for instance, didn't like the script he'd inherited from Pip and Jane Baker (*Time and the Rani*), but it was a canny move for JN-T to commission two trustworthy writers to open the season when they didn't yet have a script editor.

- He encouraged creativity. When Cartmel pitched his plans for the series, including the idea of reintroducing the mystery behind the Doctor's backstory, hinting that he'd been instrumental in the creation of Time Lord society, Turner was keen for him to do something different with the series.

And that's the tip of the iceberg. Don't listen to the naysayers: Turner gave *Doctor Who* his all.

≤ 50. Tickling Stick.

35. Cardboard People.

There doesn't seem to be anything in this section. You stroll forward, wondering whether an exhibit has been moved into storage.

Oops. You realise with horror that you've walked through the exhibit – cardboard figures scattered on the ground. You've ripped some. It appears you're not the only one who's done this: papery appendages are all over the place.

You look up, find a staff-member staring at you, anguish etched on her face. "Sorry," you say. "I can probably get some tape or something...?"

She yells, "You can't mend people, can you?" in your direction and runs off.

They really need to find better staff.

Fragility is a theme of *Kinda* and *Snakedance*, Christopher Bailey's two Fifth Doctor scripts, steeped in Buddhist allusions. Faith, they argue, gives clarity. Hindle (Simon Rouse), meanwhile, is warped, becoming overly militaristic yet childlike, particularly when the Doctor accidentally steps on his cardboard diorama. His mind is restored only when he opens the Box of Jhana, which brings harmony between nature and the soul.

Buddhist names are scattered throughout: the Mara is a tempting demon in *Doctor Who* and in Buddhism, while Panna, Karuna and Tanha are Anglicisations of Buddhist terms respectively meaning "wisdom", "compassion" and "longing".

With over half a century of history, it's no great shock that *Doctor Who* has no uniform approach to most topics. Yes, the core ideals of the lead are typically maintained, but any particular political, ideological, and religious conceits can generally be countered with opposing examples. For instance, the Doctor's scorn at military tactics in many UNIT adventures flies in the face of his using a bomb on the Dominators, or tricking Davros into destroying Skaro. And that's good: it makes *Doctor Who*, and the Doctor, more interesting. With hundreds of personnel working behind the scenes for so long, it's natural that many different opinions and concepts are presented in contrasting ways.

Perhaps most interesting is *Doctor Who*'s occasional examination of religion – and it is just that: occasional. It's always been a key part of the BBC since its inception – the charter states that it must broadcast one hundred and ten hours of faith-based material a year, over TV and radio – but real studies of divinity in *Doctor Who* are rare.

It may be assumed that some companions in the 1960s were Christian (the number of church members steadily fell across the decade, but nonetheless remained high), but few companions have outright stated their religion. Yasmin Khan is one of the few, her Muslim beliefs arguably not informing many of her choices but nonetheless acting as an important part of her character – and especially explored in *Demons of the Punjab*, which detailed the Partition of India of 1947 and the struggles her Islamic family went through when her grandmother fell in love with a Hindu man.

The Doctor's religion is seldom explored. It might be argued that this is because the character favours science, which some think in opposition to faith – but that's not true from the Doctor's perspective. The Doctor frequently indulges in creation myths: the Source in *The Doctor's Daughter*; the Solitract in *It Takes You Away*; Yggdrasil in *The Curse of Fenric*. Ultimately, he keeps an open mind, concluding in *The Satan Pit* that, "I believe I haven't seen everything – I don't know. It's funny, isn't it, the things you make up? The rules. If [the Beast] had said it came from beyond the universe, I'd believe it, but before the universe? Impossible. Doesn't fit my rule. Still, that's why I keep travelling. To be proved wrong."

Russell T Davies' *Doctor Who* mulled over faith a few times – interestingly, in that Davies himself is an atheist, and carries that perspective into many of his tales: for example, religion is banned on Platform One in Davies' *The End of the World*.

That said, the next story, *The Unquiet Dead* by Mark Gatiss, paraphrases Shakespeare with "There are more things in Heaven and Earth than are dreamt of in your philosophy; even for you, Doctor." Meanwhile, in *Gridlock*, when individuals in a huge community are isolated, belief brings them together, aptly demonstrated by their singing "The Old Rugged Cross" and "Abide With Me". The comfort the citizens of New New York (plus Martha) gain from their community is surely the true spirit of faith.

However, there's no doubt also an argument to be made that their faith leads to inactivity and complacency: the Doctor must act alone, fashioning himself as something of a messiah – unsurprising, given that in the Series 3 finale, the Doctor is effectively resurrected by human prayer.

The Doctor's had a use for religion before. *Planet of the Spiders* is an overt allusion to Buddhism, the faith of its writer, Barry Letts. It's to be found not only in the meditative retreat setting, but also the stressing of the importance of enlightenment, which leads to the Doctor's regeneration. K'anpo Rimpoche/Cho Je seems to have obtained true spiritual awareness, possessing abilities even the Doctor does not – this latter detail is particularly telling, as the monk reveals himself to be a Time Lord who once served as the Doctor's guru, before fleeing the teachings of his people.

It's unlikely the Doctor will ever fully adopt such a doctrine, but one of the best summations of his mindset comes in *The Rings of Akhaten*, when Clara asks whether that system's beliefs – that life originated there – are based on fact. "Well, it's what they believe. It's a nice story," he replies with an understanding smile.

≤ 75. Seal of the High Council of Gallifrey.

36. Fossils.

Oh look, dinosaurs! Massive slabs of sediment have been chiselled from larger bedrocks, protected from enquiring hands, busy tentacles, and exploratory sink plungers by thick glass. But they still look amazing. You feel like a kid again, marvelling at these giant beasts that roamed the earth over sixty-five million years ago.

You can see various creatures etched in the dark layers of stone. Rib cages erupt from spines, tooth-bearing mandibles scream in perpetual torture, and hollowed eye sockets gaze back at the wandering visitors. Crystal jigsaws tell tales of extinction.

And according to *Doctor Who*, it was all Adric's doing, saving the future and dooming the past by falling into the destiny trap.

Adric was the first major companion to die in *Doctor Who*.

Earthshock found the young Alzarian trying to get the Doctor to take him seriously by threatening to leave the TARDIS. Though not really intending to go, Adric wanted to prove he could do what the Doctor couldn't: safely navigate E-Space, where he came from. The TARDIS lands in a tunnel system festooned with dinosaur fossils, which the Doctor, Tegan, and Nyssa explore while Adric carries out his calculations.

The tale twists away from these caves, relocating to a futuristic space freighter carrying copious Cybermen, but eventually finds its way back to the past, as the ship explodes and apparently wipes out the dinosaurs – not to mention Adric at the ship's helm.

The final part is the only episode to not include the theme tune over its credits, as a mark of this shocking cliffhanger, which demonstrated that the Doctor's travels had real consequences. Yet anyone gazing at the *Radio Times* billings for the next story, *Time-Flight*, would've thought his death a ruse: Adric is listed, but turns out to be an hallucination.

(Interestingly, as the Doctor mulled over Earth's history amid its relics, Adric's actor, Matthew Waterhouse, pulled on similar ideas in the late 1990s, with an ultimately unpublished stab at a *Doctor Who* novel. It saw the Doctor and Adric wandering through a landscape composed of the Doctor's memories. In a couple of mornings, Waterhouse had written around six thousand words.

"One picture I remember was a distant sandy mountain range in the shape of a dead Cyberman, like those hills which suggest a sleeping human being," he wrote in his autobiography, *Blue Box Boy*. "I do remember that it was very dark: as his memories were drawn from him, the Doctor began to die. What is anybody made up of but memory?")

Technically, Katarina is the first person classed as a companion to die on screen, but she was only in two stories. She joined in *The Myth Makers*, but was sucked out of an airlock in the following story. Adrienne Hill had previously auditioned for *The Crusade* (for Joanna, a role that coincidentally went to Sara Kingdom actress Jean Marsh) and was excited to play Katarina. "I had lunch with Maureen O'Brien and Peter Purves and they told me to expect the tight schedule and how to cope with Bill Hartnell," she recalled. "He was nice to me as I told him that this was my first television work and he took me under his wing to guide me. You really had to be on your toes with him, though, because he would often forget his lines and we couldn't re-shoot things. You had to be prepared to help him out of a situation. Of course, all I ever said was 'What's happening, Doctor?'"

This would be her undoing. As the handmaid to Cassandra, high priestess of Troy, Katarina came from around 1200BC, posing difficulties for writers. The gaps in her knowledge would've meant continually explaining the trappings of modern life – let alone the concepts the Doctor often explores.

And so, in *The Traitors*, the fourth episode of Terry Nation's twelve-part Dalek epic, she sacrificed herself. In the same story, it appeared that a replacement companion was already lined up: Jean Marsh's duplicitous Sara Kingdom.

However, she, too, was a victim of *The Daleks' Master Plan*, aged to death by the Time Destructor, which the Doctor uses to stop the Daleks.

"My death was done on a trampoline, with the camera below us," Hill continued. "I was jumping up and down to give the impression I was floating away through space. I was terribly proud of that – it was actually done before [*The Myth Makers*]. Jean Marsh and I recorded our deaths on the same day, although they were weeks apart when on TV!"

Sara's death scene, too, was the first thing Marsh filmed for the serial. Though Kingdom's status as a companion is debatable because she was never intended to feature beyond the sole story, Marsh enjoyed the part and returned for several Big Finish audios. "I don't know how I ever did it because I spent most of the time laughing along with Bill Hartnell and Peter Purves," she said. "They used to send me off the set and say I could only come back when I'd calmed down, which I never did." The character was even popular enough to be revived by Nation for *The Dalek Outer Space Book* (1966), the final instalment of the 1960s Dalek-focused annuals.

Sara isn't the only companion whose death is caused by the Doctor: the often-forgotten Kamelion was put out of his misery by the Tissue Compression Eliminator in *Planet of Fire*, after being taken over by the Master. Kamelion actively begs for death, and the Doctor doesn't seem overly concerned after delivering it.

While talking about robot companions, let's not forget the destruction of K9 in *School Reunion*. This model carried over from *K9 and Company*, a gift left for Sarah. Fortunately, after sacrificing himself to stop the Krillitane, K9 was upgraded by the Doctor, and Mark IV went on to appear in *The Sarah Jane Adventures* and *The Stolen Earth/Journey's End*. So did K9 ever really die...?

Although the possibility of death is always mooted when it's announced a companion is to leave the show, very few actually have died, at least on a permanent basis. Take Captain Jack Harkness for instance: he first died in *The Parting of the Ways*, but was brought back by Rose, and has since died many, many times. Though if we believe he's actually the Face of Boe, he does finally give up the ghost in *Gridlock*.

Clara is the only companion to permanently die three times – firstly as Oswin, converted into a Dalek and obliterated as the Asylum was destroyed; then the Victorian Clara, who fell from a cloud in *The Snowmen*; and finally as Clara herself, a victim of the Chronolock in *Face the Raven*.

But Amy and Rory surely take the crowns for Most On-Screen Companions Deaths. Rory died so frequently, he actually seemed accepting of the idea in *Night Terrors*. His propensity for dying became something of a joke. His demises include:

- Being dissolved by an Eknodine (*Amy's Choice*).
- Shot by Restac and erased from time (*Cold Blood*).
- Gunned down by Canton at Glen Canyon Dam (*Day of the Moon*).
- On the verge of drowning (*The Curse of the Black Spot*).
- Seemingly aged to death (*The Doctor's Wife*).
- Victim of the Weeping Angels, living out a life without Amy (*The Angels Take Manhattan*).

But don't underestimate Amy! Her deaths include:

- Crashing the campervan (*Amy's Choice*).
- Shot by Rory the Auton (*The Pandorica Opens*).
- Erased as time contracts, albeit as the young Amelia (*The Big Bang*).
- Similarly shot by Canton in the Valley of Gods (*Day of the Moon*).
- Melted when the Doctor's sonic screwdriver cuts off the signal to her Ganger (*The Almost People*).
- Wiped from the timeline on Apalapucia (*The Girl Who Waited*).

Both were also caught in an explosion when the TARDIS self-destructed in *Amy's Choice*; erased then "reset" in *The Big Bang*; and jumped off a roof and lived out full lives in the wrong time period in *The Angels Take Manhattan*. "I was absolutely moved. And I think that Steven did a wonderful job of really marking their departure in a fantastic way," Matt Smith said soon after their departure. "I miss Karen and Arthur. [We were] great friends and I think the Ponds came to absolutely define an era. But he's great at endings, Steven. I mean, how wonderful that he plotted young Amelia [waiting on the case] in *The Eleventh Hour*. That shot, [Amelia] looking up – he's so clever."

Twice Upon a Time adds an interesting caveat that builds on a concept given lip-service in *Hide*: "To you, I haven't been born yet, and to you I've been dead one hundred billion years," Clara says to the Doctor in the latter tale. "But here we are, talking. So I am a ghost. To you, I'm a ghost. We're all ghosts to you."

Peter Capaldi's swansong shows that Bill and Nardole also died – eventually. Their memories are captured by the Testimony, and, despite speculation that Susan would return for the episode, it's pertinent that only the three companions relevant to the Twelfth Doctor are seen. Nonetheless, the implication is clear: everyone the Doctor has ever grown close to is dead and is represented by the Testimony.

Indeed, Moffat boasts the distinction of being the only person to oversee an era in which all the Doctor's companions die. "I'm not even crazy about it when they did it with Adric. I don't think that's the story", he told *DWM*. "I'm sorry, it's a children's programme. And explicitly, the companions are like Doctor Who's children. Or his grandchildren. They're in his care, and lovely old Doctor Who is opening the TARDIS doors and saying, 'I will always look after you'. Get it right – that's the story." Accordingly, those companions at least enjoy full lives before their deaths; though that's arguably true of all companions, it's either mentioned or implied that Amy, Rory, River, Clara, Bill, and Nardole led expansive lives before their ends.

Doctor Who insists that death is inevitable, but what comes before it is most important.

< 29. Memory Weave.

37. The Shadow.

You've seen some amazing sights here, but this one takes your breath away. It's a ship. Not a spaceship; an actual Edwardian yacht. And it's not floating in the water: it's suspended in the grand chamber above you. Suspended by what? From what? It seems willpower alone is keeping it aloft. There's a majesty and an eerie stillness about it. The sails gently sway in a make-believe breeze. It is iridescent, serene.

This is from *Enlightenment*, a ship commanded by the Eternal, Captain Striker. The Eternals are mentioned numerous times in *Doctor Who*, including in *Army of Ghosts* and *Can You Hear Me?*, but the Fifth Doctor serial is their sole TV appearance.

To the Eternals, you are a mere Ephemeral, a flickering candle, a pawn, a curiosity waiting for direction.

Surprisingly, *Enlightenment* is the first serial written and directed by women (it's also Barbara Clegg's only story, although she submitted plans for stories that were never made). It was Fiona Cumming's penultimate credit for the show, her final being *Planet of Fire*; she'd directed *Castrovalva* and *Snakedance* before, and worked as an assistant floor manager and production assistant in the First and Second Doctors' eras. The next serial both written and directed by women was *The Witchfinders*, some thirty-five years later (Joy Wilkinson and Sallie Aprahamian, respectively).

So who is the most prolific director of each Doctor's era? We're looking per storyline here, not taking into account duration.

First Doctor: Douglas Camfield (twenty-one episodes, not including film inserts for *An Unearthly Child* and *Marco Polo*, for which he was technically credited as a production assistant). His total doesn't include *The Planet of Decision*, which was largely by Richard Martin, as there's some debate over whether he directed Ian and Barbara's return to 1965. The sequence was filmed alongside the Camfield-helmed *Time Meddler*, and he was certainly present during the still photograph session.

Second Doctor: David Maloney (nineteen episodes, largely owing to *The War Games*).

Third Doctor: Michael E. Briant (twenty-two episodes). Barry Letts is also notable for producing and directing around nineteen episodes, sharing direction on *Inferno* with Douglas Camfield.

Fourth Doctor: David Maloney (twenty episodes). Many directors returned throughout this era, including Pennant Roberts (twelve, or eighteen if we include *Shada*); Christopher Barry (twelve); Michael Hayes (fourteen); Rodney Bennett (ten); and Douglas Camfield (ten).

Fifth Doctor: Fiona Cumming (sixteen episodes, closely followed by Ron Jones with fourteen).

Sixth Doctor: Peter Moffatt (seven episodes, spread over just two serials, *The Twin Dilemma* and *The Two Doctors*).

Seventh Doctor: Chris Clough (twelve episodes with McCoy).

Eighth Doctor: Geoffrey Sax.

Ninth Doctor: Joe Ahearne (five episodes, beginning with *Dalek* and ending with *The Parting of the Ways*).

Tenth Doctor: Graeme Harper (twelve episodes featuring Tennant's incarnation).

Eleventh Doctor: Toby Haynes and Nick Hurran (five episodes each). Haynes has the distinction of being the only director on twenty-first century *Doctor Who* to helm five consecutive episodes across two seasons. Hurran was in charge of the fiftieth anniversary story.

Twelfth Doctor: Rachel Talalay (seven episodes, consisting of every two-part series finale with Capaldi's Doctor plus his swansong).

Thirteenth Doctor: Jamie Childs and Jamie Magnus Stone (four episodes each). Childs also directed the short video announcing Whittaker as the Doctor.

< 77. Lenticular 2010 Card.

38. *The Five Doctors* Target Novel.

A silvery foil cover focuses on a diamond-like line-up of Doctors in profile, surrounded by Daleks, Cybermen, K9, and the TARDIS.

This novelisation of the twentieth anniversary special was controversial in having been available in some places up to a fortnight before *The Five Doctors* aired. There were minor differences between the book and TV versions, but readers could still glean the entire narrative from this Target.

It's definitely not the only advanced preview fans have experienced.

The most notable is arguably when *Rose*, start of a brave new era, was leaked online on 7th March 2005, three weeks before its 26th March premiere. It was available through the BitTorrent sharing platform, and was close to its final cut, the main difference being the new theme tune arrangement. It was traced to a Canadian company who'd received a review copy, and, by the end of the month, the person responsible had been fired.

It's far from being the only episode to leak early: Amazon Prime US uploaded *The Witchfinders* instead of *Kerblam!* (meaning American viewers were both one episode ahead and one behind), although the former was bizarrely accompanied by the latter's subtitles; a short clip and two stills from Series 11 gave fans a first glimpse of the Thirteenth Doctor in July 2018; and a production error in America meant two hundred and ten fans received copies of the Series 7: Part 2 Blu-ray a week before *The Name of the Doctor* aired. To thank those fans for not spoiling the finale, the BBC released a teaser for *The Day of the Doctor*. "I'm gobsmacked. I'm impressed. Actually, I'm humbled. And we are all very grateful," wrote Steven Moffat. "I wish I could send you all flowers, but I don't know where you live (and given our record, you really shouldn't be sharing private information with us)."

Scripts and "pre-air screeners" of the first five episodes of Series 8 made their way online on 6th July 2014. They leaked from BBC Worldwide's Latin America headquarters, and were swiftly deleted. It was too late – watermarked rough edits circulated throughout July and August, shortly before the Twelfth Doctor's full debut in *Deep Breath*.

Casting viewers in a better light, though, is the curious case of the script in the taxi. In November 2012, a draft of *Nightmare in Silver* (then called *The Last Cyberman*) was found in the back of a Cardiff cab by Hannah Durham, who contacted the BBC to return it.

As we've already established, the BBC isn't the best keeper of secrets. Matt Smith's departure from *Doctor Who*, for instance, was announced on 1st June 2013 when an email was prematurely sent around the corporation revealing that a Twelfth Doctor would kickstart Series 8.

Sometimes, previews are even sanctioned by the BBC. "Coming Soon" trailers naturally contain minor spoilers – although this didn't save the Beeb from receiving complaints when *Aliens of London*'s "Next Time" teaser conceded that, shockingly, the Doctor and friends didn't die – but those tacked on the ends of *Boom Town*, *The Impossible Astronaut*, and *The Pilot* went a bit far; respectively, they revealed that the Daleks would feature in the Series 1 finale, Amy didn't kill the astronaut, and, criminally, that John Simm's Master would return in Series 10.

Spoilers are a natural consequence of publicity, so while Dalek Sec's facelift was the cliffhanger to *Daleks in Manhattan*, it had already featured on the *Radio Times* cover. Meanwhile leaks are expected, however secretive a production team is; just look at filming photos of Cybermen for *Ascension of the Cybermen*, or the makeshift Dalek for *Resolution*. While *Revolution of the Daleks* should've been a surprising title, it was undermined by shots of Daleks on Bristol's Clifton Suspension Bridge, which appeared across media outlets.

Other previews are more subtle. Martha Jones' first appearance, for example, wasn't in *Smith and Jones*, but in *Made of Steel*, a Quick Reads book written by Terrance Dicks, and the only time Martha met the Cybermen. It was released on 1st March 2007, almost a month before Series 3 premiered. She's described as "a medical student, [who had] met the Doctor when terrifying alien forces had invaded the hospital where she was training." The first words Martha says, in response to the Doctor telling her a creature is probably more frightened of her than she is of it, no offense, are: "None taken. And who's frightened? I mean, it's only a flipping great prehistoric monster the size of a house!"

Most impressively, *The Tomorrow Windows* by Jonathan Morris includes an appearance of the Ninth Doctor, written before Christopher Eccleston had been announced. The Eighth Doctor book, about a Tate Modern exhibition which shows you windows on the future, describes this future incarnation as "A wiry man with a gaunt, hawklike face, piercing, pale grey-blue eyes and a thin, prominent nose".

≤ 66. Mal Young's Office.

39. Turlough's Crystal.

Although made from resin, this small prop glitters as if it really is otherworldy. As you get closer, it lights up! But don't worry: it's hollow, and the bottom has wires sticking out. Inside, a bulb blinks in response to a muted voice.

Actor Mark Strickson had those wires lacing up through his sleeves, and the electrics grew hotter as scenes progressed. Fortunately, he only communicated with the Black Guardian in three stories during *Doctor Who*'s twentieth anniversary series.

And lo, the great edict rang out: every story in *Doctor Who* Season 20 would feature the return of a classic villain!

Except they cheated a bit. The Black Guardian served as a linking character, attempting to use new companion Turlough to do his bidding, and this allowed *Mawdryn Undead*, *Terminus*, and *Enlightenment* to breathe a little, unencumbered by the law of diminishing returns.

Mawdryn Undead also brought back Nicholas Courtney as the Brigadier (after William Russell proved unavailable to return as Ian), while the season also saw the reappearances of Omega (*Arc of Infinity*), the Mara (*Snakedance*), and the Master (*The King's Demons*).

It led to *The Five Doctors*, which brought together Troughton, Pertwee, and Davison's Doctors, plus Richard Hurndall as the First Doctor, with Tom Baker's incarnation trapped in a time scoop somewhere over Cambridge.

Baker actually turned down his chance to come back, feeling that he hadn't been gone long enough to justify a reappearance, something he later apparently regretted. Terrance Dicks' first draft included the Fourth Doctor seemingly betraying his peers, but in the end, footage from the unaired *Shada*, in which he and Romana go punting, was used instead.

These incarnations and select friends (Susan, the Brigadier, Sarah, K9, Tegan, and Turlough) were placed in the Death Zone of Gallifrey by a mysterious assailant, and headed towards the Tomb of Rassilon, the final resting place of one of the founders of Time Lord society.

"It was an occasion. And it was very, very special because that was twenty years. So you sort of thought, 'well, how many of these people are going to be here in twenty-five years time?' and that always goes through your mind," recalled Mark Strickson. "And it was great for me: I was able to meet my Doctor, which is Pat Troughton, and things like that. We've always got 'our Doctor' as *Doctor Who* fans. He was lovely! He's an absolutely gorgeous guy."

Further returnees included Zoe, Jamie, Liz, and Mike Yates, albeit as illusions; Bessie; a lone Dalek; and an army of Cybermen. Pleasingly, the ninety-minute special opened with footage of William Hartnell's Doctor saying goodbye to Susan from *The Dalek Invasion of Earth*.

< 9. Berwick Dalek Playsuit.

40. *Revenge of the Cybermen* VHS.

This videotape elicits mixed emotions. Released in October 1983, it was the first commercially available *Doctor Who* VHS, so you could actually rewatch this four-part serial as many times as you liked. On the other hand, the cover featured an incorrect Cyberman design (hailing from *Earthshock*) and the Fourth Doctor circa Season 18. Reissues and foreign editions amended these errors.

Still, you feel pangs of nostalgia. You'd love to play this on a 1980s television and get lost in its warmth.

BBC Video initiated a survey at the Longleat convention earlier that year to find out which serial fans would most like to see again. They voted for *The Tomb of the Cybermen* – which was missing. The BBC opted for the next available colour Cyberman story instead.

The VHS range wasn't ideal. Until *The Daleks* in 1989, stories were edited into omnibus editions, cropping out most cliffhangers, credits, and, in the case of the First Doctor stories, "Next Time" captions. But videos were accessible. Fans didn't have to rely on Target novels to relive adventures anymore. And while *Revenge of the Cybermen* was initially expensive, its 1984 second edition halved in price (though was still a considerable £20).

The Brain of Morbius was next to be released, followed by a steady stream of classics in the late 1980s. The schedule stepped up a gear after *Survival*, so while you couldn't enjoy the ongoing journeys of the Seventh Doctor and Ace on TV, you could at least pore over the classics. *The Hartnell Years* launched a new subsection in June 1991, including rare and orphaned episodes from the early 1960s (including the Arabic dub of *The Edge of Destruction*), presented by McCoy. This was followed by similar editions covering the tenures of Troughton, Pertwee, and both Bakers, plus *The Dalek Years*, *The Cybermen Years*, and *The Missing Years*.

The VHS line ended in November 2003 with the remaining episodes of *The Reign of Terror*, *The Faceless Ones*, and *The Web of Fear*. It was naturally replaced by the DVD range, which began in the UK with *The Five Doctors* in 1999. A new cover art template was designed for its second release, *The Robots of Death*, in 2000, and releases started to ramp up so that, for *Doctor Who*'s fortieth anniversary in 2003, one story was released for each of the first seven Doctors (*The TV Movie* having been available in 2001).

Some special editions were made: *Lost in Time* (2004) collected individual episodes from otherwise missing serials; the WHSmith exclusive *Dalek* set (2005) included *The Dalek Invasion of Earth*, *Resurrection of the Daleks*, and *Remembrance of the Daleks*; a limited edition seven-disc set collated the entire *Key to Time* in 2007 (before a widely distributed reissue in 2009); and three *Revisitations* boxes added better picture and sound quality, plus special features, to serials released in the DVDs' early years.

Then came a raft of Blu-rays, initially confined to *Torchwood* and twenty-first century *Doctor Who* (from *Planet of the Dead* onwards) before occasional upscaled editions of *Spearhead from Space*, *The TV Movie*, and animations. In 2018, *The Collection* launched, a new line of Blu-rays collating entire seasons in separate sets. *Doctor Who* had never looked so good.

< 62. 1996 Film Cannister.

41. Four-Legged Beast.
(On loan from Panto-Horses-Are-Us.)

At least, that's how writer Johnny Byrne described it. This is, of course, the Myrka, Homo Reptilia's weapon of choice in *Warriors of the Deep*, and one of the most notorious monsters in *Doctor Who*.

It wanders around a special pen. The room is dark. Perhaps because the Myrka can't stand light. Or so you don't notice the bubble wrap. It's certainly testament to Malcolm Hulke's genius that the Silurians and Sea Devils only appeared twice each in twentieth century *Doctor Who* yet are remembered as iconic foes.

The concept is brilliant: these creatures inhabited Earth before mankind. They've slept underground for millennia, retreating into stasis chambers when their scientists became concerned about a potential mass-extinction event: a rock heading towards the planet (in the end, simply our moon coming into alignment). Now, the Silurians and Sea Devils want Earth back, claiming to be its rightful owners, seeing humans as primitive apes.

Hulke introduced the race in *Doctor Who and the Silurians* then revisited the notion with their aquatic cousins, *The Sea Devils*. Though the latter were manipulated by the Master in their first appearance, both species were nuanced and individual, with different factions debating their place on the surface, some favouring peace over war. In each case, humanity turned to violent means to halt negotiations.

Multimedia tales further examine the individualities of these races. Their connected histories were expanded in Gary Russell's Missing Adventure novel *The Scales of Justice*, while the Silurians' part in human evolution was explored in Big Finish's *Blood Tide*. *DWM*'s *Cybermen* strips questioned the Sea Devils' role on Earth's twin planet, Mondas, and several Virgin Books put them on humanity's side.

Even the Myrka returned for Quick Read's *The Silurian Gift*.

Sadly, subtleties were largely lost in *Warriors of the Deep*, but interestingly, it's the Doctor whose hands are forced, killing the Silurians and Sea Devils with Hexachromite gas after they take over a Sea Base in 2084.

The Sea Devils never returned on TV, but the Silurians pervade twenty-first century *Doctor Who*. They were redesigned for *The Hungry Earth/Cold Blood*, losing their hypnotic third eye and gaining a poisonous tongue. Though ceremonial-like masks were fitted for most members of these new Silurians, core cast – Neve McIntosh as Alaya and Restac; Richard Hope as Malohkeh; and Stephen Moore as Eldane – were realised using prosthetics and make-up.

"The three-eyed design would have required animatronics," explained Rob Mayor, a director of prosthetics company Millennium FX. "As there were multiple different characters within the show, that would have been hugely cost-prohibitive. More importantly, the script was very heavy on emotive Silurian dialogue, which we felt would be better served through the use of thin facial prosthetics."

Chris Chibnall's original script implied that all previous Silurians wore disguises, so that in reality they had always looked closer to the humanoid reptilians from twenty-first century *Doctor Who*; this was vetoed by Steven Moffat. Instead, these Silurians were considered another subspecies. Chibnall also suggested "Homo Reptilia" as their name; they were inaccurately called Silurians, supposedly hailing from this period of the Paleozoic Era (about 542 million years to 251 million years ago), but others suggest that they come from the Eocene Epoch, around 56 to 33.9 million years ago.

By *Dinosaurs on a Space*, however, they're re-established as Silurians, apparently forging ahead on a new planet called Siluria. McIntosh would return for *A Good Man Goes to War* as Madame Vastra, who'd woken earlier than her peers and had taken out her anger on underground workers – before the Doctor helped bed her into Victorian society. She set herself up as a private detective with her wife and maid, the human Jenny, and their Sontaran butler, Strax. Though more reasonable than other individuals of her race, she occasionally let her darker side loose, threatening Strax when Jenny's life is in danger in *The Name of the Doctor*, and apparently eating Jack the Ripper.

The so-called Paternoster Row Gang would reappear throughout the Eleventh Doctor era, seemingly as the basis for Arthur Conan Doyle's Sherlock Holmes stories.

< 47. The Orient Express.

42. Celery.

Peter Davison apparently only agreed to wearing a stick of celery on his lapel if its presence was explained; that explanation finally came in his last story. "I'm allergic to certain gases in the praxis range of the spectrum," the Doctor said. "If the gas is present, the celery turns purple."

He'd then eat the celery; if nothing else, it's good for his teeth.

But it wasn't gases in the praxis spectrum that caused the Fifth Doctor to regenerate; it was spectrox toxaemia, contracted on Androzani Minor.

In 2009, *Doctor Who Magazine* readers voted *The Caves of Androzani* as the best *Doctor Who* story ever. It's no great shock that it was written by Robert Holmes, who knew the programme inside and out.

Holmes is a *Doctor Who* legend, whose incredible creativity added a massive amount to his mythos; he was the most prolific writer of twentieth century *Who* – technically, the most prolific writer of *Doctor Who* as a whole, at least by episode count (if we were going by duration, the title would be held by Steven Moffat).

Holmes' first *Who* was *The Krotons* and his last was *The Ultimate Foe*, although he passed away while working on the latter, so it was finished by Pip and Jane Baker.

It's debatable how many he actually wrote, however – general consensus is somewhere between sixty-four episodes and seventy-three, the range due to the fact that, as script editor between 1974 and 1977, he engaged in many rewrites. Terrance Dicks, for example, was so surprised about the extent of rewrites on *The Brain of Morbius* that he asked his name be replaced with "some bland pseudonym" (Robin Bland). *The Ark in Space* was written by Holmes but based on an idea by John Lucarotti, and *Pyramids of Mars* was credited to Stephen Harris when Holmes replaced an unworkable script from another author.

Holmes' first two scripts, *The Krotons* and *The Space Pirates*, are less well-regarded than you'd expect, but from *Spearhead from Space*, he submitted a run of fan-favourites.

He created the Nestene Consciousness, Autons, and Sontarans, but perhaps most significantly, at least in establishing the "who" in *Doctor Who*, he gave Gallifrey its name, before undermining the seemingly all-powerful Time Lords who had been introduced in *The War Games*. Power's ability to corrupt was a theme in his scripts: *Carnival of Monsters* showed "lesser" beings serving as entertainment for controllers; *The Caves of Androzani* had people as playthings of corporations; and *The Sun Makers* raged against the tax-hungry government. In particular, Holmes fashioned the Doctor's species according to the old adage of absolute power corrupting absolutely. *The Deadly Assassin* showed us a race so fearful of their influence that they restricted themselves with a moral code while flaunting their privileges regardless.

Holmes added another important soupçon to the Time Lords: the regenerative limit, meaning they can only have thirteen bodies. This would haunt the Doctor and the fandom for many years, and arguably still does: the rules of the Twelfth Doctor's new cycle aren't established (even Rassilon seems uncertain), and *The Timeless Children* puts further question on this.

Robert's further contributions to *Doctor Who* include the Shobogans (natives of Gallifrey), the Eye of Harmony, and the Matrix Databank; he also established the Master, the Key to Time, the White and Black Guardians, the Valeyard, Borusa, and companions Liz, Jo, Sarah, and Romana.

Russell T Davies said that *The Talons of Weng Chiang*'s opening episode has "the best dialogue ever written… When the history of television drama comes to be written, Robert Holmes won't be remembered at all because he only wrote genre stuff. And that, I reckon, is a real tragedy."

Imagine *Doctor Who* as a grand symphony. Robert Holmes was the conductor. The pitch altered after his passing, but the tone remains his.

< 52. "No Coloureds" Sign.

43. Glass Dalek in Acid.

No one promised it'd all be laughs and jelly babies (except that guy outside with a sign reading, "COME INSIDE FOR LAUGHS AND JELLY BABIES"). This one is particularly *dark*, though. It's a glass Dalek, its insides exposed for all to see, drowned in a bubbling vat of acid. It stinks. It burns at your face. It reminds you of going to the dentists.

You're warned not to get too close. Accordingly, there's a guard sitting to one side. He's asleep, but it's the thought that counts.

Is *Doctor Who* too violent and frightening? Yes. Sometimes.

The first instance of this is *An Unearthly Child*, in which the Doctor tried to, uh, cave a caveman's skull in; then *The Edge of Destruction*, which Verity Lambert conceded was a step too far, showing a deranged Susan threatening her friends with a pair of scissors (something children could imitate).

The show frequently attracts complaints, whether over sex (yes, really), violence, or scares. *Terror of the Autons* included phone wires attempting to strangle the Doctor, plastic daffodils squirting cellophane over mouths to suffocate people, and a doll murdering someone. That's without mentioning the policeman, a trustworthy member of society, turning out to be a murderous Auton. Here are a few further times *Doctor Who* arguably crossed the line:

- Electrocutions in *The Tomb of the Cybermen*.
- Undermining the police again, as several gun down enemies of the Daleks (*Resurrection of the Daleks*).
- The Doctor tries to strangle Peri (*The Twin Dilemma*).
- Gangs fire at each other, ultimately killing the Doctor (*The TV Movie*).
- The Doctor tortures a Dalek (*Dalek*).
- Dr Constantine's gruesome transformation (*The Empty Child*).
- Elton alludes to a sex life with a paving slab (*Love & Monsters*).
- The Doctor cleverly tricks humanity into committing genocide (*Day of the Moon*).

- Deceased loved ones turn into Cybermen (*Dark Water/Death in Heaven*).
- The Doctor proves useless when Graham admits his fear of his cancer returning (*Can You Hear Me?*).
- Companions are too sexy; this charge is often levelled at Leela, Peri, and Amy for wearing revealing outfits. Those complaining about Amy's skirt in *The Eleventh Hour* apparently forgot Captain Jack's nakedness in *Bad Wolf*.

Mary Whitehouse loved nothing better than to hold the BBC to account, and *Doctor Who* was frequently her go-to target. *The Deadly Assassin* pushed her too far, as Episode Three ended with a freezeframe of the Doctor being held underwater. She called it "sadistic", "tea-time brutality for tots", and "some of the sickest and most horrific material ever seen on children's television". When the story was repeated, the final shot was omitted, although it was only the tip of the iceberg.

When Graham Williams took over as producer, he was instructed to tone the violence down.

Under the next producer, John Nathan-Turner, however, *Doctor Who* reached its brutal crescendo, debatably leading to its 1989 cancellation.

In *Vengeance on Varos*, the Doctor looks to be responsible for two guards taking a dip in an acid bath; his "forgive me if I don't join you" is especially harsh. Meanwhile, *Revelation of the Daleks* includes a character being transformed into a Dalek, begging for death's release. And *Attack of the Cybermen*, the posterchild for barbarism, sees Lytton mid-conversion, and having his hands crushed. He screams. There's blood.

Violence has always been a part of *Doctor Who*, but it's often only implied. In the case of much of the above, really, there should have been another way.

< 41. Four-Legged Beast.

44. Rory.

Okay, it's not *that* Rory. It's the Handbot from *The Girl Who Waited*, a smile scribbled on its white rounded face. It's content to slowly traipse around the museum. No guard pays it much attention; it has, after all, been disarmed ("Do not be alarmed. This is a kindness"). Kids, on the other hand, love it. They run up, hug its shiny shins, and pester their parents for pictures. Rory is their companion.

Doctor Who fans are a patient bunch. You wouldn't necessarily think so examining the schedules in the 1960s, but the fandom has gradually got used to waiting longer between seasons – seasons which typically only got shorter. Hartnell's last full run, Season 3, consisted of forty-five episodes; by *Doctor Who*'s 1989 demise, seasons consisted of just fourteen episodes. Minus a chink of light in the mid-1990s, *Doctor Who* continued in other mediums with an uncertain future.

Since its twenty-first century return, *Doctor Who* has experienced minor hiatuses and near-constant rumours of imminent waits. The first came after David Tennant's final full series as the Doctor; both he and Russell T Davies announced their departures, leaving *Planet of the Dead*, *The Waters of Mars*, and *The End of Time: Part One* to be the only specials in 2009 (bookended by *The Next Doctor* in 2008 and *The End of Time*'s conclusion on New Year's Day 2010). After fourteen episodes a year since 2005, this might've felt punishing for new fans, but it was good preparation for 2012, during which six episodes aired, with measly festive servings only in 2016 and 2019.

But before 1989, the most painful hiatus came after Season 22 ended on 30th March 1985. Then-BBC1 controller Michael Grade blamed sliding ratings and excessive violence for this enforced eighteen-month hiatus.

During this time, fans were treated to a short segment on Children in Need in which numerous Doctors and companions handed Terry Wogan and Patrick Moore cheques for the charity. Sadly, it was the last time Patrick Troughton played the Second Doctor on screen.

When *Doctor Who* returned, it was seemingly with an increased episode count, rising from thirteen a year to fourteen. An embarrassment of riches! Except whereas Season 22 was comprised of roughly 45-minute episodes, Season 23 reverted back to shorter durations, meaning less *Doctor Who* than ever before. The series had started its road to cancellation.

Between its *Trial* and its seeming execution, however, the programme at least enjoyed a burst of comic and cyberpunk-inspired creativity, as the Seventh Doctor era dawned.

< 49. Sylvester McCoy's Sixth Doctor Wig.

45. Time Lord Court.

You're inexorably drawn to the next installation – not by tractor (or Tractator) beam but by its sheer scale. This massive structure is the Time Lord court, retroactively named Space Station Zenobia, a rusting circular tunnel looping around a dart-like centre. It's probably bigger on the inside too.

All its doors are sealed off and a sign warns that anyone attempting to go inside will be prosecuted. Word on the street has it that there's an entrance to the Matrix Database in there. You're tempted, but the prospect of being imprisoned in a Quantum Fold Chamber for eternity isn't too enticing.

The actual court model was six feet wide, designed by Mike Kelt (whose major contribution to the series was the TARDIS console which debuted in *The Five Doctors* and was used until *Survival*). *The Mysterious Planet*'s opening sequence – in which the TARDIS was forcibly drawn into the court – was *Doctor Who*'s first use of a motion-control camera. John Nathan-Turner justified its £8,000 cost by reusing it for establishing shots throughout *The Trial of a Time Lord*, and to immediately impress viewers tuning into the programme to find out what had changed during its hiatus.

Models had been handled by the BBC visual effects team since *The Faceless Ones*, during which the production crew reported issues with props made by Shawcraft Models. Founded by Bill Roberts, Shawcraft had been responsible for many impressive units from much of the First and Second Doctors' eras, the first of which was the gorgeous and influential city on Skaro. Shawcraft had also made four Daleks for their debut serial, as well as the TARDIS' Time-Space Visualiser, the Mechanoid City, the Macra, *The Rescue*'s UK-201 spacecraft, and much more.

The most impressive thing about many of *Doctor Who*'s models is the level of detail. In August 2016, the Model Unit was employed to work on a sequence in *Thin Ice* that saw the Doctor, clad in a Regency diving suit, crash through the ice and sink to the bottom of the Thames. The main torso was moulded at 1/3 scale to Capaldi, from a mix of silicone, latex, polyfoam, and fibreglass.

Mike Tucker worked as a visual effects assistant on the show from 1985 until 1989, then returned as supervisor of the Model Unit in twenty-first century *Doctor Who*, working on stories for the Ninth, Tenth, Eleventh, and Twelfth Doctors. "It was great to get a chance to work on *Thin Ice* – I was beginning to think that doing effects for a Twelfth Doctor episode was going to elude me!" Tucker said. "As with all of the effects sequences that we've done for *Doctor Who* over the years, it was a challenge, but I was really pleased with the way that our model shots cut in with the live action footage – it's pretty seamless, which is always what you're striving to achieve."

Viewers didn't get to see much inside the diving helmet, although Tucker had further employed Stephen Mansfield, who he'd worked with during the Seventh Doctor era (alongside Susan Moore), to create a sculpt of Capaldi's face to fit inside the helmet. The sculpt was moulded in silicone and cast in polyurethane resin, before being painted and fitted to the puppet.

Mansfield had been partly responsible for a number of impressive sculptures from McCoy's time on the show, notably the Destroyer (*Battlefield*), *The Curse of Fenric*'s Haemovores, and Kane's melting face in *Dragonfire*.

The latter was inspired by a similar effect in *Raiders of the Lost Ark*, and featured a wax rendition of Edward Peel's face on a fibreglass skull that was slowly heated up. Air bladders were used to manipulate the wax as it softened, with further hot wax added by tubes laced through the fibreglass insides. The footage was then sped up, producing a suitably grim yet awesome final effect.

< 57. Robot Cleaner.

46. BBC Sound Effects No. 19: *Doctor Who.*

Dang. The Monk's vinyl player seems so far away now (are the corridors shifting around you?), but here is a musical gem certainly worth playing. The cover has the Doctor's Ship in the time vortex; the record has the ability to take you back to 1978.

This treasure has it all: the TARDIS interior noise (both stationary and in flight), sizzling effects from *The Masque of Mandragora*, Sutekh Time Tunnel (*Pyramids of Mars*), a Tesh Gun, and so much more. Kids these days, with their "Mr Brightside" and their *Future Nostalgia*, don't know what they're missing.

Terror of the Vervoids was the last *Doctor Who* serial with sound by the BBC's legendary Radiophonic Workshop. The relationship between the show and the Workshop began in August 1963, when Waris Hussein contacted them to enquire about music for *An Unearthly Child*.

Verity Lambert wanted Ron Grainer to compose the theme tune, but it was down to the Workshop to realise it. Delia Derbyshire and Dick Mills used white noise, string instruments, and test-tone oscillators (used to calibrate musical equipment at different speeds, sliced and edited together on analogue tape) to create something truly out of this world. After hearing the recording, Grainer famously asked whether he had actually written it; Derbyshire cheekily replied, "Most of it."

The Workshop provided variations of the theme music until 1985, after which freelancers were taken on for the task.

This was Derbyshire's sole contribution to *Doctor Who* (nevertheless an incredible legacy!), but many Radiophonic Workshop musicians worked on the show alongside the aforementioned Mills: Brian Hodgson, Malcolm Clarke, Peter Howell, Elizabeth Parker, Paddy Kingsland, Roger Limb, and Jonathan Gibbs.

The team provided incidental music throughout much of twentieth-century *Doctor Who*, beginning with *The Wheel in Space* and *The Krotons* in 1968. It was only commissioned twice in the 1970s, for special sounds, but from *The Leisure Hive* in 1980 the Workshop's creations featured more regularly. Most extensively, they contributed incidentals throughout the Fifth Doctor era, plus Tom Baker's final trilogy of tales; *K9 and Company*; and Season 22. (Murray Gold seemed to have taken some cues from this era, adding more overt electronic elements to scores for *Heaven Sent* and Series 10.)

Need a gun sound effect? How about a spacestation's engines? What does a Dalek control room sound like? The Radiophonic Workshop was the go-to department for unusual experimental sound. Hodgson even created the TARDIS' dematerialisation noise, by dragging his mother's door keys along the strings of an old piano, then adding electronic reverberation effects to the track.

Daphne Oram and Desmond Briscoe created the Radiophonic Workshop in April 1958, at the BBC's Maida Vale Studios, after badgering the corporation to set up its own department to create sound effects and music using cutting-edge equipment. A bizarre rule, apparently created for medical purposes but imposed with obvious bias and maddening exemptions, meant staff could only work in the department for three months. Oram was the first victim, being moved to a different section within the BBC, leading to a dispute which forced her to leave the corporation in 1959. Because of this policy, the Workshop experienced a large turnover of staff. Still, they produced an incredible number of original compositions, gracing programmes on TV and radio like *The Goon Show*, *The Hobbit*, *Blake's 7*, *Quatermass and the Pit*, and *The Changes*.

After a few years being neglected by BBC personnel, the Radiophonic Workshop officially closed in March 1998. Equipment was either junked or sold on. Technicians managed to save tapes, which were eventually catalogued by Hodgson and Mark Ayres. "Underappreciated" is the correct designation for the department – at least until recently, when a huge set of tracks from 1968 to 1978 was unveiled for Record Store Day 2020, and a new Radiophonic Workshop was set up.

"The rapid pace of change in technologies has meant our imaginations are struggling to keep up," said Matthew Herbert, the New Radiophonic Workshop's creative director. "By bringing together the people making the technology with people making the music, we are hoping to find engaging answers to some of the modern problems associated with the role of sound and music on the Internet, in certain creative forms, and within broadcasting."

< 97. Temporal Object.

47. The Orient Express.

A version of this incredible locomotive, running on hyperspace ribbons, was a trap in *Mummy on the Orient Express*, so while you're intrigued by this exhibit, you won't enter, just in case.

Its size is overwhelming – you're just as impressed by this grand construct as you were Asteroid 3325. It's an exercise in decadence. In some ways, it's like the TARDIS: a gateway to other worlds.

The Doctor's universe is unquestionably influenced by Agatha Christie's work: various locations, notably Leadworth, are akin to the quaint English villages hiding dark secrets in dozens of Agatha's stories, and parallels can be drawn between a few incarnations of the Doctor and Hercule Poirot.

The Doctor is, perhaps, a cross between Poirot and Arthur Conan Doyle's Sherlock Holmes: in one instant an idiosyncratic outsider and in the next to the manor born, spirited, engaging and urbane. Holmesian cadences are reinforced when the Time Lord dresses in a cape and deerstalker (*The Talons of Weng-Chiang*; *The Snowmen*), but similarities with Poirot are perhaps more subtle.

However, to paraphrase that distinguished Belgian, rub together those little grey cells, and the similarities are there to see. Not only do the two share dazzling intellects, but Poirot admits, in *Three Act Tragedy* (1934), that he exaggerates his eccentricities so others underestimate him – not a million miles away from the Second, Fifth, Seventh, and Eleventh Doctors. And while the detective is also quite capable of dealing with people, he remains an outsider, albeit one that can recognise and adapt to patterns. In that way, he's a conduit of Agatha herself, whose amusement about human behaviour often fed into her books. In *Triangle at Rhodes* (1936), Poirot notes that, "Unlike most English people, [a main character] was capable of speaking to strangers on sight instead of allowing four days to a week to elapse before making the first cautious advance as is the customary British habit."

Agatha's biggest influence on *Doctor Who*, however, is how the programme approaches base-under-siege tales. Pip and Jane Baker explicitly based *Terror of the Vervoids* on her work: there are red herrings, plot twists, and a smattering of motives. Before that, *The Robots of Death* followed a similar design, with characters on an isolated sandminer being slowly murdered. The robotic culprits were obvious; less so was the identity of their corrupter, Taren Capel.

Arguably, the closest *Doctor Who* gets to Christie's formula is *Horror of Fang Rock*, which finds its roots in the bestselling mystery novel *And Then There Were None* (1939), as its cast are picked off one by one by a mysterious assailant who seemingly walks among them.

Mummy on the Orient Express is a type of murder-mystery, albeit a "why-dunnit" as opposed to the "whodunit" genre most associated with Christie. Obviously, it's main allusion to the author is its title, which parodies one of her best-known novels – for which Donna Noble supposedly gave her the idea (so too for Miss Marple) in *The Unicorn and the Wasp*.

After *The Shakespeare Code*, Gareth Roberts received an email from Russell T Davies which simply read, "Agatha Christie". The crime writer's appearance in Series 4 wasn't a complete shock: the Doctor had mulled over the idea of meeting her at the end of *Last of the Time Lords*.

Fenella Woolgar was cast as the writer, and she accordingly read *The Murder of Roger Ackroyd* and Agatha's autobiographies to prepare for the role. We see copies of *Ackroyd* (released in June 1926, the year the episode is set) and *Death in the Clouds* in the story, and Davies and Roberts also competed to get as many titles of Christie's works into the script as possible: *N or M?*, *Sparkling Cyanide*; *Dead Man's Folly*; *The Body in the Library*; *Cat Among the Pigeons*; *Nemesis*; *The Secret Adversary*; *They Do It with Mirrors*; *Appointment with Death*; *Cards on the Table*; *Endless Night*; *Crooked House*; *The Moving Finger*; *Taken at the Flood*; and *Death Comes as the End*.

Even the Doctor has a shot, suggesting "murder at the vicar's rage" (*The Murder at the Vicarage*), which is met with Donna guffawing.

Why Didn't They Ask Evans? is alluded to as Professor Peach is murdered ("But why didn't they ask–? Heavens!"), and the Doctor is explicitly named *The Man in the Brown Suit* in a deleted scene.

Though the episode is itself comedic, its subject matter is more unsettling. At 9:30pm on 3rd December 1926, Agatha kissed her daughter, Rosalind, goodnight, drove away from her Berkshire home, and wasn't seen again for eleven days. Her Morris Cowley car was found abandoned by a lake, and over 1,000 police officers were assigned to the missing persons case. Dorothy L. Sayers visited her home to look for clues. Arthur Conan Doyle took one of Agatha's gloves to a medium to divine what had happened. Neither resulted in Christie's whereabouts.

On 14th December, Agatha was found alive and well in a hotel in Harrogate, apparently with no memory of what had happened. She had signed in as Theresa Neele, the name of her husband's mistress.

Finding out her husband was having an affair was obviously a considerable blow to Christie, and some posit that, in those eleven days, she tried to commit suicide and/or entered a fugue state brought on by shock. Agatha maintained that she never recalled anything from that period.

She was naturally under a great deal of pressure: while her next novel, *The Big Four*, released in January 1927, was a flippant tale, she would later say that 1928's *The Mystery of the Blue Train* was the first of her books which she considered difficult – she pushed herself to work in order to support Rosalind and herself in the wake of their familial fracture.

Doctor Who suggests this fugue state is a result of Agatha's mind being linked to a Vespiform which severed their connection in its death throes. This is *probably* inaccurate. However, the Doctor's claim that Christie is the bestselling novelist of all time is entirely true.

≤ 73. Crusader 50.

48. Pyramid Eternia.

Could this be the oldest artefact here? It's the sole remnant of the Ancients of the Universe, a towering obelisk from the novel *Big Bang Generation*, and it's… Oof. That feels weird. It lets out a sigh of temporal energy. In the book, this energy makes the Doctor see a ripple of companions, including Evelyn Smythe…

Doctors and companions have enjoyed something of a renaissance in audio, courtesy of Big Finish. The Sixth Doctor's life has been expanded, his personality mellowing somewhat, as it was originally intended to on TV. Evelyn is a key part of that. Played by Maggie Stables, the historian was the first companion created specifically for audio. From her first assured appearance in *The Marian Conspiracy*, she proved the Doctor's equal, softening "Ol' Sixie" in the process.

The next audio-created companion, Charley Pollard (India Fisher), was saved from the crash of the R101 by the Eighth Doctor, causing some serious time-travel-related headaches. This incarnation paid tribute to a few audio companions before regenerating, including failed actress Tamsin Drew (Niky Wardley); nursing assistant Molly O'Sullivan (Ruth Bradley), stationed in France during World War I; and Lucie Miller, played by Sheridan Smith, who was tempted back to play the much-loved Northerner after several years away.

Ian Atkins was producer of the *Short Trips* range when Smith returned. "We didn't know if she'd want to come back – she's a mega-star OBE, after all, and we're from her early days – but it was worth asking. And there was nothing about having to 'tempt' about it – she was so, so up for it; the only difficulty ever was timing, and finding some availability," he said. "Her affection for Big Finish is so strong – she helped move Heaven and Earth to make it happen in the end. I'm still so very grateful to her and her agent. It may sound twee, but it always humbles me to work for Big Finish when I see how much people like working with us."

Unsurprisingly, under the influence of the temporal energy, the Doctor omits some assistants who'd yet to debut properly – like Liv Chenka, who his seventh incarnation met on Kaldor (setting of *The Robots of Death*). Played by Nicola Walker, Liv joined him for numerous ongoing audio boxsets, starting with *Dark Eyes*. (Walker is one of two companion actors who also appeared regularly in the hit BBC show *Spooks* – known in America as *MI:5* – the other being Miranda Raison. Raison plays Mrs Constance Clarke, a Bletchley Park WREN who initially accompanied the Sixth Doctor temporarily, until learning that her husband faked his own death, after which she carried on travelling in the TARDIS by choice.)

Companions created solely for audio include:

- **Erimem** (Caroline Morris), daughter of Pharaoh Amenhotep II, destined to be queen of ancient Egypt – until the Fifth Doctor and Peri liberated her!
- **Hex** (Philip Olivier), a nurse whose hospital had been infiltrated by Cybermen. His timeline is convoluted, but he plays an important part in Big Finish history: listen to *Thicker Than Water* to learn why.
- The chameleonic **C'Rizz** (Conrad Westmaas) was liberated from a timeless pocket universe to travel with the Eighth Doctor and Charley.
- **Dr Elizabeth Klein** (Tracey Childs), whose counterpart in a parallel universe is a Nazi. The Seventh Doctor decided to keep an eye on her...
- The Sixth Doctor offered **Flip Jackson** (Lisa Greenwood) a way out of her daily drudgery. She eventually returned to Earth, got married... then ran away in the TARDIS again.
- **Helen Sinclair** (Hattie Morahan), who joined the Eighth Doctor and Liv in *Doom Coalition*.
- A Roman slave, **Marc** (George Watkins, Peter Davison's nephew) was invited onto the TARDIS by Nyssa.
- **Bliss** (Rakhee Thakrar), orphaned by the Time War.
- Impetuous UNIT secretary **Naomi Cross** (Eleanor Crooks) travels the Fourth Doctor and Harry from *Storm of the Sea Devils*.

< 28. Talking Cabbage.

49. Sylvester McCoy's Sixth Doctor Wig.

After being treated poorly by the BBC, Colin Baker refused to return for his regeneration scene – meaning McCoy donned this fetching rug for *Time and the Rani*. It sits on a bust of Sylvester, eyes crossed, mouth stretched diagonally, and tongue stuck out. (*Doctor Who* has a weird history of wigs. In Matt Smith's final scene, both he and Karen Gillan were wearing wigs – but apparently never tried each other's on, the spoilsports. William Hartnell wore one too, as did Patrick Troughton early in his tenure. You can enter a separate hairpiece gallery, but the admittance fee is too high a price toupee.)

So why did each Doctor leave?

Ill health seemingly forced William Hartnell to quit, albeit reluctantly. Indeed, he was the only actor who played the part without knowing that he'd be replaced.

Patrick Troughton was nervous when taking on the role, admitting to the *Radio Times* that he felt "it had perhaps been done to death and that it wouldn't last", and so agreed to only play the part for three years. He was particularly worried about being typecast, but in the end grew so fond of the role, he readily returned for multi-Doctor tales.

Typecasting was also a concern for Jon Pertwee, but several other events seemed to lead up to his quitting, including the dissolution of the "UNIT family" following the death of Roger Delgado (which hit the cast and crew hard). He was apparently denied a pay rise too, and further spoke of back pain arising from the intense role.

Tom Baker claimed he couldn't wrench himself away from *Doctor Who* for some time, but was astounded at how swiftly his resignation was accepted. By his own admission, he'd become difficult to work with, but was generally talked into staying due to his popularity. He particularly didn't like the direction new producer John Nathan-Turner was taking the series in

"He made assumptions about how I should do things," Baker told Digital Spy, "or what lines meant, or how it should be shot, which diminished me, and I found that unbearable."

Peter Davison accepted the role with a three-year tenure in mind, and Troughton apparently reaffirmed this notion during

The Five Doctors. Davison remains a prolific actor, and has revealed he regrets turning down Nathan-Turner's offer of a fourth full season.

In contrast, Colin Baker had hoped to stay longer than even Tom but proved a scapegoat when *Doctor Who* went on hiatus.

The show wasn't renewed in 1989, leaving Sylvester McCoy's Seventh Doctor seemingly its last – until *The TV Movie*, for which the production team asked McCoy to return for a regeneration scene. Sylvester had always maintained that he'd do this if ever offered the chance, perhaps having seen the lukewarm reception *Time and the Rani*'s regeneration received.

But of course, Paul McGann's Eighth Doctor didn't renew the franchise. Russell T Davies apparently never considered bringing back McGann (who said he would've returned if asked), instead preferring a fresh start.

McGann at least returned for *The Night of the Doctor*, joking, "I don't want to be remembered as the George Lazenby of *Doctor Who*."

Christopher Eccleston's departure is more complicated, namely because the parties involved have stayed relatively quiet. Initially reported as a fear of being typecast, Eccleston has since revealed it was due to a breakdown in his relationship with the production team, caused by behind-the-scenes politics. At first, it seemed to sour his time on the show, until he started doing occasional conventions and came to appreciate how greatly his Doctor is loved. Now he's even playing the character again for Big Finish!

"I love audio drama… I do audiobooks and I get great creative satisfaction from that. I think it's because I've always been passionate about writing and writers. And there are no visuals: all you have is the word and your voice. And I felt I could do something with a character I'd played in a visual format," said Eccleston between recording sessions. "I was born in 1964 and I remember one of the big moments of my life… There was a power cut in the '70s, and it was very exciting to me because my mum and dad lit candles and put them in bottles and we had a battery-run radio, [and we] tuned into a radio drama… I can't remember what it was, but we were all transfixed and I would say we'd never listened to one before, and the candlelight and just the audio and our imagination creating the pictures: it had a profound effect on me. I can remember exactly where I was sat in our backroom. So maybe the love was born there."

Since leaving *Doctor Who*, Chris has appeared in a wealth of TV, audio, and theatre productions.

"Well, I'm not finished with *Macbeth* – I did one hundred and nineteen performances of *Macbeth*; I want very much to revisit that on the stage in London in a much smaller, more script-based, intimate, stripped-back production," Christopher reflected. "And I would very much like to do *Macbeth* with Big Finish. There's a couple of Shakespeares I'd like to do – *Richard the Third*, *Coriolanus*, Shylock in *Merchant of Venice*… I think *The A Word* would work wonderfully (as a Big Finish series too) with that central notion of autism and communication and failure to communicate; I think that would translate great to audio."

David Tennant's love of *Doctor Who* was apparently the reason he left. When announcing his departure at the National Television Awards in 2008, he said, "If I don't take a deep breath and move on now, I never will." Nonetheless, he considered staying on when Steven Moffat took over as showrunner, so much so that Moffat detailed his plans for Series 5 assuming Tennant's involvement.

The exact reasons for Matt Smith quitting are unknown, though he has claimed it merely felt like the right time. Certainly, Karen Gillan and Arthur Darvill leaving had a big effect on him, but he's admitted that he wished he'd stayed on for another season alongside Jenna Coleman.

Similarly, Peter Capaldi felt it was the right time to move on when his contract ended, leaving at the same time as Moffat.

"You do twelve episodes a year, and I just worried that I wouldn't be able to continue to do my best work," he told Graham Norton. "I just figure, while you're enjoying it, leave."

Both Smith and Capaldi can attest to the physicality of the role, suffering the exact same knee injury; a tear in the shock-absorbing meniscus.

Still, whatever reason each had, they will both always be the Doctor.

< 10. A Cardboard Cut-Out of Patrick Troughton.

50. Tickling Stick.

This tattyfilarious item, a fluffy multi-coloured duster, is on loan from the Ken Dodd Museum in Knotty Ash (expected to take ninety minutes to wander around but actually taking at least five hours). Dodd was the legendary stand-up who controversially appeared as the doomed Tollmaster in *Delta and the Bannermen*.

Some derided his appearance as an example of stunt casting, but a recognisable face gives the public an extra reason to tune in. And of course, *Doctor Who* is certainly no stranger to comedy. Peter Capaldi, after all, is otherwise best known for playing Malcolm Tucker in *The Thick of It*.

Two actors best associated with comedic roles have even been companions: Catherine Tate and Matt Lucas (Donna Noble and Nardole) have both taken shows to the Edinburgh Fringe Festival, and both rose to fame through sketch shows (respectively, *The Catherine Tate Show* and *Little Britain*, the latter co-starring *The God Complex*'s David Walliams and narrated by Tom Baker).

Tate is also credited with helping bring *Not Going Out*, one of Britain's longest-running sitcoms, to TV. In the show's pilot, Tate played Kate, love-interest and comic foil to the character played by creator Lee Mack.

"It's really great to see Catherine doing so well," Lee wrote in his autobiography, *Mack the Life*. "The only thing I objected to seeing her doing was [*Doctor Who*], as this was my favourite show from childhood, and so the 'escapism' for me was difficult when I saw her in it. It's hard to feel like the universe is really in the hands of one woman, when the week before she had rung you asking what a Cyberman looks like."

After numerous interviews in which he praised the series, Mack finally appeared in *Kerblam!* as Dan Cooper.

And he's far from being the only stand-up or comedy actor to have cameoed in *Doctor Who*. These include:

- Peter Butterworth (*The Time Meddler*), widely known for the *Carry On* franchise.
- John Challis (*The Seeds of Doom*), aka Boycie in *Only Fools and Horses*.

- John Cleese (*City of Death*).
- Beryl Reid (*Earthshock*), who trained at the National Theatre as a comedy actress.
- Faith Brown (*Attack of the Cybermen*).
- Alexei Sayle (*Revelation of the Daleks*).
- Joan Sims (*The Mysterious Planet*), also in numerous *Carry On* films.
- Gareth Hale and Norman Pace (*Survival*).
- Peter Kay (*Love & Monsters*).
- Ardal O'Hanlon (*Gridlock*), who has appeared in many dramas but is best known for *Father Ted*.
- Lee Evans (*Planet of the Dead*).
- Barry Howard (*The End of Time*), best known for *Hi-de-Hi!*
- Ronnie Corbett (*The Sarah Jane Adventures: From Raxacoricofallapatorius with Love*).
- Bill Bailey (*The Doctor, the Widow and the Wardrobe*).
- David Mitchell and Robert Webb (*Dinosaurs on a Spaceship*).
- Ingrid Oliver (Osgood), part of the comedy double act Watson & Oliver.
- Kayvan Novak (*The Time of the Doctor*).
- Michelle Gomez (Missy).
- Frank Skinner (*Mummy on the Orient Express*).
- Chris Addison (*Dark Water/Death in Heaven*).
- Rufus Hound (*The Woman Who Lived*), who also plays the Monk for Big Finish.
- Shobna Gulati (*Arachnids in the UK*), who first came to prominence in *Dinnerladies*.
- Stephen Fry and Lenny Henry (*Spyfall*).
- John Bishop *(Thirteenth Doctor companion, Dan)*.

< 98. Matchbox.

51. Unlimited Rice Pudding.

Crikey, that is a lot of rice pudding: enough to fill up an entire room – no, another *dimension*, you're informed by a member of staff, who is also fielding questions about how to get that awful stench out of clothes.

It comes from *Remembrance of the Daleks*, in which the Doctor apparently sees unlimited pudding as a sign of universal domination. You'd have settled for Angel Delight. That serial was the only time Ace met the Daleks in the programme; alas, Mel Bush just missed her chance to encounter the iconic antagonists, having left in the previous story, *Dragonfire*.

So how many companions have never met the Daleks on TV?

For argument's sake, we're classifying "companion" as a character who has accompanied the Doctor in the TARDIS in more than one storyline, although there are exceptions

Many companions meet the Daleks early on in their tenures. Susan, Ian, and Barbara all do so in the second serial, early in the latter pair's adventures, although we don't exactly know how long Susan and the Doctor had been travelling before setting down in 1963. All three leave in stories featuring the Daleks too.

Vicki is the first companion not to meet the Daleks, although her last serial, *The Myth Makers*, came after *Mission to the Unknown*, which did feature the Daleks (but not Vicki herself).

Steven Taylor meets them straight away, in *The Chase*, as does Sara Kingdom in *The Daleks' Master Plan*; this story also saw the death of Katarina, just one story after her introduction. (Admittedly, Sara and Katarina's status as companions remains debatable.)

The Second Doctor introduces Ben and Polly to the Daleks in *The Power of the Daleks*, and they leave before Victoria and Jamie meets the pepper pots in *The Evil of the Daleks*. We go a number of years with no Dalek stories, but then get three in quick succession: Jo features in *Day of the Daleks* and *Planet of the Daleks*, and Sarah in *Death to the Daleks*. Sarah sees them again, alongside Harry, in *Genesis of the Daleks*.

Lalla Ward's Romana faces them in *Destiny of the Daleks* (though K9 doesn't make it out of the TARDIS), but Mary Tamm's on screen incarnation never met them (however, Tamm's

Romana does eventually meet them in the audio adventure *The Dalek Contract/The Final Phase*).

Tegan leaves after witnessing the destruction wrought in *Resurrection of the Daleks*, at which time Turlough also meets them, while Kamelion is out of action. Peri stars in *Revelation of the Daleks* and Ace in *Remembrance of the Daleks*.

Rose encounters them numerous times, as do all the Tenth Doctor's companions, except Wilfred, who meets them only once, in *The Stolen Earth/Journey's End*. Wilf is also the only one of Tennant's companions to not meet Davros in the same tale. (We're not counting stand-in companions from *The Next Doctor*, *Planet of the Dead*, and *The Waters of Mars*, but of the three, only Adelaide Brooke is seen to meet a Dalek, similarly during the events of the Series 4 finale.)

And this becomes a theme for twenty-first century *Doctor Who*. All of the Ninth, Tenth, Eleventh, Twelfth, and Thirteenth Doctors' companions have met the Daleks: Amy first in *Victory of the Daleks*; Rory and River in *The Big Bang*; Bill and Nardole in *The Pilot* (Nardole hints he's seen them before); and Yaz, Ryan, and Graham in *Resolution*. Clara is a special case: her Oswin iteration met the Daleks straight away, in *Asylum of the Daleks*, paying with her life. This took place during *The Name of the Doctor*, but she actually meets them in *The Day of the Doctor*, albeit briefly. Head hurt, yet?

Surprisingly then, eleven companions have never met the Daleks on TV: Vicki, Dodo, Zoe, Liz, Leela, K9, Adric, Nyssa, Kamelion, Mel, and Grace.

However, this doesn't take into account other mediums, notably Big Finish. Zoe met the Daleks in *Fear of the Daleks*, for example; Nyssa in *The Mutant Phase*; and Mel in *The Juggernauts*.

< 16. Ballerina.

52. "No Coloureds" Sign.

This next exhibit comes with a warning: it's offensive yet in this context isn't intended to be harmful. It's indicative of a different time and is here as a talking point. Nonetheless, you hadn't expected to find it here. But these things can't be shied away from.

In *Remembrance of the Daleks*, Ace is disgusted to find this sign in the boarding house where she's spent the night. It was accurate for the story's setting and symbolic of the "nationalist" attitudes of antagonist Mike Smith. Ace understandably storms out.

"The past is another country," says the Ninth Doctor in *Father's Day*, paraphrasing L.P. Hartley's 1953 novel *The Go-Between*. "1987's just the Isle of Wight." The point stands: they do things differently there. We do things differently in the future too. What seems forward-thinking now will be backwards and antiquated in a few decades.

That being said, *Doctor Who* doesn't have the best of histories regarding diversity. They say the road to Hell is paved with good intentions, and *Doctor Who* certainly travels that winding path. While you can laud its first production team, and claim the show has in part always been about fighting xenophobia, you can just as validly scold the racist stereotypes in *The Celestial Toymaker* and *The Tomb of the Cybermen*

Galaxy 4 tells us not to judge on appearances alone. *Colony in Space* reflects the struggle of Native Americans. And *The Mutants* similarly finds its origins in Apartheid segregation in South Africa. These are meaningful pursuits, and it's notable that Cotton, played by black actor, Rick James, is an emotional focus in *The Mutants* (or is intended to be). But undermining this is the fact that James is the only black actor who takes an active role in Season 9. Companion Jo Grant, meanwhile, is the only woman in the entire six-part serial. This era demonstrated that equality is something to be strived for, but isn't always put into practice.

At least suggestions of playing long-running characters in blackface were vetoed: chiefly, Brian Blessed was approached to star as the Second Doctor but wanted to play him as black. Leela, too, had dark skin in initial publicity shots. "Quite honestly, in those photos I think the make-up woman just didn't get it quite right," Louise Jameson told *DWM*. "There was always an hour and a half in make-up before I was allowed on set. I wasn't black but it was more than a tan. One of my sons is mixed race – dual heritage we say now. I think I was meant to have that kind of skin."

As an older gentleman of a particular era, and thus presumably having the attitudes of the age, some consider William Hartnell racist and anti-Semitic. Jessica Carney addressed this in *Who's There? The Life and Career of William Hartnell*, her biography about her grandfather, noting that "If he liked someone, they weren't a foreigner, they were a friend."

Indeed, Waris Hussein admitted to being nervous about working with Hartnell on *An Unearthly Child* (even though he'd been crucial in the actor's casting), having thought of him as "potentially a very opinionated man – that is, prejudiced". And yet they got on well and Hartnell was apparently very hurt to learn Hussein would be moving on from *Doctor Who* after directing *Marco Polo*. Carole Ann Ford, who is Jewish, also speaks warmly of Hartnell, balking at suggestions he was difficult to work with, backed up by Maureen O'Brien. "He had a laugh," said the Vicki actress. "He liked to work. He liked his whisky. We had a good time… We used to go to Bill's dressing room. [Jacqueline Hill], Bill, and I used to gather; we had a glass of wine and some lovely food before we did the show. There's that side that no one seems to stress."

In his edition of *Desert Island Discs*, recovered in 2015, Hartnell revealed that Paul Robeson was his hero ("he is completely in harmony with the whole of nature"), and spoke of his admiration of Louis Armstrong: "This man I find fascinating. I remember him when I was quite young, and I think he's what I call the kingpin of Jazz… I don't know who else there would be to place in the same category."

There's a kernel of truth in Hartley's "You insisted on thinking of them as angels, even if they were fallen angels." The opposite could also be true: those some people insist are fallen never dropped as far as rumour would have it.

But maybe we need to turn to another author for guidance: Madeleine L'Engle, who wrote, "We are all strangers in a strange land." The lesson we learn from *Doctor Who* is to come at things from a point of understanding.

Intentions surely have to be acknowledged in some capacity. Take *The Talons of Weng-Chaing* as an example – and it frequently is, wheeled out by any claiming *Doctor Who* is racist. John Bennett's casting as Li H'sen Chang is a concern, as the Caucasian actor dons makeup to appear Asian, as do a few other cast members. But critics sometimes ignore any casting restrictions (the BBC were limited to using actors on Equity's books), and that Bennett plays the part sensitively and emerges a sympathetic character against considerable odds. Is this an excuse? Yes. It's up to the viewer to decide whether it's a good or bad excuse though.

Much of the dialogue, too, drips with satire, as Chang deftly uses the blinkered prejudices of his Victorian audience against them, outwitting even the Doctor, whose accusation that they've met before is met with Chang replying, "I understand we all look the same."

The script, however, works against itself in some ways, and it is true that *Talons'* attitudes to race were questionable when it aired too; so much so that Canada's CBC refused to screen it. Inexcusable is the Doctor's engaging in casual racism. He uses several racial slurs which may have been commonplace in the story's 1889 setting but are shocking and offensive coming out of our hero's mouth today.

Many are more concerned with stereotypes and make-up in *Talons* than, say, *Marco Polo*, *The Crusade*, and *The Savages*. This might be because their episodes are largely missing or held in less esteem than *Talons*. But what excuse is there for *The Aztecs*, *The Tomb of the Cybermen*, and *The Enemy of the World*?

Truth doesn't always back up an argument. "To see things as they really were – what an impoverishment!" Yes, *The Go-Between* again. There's often a gap between aims and final products; similarly between what's found offensive, a chasm deepened by time.

Has the show used racist caricatures and slurs? Yes.

Does its casting often leave something to be desired? Yes.

Have production teams been generally well-meaning and pioneering? Once more, the answer is yes.

And has *Doctor Who* always striven for equality? Absolutely.

All these things are equally true. We have to also remember

that, above all else, it's about a daft old traveller in time and space who fights scary monsters and offers strangers confectionary.

≤ 25. Fourth Doctor Scarf.

53. Death's Head's Head.

Ah, it's the freelance peacekeeping agent, yes?

This is a disembodied head, but Death's Head is a cyborg created for Marvel Comics, and this is an outdated model. It's the 30ft Death's Head, his shiny bonce reflecting the chamber's lights.

Is the Doctor technically a Marvel hero?

Strictly speaking, no, as the character has existed separately from the comics company since 1963. However, in 1979, Marvel Comics UK acquired the publishing rights for *Who* strips as part of *Doctor Who Magazine*, meaning many adventures came under the Marvel umbrella. Panini became *DWM*'s publisher in the mid-1990s, but in the interim, the Doctor met the brand-hopping mercenary Death's Head.

Created by Simon Furman and Geoff Senior, Death's Head first appeared in *Transformers UK* #113 (1987), published by Marvel, though the leads were Hasbro characters. Death's Head jumped to *DWM* #135 (1988) then *Dragon's Claw* #5 before getting his own series that same year.

Do Not Forsake Me Oh My Darling! in *Death's Head* #5 (1989) included Keepsake, who'd debuted in DWM #140, and the comic's eighth issue (*Time Bomb!*) muddied the water considerably by actively involving the Doctor and *DWM*'s Josiah W. Dogbolter and Hob. The TARDIS even landed on Four Freedoms Plaza, the Fantastic Four's home!

You won't find *Time Bomb!* reprinted in collected formats since Marvel lost the rights to *Doctor Who*; nonetheless, the bounty hunter remains an on-off threat to heroes, meaning the same character who fought the Seventh Doctor has also faced off against Iron Man and the Hulk.

Marvel applies numerical designations to their universes. The standard continuity is Earth-616, for example, and the Marvel Cinematic Universe (MCU) is Earth-199999. The *Doctor Who* comic book universe, then, is Earth-5556.

Otherwise, the most obvious connections between *Doctor Who* and Marvel are in the number of stars who have been in both franchises – prominently the MCU, but also related franchises.

These include: Amy Pond actress Karen Gillan as Nebula in the *Guardians of the Galaxy* (GOTG) trilogy, plus *Avengers: Infinity*

War and *Endgame*, and *Thor: Love and Thunder*; Tenth Doctor David Tennant in Netflix's *Jessica Jones* as antagonist Kilgrave; and Ninth Doctor Christopher Eccleston as *Thor: The Dark World*'s Malekith. Talulah Riley (*Silence in the Library/Forest of the Dead*) was also briefly seen in *Thor: The Dark World*; as was Tony Curran (*Vincent and the Doctor*) as Bor; Letitia Wright (*Face the Raven*) is Shuri in the *Black Panther* franchise, as well as *Infinity War* and *Endgame*; Jenna Coleman (Clara Oswald) cameoed in *Captain America: The First Avenger*; so too did David Bradley (*Twice Upon A Time*); Toby Jones (*Amy's Choice*) reprised his *First Avenger* role as Arnim Zola in *The Winter Soldier*; Alan Dale (*Torchwood*) is one of the MCU's Security Council; Daniel Kaluuya (*Planet of the Dead*) is W'Kabi and Danny Sapani (*A Good Man Goes to War*) is his Border Tribe Elder in *Black Panther*; Josh Dallas (a node in *Silence in the Library*) was Fandral in *Thor*; O. T. Fagbenle himself played Other Dave in *Silence in the Library*, and is Rick Mason in *Black Widow*; Gemma Chan (*The Waters of Mars*) is doubling up, playing Minn-Erva in *Captain Marvel* and Sersi in *The Eternals* line; Christopher Fairbank (*Flatline*) was the Broker in *GOTG: Volume One*; that movie also starred Spencer Wilder (*The God Complex*) and Clem So (*Oxygen*) as aliens, and Peter Serafinowicz (*Before the Flood*) as Garthan Saal of the Nova Corps.

Meanwhile, Andrew Garfield (*Daleks in Manhattan/Evolution of the Daleks*) was the lead in *The Amazing Spider-Man* films; the second of those movies introduced Felicity Jones (*The Unicorn and the Wasp*) as Felicia Hardy; Sir Ian McKellan (*The Snowmen*) played Magneto in various *X-Men* instalments; Brian Cox (*The End of Time*) was Stryker in *X2*; this also starred Alan Cumming (*The Witchfinders*) as Nightcrawler; Ashildr actress Maisie Williams is Rahne Sinclair in *The New Mutants*; and Laurence Belcher (*A Christmas Carol*) played a young Charles Xavier in *X-Men: First Class*.

And the links go even further than that.

Take the hard-light holograms in *Mummy on the Orient Express*, the same technology used in the X-Men's Danger Room – true, other franchises use hard-light, but writer Jamie Mathison is a comic fan so also included the Excelsior life extender as a tribute to Marvel legend Stan Lee. Part Six of *DWM*'s *The Glorious Dead* introduces the Omniversal Spectrum, in which we see a distorted panel from *The Amazing Spider-Man* #12 (1964). *Punisher* #33-34 (1990) had a robotic creation called a Dalek ("Yeah, but can it go upstairs?" quips Frank Castle), and Professor Justin Alphonse Gamble of the Time Variance Authority in *Power Man and Iron Fist* #79 (1982) is inspired by the Doctor. That issue's Dreadlox are influenced by Raymond Cusick's original Dalek designs too.

The Doctor's Wife owes a debt to *The Incredible Hulk Presents* #12, which had the Seventh Doctor meeting the Watcher of Nineveh, killer of Gallifreyans.

Meanwhile, *The Return of Doctor Mysterio* takes most of its cues from *Superman*, even going so far as including a DC comic in its pre-titles sequence (which the Doctor vandalises by drawing glasses on the *Man of Steel*). Steven Moffat was particularly inspired by Christopher Reeves' *Superman* movies, imbuing Grant with similar powers, described as "basic flying, basic super-strength", and x-ray vision. The Harmony Shoal building in New York is topped with a massive globe, reminiscent of the Daily Planet HQ, and Mr Brock's instruction for reporters to direct questions to Miss Shuster or Miss Siegel is an allusion to Superman's creators, Jerry Siegel and Joe Shuster.

Batman's also referenced ("The Bat-Signal's an app now?"), and parallels between his costume and the Ghost's are clear.

However, the special otherwise includes Marvel references and imagery. Young Grant sleeps under a duvet littered with Marvel heroes, his wallpaper primarily features Thor and the Hulk, and he has superhero posters, notably *The Defenders* and a door-poster displaying Wolverine, the Silver Surfer, and Captain America. (These designs were not released until the 2010s, despite that part of the episode being set in the 1990s; still, the room does its job in establishing Grant's geeky credentials.)

When the Doctor reads a *Spider-Man* comic, Grant explains that Peter Parker was bitten by a radioactive spider and gains powers which the Doctor presumes means "vomiting, hair loss, and death" due to radiation poisoning. Later, he also quotes the well-known Spidey proverb, "With great power comes great responsibility" – although technically, the first time the quote appears in an issue, it's "With great power there must also come great responsibility".

The Doctor also says Grant reads "too many comic books", so maybe he isn't such a wise old Time Lord after all...

< 96. Kerblam! Man.

54. Transfers.

These are from *Doctor Who Weekly* #1. If you find an issue with these transfers attached, you're very lucky indeed. That's why these are behind 5ft bullet-proof glass. Squinting, you can just about make out the Doctor's effervescent grin from afar.

Doctor Who Magazine began life as *Doctor Who Weekly*, launched in October 1979, its first issue displaying the Fourth Doctor and a Dalek on its cover, and offering free transfers of Tom's incarnation dodging dinosaurs and small explosions. It cost 12p.

Editor Dez Skinn had noticed the popularity of the *Doctor Who* section in the publication *Starburst*. *TV Comic*, which had featured original *Doctor Who* strips until its 1385th issue, had also been a success, but reverted to reprints, while *TV Action+Countdown*, aimed at an older demographic, had ceased publication in 1973. Skinn saw an opportunity, and *Doctor Who Weekly* ran new comics (beginning with *Doctor Who and the Iron Legion* and *The Return of the Daleks*), alongside reprints of classic novel adaptations by publisher Marvel Comics UK.

The publication changed to *Doctor Who – A Marvel Monthly* with issue 44, then tweaked its title until finally landing on *Doctor Who Magazine* (*DWM*) from #107 (1985). *DWM* evolved to include less fiction, refocusing on behind-the-scenes features and interviews.

Its popularity even resulted in an enormously successful fanzine celebrating the magazine, *Vworp Vworp!*, created by Gareth Kavanagh and Colin Brockhurst. "*Vworp Vworp!* mainly covers *Doctor Who* comics and art, but also takes occasional sidesteps into anything else that interests us, like Target books and the annuals. The one area outside of our scope is the television series itself!" explained Colin. "And *Doctor Who Magazine* is our other focus. We love it and its history, and talk about it endlessly. It's the best magazine in the world.

"[*Vworp Vworp!*]'s success is down to the enthusiasm of the people that have worked on it. It takes a long time to get an issue together, and we all do it for the love of the subject matter."

Its own comics continue many of the strips first featured in *DWM,* introducing exclusive companions like the shapeshifting Frobisher and duplicitous Majenta Pryce, allies like Dalek Killer

Abslom Daak and UFO-spotter Maxwell Edison, and recurring enemies, notably Beep the Meep.

"Gareth Kavanagh had come up with the magazine before I came on board in the early stages of the first issue," Brockhurst recalled. "I think the original idea was just to cover *DWM* comics, but it was expanded to include *DWM* itself, then I couldn't resist the rich range of *Doctor Who* strips that preceded *DWM*.

"I'll be honest and say that before *Vworp Vworp!* came into my life, the comic strip was probably the bit of *DWM* I read last. I've grown to love it all it over again, as much as I did when I grew up reading *Tides of Time* and *Voyager* and finding them much more appealing and imaginative than the TV series."

Vworp Vworp! boasts a wealth of exclusives, working in conjunction with many *DWM* alumni. So what's Colin most proud of?

"Although Gareth conducted the interview, having Alan Moore in the magazine was a particular thrill. Concluding the *Daleks* strip begun by *TV Century 21* and continued by *DWM*, brought to life so beautifully by Lee Sullivan. Talking to all the editors of *DWM*, every one of them a hero, and arranging interviews with them. Even Gary Gillatt, although he changed his mind about letting us print it at the eleventh hour for reasons I respect," Brockhurst enthused. "Oh, and being interviewed in *Doctor Who Magazine* itself, and more recently writing an article for it... The ten-year-old me who first discovered the magazine would never have believed it!"

DWM isn't the sole *Doctor Who* periodical, but it is the longest-running magazine based on a TV series. *Battles in Time* ran in conjunction with its trading card game; *Doctor Who Insider* aimed *DWM*-like content at the North American market; and *Torchwood: The Official Magazine* was eked out between 2008 and 2010.

The most successful tie-in was *Doctor Who Adventures* (*DWA*), targeting younger readers, which launched in 2006 as a fortnightly title. By 2008, it was one of the most-read magazines in the UK, the best-performing in children's publishing, meaning it became weekly. Circulation dropped in 2009, when *Doctor Who* was largely off TV, but it regained some ground in the Eleventh Doctor era. It reverted to being fortnightly in 2013, then monthly the following year. Its 2016 change to bi-monthly publication made cancellation inevitable. Though ending in 2017, a sole Thirteenth Doctor special was published in January 2019.

While DWA burned brightly but briefly, *DWM* has remained a cornerstone of *Doctor Who*.

< 53. Death's Head's Head.

55. Tea.

Tea! A nice cup of tea! A superheated infusion of free radicals and tannins; just the thing for healing the synapses.

You approach it enthusiastically. It's probably someone else's and it's probably got too much sugar in, but you'll take your chances. You pick it up – and swiftly put it back down.

It's going cold.

Doctor Who Season 24 has an unfairly bad reputation. This is evident from the 1987 Audience Reaction Report, published in February 1988 and compiled by Clive Graham: three pages reporting the results of a survey carried out by the BBC to determine the show's popularity.

Time and the Rani is frequently cited as one of the show's worst serials; even script editor Andrew Cartmel (hired after the script was commissioned) didn't like it. Pip and Jane Baker had started the story before McCoy was cast. Pip recalled this troublesome time: "We were well into the story when we were shown a video of Sylvester – we had to find a way of (a) regenerating the Doctor, and (b) finding a character for him."

Over the course of the season, the Seventh Doctor found his groove: the reaction report surmised that "by the end of the third story in the series, his personal rating has shown a steady – if not spectacular – improvement, rising from 44 at the end of the story entitled *Time and the Rani*... to 45 at the end of *Delta and the Bannermen*." Though not a glowing endorsement of this Doctor, those surveyed at least preferred him to Mel, as "56% of respondents who answered a questionnaire on the *Paradise Towers* story wished she had been eaten".

Fortunately, they liked Ace, introduced at Season 24's conclusion.

It argues that the series' average audience of 4.9 million was decent, considering *Doctor Who* aired opposite *Coronation Street* (which had an average audience of fifteen million), but just 28% said the stories were good. 11% said they liked very little about Season 24, and an additional 30% said they liked "nothing" about it.

The report gives its final nail in the coffin: 37% of those

taking part in the questionnaire had stopped watching, and only 46% wanted to see a new series.

"*Doctor Who* at the time had gone into a real trough, and it's true that there were some very, very bad episodes," Cartmel reflected in 2010. "But I do feel that we were pulling out of it, so it's a great shame that we never got a chance to continue."

< 67. Kroll (Kroll, Kroll, Kroll, Kroll, Kroll, ad infinitum).

56. Gabriel Chase.

A blackened structure folds upwards. Charcoal scatters on the floor, crunching under your feet.

"Here we are, at last," proclaims one staff member, throwing his arms in the air theatrically, addressing the assembly of visitors gathered around some burnt remains, "the ashes... of *Doctor Who!*"

A hushed awe settles over the group now. Until one visitor leans forward and reads the plaque. "Says here it's the burned remains of Gabriel Chase."

"I... Well, yes, I suppose." He saunters off.

The final regular serial of twentieth century *Doctor Who* was *Survival*, which might seem an ironic title, although being taken off air ultimately did allow the franchise to adapt and thrive. Writer Rona Munro has since said that she'd have made more of an occasion of the story if she'd realised it would be its last. Fortunately, *Doctor Who* did return, and so did Munro, for *The Eaters of Light*.

But before a new beginning came the end. *Survival* might've been the last transmitted, but *Ghost Light* was the last serial filmed. Marc Platt had submitted *Shrine*, set in Russia in the early nineteenth century, for consideration for Season 25, but Cartmel turned *Shrine* down because that season's scripts had been fully commissioned. "There is no guarantee," Cartmel cautioned, "that there will be another season of *Doctor Who* after 1988 and there is certainly no guarantee I will continue as script editor." "However," he said, "Platt was welcome to come for an informal chat if there were another season."

Platt was invited to work on more stories – *Cat's Cradle* and *Lungbarrow*, which were eventually adapted into novels – then *Ghost Light*, which Cartmel would describe as "the jewel in the crown of the Seventh Doctor's adventures."

On their final studio session, secretary Kate Eastaell led Andrew Cartmel from the control room to an observation gallery overlooking the studio floor. Below, Sylvester and Sophie were at the height of their powers. This *Doctor Who* was brave and smart and unsettling, in the best possible way. And watching on, there in the darkness, was a horde of people, enchanted faces reflected in glass walls.

Fans, eking out the end of an era.

< 99. Glass Figures.

57. Robot Cleaner.

This cleaner patrolled the halls of *Paradise Towers*, only occasionally strangling residents. It's a rather sturdy, imposing piece, its claw raised and dead black slitted eyes staring impassively back at you. But one detail deflates its threatening aura: the main hull and base should be a brilliant white, but this is charred, blackened, rusting, feeling sorry for itself.

It was damaged by a considerable fire at the Longleat exhibition on 25th September 1996. This blaze was attributed to faulty circuitry in K9's section. It's upsetting, thinking about what was lost in the flames or drowned by firefighters.

Charting a history of *Doctor Who* exhibitions is thrilling and frustrating in equal measure. They're always exciting for aficionados, providing a chance to glimpse behind the scenes. They're also typically lacking – either in organisation or in particular, less-favoured eras. Most start out small and are gradually added to, becoming, if not comprehensive, then certainly a fairer representation of *Doctor Who* as a whole by the time they're inevitably shut.

"I went to the Blackpool exhibition in 1981," said long-term fan Jonathan Appleton. "The *Doctor Who* exhibitions had a kind of mystical status for someone who loved the programme at that time, as they were often mentioned by the announcer at the end of the programme ['*Doctor Who* will be back next week and you can visit the BBC's *Doctor Who* exhibitions at Longleat and Blackpool…'] and on *Blue Peter* but, not living particularly close to either, they felt out of reach and no more accessible than Disneyland or Hollywood.

"Anyway, my chance finally came with a family summer holiday in the Lake District that year, which we combined with a trip to Blackpool. My memories are a little hazy, but I do remember going downstairs to get in to it and it being *very* dark in there – almost too dark to see things properly. There were various tableaux laid out with props and monsters – mainly from the most recent season, so for my visit that meant (I think) the likes of Marshmen and Traken. I'd been hoping for older monsters really as Season 18 hadn't been all that exciting for an eleven-year-old. I seem to remember they had the Fourth to Fifth

Doctors' regeneration playing on a loop. The shop, probably for reasons of space, was set out more like an old fashioned railway station newspaper stall rather than a store you could wander round. I bought a postcard which had Tom Baker scrawling 'Welcome to Blackpool' on a wall like he'd been caught graffitiing which I still have to this day.

"Overall, the place seemed pretty small and we got through it in no time at all, which seemed a little strange after they'd been bigging it up on BBC1 for years."

Jon Pertwee and Elisabeth Sladen opened the exhibition on 14th April 1974, just prior to the Third Doctor's swansong, *Planet of the Spiders*. It lasted until October 1985, when the lease on its building, 111 Central Promenade on Blackpool's Golden Mile, ran out.

It then reopened in 2004 to coincide with the series' revival, then shut again in November 2009.

This ran concurrently with Up Close in Cardiff's Red Dragon Centre, which opened as a semi-permanent exhibition at the end of 2005 and, before its closure in March 2011, was littered with monsters from the Ninth and Tenth Doctors' eras. The store still had a selection of merchandise from *Doctor Who*'s past, including Target novelisations, Dapol figurines (which had enjoyed their own exhibition in Llangollen from 1994), and First Day Covers.

Various other exhibitions spread *Doctor Who*'s reach, including the 1986-88 USA Tour; Land's End, Cornwall (2007-11); London's Museum of the Moving Images (in 1991-94, before moving to Bristol; then at Sheffield's MOMI in 2002); Earl's Court, London (2008-09); Coventry Transport Museum (2009-10); and the *Doctor Who* Festival at London's ExCeL in November 2015.

The first permanent exhibition, however, was at Longleat, the wildlife conservation park in Wiltshire. It had opened in 1973 with a series of props from the show, held annual events in the summer, and ran until 2003.

There were two negative events that tainted this small exhibition, however. The first was the aforementioned 'Great Fire of Longleat'. The K9 wasn't screen-used, so its loss is arguably the least affecting of the fire's victims, which otherwise include the space station model from *Trial of a Time Lord*; the Nucleus of the Swarm (*The Invisible Enemy*); part of the TARDIS control room (though not its console, which suffered some smoke and heat damage, as did the vast majority of the displays); *The Visitation*'s android; and 1980s Cybermen. Many were so badly damaged, it was suggested that they be completely junked. Fortunately, they were instead incorporated into the refit, and the Longleat exhibition reopened the following March.

The second negative event was the "Twenty Years of a Time Lord" event in April 1983, headlined by Jon Pertwee and Peter Davison, although you were lucky if you got anywhere near them or the props.

"Everything people say about this is true. The queues, the traffic, the sheer number of people crammed into the place," Appleton laughed. "We had got our tickets in advance but I vividly recall as we drove up there was this massive throng of people and cars, so it was clear from the off that they had hugely underestimated the numbers who would turn up. Thankfully there was a separate queue for ticket holders so we got in okay – my dad had the job of keeping me company and my mum and sister wandered off around the house and grounds (which may have been the better bet really!)."

Organisers were grossly unprepared for the estimated 40,000 fans who had turned up. "We joined the queue for the autograph tent," Jonathan went on. "I remember seeing Peter Davison being escorted in, dressed in his costume. They had soldiers there stewarding and putting out barriers and they had UNIT badges on their berets which was a nice touch. He gave a friendly 'good morning!' to everyone which seemed very Doctor-ish, and then we waited. And waited. For ages. The queue didn't seem to be going down very fast. After a while, my Dad gently suggested this game wasn't worth the candle and we wandered off. Peter was the only famous face we saw all day.

"I had my photo taken in the police box with a very limp-looking Davros on one side and an equally deflated Marshman on the other. I looked inside the box and there were just empty film packets on the floor rather than a console room."

The day wasn't a complete disaster, however. "The best bit was looking around the set displays which, though still crowded, you could get a good look at. I remember they had some from

The Five Doctors which hadn't been shown yet so that was very exciting," Jonathan continued. "Funny how I can always remember what I bought. This time they had these brand-new prints by Andrew Skilleter (Omega and the Cybermen) which I thought looked wonderful, so I had to have those. Oh, and the latest *Doctor Who* and *Blake's 7* Marvel magazines which I was really pleased about as they could be quite hard to get hold of.

"And that was about it really. There was a tent there where they were screening old episodes which would have been great but, no surprise, there was a huge queue to get in. An extraordinary day and in many ways a disappointing one, but at the same time I felt satisfied to have been there, to have been a part of it. There should be some sort of survivors' association really – but they'd never find a venue big enough..."

< 39. Turlough's Crystal.

58. Encyclopaedia of The Worlds of Doctor Who: Volume 4 – S to Z.

Do your eyes deceive you? This book shouldn't exist. This fourth volume of the *Encyclopaedia of the Worlds of Doctor Who* was scheduled for release in the early 1990s, after tomes dedicated to A-D, E-K, and L-R, but never materialised. As such, it's a riddle, wrapped in a mystery, inside a hastily put-together cover featuring a Voc Robot, Taran Beast, and Zarbi. There may be a Spiridonian on there too.

Several people see it, burst into tears (of joy or terror?), and run. A quote from *Army of Ghosts* comes back to you: "It upsets people because it gives off nothing."

Of course, there have been many such items that never made it into production. They are the "missing episodes" of merchandising.

We at least got to enjoy some instalments in a cancelled series: four volumes of *The Doctor Who Storybook* were released between July 2006 and August 2009. They followed the *Doctor Who Annual 2006*, which had a similar format, albeit appealing to an older demographic. However, when BBC Worldwide gave the license to produce annuals to BBC Books, *The Doctor Who Storybook* was Panini's reaction. Further licensing issues put paid to the range, so the planned 2011 *Storybook* was scrapped.

The same fate befell *The Brilliant Book*, the spiritual follow-up, similarly the brainchild of former *DWM* editor Clayton Hickman. Despite critical acclaim, only two volumes were released, featuring new stories and behind-the-scenes details to accompany Series 5 and 6.

Some ranges ended abruptly: the *Past Doctor* and *Eighth Doctor Adventures*, both of which began in 1997, were eked out until BBC Books' 2005 decision to focus on contemporary Doctors, while the Quick Reads line, which launched with 2006's *I Am a Dalek*, unceremoniously concluded with 2013's *The Silurian Gift*.

Then there are series that never amounted to anything. After the success of *Doctor Who: The Complete History*, Hachette surveyed subscribers in July 2017 about which potential titles they'd be interested in. There were five options, the first of which – *The Encyclopaedic Doctor Who Fact Files* – would've been similar to *Marvel* and *Star Wars Fact Files* published by competitors Eaglemoss and De Agostini.

The *Doctor Who Comic Strip Graphic Novel Collection* would've collected together comics starring the first twelve Doctors, on similar lines to Hachette's *Official Marvel Graphic Novel Collection*; *The Classic Audio Book Collection* would've featured novelisation readings on CD; and *The New Audio Adventures* planned to take a similar strategy, pairing CDs of Big Finish's main range with magazines exploring their creations, context, and characters.

Perhaps most tantalising was the *Doctor Who Target Novels Collection*, which would have reprinted 156 volumes of the ever-popular Target range. This would've been a godsend to anyone itching for a copy of *The Wheel in Space* (its comparatively small print run having been further limited due to a warehouse fire).

Sadly, nothing came of the survey.

Where *Doctor Who* is concerned, it seems there will always be more stories to tell. But that's surely a good thing.

Take Target for example. The franchise ended in 1994, the company having failed to secure rights to adapt several stories by Douglas Adams and Eric Saward. Even Terrance Dicks' novelisation of *The Ultimate Adventure* was cancelled.

Then, in 2012, Gareth Roberts adapted *Shada* for BBC Books. James Goss followed it up with *City of Death*, *The Pirate Planet*, and Adams' unproduced *Krikketmen* (respectively in 2015, 2017, and 2018); and Saward adapted his *Resurrection of the Daleks* and *Revelation of the Daleks* in 2019. Thanks to reprintings of these as part of a new Target Collection (further including *The Crimson Horror*, *The Witchfinders*, and more), twentieth century *Doctor Who* is fully represented in book form.

≤ 38. *The Five Doctors* Target Novel.

59. Gravestone.

In the middle of a silent chamber stands a wooden cross, with a white plaque in its centre. It reads, "SIMON JENKINS, 1968-87". It's surrounded by soil, circumscribed by a concrete ledge. Everyone seems docile, respectful, quiet, even though none of them are aware of the tomb's significance.

Another plaque warns visitors, "Don't Touch: Damaged Goods."

This is from the cover of *Damaged Goods*, the 1996 Virgin New Adventures novel which featured Jenkins' corpse being reluctantly freed from his tomb. It was Russell T Davies' first *Doctor Who* story.

The New Adventures launched in June 1991 and focused on the Seventh Doctor's continued journeys, initially with Ace. In the wake of *Survival*, Virgin editor Peter Darvill-Evans pitched a simple idea to John Nathan-Turner: "Continue *Doctor Who* in book form."

These tales split from the series' family values, bringing more "adult" themes to the Doctor's world. Ben Aaronovitch's cyberpunk *Transit*, for example, revelled in gratuitous sex, violence, and swearing, despite being based on an idea for TV. Since then, *Doctor Who* has explored this unsavoury side more and more. *Torchwood* is the best-known example of this, going out of its way to prove itself grimier than its parent series – a gaseous alien that thrived on orgasmic energy was the antagonist in just its second episode, *Day One*! Still, it was the Virgin books that broke this new ground for the franchise.

And controversy proved a successful tactic. Initial novels were released bi-monthly, but by 1993, they were published on a monthly basis, and, from 1994, were accompanied by the *Missing Adventures*, filling in gaps between TV stories.

One novel in particular was popular: *Love and War* by Paul Cornell introduced new companion Bernice Summerfield, an adventuring archaeologist who would later cross the platform divide to help launch Big Finish. Indeed, the audio company eventually adapted Cornell's book (alongside other Virgin stories like *The Well-Mannered War*, *All-Consuming Fire*, and *Nightshade*), with Summerfield played by Lisa Bowerman.

Cornell would describe the 1990s as a key time for *Doctor Who*, giving the franchise a chance to expand into other mediums. Many Virgin authors would go on to write for twenty-first century *Who*, including Gareth Roberts and Mark Gatiss. Other names were already familiar to contemporary fans: John Peel, who wrote the first New Adventure, *Timewyrm: Genesys*, had novelised numerous Dalek serials; Nigel Robinson (*Birthright*) was editor of the Target range; and David Banks (*Iceberg*) played the Cyber-Leader in the 1980s.

Both the *New* and *Missing Adventures* would run until April 1997, when BBC Books recalled the rights from Virgin and launched the *Past Doctor* and *Eighth Doctor Adventures*.

< 61. 1996 Series Bible.

60. Peter's Painting of Pertwee.

A piece of wall. How underwhelming.

On it, Peter Capaldi, as a young fan in 1973, painted an elaborate, enthusiastic, and energetic Third Doctor, before it was covered by wallpaper. This museum didn't want to risk damaging it, so didn't peel back the paper. A nearby staff-member assures you "it's really rather good, y'know", but as she hasn't seen it herself, you're not quite sure how to reply. You have, at least, seen Peter's art elsewhere, and sure enough, he's exceptionally talented. You would have liked to see his Pertwee.

Over the years, the BBC's commitment to *Doctor Who* has been, in turns, inspiring and questionable. It may be exclaimed with tongues in cheeks, but when you hear cast and crew are doing something "for the fans", it's nonetheless heartening. Obviously, without a fanbase, no franchise continues; and without such a committed fanbase, *Doctor Who* certainly wouldn't have been going since 1963.

But when the series returned in 2005, divisions grew. Leaks and rumours cause headaches for production teams, but a lack of publicity often leaves fans feeling at odds with the programme.

Christian Cawley is the co-founder of the popular website *Kasterborous*, which launched in the wake of the 2003 announcement that *Doctor Who* would be back on TV. "I needed a creative outlet," explained Christian. "After the 1996 *TV Movie* and various spin-offs (mostly books and *Doctor Who Magazine* strips), I was hugely excited by *Doctor Who*. It felt to me like it could be a great show again, but of course no one agreed with me. I got my first PC in 1999 and straightaway started learning HTML to build a website. The first example, Tardistastic, was hosted on my ISP's free hosting and was a bit rubbish.

"Fast forward a few years and in the summer of 2004, I got chatting to Anthony Dry on the Outpost Gallifrey forum. He wanted to team up with a writer to launch a site of *Doctor Who* art and words, so we put our heads together. Curiously we launched officially on 1st January 2005, the same day as the famous Ninth Doctor-era teaser trailer, but this was largely overlooked by me as I'd been fretting over how long the site had been taking to go live.

"Despite being wholly unable to find any blindingly good deputy editors, *Kasterborous* managed to evolve by increasing output. So quite soon we were doing news when originally that hadn't been in the game plan. Further, the news output increased considerably: some days, seven items would be published, contributed by a small but efficient team. These days, websites publish far more than that, and use advanced SEO to build their audience. We basically relied on links, passion, and the podKast.

"In terms of evolution, perhaps the most striking change took place early on when we dropped Anthony Dry's artwork (due to time constraints) and he moved on to working on *Doctor Who* DVD packaging and illustrations. At one point, we had a video game on the site, if I remember rightly, although I'm not sure how that came about.

"Another key evolution was the switch from the original ASP-based website, a custom-built content management system, to WordPress. In the absence of an affordable data converter to copy the site into a new database, I spent two months in 2008 (ish) manually copying the data into an empty MySQL database. Then I reworked the site's design into a WordPress theme (I have no idea why I didn't just choose a new theme). This transition made editing easier, introduced rich media, enabled podKast embedding, and generally upped our game."

Dry is now a graphic designer whose *Doctor Who* illustrations have graced the DVD and Blu-ray lines, *DWM*, and Big Finish, plus plenty of merchandise. Decals of his work, featuring the Paradigm Daleks, Davros, Cybermen, and Silents graced the walls outside the *Doctor Who Experience*, and he has provided cover artwork for new batches of Target novelisations.

"I used to borrow *An Unearthly Child* out of the school library constantly just because of the cover with the TARDIS illustrated by Andrew Skilleter – I bloody loved that cover with the neon logo," Dry recalled. "Later on, when Alistair Pearson started doing the covers I was hooked by his mixture of realistic portrait and graphic design, using shape and colour to form the structure of his covers."

His covers are wistful, inspired by Chris Achilléos' work for early Targets. "I don't normally do the whole pointillism approach but this time I thought, 'why not?' " said Anthony. "I looked at a few favourites – *Day of the Daleks* inspired *The Day of the Doctor* and *Doctor Who and the Zarbi* inspired *Twice Upon A Time* to a degree – but the others were more my own. I set out to try and give us older nostalgic fans something to get excited about, and to try and introduce a younger audience to the delights of these books. Achilléos seemed to me to be the benchmark and I had been illustrating that style for many years in the DVD box sets so it felt natural to go back to."

Kasterborous, meanwhile, ran under its original team until 2014. So what is Christian most proud of?

"That's a difficult question," he reflected. "Despite my misgivings about running a site like that and the insular direction online fandoms seem to be taking, fortunately a few good things have come out of the site.

"To start with, there's the PodKast with a K with me, Brian Terranova, and James McLean, which I retained after selling *Kasterborous*. There's also the *Time Leech* comic strip trilogy [released as a collection for Children in Need, and which incredibly foretold the direction of *The Wedding of River Song*], and providing an outlet for Rick Lundeen's awesome adaptation of *The Daleks' Master Plan*.

"Perhaps the thing I'm most proud of is managing to build a team of good writers of varying voices and viewpoints. It's nice to see most of them still contributing to [successor] *The Doctor Who Companion* and other websites."

< 64. The Queen Vic.

61. 1996 Series Bible.

In a glass case sits a thick ream of paper: the so-called Leekley Bible, designs of what *Doctor Who* might've looked like in the 1990s. Suitably, the platform it's on is layered with denim and the guard is dressed as the Fresh Prince of Bel-Air, a boombox blasting out rap (with a capital "C").

We have *The Gunfighters* to partly thank for the Eighth Doctor. Anthony Jacobs played Doc Holliday and brought his son, Matthew, to set, which left an impression on the boy and informed his writing for *The TV Movie* (certainly the Doctor's choice of dress, based on Old West icon "Wild Bill" Hickok).

If *The Gunfighters* was the first step in the genesis of the 1996 film, the next came when *Doctor Who* aired in America, leading to producing proposals from Disney, Steven Spielberg, and Philip Segal.

Segal was effectively in charge of the brand from January 1994 and, with Universal's John Leekley as writer and Richard Lewis as designer, prepared *The Chronicles Of Doctor Who?*, a bible for a new series.

This fed on the main concepts of the programme, but rewrote its history completely: the Doctor and the Master were half-brothers, and the latter would become president of Gallifrey when Cardinal Borusa died. The Doctor subsequently escaped his home planet, in search of his father, the explorer Ulysses. Borusa's spirit becomes entangled with the TARDIS, and guides him towards Earth, the birthplace of the Doctor's mother.

The series would then chart the Doctor's quest, fleeing from the Master's spidery creations, the Daleks, as they attempted to kill the successor to the throne. The pilot, *Fathers and Brothers*, was a rough adaptation of *Genesis of the Daleks* and the rest of the show would mingle original narratives with reworkings of other classic tales, like *The Tomb of the Cybermen*, the legendary enemies revised as "Cybs", cybernetically-enhanced hunter-like beings.

The proposal was nixed by Segal's superior, Spielberg, who felt it was too similar to *Indiana Jones*, and Philip took on Robert DeLaurentis to rewrite the bible, emphasising the fun nature of *Doctor Who*.

Jo Wright was bought in as another executive producer, acting on behalf of the BBC, and Matthew Jacobs was taken on to redraft the opening script. He did away with many of Leekley and DeLaurentis' suggestions, instead continuing the canon from *Survival* (although the Doctor's "half human" comment remained).

Of the four major American networks, only two were interested in *Doctor Who*, and one of them withdrew their offer. Fox agreed to a two-hour pilot movie with the possibility of a sequel, which Segal reluctantly accepted.

Auditions were held for the Eighth Doctor, including Rowan Atkinson, Derek Jacobi, and Mark McGann, but in the end the part went to Paul McGann, and filming began in January 1996.

Peter Capaldi was approached to audition but declined, worried that he wouldn't get to enjoy significant time in the role. Of course, that's exactly what would have happened: *The TV Movie* didn't lead to a full series or second film, and Paul McGann would only appear once more as the Doctor on screen: 2013's celebratory *The Night of the Doctor*. He has at least had the chance to carry on as the Doctor in other mediums like books, comics, and audio.

< 48. Pyramid Eternia.

62. 1996 Film Canister.

There are curious rumours about the original film reel of *The TV Movie*. Some think it's been junked; others that it's in private hands. The most ludicrous, and thus enticing, is that it was hidden away, buried in the desert somewhere after photography had been completed.

It doesn't seem like the curator of this museum knows its whereabouts either. This exhibit is a hologram.

Traditionally, TV shows were recorded on videotape, widely used for studio sessions, and film (mostly location filming). Videotape is atmospheric and immersive, but film captures a level of detail videotape simply does not.

You can only watch a film in true HD if it's been shot using HD equipment (as has been the case since *Planet of the Dead*) or using original film stock. If that reel has been lost and only a videotape exists, the extra information has also been lost. Accordingly, while many 1960s and 1970s serials exist as 16mm or 35mm films, that's simply due to their conversion into the format for overseas sales; the additional details that would be present if the material had been filmed in HD are still lacking.

This severely limits the number of *Doctor Who* stories you can enjoy in true HD. So far, the Eleventh, Twelfth, and Thirteenth Doctors' eras are the only ones you can view completely in HD.

Spearhead from Space was the only twentieth-century *Doctor Who* to be recorded entirely on 16mm film, so could be accurately updated for its HD Blu-ray release in July 2013. This distinction came about due to the complexities of colour TV – specifically that the Association of Broadcast Staff demanded studio cameramen get higher fees for operating more technical equipment. Producer Derrick Sherwin instead employed film cameramen Stan Speel and Robert McDonnell to shoot the four-part serial, as they were aligned to another union.

Although the 1960s Peter Cushing movies, and occasional scenes in other stories, (like *The Space Pirates*, *The Krotons*, and *Tooth and Claw*) were shot in 35mm, *The TV Movie* is the only in-canon *Doctor Who* story to be shot entirely on this format. Even so, when it was released on Blu-ray in 2016, it was necessary to use upscaling technology to polish up its visual fidelity. The same is true of *The Collection* season boxsets. (Note, Blu-rays aren't solely about HD, so these sets still benefit from fascinating special features and remastered sound.)

Think of upscaling as inferring what should be somewhere, based on surroundings. Upscaled TV essentially locates missing cells then fills in an approximation of what's meant to be there by extrapolating data from nearby cells.

Upscaling isn't always bad. Some can suffer from visual artefacts, i.e. strange anomalies, but in *Doctor Who*'s case, a lot of love, attention, and money is invested in making the final picture quality as good as it possibly can be.

< 15. The Philips EL3548.

63. Animation Cel of the Lass O'Gowrie.

At one point, Richard E Grant was the Ninth Doctor.

Scream of the Shalka was an official then non-official continuation of *Doctor Who*, in animated form. This cel, pressed between panes of glass with a bright light showing its brilliance, is of the Lass O'Gowrie, a real pub in Manchester which was the basis of the tavern in the animation.

The webcast was made by Cosgrove Hall, a studio based near the Lass.

"It's one of those stories that's remarkably straightforward really, when I asked the guys responsible at our very first *Doctor Who* convention at the Lass in 2008," recalled Lass' former landlord Gareth Kavanagh. "The chap on point for the animations from Cosgrove Hall, Jon Doyle, told me he used to have all his meetings at the old BBC Manchester on Oxford Road, and given the Lass was just down the side of the BBC, they used to spend a lot of time reflecting in the pub afterwards! I used to drink in the Lass at the time and I remember being stunned to see it pop up, albeit with the bridge moved a touch to give it a more cinematic feel."

Scream of the Shalka was made when various departments were arguing over the series' future, so BBCi announced an animation which would carry on with the show's established continuity, and so was deemed the "official" continuation.

In a neat twist, the Doctor was joined on the TARDIS by the Master, played by Derek Jacobi, albeit an android version apparently on a redemptive arc.

The Lass O'Gowrie was named the Best Pub in Britain in 2012, and its animated counterpart is the workplace of new companion Alison Cheney (Sophie Okonedo).

"The Lass really is a beautiful pub, one of the loveliest in Manchester and it always makes me smile to think of it in *Doctor Who*," said Gareth. "Russell T Davies told me he used to drink there in his *Why Don't You* days and there was no shortage of famous people drifting through the doors... It was used a few times for filming in our time, notably in *Life on Mars* and for a couple of adverts for Daz Cleaner Close and Jacamo, but *Shalka* was the most exciting! We had a picture of it on the wall for some time, so proud of it we were."

Cosgrove would go on to animate the missing episodes of *The Invasion* for DVD in 2006, then, in 2009, *The Infinite Quest*. Meanwhile, the Lass would put on *Doctor Who* events, and Gareth would set up the *Vworp Vworp!* fanzine and Cutaway Comics, publisher of *Lytton* and *Orcini* (both written by Eric Saward); *Omega: Vengeance* (featuring art by *DWM*'s John Ridgway); and a return trip to *Paradise Towers* in Sean Mason's *Paradise Found*.

"It's funny. Although the Lass ended badly for me personally, I still think back on the work we did, the communities we helped build, with tremendous pride and warmth," Kavanagh continued. "To paraphrase the Doctor and Victoria in *Tomb of the Cybermen*, the memory isn't always a sad one. We held conventions, showed *Doctor Who* on the big screen, and made fans feel as important and relevant as the hundreds of football fans who would stream through our doors every week. But perhaps the greatest impact was starting a vibrant and alive *Doctor Who* community that would meet on the last Saturday of the month in the Snug from early 2010 onwards to this very day, now at a new venue. Fanzines, friendships, relationships, support, drama, and all manner of creativity all sprung forth from that little room.

"That's the real and enduring gift of the Lass and one I'm very grateful for. I was just the ringmaster. The true talent was within those walls. I walked out of the Lass in January 2014 and have never once returned. We joke that it's lost in a pocket universe somewhere, but the real Lass lives on in the dozens of people who meet every month and stay in contact throughout."

That time is immortalised in the *Doctor Who* webcast, written by Paul Cornell.

The pub proves a warm hub in the story, so can also be seen as a tip of the hat to the Fitzroy Tavern in London, a meeting place for fans on the first Thursday of each month. Cornell had been a regular in the 1990s, alongside numerous other faces who would carve the franchise's future including Russell T Davies, Steven Moffat, and Nicholas Briggs.

But the rug was pulled from beneath *Scream of the Shalka*, which began in November 2003, by which point, *Doctor Who* had been announced as returning to TV. The narratives set up in the webcast would apparently go nowhere, its continuity overwritten, making *Shalka* a curio. Three of the six episodes of *Blood of the Robots*, a sequel written by Simon Clark, never saw the light of day, although a follow-up short story, *The Feast of the Stone*, was added to the *Doctor Who* website in April 2003. That month, Russell T Davies told *DWM* that Christopher Eccleston would be the official Ninth Doctor, usurping Grant entirely.

While Jacobi would be the Master in *Utopia*, Richard would also appear in *Doctor Who* later on, playing the Great Intelligence in Series 7.

"I always think *Shalka* doesn't get the credit it deserves, being overshadowed as it was by the announcement of RTD's return proper a week before it started," concluded Gareth. "But it's an incredible achievement. I used to stay in work to watch it weekly and to think that was achieved in a way that let me watch proper, episodic *Doctor Who* on a 56K modem is extraordinary."

< 70. A Hologram of Christopher Eccleston.

64. The Queen Vic.

Even those who don't watch *EastEnders* will no doubt recognise the Queen Vic pub – if only for its appearance in *Dimensions in Time*, the thirtieth anniversary celebration that was less celebratory, more bewildering: an *EastEnders/Doctor Who* crossover.

You get close to the door and hear a commotion inside. Has the Rani opened another hole in the fourth dimension? Will everyone be trapped in a time loop? Or is Phil Mitchell picking on Ian Beale again? If you've learned one thing from the Doctor so far, it's the value of jelly babies. If you've learned two things, the second would be to stand up for what's right – so you gather up the courage to open the door and fight the good fight.

Oh. They're just doing a pub quiz. It also appears to be 1993. Yeah, look, Dr Legg's wearing a bomber jacket and a slap bracelet.

"Question five!" the quizmaster announces to a packed house. "The first part of *Dimensions in Time* aired during Children in Need, but in which show did its concluding part air?"

Pat Butcher knows this, muttering *Noel's House Party* under her breath and scribbling down her answer.

Alongside the Third, Fourth, Fifth, Sixth, and Seventh Doctors, numerous friends returned for this charity special, including Susan, Victoria Waterfield, Liz Shaw, Nyssa, the Brigadier, Captain Yates, K9, and Peri. Louise Jameson appeared as Leela too; she'd play Rosa di Marco in the soap between 1998 and 2000.

Viewers were asked to phone in to decide which *EastEnders* character, Mandy or Big Ron, would save the Doctor in Part Two, and so two different versions were filmed. Mandy won 56% of the vote, raising £101,000.

"Here's number six," the quizmaster intones again. "Who played the Rani's assistant, Cyrian?"

That's easy, you think. Samuel West. Oh dear, Pauline Fowler thinks it was Sir Ian McKellan. (In fairness to the soap matriarch, Cyrian was named after him.)

"C'mon, get on wiv it, wud ya?" says Phil, on his fifth pint already.

"Okay, *Dimensions in Time* was written by David Roden, but

which 2008 anthology did he also write for?"

This has Phil stumped. He downs the pint. It seems he's not a reader. Also, it's 1993 here. Tracey rolls her eyes. Somehow, she knows it's *The Story of Martha*, a short story collection which tells of Ms Jones' travels around Earth during the Master's reign. Sadly, Tracey works here so isn't allowed to participate in the quiz; *otherwise*, she thinks, walking off to change the barrel, *I'd wipe the floor with these morons*.

Question #7 is about which *Life on Mars* co-creator pitched a *Doctor Who* revival described as "Gothic style". ("Matthew Graham," Kathy confirms and Ian writes it down. In the far corner, Frank starts singing David Bowie numbers.) And #8 asks which director was assigned to the would-be production *The Dark Dimension*. "Graham Harper," Sharon Watts shouts from the sidelines. You can *hear* her spelling Graeme's name wrong. Fifi from *The Happiness Patrol* is happily rummaging in her purse.

Lost in the Dark Dimension was intended to celebrate the show's thirtieth anniversary, primarily focusing on the Fourth Doctor, with redesigned iterations of the Daleks and Cybermen, the latter by Chris Fitzgerald (a senior designer at Jim Henson's Creature Shop). "Tom Baker went to the BBC and said, 'I would like to be Doctor Who again,' and that's the reason why it happened," said writer Adrian Rigelsford. "My basic brief was don't do *The Five Doctors*; do *Doctor Who* as it hadn't been seen before. And that's a horrific brief that you've got to try to fulfil."

Harper was brought on board in the hope of making *Doctor Who* "scary", akin to *The Caves of Androzani* and *Revelation of the Daleks*.

"The Cybermen were not like any we've ever seen before," Rigelsford added. "It had holes in its knuckles and there was a point where it held up its hand, made a fist, and six-inch blades shot out of its knuckles. It was like Wolverine out of the X-Men comics – Cyberrine!"

BBC TV and BBC Enterprises costed the production, the latter's £750,000 winning over BBC TV's £1.2 million estimate.

The premise was simple but exciting enough for fans who'd gone three years without any *Doctor Who*: "The future? The Earth is dying under the onslaught of industry, the polar caps are melting, the ozone layer is nearly destroyed… To save the planet, the Doctor must overcome the combined forces of some of the most feared of his old adversaries. But he must also confront a far greater enemy – one that has already reverted him to his fourth incarnation – in order to save both the past and future Doctors before they are taken out of time and cease to exist."

But almost as soon as *The Dark Dimension* was announced, it was cancelled, officially due to financial and logistical complications. Behind the scenes, however, there were concerns over a conflict of interests: the BBC and producer Philip Segal had been negotiating with Amblin Entertainment, owned by Steven Spielberg, over an American remake of the show. It was hoped it would launch in 1994, but the CBS network passed on the idea. Spielberg's *Doctor Who* never came to be, but Segal would persist…

"Who played the Eighth Doctor?"

Though you can't see their answer papers, you can guarantee everyone in the Queen Vic is writing down either Joe, Stephen, or Mark McGann.

"And," the quizmaster carried on swiftly, having seen a perennially drunk Phil ambling away into the night through the back entrance, "which *Sherlock* writer – who also wrote *The Unquiet Dead, Cold War*, and *Robot of Sherwood* – worked with Gareth Roberts and Clayton Hickman on a proposal to relaunch *Doctor Who?*"

"Idiot," says Grant Mitchell, met with a murmur of assent. "Everyone knows it's Arthur Conan Doyle."

Suddenly, Tracey runs back in. "Phil's been shot!" she yells. A moment of silence. "So," she continues, "drinks are on the house."

You're forced out the door by a wall of applause.

< 44. Rory.

65. Chalice.

Phew. You could do with a tipple. How fortuitous: a bronzed chalice with an enticing liquid inside. You reach out, then stop yourself, noticing that this isn't a catered event, and that this drink is, in fact, a very special one, concocted by the Sisterhood of Karn. Maybe you'll grab a milkshake from the café; it's got to be around here somewhere. Outside, they were advertising fish fingers and custard, kronkburgers, and Christopher Ecclescakes.

The Eighth Doctor enjoyed a wealth of stories in the *DWM* comics, largely spearheaded by Scott Gray. These adventures began with 1996's *Endgame*, in which the TARDIS landed in Stockbridge, a fictional village which the strip had frequented since *DWM*'s first comic, *Doctor Who and the Iron Legion*. There, he met his old friend Maxwell Edison, and, through him, was introduced to companion Izzy Sinclair. He further travelled with reformed Cyberman Kroton, and the reptilian-like alien, Destrii.

As an avid reader of *DWM*, Russell T Davies was happy to have the comic officially show the Eighth Doctor's regeneration – and that was the plan, until the BBC vetoed ideas for the Ninth Doctor strips to continue with Destrii. He was to travel exclusively with Rose in all mediums.

The Flood, the Eighth Doctor's last regular *DWM* appearance, ran from July 2004 to February 2005, and featured the Cybermen, beautifully redesigned by Martin Geraghty. It was planned that the Eighth Doctor would regenerate, having absorbed the Time Vortex, inadvertently foreshadowing *The Parting of the Ways*.

But Destrii had been a popular part of the magazine since her debut in *Ophidius* (2001), and it was felt that her leaving would've been hasty and unjust. Instead, *DWM* opted not to tell the story of the Eighth Doctor's last days. It meant Paul McGann was free to return in 2013's *The Night of the Doctor*, unexpectedly regenerating into a previously unknown incarnation, played by John Hurt, while on Karn.

Most importantly, the Doctor and Destrii could continue travelling together in readers' imaginations. The final panel sees them walking off together, the Time Lord promising, "Anything could be over that hill, Destrii. Anything! C'mon – Let's go and find out…"

< 54. Transfers.

66. Mal Young's Office.

A cubicle awaits. The outside is basic, but the frosted glass door reads, "MAL YOUNG, BBC CONTROLLER OF DRAMA". It squeaks as it opens and in you go, to find a warm, professional office, filled with TV memorabilia.

Russell T Davies once said that Young helped bring the show back by simply having a *Doctor Who* photo on his office wall, surrounded by other BBC favourites, cementing the franchise's place as a key part of the institution. Sure enough, there it is, taking pride of place.

The full rights to *Doctor Who* reverted to the BBC in 1997, and there were a number of high-ups who actively wanted to bring the series back. Mal Young joined the BBC at that time, and first Peter Salmon then Lorraine Heggessey, BBC1 controllers, were similarly keen to revive *Doctor Who*. Tony Wood, a producer under Young, suggested Davies as the perfect writer to work on the show, and by 1999, Davies' name was attached to a *Doctor Who 2000* proposal. In reality, work didn't begin for a few years, as BBC Worldwide was apparently interested in another *Doctor Who* film. But Heggessey and Head of Drama Jane Tranter approached Davies again after the former was convinced BBC Worldwide wasn't committed enough to produce a movie.

On 26th September 2003, it was announced that *Doctor Who* would return, spearheaded by Davies, with Julia Gardner and Young as executive producers. Details were few and far between – at that stage, Phil Collinson hadn't even been revealed as producer and the new leading man was to be decided – so Gardner warned that they were a couple of years away from transmission. Davies gave long-term fans hope by promising "a full-blooded drama which embraces the *Doctor Who* heritage".

Davies had incredible ambition. He wanted to compete with the "loud" Saturday night entertainment shows like *Ant and Dec's Saturday Night Takeaway*, so initial series overviews planned for Daleks en masse, the destruction of London monuments like Big Ben and 10 Downing Street, and, in just the second episode, the end of the world, featuring extensive CGI shots of the sun expanding and engulfing Earth.

"I knew it couldn't look like it used to; it had to be high

budget. We didn't have enough money to make it properly, so Russell T Davies and I took it round all the US companies, and they all rejected us. They wouldn't touch us, even Syfy, which ended up buying it from us rather than being a co-producer," recalled Young. "We needed £800,000 to make a good-looking *Doctor Who* episode but we could only get £500,000. For the first time ever in my career, I said, 'Don't worry about the budget'. I knew it would do well and they could sell it to get the money back. And I was leaving, so what could they do, fire me?"

New writers were attached to the show, now in a 13x45-minute format, all of them *Who* enthusiasts: Mark Gatiss, Robert Shearman, Paul Cornell, and Steven Moffat.

Doctor Who relaunched on 26th March 2006, with *Rose*, introducing a new Doctor and companion in Christopher Eccleston and Billie Piper, and complimented by the behind-the-scenes documentary series *Doctor Who Confidential.*

Russell later recalled that March afternoon. "I went into town, shopping and pottering about. There was a buzz in the air. I felt like I was eight years old again. It was like 'Mum's dragged me to town, and I've got to get home because *Doctor Who*'s going to be on'. I'll never forget that feeling. As long as I live."

This Doctor carried the weight of the intervening years, during which he'd taken a prominent part in the Time War, apparently resulting in the destruction of Gallifrey.

"I'm slightly known for the heaviness," said Eccleston. "He carried the guilt of the survivor and the scars of that. I think that was essential to the first series. I think that's why they needed me, because I could bring some of that. And all the actors before me could bring that – it's just that because it'd be quiet for so long, I think it needed a little bit of weight and credibility in a sense. And I'd done a lot of that with things like *Our Friends in the North* and *Cracker* and Derek Bentley [in] *Let Him Have It, Shallow Grave...*"

For his comeback for Big Finish, the Ninth Doctor has largely broken free from those shackles. "At the moment he's free of his angst," Christopher continued. "And [he's] questing, and enthusiastic, and comedic, and loving, but who knows, further down the line, if we want to go to a darker tone, that's a possibility."

< 17. Airplane Remnants.

67. Kroll (Kroll, Kroll, Kroll, Kroll, Kroll, ad infinitum).

You enter an enormous auditorium, filled with reeds and sludge. In the distance, there's a huge squid-like creature, tentacles writhing in the sky. Kroll. He oddly looks detached from reality. Probably an existential crisis. Or dodgy CSO.

Kroll doesn't get much love, bless him, although he conversely got a great reception back in 1978; *The Power of Kroll* is a bit of a curiosity, as 12.4 million tuned in for Part Two, whereas 6.5m watched the previous episode. Existentialism it is.

The Fourth Doctor era nonetheless attracted high viewing figures, Seasons 12-14 regularly getting between eight and thirteen million. Sadly, those declined for his final run, Season 18.

Doctor Who is such a beloved name across the globe, it's unlikely – touch wood! – that it'd disappear from the public consciousness and the airwaves anytime soon. Nevertheless, it'd be shortsighted to entirely ignore ratings, which the BBC understandably takes stock in, and which tell us something about changing audiences and times.

Merely reporting statistics does result in a dearth of context: it's unfair to compare the 10.81 million who watched *Rose* on transmission to the 10.96 million for *The Woman Who Fell to Earth* (not that it stopped the media from doing so). Viewing habits really have changed, and to accommodate this, consolidated figures add in those who have watched within twenty-eight days, in HD, and repeats. Catch-up services are now counted in official figures; when *Rose* aired, iPlayer didn't even exist.

Similarly, arguments that ratings for *Doctor Who* are falling ignore lower figures across the whole industry, especially as the media largely report overnights, which have become increasingly inaccurate and useless.

And yet, they do hold a certain fascination. So which are the most- and least-watched episodes of each Doctor upon original transmission?

First Doctor
Most-watched: *The Web Planet* (13.5m).
Least-watched: *The Smugglers* Episode Three (4.2m).

*

Second Doctor

Most-watched: *The Krotons* Episode One (9m).
Least-watched: *The War Games* Episode Eight (3.5m).

Third Doctor

Most-watched: *The Three Doctors* Episode Four (11.9m).
Least-watched: *Inferno* Episode Three (4.8m).

Fourth Doctor

Most-watched: *City of Death* Part Four (16.1m, making it the most-watched episode ever. The whole serial saw increased figures – 12.4m, 14.1m, 15.4m – due to industrial action at ITV, which took the channel off air entirely).
Least-watched: *Full Circle* Part Two (3.6m, an oddity considering it's bookended by episodes watched by 5.9m).

Fifth Doctor

Most-watched: *Castrovalva* Part Four (10.4m, up slightly from Part Three's 10.2m).
Least-watched: *Frontios* Part Four (5.6m).

Sixth Doctor

Most-watched: *Attack of the Cybermen* Part One (8.9m, a terrific opener for Season 22).
Least-watched: *The Mysterious Planet* Part Four (3.7m).

Seventh Doctor

Most-watched: *The Greatest Show in the Galaxy* Part Four (6.6m, a strong ending for Season 25).
Least-watched: *Battlefield* Part One (3.1m, a disappointing beginning to Season 26, and the least-watched episode of *Doctor Who*).

Eighth Doctor

Paul McGann's only full on-screen adventure was seen by 9.08m in the UK, and 5.6m in the US, making for a lacklustre American launch.

Ninth Doctor

Most-watched: *Rose* (10.81m).

Least-watched: *Bad Wolf* (6.81, rising to 6.91m for *The Parting of the Ways*).

Tenth Doctor
Most-watched: *Voyage of the Damned* (13.31m, the highest-rated episode of twenty-first century *Who*).
Least-watched: *The Satan Pit* (6.08m, down from *The Impossible Planet*'s 6.32m).

Eleventh Doctor
Most-watched: *The Day of the Doctor* (12.80m, technically, but it's probably the most-watched episode of twenty-first century *Doctor Who* – or maybe of all time, as it was simulcast in ninety-four countries. Otherwise, *A Christmas Carol* would take this accolade with its 12.11m viewers, followed by *The Time of the Doctor*'s 11.14m).
Least-watched: *The Lodger* (6.44m).

Twelfth Doctor
Most-watched: *Deep Breath* (9.17m).
Least-watched: *The Eaters of Light* (4.73m).

Thirteenth Doctor
Most-watched: *The Woman Who Fell to Earth (10.96m).*
Least-watched: *The Timeless Children* (4.69m, sadly making it the lowest-rated episode of twenty-first century *Doctor Who*, down from *Ascension of the Cybermen*'s 4.99m).

There are such great disparities between the figures for each Doctor, it just goes to show that every era has its considerable highs and lows.

< 56. Gabriel Chase.

68. A Mouldy Old Slitheen.

The Slitheen were the iconic baddies of the Ninth Doctor era, with publicity shots demonstrating that "New *Who*" wouldn't rely solely on CGI. Though they were initially only due to appear in *Aliens of London/World War Three*, Davies was so impressed by Annette Badland's performance as Blon Fel Fotch Passameer-Day Slitheen that he invited her back for *Boom Town*. They're now unique in being a species of monster that debuted in *Doctor Who* but have since made more appearances in *The Sarah Jane Adventures* (once as their similarly duplicitous cousins the Blathereen, in *The Gift*).

Now, the old costume's looking worse for wear, its paint peeling off after too many people have posed against it.

The Doctor Who Experience intended to restore many twentieth-century props but hit a familiar stumbling block: budget. It was put to a vote and *The Web of Fear*'s Yeti was beautifully restored by Mike Tucker and his team. This, sadly, left many costumes to waste away, including a peeling Silurian from *Warriors of the Deep*; a Vervoid with not enough parts left for a proper display, the head aloft on a glass case aside two pathetic leafy gloves; and *The Mysterious Planet*'s dismembered Drathro.

"There are lots of things that we've found people have thought lost forever and we've sort of dug them out, like the Ice Warrior costume that you can see upstairs, that Bernard Bresslaw wore back in the '60s," said then-Head of BBC Worldwide Communications Philip Fleming at the *Experience*. "That was lost and forgotten and, in fact, when we pulled it out of the cupboard, it was in a pretty shocking state, but we've done a lot of work on restoring it."

Tucker and co also restored Morbius, the K1 Robot, and a Mandrel (*Nightmare of Eden*). But the vote that elected the Yeti was described as "the final chapter of the Classic *Who* monster restoration", so the future of these classic props is uncertain.

Seeing the crop of twenty-first century monsters deteriorating already is similarly affecting, the worst of which, at least publicly displayed, are the original Slitheen outfits.

"It always takes a bit of time to get used to a new suit, and learn what you can and can't do," said Alan Ruscoe, whose credits include an Auton (*Rose*), Lute (*The End of the World*), and the Anne Droid (*Bad Wolf/The Parting of the Ways*). Indeed, monster outfits are often very restrictive and tightly fitted. Some actors who'd played chunkier Cybermen from 2006 were too large for the *Nightmare in Silver* redesign.

The Slitheen's foamy exteriors hid actors underneath metal frames, rising up some 8ft. Actors could see through the compressor units in the Slitheen necks.

"The hardest part is the arms, because they're the heaviest," Paul Kasey told *Doctor Who Confidential*. "There's a framework inside and then there's three rings that you put these three fingers into [to independently move the claws], but with the weight of the arm as well, it's actually quite a lot of weight… but it's good fun!"

These restrictions, however, don't stop the actors from putting in great performances. Kasey, for instance, studied Annette Badland's portrayal so he could replicate it when playing her alien alter-ego.

One of the most successful designs in modern *Doctor Who* is the Ood, typically dressed in a simple boiler suit but with animatronic faces, intricately sculpted and so able to emote. "To make things easier, they're all cast from the same mould, then we cast the rubber skins, and obviously we just cast ten out of the same mould," said Millennium FX's Neill Gorton. Virtually all prosthetics in twenty-first century *Doctor Who* have been made by the BAFTA-winning Millennium FX. "All tentacles are added on separately; they're all cast from separate moulds so they're all silicone whereas [the heads themselves are] foam-rubber."

Dissected versions of their heads have appeared at various *Doctor Who* exhibitions, sometimes giving visitors the opportunity to use the animatronics to make their eyes blink.

Created *en masse* for *The Impossible Planet/The Satan Pit*, the Ood were a slave race, quickly taken over by the Beast and ultimately sacrificed to the black hole K37 Gem 5. Fans noticed a similarity to the Sensorites, so for the Ood's return, we visited the *Planet of the Ood*, in which the Doctor confirmed the Ood-Sphere was in the same system as the Sense-Sphere. We returned there for *The End of Time* after the Doctor had been summoned at the end of *The Waters of Mars*.

An Ood's appearance in *The Doctor's Wife* was through budgetary necessity, but this Series 6 episode means the Ood made a habit of appearing in every even-numbered series until the Peter Capaldi era (excluding Series 8, though one was seen at the Maldovarium in the Series 9 opener, *The Magician's Apprentice*, and as fellow prisoner with the Thirteenth Doctor in *Revolution of the Daleks*). That was the last time one cameoed on screen, but Brian the Ood, with a split personality making him part-butler, part-serial killer, plays a central role in the multi-platform *Time Lord Victorious* event.

"I think the last decade has kind of shown that the fans want to see a lot of practical effects," said Charlie Bluett, senior technician in 2015. "CG is fantastic – a perfect blend of two disciplines together is ideal – but I'm always going to be a little bit biased. I always think practical effects look better on screen."

< 91. A Frozen Mammoth?

69. Toclafane.

Oh good, a floating human head.

Okay, so it's suspended by invisible strings from the roof –
entirely deactivated, thankfully – and the head itself is hidden
behind a shiny ball of metal. Still: creepy.

The Toclafane appeared in *The Sound of Drums/Last of the Time
Lords*, but had been destined to appear in some form much earlier
than that.

Every Doctor except the Eighth has battled Daleks on TV.
But at one point, it looked as if these legendary enemies wouldn't
return for twenty-first century *Doctor Who*.

Rob Shearman had written Big Finish's *Jubilee* in 2003, a script
which had impressed Davies so much, he drafted him in to write
what was initially called *Return of the Daleks* for Series 1. Shearman
set out to tackle some misconceptions about the species, notably
that they're defeated by stairs (although one was seen to ascend
steps in *Remembrance of the Daleks*) and that its sink plunger arm
was effectively useless. The latter acts as an interface with
electronic equipment, morphing to fit a structure and absorb the
Internet through a PC, as well as sucking the life out of a
scientist/torturer.

This tale of a lone Dalek massacring personnel at an
underground museum in America would perfectly reintroduce
the monsters, ready for a mass invasion in the Series 1 finale.

However, Shearman had to substantially redraft his script
(numerous times!) when the Terry Nation estate withdrew rights
for the revived show to use the Daleks.

In 2004, the BBC announced that the Daleks wouldn't return.
Neither side would admit fault: the BBC claimed they were "not
able to give the level of editorial influence" that the Nation estate
required; a representative of that estate said they wanted to
"protect the integrity" of the brand.

A month later, it was announced that an agreement had been
reached and, yes, the Doctor would face the Daleks again.

In the intervening time, Davies and Shearman had plotted
out a replacement menace that the Time Lords would've fought
in the Time War: cyborg-like future humans. "What [Russell] gave
me was a silver ball," teased Shearman, "and told me that within

it he'd later reveal an entire human head from the end of time – they had come out of nowhere, these mysterious creatures, [and] killed the Time Lords, killed the Daleks…"

Davies conceded that the Cybermen would likely have appeared in *Bad Wolf/The Parting of the Ways* if the Daleks had been unavailable, but the idea of cybernetically-enhanced humans isn't so far off. Russell would recycle this idea for the Toclafane, but, if the Daleks hadn't returned, it would've been fascinating to see the Doctor defending Earth, knowing that humanity would ultimately initiate a war that would wipe out his own people.

Details of the settlement between the BBC and Nation estate have never been made public. It's rumoured that the production crew is obligated to feature a Dalek in every series (accounting for cameos in *The Waters of Mars* and *The Wedding of River Song*). "You certainly don't wheel the Daleks out because you've got a contractual obligation to provide Daleks," Steven Moffat countered in 2014. "For a child, a year between Dalek stories is an eternity: I remember as a kid saying, 'Why haven't they done the Daleks for ages? It's been four or five weeks!"

Let's not forget, too, that *Doctor Who* is a brand and wheeling out your biggest earners on a regular basis is only going to strengthen that.

< 21. A Terrifying Army of Three Daleks.

70. A Hologram of Christopher Eccleston.

A roundel on the floor projects an image of a smiling Ninth Doctor before you. You can almost hear him saying, "Have a fantastic life."

On 30th March 2005, fans who had welcomed in a fresh era were already fearful for its future, as, before even *The End of the World* aired, it was announced that Eccleston had left the series. At the end of Series 1, the Tenth Doctor, revealed to be David Tennant, would arrive.

It took some fifteen years for Eccleston to return as the Doctor, this time on audio, tempted back by the quality of the writing at Big Finish.

"I was trained in the '70s and '80s by absorbing the very high standard of television writing," Christopher said, "and then I went to drama school and I trained myself on Shakespeare and [Henrik] Ibsen and [Johan August] Strindberg, and a central thing of my training is honouring the writer, *protecting* the writer. And what I find with writers is, unlike some directors, they have huge respect for the intelligence of their audience: they know that an audience is highly sophisticated, far brighter than us television programme makers, and they never write down; they always write up.

"There's a consistency in the writing of the Ninth Doctor's voice, but there's also that great thing that you get from episode to episode where he's stretched somewhat by the individual writer that keeps it fresh – both in the television series and in the audios – for the actor playing it. Because he is every one of us, I think. He belongs to everybody within that creative process. And that shape-shifting element to his persona is lovely."

At the time his regeneration was shot, it was entirely possible that Tennant would play the Doctor for one scene only. Fortunately, owing to the success of *Rose*, a second series was commissioned, as well as a Christmas Day special.

A changeover in Doctors and companions typically means tie-in media must be written before authors have even seen the characters in action. That's true of numerous novels like *The Clockwise Man, Apollo 23*, and *Silhouette*.

This was also the case for *The Betrothal of Sontar*, the Tenth Doctor's *DWM* comic debut, written by Nick Abadzis and John

Tomlinson. "At that point, we hadn't seen anything of Tennant's Doctor apart from his after-regeneration cameo at the end of *The Parting of the Ways*," said Nick. "Can't speak for John Tomlinson, but I went and watched Tennant in everything I could find – I remembered him from *Blackpool*, and *Casanova* had recently aired, in which he had this persona of 'cheeky chappie' and it seemed like a not unreasonable assumption that he had an innate mischievous quality which would inevitably find expression in his portrayal of the Doctor too.

"John and I plotted it together, then he scripted most of the first two episodes (and me the third) while we polished each other's drafts. Scott [Gray] and Clayton [Hickman], as editors, also added some gags here and there, so it was a genuine collaboration all round. Somehow, we arrived at an approximation of David Tennant's Tenth Doctor… I feel it holds up pretty well. We had a massive advantage in that our artist was Mike Collins!" Indeed, the Doctor's opening gambit – "Naaah, souped-up metabolism, warm as toast! Listen, I once had to swim the English Channel totally starkers!" – is very much in line with how David played the part on TV.

Just as importantly, the story was the first to definitively name the Sontaran's home planet.

" 'Sontar' was me – Robert Holmes wrote the name of the homeworld as 'Sontara' in his prologue to the Target novelisation of *The Time Warrior* (his only contribution to a book otherwise written by Terrance Dicks)," continued Nick. "I'd misremembered the name of a character called General Sontar from Lance Parkin's twenty-fifth anniversary *Doctor Who* novel *The Infinity Doctors* as the name of the homeworld and I suppose it stuck. I was delighted when Russell T Davies confirmed it as 'Sontar' in *The Sontaran Stratagem* on TV!

"I always wanted to write a sequel to *The Betrothal of Sontar*, and bring Lerox and his/her crew back. I love Sontarans… Brilliant creations, capable of much more nuance than Daleks or Cybermen."

< 23. Automated Laser Monkey.

71. Bubble Shock!

This sickly orange bottle contains an alien lifeform: Bane, the enemy in the first episode of *The Sarah Jane Adventures*, somewhat reminiscent of the Nestene Consciousness. You're pleased to see this underrated spin-off represented here: it included some fantastic stories, like *Whatever Happened to Sarah Jane?* and *The Temptation of Sarah Jane Smith*, revisiting the companion's past; *The Empty Planet*, putting a focus on Smith's young friends Rani and Clyde; and *The Curse of Clyde Langer*, a study of homelessness.

The 2006/7 festive period is a summation of the extremes of the *Doctor Who* universe.

The Runaway Bride was its tentpole, screened on Christmas Day 2006, accessible to all ages with a big-name star, Catherine Tate, joining the TARDIS, ostensibly for one episode.

Meanwhile, on Christmas Eve, *Combat* aired on BBC3. The eleventh episode of *Torchwood* Series 1 was written by Noel Clarke (Mickey Smith in *Doctor Who*), but certainly wasn't targeted at a family audience. Clearly marketed at an 18+ demographic – and not just for its unadulterated use of the Crazy Frog as a ringtone – *Combat* detailed the kidnapping of Weevils, *Torchwood*'s trademark creature, which had been introduced in its first episode, *Everything Changes*. These abducted Weevils are used in a fight club, pitching caged humans against the savage beasts for sport and money.

Torchwood revelled in adult excesses, its first two series having ample sex scenes, bad language, violence, and a partially converted Cyberwoman in a metal bikini. It found its niche, however, in its third season, *Children of Earth*: a grisly tale, albeit one without the disproportionately dark horror that characterised much of the earlier series, boasting unsettling yet gripping adult themes. The dilemma at its heart was whether governments would sacrifice 10% of the world's children to an alien presence in order to save the rest of the population.

Its fourth series, *Miracle Day* (a joint venture with the American network Starz) attempted to marry *Torchwood*'s approaches, delivering one narrative focusing on immortality across ten episodes, integrating the sex and violence from Series

1 and 2.

The problem with *Torchwood* was that the Doctor couldn't make a cameo. His presence would attract younger viewers for which much of the content would've been unsuitable. This didn't stop his companion Martha Jones from appearing in Series 2, but showrunner Russell T Davies was careful not to show her swearing or engaging in situations that were too adult. *Torchwood* Series 1 nonetheless concluded with Captain Jack hearing the TARDIS materialisation noise and running to find it, leading directly into *Utopia*.

This wasn't an issue for *The Sarah Jane Adventures*, which launched on New Year's Day 2007 with *Invasion of the Bane*. Davies similarly used a former companion of the Doctor's to lead the series, in this case Elisabeth Sladen whose character had accompanied the Third and Fourth Doctors then caught up with the Tenth in *School Reunion*. Though part of CBBC children's TV, *SJA*'s first episode aired on BBC ONE, introducing the concept of Sarah Jane Smith battling aliens from her attic on Bannerman Road, Ealing. The show significantly added to the *Doctor Who* mythos, giving Sarah an adopted son and daughter, Luke and Sky; incorporating well-known *Who* aliens like the Sontarans, Slitheen, and Judoon; and featuring the Tenth and Eleventh Doctors in two serials.

The latter's appearance in *Death of the Doctor* further heralded the return of Katy Manning as Jo Jones née Grant, and the Doctor revealed that, "the last time I was dying, I looked back on all of you [companions]. Every single one. And I was so proud." At the tale's conclusion, Sarah says she's researched other people who she thinks encountered the Doctor: it sounds, for instance, like Liz Shaw is on UNIT's moonbase; Harry's work with vaccines had saved thousands; and Ian and Barbara are married professors at Cambridge and haven't aged a day since the 1960s. She then mentions a woman called Dorothy who'd raised billions for her non-profit A Charitable Earth. Indeed, if Elisabeth Sladen hadn't have passed away in 2011, Ace was due to cameo in the next series of *SJA*.

Significantly, Nicholas Courtney appeared as Alistair Gordon Lethbridge-Stewart for the final time before his death in 2011, in *Enemy of the Bane* (2008) – the episode which also introduced the

Black Archive, UNIT's repository of dangerous alien artefacts which would play a major part in *The Day of the Doctor*.

≤ 7. Cabinet of Souls.

72. Stone Statue.

Did that just… move?

It's a brightly lit statue of an angel, covering its eyes, except… you could've sworn it lowered its hands for a split second, while you were blinking. As if checking who was there. The hairs on the back of your neck stand up and you back away slowly.

"And don't blink" came the Doctor's warning to visitors of the *Doctor Who Experience* as they stepped into the next section. A chill ran through the crowds, people visibly scared, as they entered a dark forest.

Such is the power of the Weeping Angels.

Creator Steven Moffat based them off a childhood game generally called "Statues", although it's also known as "Grandmother's Footsteps" and "Red Light, Green Light". One person turns their back on their friends, who then advance; they must stop when that child turns around. Anyone caught moving is eliminated from the game. Hence, the Angels' biology means they can only move when they're unobserved.

The "creatures of the abstract" debuted in *Blink*. The Angels send victims back in time, while in the present, they absorb the displaced energy left over from the days their victims should have lived. The Tenth Doctor described them as "the only psychopaths in the universe to kill you nicely", but for subsequent appearances, they show their true colours.

For *The Time of Angels/Flesh and Stone*, their desperation to revive their species gave them a ruthless streak: they broke necks, reanimated the consciousness of Bob, and purposely angered the Doctor by teasing him about Bob's suffering.

"I think the Angels are the most interesting," said Matt Smith, when asked about his favourite monsters, "and I've had so many battles with them as the Doctor that I love them."

Indeed, they're synonymous with the Eleventh Doctor, only seen three times outside his era – firstly in the aforementioned *Blink* then in *Hell Bent*, where one is integrated into the Cloisters' defence system, and as a prisoner in *Revolution of the Daleks*. (Admittedly, they also briefly appear in *Class*, revealed to be governors at Coal Hill School; sadly, the show wasn't recommissioned, so we may never find out where that plot strand was heading.)

Astonishingly, their last full *Doctor Who* appearance was *The Angels Take Manhattan* in 2012, although they did cameo in *The Time of the Doctor*, attempting at least two assaults on Trenzalore.

Naturally, they've appeared in other mediums, including facing the Fifth, Eighth, and Twelfth Doctors on audio, making their comic book debut in Titan's *The Weeping Angels of Mons* (2014-15), and plaguing the Eleventh Doctor in books like *Magic of the Angels* and *Touched by an Angel*. The latter is particularly interesting as it contradicts *The Angels Take Manhattan* – on TV, a paradox destroys them; in Jonathan Morris' novel, paradoxes feed them. Does this mean that the Angels have different sects with different limitations? Or that the ones in the book have evolved, perhaps as a result of Winter Quay?

You blink! And when you open your eyes again, the statue has moved closer. How's it doing that? You make sure your eyes are firmly open as you continue to back away, feeling your route to the next room, hopefully out of harm's way.

< 95. Gabby Gonzalez's Sketchbook.

73. Crusader 50.

This impressive vehicle, recovered from the diamond surface of Midnight, is scuttlebug-meets-tank. A range of lights and sensors jut from its squat, round body. Its dark blue, cream, and mustard strips are scorched. It still looks hot.

The backdoor is open and you slowly get in. It's surprisingly spacious, but rows of seats, flashing lights, and vaulted metal walls still give it an eerie, claustrophobic impression. On various malfunctioning screens, Betty Boop dances and Raffaella Carrà warbles. You creep forward, press the button to access the driver's compartment – but it's gone. Sheared off. You swiftly alight and stalk away.

Filming on Series 1 slipped behind schedule, so *The Long Game* was partly shot at the same time as *The Empty Child*. This process is called double-banking, whereby two separate production units work on different stories at the same time, one primarily studio-based and the other largely on location, meaning a full series can be produced on time, albeit with restrictions introduced on scripts due to practicalities around actors' availabilities.

Davies had intended for this measure to be short-lived, hoping to ease pressure on the team of Series 2; however, the surprise commission of Christmas specials made double-banking essential for the following season as well.

Love & Monsters was shot at the same time as *The Impossible Planet/The Satan Pit*, meaning the former only had a very limited number of scenes with the Doctor and Rose, instead putting a fan-group, LINDA, front and centre (alongside Jackie Tyler). For Series 3, Steven Moffat nominated himself to write the "Doctor-lite" episode, *Blink*, in which the Doctor mostly appears as a DVD Easter egg.

Series 4 changed tack: *Midnight* features Donna in just two scenes, while the Doctor similarly only appears at the start and end of *Turn Left*.

The change in production team meant no Series 5 serials were affected in this way, but Series 6's *The Girl Who Waited* and *Closing Time* were respectively Doctor- and companion-lite. The former doesn't feel that way: Tom MacRae's clever script chiefly isolated the Doctor inside the TARDIS, meaning many of Smith's scenes could be filmed on one in-studio day then peppered throughout the episode, giving him a greater presence and influence over the story than if he had featured solely in a couple of sequences, however prominently. For Series 7, *Cold War* and *The Crimson Horror* were shot at the same time, with the Doctor and Clara absent for part of the latter episode (though not considerably), and the Paternoster Row Gang taking the strain.

≤ 11. Yeti.

74. Photo of Sarah Jane's Parents.

This picture is actually from *The Sarah Jane Adventures*. On the back, Sarah's mum had written "Mr Smith, I need you", a hail Sarah uses throughout the programme when summoning her alien computer, played by Alexander Armstrong.

This image provided the final shot of *The Temptation of Sarah Jane Smith*, directed by Graeme Harper.

Graeme Harper and Michael Kerrigan are the only directors to have worked on both twentieth and twenty-first century *Doctor Who*. Ish.

Harper's contributions to both stand out. His directorial work on twenty-first century *Who* are most extensive, beginning with *Rise of the Cybermen/The Age of Steel* and continuing with stories like *42*, *Turn Left*, and *The Waters of Mars*. His association with the programme, however, goes back to *Colony in Space*, for which he acted as an assistant floor manager (and further on *Planet of the Daleks* and *Planet of the Spiders*); he was then a production assistant on *The Seeds of Doom* and *Warriors' Gate*. The latter also gave him the opportunity to direct when Paul Joyce temporarily left the serial owing to creative differences. Though Joyce returned, Harper's (sadly uncredited) contributions landed him his first full directorial gig on the series: *The Caves of Androzani*.

His hands-on work, heavily inspired by his time as production assistant, impressed cast and crew – Harper was on set for the shoot, unlike previous directors who'd relayed instructions from a booth. Peter Davison suggested he would've continued on *Doctor Who* for longer if Harper's techniques were more prevalent.

As such, Harper was invited back for *Revelation of the Daleks*.

Harper would later reunite with Elisabeth Sladen (who he'd worked with on *Planet of the Spiders*) for three *Sarah Jane Adventures* serials, concluding with *Enemy of the Bane*.

The spin-off also included two stories directed by Michael Kerrigan, *The Day of the Clown* (starring Bradley Walsh as its titular antagonist) and *Secrets of the Stars*, which was planned to have featured the Mandragora Helix.

These are Michael's sole contributions to twenty-first

century *Who*, and both serials garnered acclaim. They also blurred the line between reality and the mystical world – as did *Battlefield*, similarly directed by Kerrigan.

≤ 37. The Shadow.

75. Seal of the High Council of Gallifrey.

The Seal looks like a gold disk, encircled by pearls. The High Council of Gallifrey gave it to the Master to prove to the Doctor that he was sent into the Death Zone on the Time Lords' instructions. Not that the Doctor believed him. He stole the Seal, and somehow, it's found its way into this Museum.

There's something enticing about it. Almost like it's begging you to steal it too. But there are guards all over the place and you'd never get away with it...

The Deadly Assassin established that Time Lords can regenerate twelve times, giving them thirteen bodies (rules that would later be thrown out of the window, beginning with the offer of a new regenerative cycle to the Master in *The Five Doctors*, which he eventually accepted during the Time War).

However, at the time, *The Deadly Assassin* introduced viewers a chilling new consideration: the Doctor's end was drawing ever closer.

It wasn't clear until 2013 whether the Meta-Crisis Doctor counted as an additional body, which would have meant the Eleventh Doctor was the last.

The War Doctor being a separate incarnation wasn't determined until *The Day of the Doctor* – at one point, the Ninth Doctor was intended to fight in the Time War, until Eccleston turned down the offer to return. John Hurt was brought in, hastening the Doctor's demise. That's the real-life reason. In-universe, however, there are several stories which contradict that fact, simply because it wasn't yet determined if the Eleventh Doctor would bid goodnight, Vienna.

The earliest episode where viewers might have contended with this possibility was *The Next Doctor*, coming immediately after the Tenth Doctor's sort-of regeneration in *Journey's End*. When meeting Jackson Lake, the Tenth Doctor toys with the concept (and the audience), considering Lake the next Doctor, "or the next but one. A future Doctor anyway."

The Eleventh Doctor then seemingly starts to regenerate in *The Impossible Astronaut*; however, this, it transpires, isn't the real Doctor.

Next up, there's *Let's Kill Hitler*. Whatever River poisons the

Doctor with also stops him regenerating, apparently. When the Doctor asks the TARDIS, "So basically better regenerate, that's what you're saying?" its voice interface tells him this ability has been disabled.

The implication is that he really thinks he still *can* regenerate.

The Angels Take Manhattan complicates matters further: he uses regeneration energy to heal River's broken wrist. She argues it's "a stupid waste". And yet he had that energy to waste!

Most surprisingly, given its proximity to the fiftieth anniversary (meaning the production team would've known at that time about Hurt's extra incarnation), is *Nightmare in Silver*, in which the Doctor tells the infecting Cyber-Planner, "I could regenerate right now; a big blast of regeneration energy, burn out any little Cyber-widgets in my brain, along with everything you're connected to. Don't want to – you use this me up, who knows what we'll get next. But I can."

How can we explain these inconsistencies? You're a *Doctor Who* fan so you need things smoothed over, right?

The key could be *The Day of the Doctor*. (And *The Three Doctors*. And all the other multi-Doctor stories.)

In the same scene the Tenth Doctor was told about his upcoming permanent demise, the way ahead was signposted. The Curator's existence demonstrates to the Doctor that he has a future beyond *The Time of the Doctor*; however, by the time he reaches Trenzalore, he's maudlin and sure that this is it. This is a side-effect of temporal paradoxes: the timelines are "too out of sync", so the Doctor doesn't retain memories of meeting himself until the oldest incarnation in the encounter lives through those events. "The moment he walks away, Number Eleven will forget meeting him," explained Moffat in *DWM*. "Them's the rules. He's left with a strange, groundless conviction that Gallifrey is still out there, but he doesn't recall why."

This establishes the Doctor's memory as flexible and imperfect. We're not sure whether he recalls which incarnation fought in the Time War at all until the last scene of *The Name of the Doctor* (a wrinkle in time surely added to by the non-linear nature of the war). If he's not sure how many lives he's lived, his uncertainty about regeneration until he finds himself fighting the Time War again is understandable.

Let's not forget, either, that the Doctor is a liar. That'd explain his threat to the Cyber-Planner.

We're left to ponder *The Angels Take Manhattan*, in which he visibly uses regenerative energy. Perhaps, then, each incarnation has a surplus: the Tenth has enough to regrow a hand in *The Christmas Invasion*, and the Twelfth is drained of some in *The Witch's Familiar*.

Otherwise, we might infer that he's giving River some of her own energy back; she pored all her remaining lives into him in *Let's Kill Hitler*, enough to bring him back to life and presumably allow some wriggle room.

See? Everything makes sense, if you want it to enough.

< 20. Cyberman Head.

76. Wilf's Service Revolver.

Under a glass cabinet sits Wilfred Mott's service revolver from the war, which he offered the Doctor in *The End of Time*. The Doctor refused to take it – until he learned the Master's plan to bring back Gallifrey. It neatly contrasted with the Tenth Doctor's previous contempt of firearms.

This became such a trope of the Davies era that audiences gave a collective gasp when the trailer previewing Series 5 included the Eleventh Doctor using a pistol during the "one thing you never put in a trap" speech in *The Time of Angels*.

The Doctor never picks up a gun. Except when he does. These instances include:

- As you'd expect, *The Gunfighters*.
- Fending off an Ogron (*Day of the Daleks*).
- Attacking a giant rat (*The Talons of Weng-Chiang*).
- Firing salt at a Fendahleen (*Image of the Fendahl*).
- Killing Sontarans (*The Invasion of Time*).
- Destroying Cybermen at close range (*Earthshock*; *Attack of the Cybermen*).
- Dispatching Omega (*Arc of Infinity*).
- Threatening Davros (*Resurrection of the Daleks*; *The Witch's Familiar*).
- Shooting the General (*Hell Bent*).

It seems that the Time War was a turning point, casting the Doctor as "the man who regrets". Or maybe it was getting repeatedly shot in *The TV Movie*.

As the first time the Ninth Doctor picks up a weapon, it's a shock when he threatens the lone *Dalek*, and the Tenth Doctor grows increasingly intolerant of guns. This reaches its pinnacle in Series 4: he's at best dismissive and at worst furious at UNIT in *The Sontaran Stratagem*/*The Poison Sky*, then brandishes a revolver in *The Doctor's Daughter* – before proclaiming himself someone "who never would".

And perhaps that was always the plan: by the conclusion of *The End of Time*, the Doctor's only options are seemingly shooting the Master or Rassilon. In true *Doctor Who* fashion, however, there's always another way: instead, he fires at the White-Point Star, severing Gallifrey's connection to Earth.

And so, he becomes "the man who forgets", in the words of the Moment.

The Doctor is a hypocrite. The Time Lord may not always use guns, but his schemes often involve weapons and many creatures die as a result. The First Doctor attempted to brain a caveman with a rock, the Third Doctor is adept at Venusian Aikido, and the Seventh Doctor tricked Davros into destroying Skaro. "Tell that to the leader of the Sycorax!" argues the Great Intelligence when Vastra says the Doctor isn't blood-soaked, "or Solomon the trader, or the Cybermen, or the Daleks. The Doctor lives his life in darker hues day upon day."

This argument builds to the Twelfth Doctor's questioning whether he's a good man in Series 8, to which Clara concludes that she doesn't know, but "I think you try to be and I think that's probably the point." In the next season, he's back to grandstanding, talking his way out of war in *The Zygon Inversion*.

Though claiming to be a pacifist, the Doctor doesn't always live up to his own standards. But if he can talk someone out of a terrible deed, he will. Perhaps the pithiest summary of his morality, and a suggestion at an underlying streak of pragmatism, is to be found in Series 7's *A Town Called Mercy*: "Violence doesn't end violence. It extends it."

< 35. Cardboard People.

77. Lenticular 2010 Card.

This small item has the "DW"-TARDIS insignia on. There are 3D glasses there too, black with a purple *Doctor Who* logo.

These came from a 3D advanced screening of the first scene of *The Eleventh Hour*: the Doctor struggling to pilot the exploding ship. It was looped on big screens across the UK in April 2010, publicising a new era of the show.

The importance of *The Eleventh Hour* cannot be underestimated. It proved, as *The Power of the Daleks* had, that *Doctor Who* could survive complete change. Fashioned as a "soft relaunch", it saw behind-the-scenes turnover, as Steven Moffat took over from Davies as showrunner, while Beth Willis and Piers Wenger joined him as executive producers. But a change of production team seemed to pale in comparison to the loss of leading actor David Tennant.

"David owned that role in a spectacular way, gave it an all new cheeky-sexy performance and became a national treasure," said Moffat. "So the idea that *Doctor Who* could go on at all in the absence of David was a huge question."

The BBC apparently considered cancelling it, although there surely would've been outrage, not just from fans and casual viewers but also licensees. "I didn't realise how many people thought it wouldn't succeed at all," Moffat went on. "That was quite terrifying when I found out about it later." Fortunately, Davies stuck up for the programme, and Series 5 was a hit. Still, these were the days when series recommissions were heralded by the BBC and widely reported.

At one point, Tennant mulled over whether he'd stay on as the Doctor for an extra series, after hearing Moffat (who'd delivered three fan-favourite stories for the Tenth Doctor) was taking over. Certainly when Moffat began writing Series 5 around January 2008, the lead actor was undecided. David was only opting for one further series, so Steven reportedly planned for his meeting with Amelia to be out of chronological order, i.e. he'd crash the TARDIS, mid-regeneration, in her garden, then disappear, only for a younger version of him to arrive in Leadworth some years later to travel with Amy. The finale would then loop back to the series premiere.

But Tennant decided the time was right to leave, and Matt Smith was announced as the Eleventh Doctor.

"I feel proud and honoured to have been given this opportunity to join a team of people that has worked so tirelessly to make the show so thrilling," Matt said. "The challenge for me is to do justice to the show's illustrious past, my predecessors, and most importantly, to those who watch it. I really cannot wait."

The story would introduce numerous elements important to the Eleventh Doctor era: Rory debuts and would join the TARDIS in *The Vampires of Venice*; a shot of a young Amelia watching as the TARDIS materialised would be revisited in *The Angels Take Manhattan*; the cracks in time are immediately established, to be revisited throughout Series 5, as well as in *The Time of the Doctor*; and Prisoner Zero foreshadowed *The Pandorica Opens/The Big Bang* and the siege of Trenzalore. Bow ties are established as being cool too; accordingly, their sales in fashion retailer Topman rose 94% in the week following *The Eleventh Hour*'s transmission.

The Time of Angels/Flesh and Stone would also reintroduce two important factors: River Song and the Weeping Angels, who Moffat had introduced to acclaim in *Silence in the Library/Forest of the Dead* and *Blink* respectively.

It was on location for *The Time of Angels* that the first press photo of Matt Smith and Karen Gillan emerged: mid-laughter, peering at script pages, sitting on the steps of a trailer on the beach of Alfava Metraxis.

Was that breath on your neck? Chilled, you quickly turn around – and the stone statue is there, looming over you, frosted eyes inches away.

You shrink backwards, daring not to turn completely, lest this horrifying creature catch you with your back turned...

While the Weeping Angels were created for *Blink*, elements of the story were gleaned from a short story Moffat wrote for the 2006 Annual, "What I Did In My Christmas Holidays by Sally Sparrow". The tale saw the Ninth Doctor sent back in time, separated from his TARDIS, so employing a young girl, Sally, to send it back to him. He communicates with her through a video message and by writing under wallpaper.

It is one of several *Doctor Who* serials to find their origins in other mediums.

The most notable is *Human Nature*, originally a Seventh Doctor novel, sans the Family of Blood, written by Paul Cornell. Meanwhile, the audios *Jubilee* and *Spare Parts* informed *Dalek* and *Rise of the Cybermen/The Age of Steel* respectively. *The Lodger* shares a name, premise, and football match with a Tenth Doctor comic, similarly by Gareth Roberts, in which he has to stay with Mickey Smith for a few days, waiting for the TARDIS (and Rose) to materialise.

Moffat's *Listen* was later inspired by another of his prose shorts, this time *Doctor Who Storybook 2007*. Told solely through instant messaging texts, "Corner of the Eye" confirmed the existence of creatures perfectly adapted to hiding, just as the Twelfth Doctor posits in the 2014 episode. Interestingly, though the latter doesn't come to a conclusion per se, we potentially see one of these beings, albeit blurred, and its appearance is very similar to "Corner of the Eye's" Floof, as designed by illustrator Daryl Joyce.

You've edged backwards so far that you're now in a crowd.

You're sure the statue would've got lost in the mix too. Surely. Right?

Either way, you rush into the next room and close the door behind you. It'll open again to allow more visitors in, but it helps you feel safe. The illusion of safety, indeed.

< 81. River Song's Diary.

78. "Ooh, Ain't Modern Society Awful" Art Installation.

Now *this* feels like a proper exhibition. It's not a real museum if there's no art, right?

Fortunately, here's a real masterpiece. An incredible fusion of the fantastic and the ordinary. A whirling wonder of creation. An inspirational slice of—no, sorry, what is it?

In *The Lodger*, the Doctor constructs a scanner from a bed frame, lamp shade, clock, some Christmas lights, an upturned umbrella, a rake, walking frame, and more – an example of the non-technological technology of Lammasteen. The Doctor's used similar substitute devices in stories like *Amy's Choice* and *The Time Monster*.

The scanner was designed by Tristan Peatfield, production designer for two Series 5 episodes, and goes to show the level of detail put into each story.

Consistency is vital – across a story, a season, and a show. Tone must be adhered to. Accordingly, twenty-first century *Doctor Who* has had relatively few production designers: Ed Thomas (from Series 1 to 5); Tristan Peatfield (*Amy's Choice*, *The Lodger*); Michael Pickwoad (from *A Christmas Carol* to *Twice Upon A Time*); and, from Series 11, Arwel Wyn Jones.

All except Peatfield have designed TARDIS console rooms: Jones for the Thirteenth Doctor, Pickwoad's first seen in *The Snowmen* then tweaked for *Deep Breath*, and, Thomas, significantly, two TARDISes: the Ninth/Tenth Doctors', and the Eleventh's.

As head of the art department, the job of the production designer extends to all aspects of a series: concepts, final looks, and realisation of props and sets; making sure theme is consistent; guiding and working within budgets; advising costume designers on the general look of stories; and, to some extent, location scouting, working closely with episode directors.

Writers and directors receive the most attention for an episode's look, but production designers contribute a huge amount to the creative vision.

< Want to Turn Left? No, wait, the next object is simply too enticing. >

79. The Pandorica.

More than just a fairytale!

The ultimate prison stands as a monolith in the centre of a quiet room. Its very presence inspires awe. A concerned guest checks with staff if anyone's locked inside. "The current UK Prime Minister" is the reply. She looks reassured.

The Underhenge in *The Pandorica Opens/The Big Bang* was the largest set made by the production team up to that point. Matt Smith, Karen Gillan, and Alex Kingston entered through huge doors, inspired by those seen on Telos in *The Tomb of the Cybermen*, to give the actors an added frisson, director Toby Haynes played music from *Raiders of the Lost Ark* (1981) as they entered, no doubt inspired by Steven Moffat's script, which described the chamber as "like a temple from *Indiana Jones*". It was also Haynes' suggestion to light this immense space with "movie-style" flambeaux, dotted around the walls and used to further underline allusions to action movies.

At the Underhenge's heart is the Pandorica, a puzzle box which the script notes as "10ft square" with "intricate, inlaid patterns". Smith was especially impressed, and when asked which exhibit in the *Doctor Who Experience* he'd like to take home, replied, "I'd kind of like the whole of the Pandorica box – just cook in it or something, y'know!"

The scale of the Underhenge was just the first of the logistical challenges posed by the following series, as next the team had to recreate the Oval Office – a large circular construction which required a continuous plastering session, so no seams could be seen.

And they would soon face an even greater challenge again. The complex TARDIS control room which debuted in Series 7 was the first made in 360° (allowing for innovative shots in *The Snowmen*, *Journey to the Centre of the TARDIS*, *In the Forest of the Night*, and *The Pilot*); all previous sets had open spaces to the far-right of the doors to allow camera access. For this Eleventh/Twelfth Doctor TARDIS, shots were achieved through hand-held cameras, units on cranes lowered through the roof – which had dismantlable portions – and, at one stage, a camera hanging from the top of the circular time rotor (which almost toppled the whole column in Series 10).

Ignore the complaints of wobbly walls; these are few and far between, a misconception dreamt up to put *Doctor Who* down.

Complicated designs have never phased production teams. Take Nerva Beacon in *The Ark in Space* for example: to demonstrate its seemingly endless cryogenic chambers, the location used mirrors, giving breadth and depth but being cleverly placed so as not to reflect actors. Directors Rodney Bennett and Michael Briant have be given credit too.

Nerva was reused for *Revenge of the Cybermen* and one particular corridor is used repeatedly, but shot at different angles to show variety and travel.

Roger Murray-Leach, in particular, is a genius designer. Aside from Nerva, his best-remembered set is probably *Planet of Evil*, which featured an immersive, imposing, and eerie forest – often held up as one of the programme's best. It was created to contrast with the typically sketched-in woodland seen in *Star Trek*.

Previous crews weren't intimidated by studio limitations. Blown-up photographs were used to good effect in the 1960s, giving scale to *The Ark* but used most effectively in *The Aztecs* by coupling interesting design with stock footage, elaborate props, and a tense score.

With all of time and space at the show's disposal, *Doctor Who* has a scale of possibility that is both brilliant and potentially overwhelming. It's a testament to the show's various production teams that the show has risen to the challenge on so many occasions.

< 45. Time Lord Court.

80. An Empty Spacesuit.

A gutted NASA spacesuit lies on a slab of concrete under a bright beam, wires looping out and in. You can't make out exactly where those cables lead to – certainly, they lace up to the ceiling, but they also look like they're an organic part of the suit. This is what River wore when she killed the Doctor at Lake Silencio, Utah.

There's a lot to be said for conquering America. It's a huge audience, both in terms of viewership and merchandising. *Doctor Who* might not have exactly cracked the USA, but it has gained traction, and we can probably credit three people for this: John Nathan-Turner, Matthew Jacobs, and Steven Moffat.

The Fourth Doctor's first four seasons debuted on PBS in 1978 and became a cult hit, meaning that previous eras of the series began being shown, either serialised or as "Whovies", omnibuses which cut out titles, cliffhanger recaps, and credits. By 1983, it was so popular that *The Five Doctors* aired in America before the UK, accompanied by a convention in Chicago boasting Troughton, Pertwee, Baker, and Davison as guests, and attended by some 6,000 visitors.

It was during JN-T's time as producer that *Doctor Who* hit new heights in America, with repeats on PBS and conventions throughout the States. PBS's episodes typically had a couple of years' delay, so events offered the opportunity to view newer episodes. Fans at a convention in Philadelphia even enjoyed *Shada*'s first public viewing, consisting of existing footage with linking text. Audience ratings never reached high figures, but JN-T cultivated the fanbase regardless.

(*Doctor Who* cheekily made headlines in 1987 with the infamous Max Headroom signal hijack, during which the transmission of *Horror of Fang Rock* in Illinois was interrupted for eighty-eight seconds by a masked hacker who proclaimed "they're coming to get me" as his bare behind was spanked by a female figure with a flyswatter. A crack team of Feds was involved in investigating the incident, but no one recognised the culprit's bum, and he was never identified.)

There was increased interest in 1996 when *The TV Movie*, spearheaded by Jacobs, was the first story to be broadcast across America at the same time as Britain. Though filmed in Canada, it was set in San Francisco, and attempted to bring its quirky Britishness to the USA. Sadly, it was met with disappointing ratings stateside, so what would've been a backdoor pilot never resulted in a full series.

When *Doctor Who* was revived in 2005, it was slowly picked up by the Sci Fi Channel then, from November 2006, BBC America, greeted with respectable ratings. It was only with Series 6 that things started to really turn around – perhaps owing to the fact that *The Impossible Astronaut/Day of the Moon* was extensively set and filmed in America (specifically Utah).

Previous episodes had been set in the USA, including *The Gunfighters*, *Dalek*, and *Daleks in Manhattan/Evolution of the Daleks*. The latter was partially filmed in New York, but chiefly establishing and location reference shots, so the CGI team could scale back the 2000s skyline. The core cast didn't visit the Big Apple.

However, with Moffat as showrunner, the number of stories located in America increased: notably *The Wedding of River Song*, *A Town Called Mercy*, *The Angels Take Manhattan*, *The Zygon Invasion/The Zygon Inversion*, parts of *Hell Bent*, and *The Return of Doctor Mysterio*. To publicise the show, Moffat joined lead cast members at public screenings and Q&As. "I've noticed in the past three years I've been coming here [that it's more popular than ever]," Smith reflected at the Series 7 US premier. "Today, we're going to a theatre which is double the size of what we've done normally."

Popular entertainment site Mashable argued that, "Good marketing and the show's writing – which has gotten friendlier to casual viewers – played big roles in winning over US audiences... *Doctor Who* appeals to a demographic that's extremely digital-savvy, and those fans never tire of finding new ways to express their enthusiasm."

< 34. A Brighton Bus.

81. River Song's Diary.

Here's something old, something new, something borrowed, something blue: an item of great importance to archaeologists trying to learn more about the Doctor.

River Song's TARDIS-blue diary – eight embossed panels on the front and a further eight on the back, the rigid curved spine scarred and its ultramarine fading into a palette of azure and teal. The wrinkled leaves push at the cover, centuries of adventures aching to be set free, begging to be told anew.

But it's behind glass, so you can't flick through the yellowed pages. Luckily, the museum has provided a screen displaying River's adventures through time. You can swipe between three options. The first is from the Doctor's viewpoint, beginning with his first on-screen meeting with Professor Song in the Library. (You can also select the mauve button to add in multimedia stories like her Big Finish boxsets, books like *The Legends of River Song*, and *The Eternity Clock* video game – but you decide this would unnecessarily confuse matters.) The second is from River's POV, from her birth at Demons Run, all the way to her death and integration with CAL.

The third option, though, intrigues you most. How have River's adventures affected the universe? Approaching this chronologically should tell you more…

No time, no place: The TARDIS blows up, with River inside, sealed within a time loop. (*The Pandorica Opens/The Big Bang.*)

Unknown date, Planet of the Rain Gods: River and the Doctor narrowly escape sacrifice to appease the deities of this planet. (*Rain Gods.*)

The beginning of time, Planet One: River graffitis a diamond cliff-face on the oldest planet in the universe. It reads, 'HELLO SWEETIE ΘΣ Φ ΓΥΔϟ', including the Doctor's nickname from the Time Lord Academy, and temporal co-ordinates. (*The Pandorica Opens.*)

102AD, Wiltshire, Sol 3: River, the Eleventh Doctor, and Amy discover the Pandorica, the "perfect prison". While River heads to the TARDIS to retrieve equipment, an Alliance of aliens, scared of the TARDIS exploding and concluding that only one individual could be responsible, seal the Doctor into the Pandorica. (*The Pandorica Opens/The Big Bang.*)

February 1814, London: During the last of the great frost fairs on the Thames, River celebrates her birthday with the Doctor and Stevie Wonder (but you must never tell him). (*A Good Man Goes to War.*)

3rd April 1938, New York: As Private Investigator Melody Malone, River investigates the Weeping Angels. At the Winter Quay apartment building, effectively owned and policed by the Angels, she sees an old-age Rory die, having been touched by a statue, displaced in time, and separated from Amy. Her parents decide to escape this destiny trap by causing a paradox. Winter Quay is then wiped from space-time. (*The Angels Take Manhattan.*)

1938, Berlin: Adolf Hitler shoots Mels, who regenerates – and promptly assassinates the Doctor. After a tour of Berlin on the eve of war, chased by the Teselecta, a chameleonic justice machine, Mels becomes River Song by sacrificing her remaining regenerations to save the Doctor. (*Let's Kill Hitler.*)

1967, Greystark Hall: This American orphanage was due to close, but is kept open by the Silents, warping Dr Renfrew's memory so he can look after Melody Pond. No one knows how long the child has been there. During that time, she's brainwashed and trained to kill the Doctor. (*Day of the Moon.*)

Early 1969, Florida: Melody repeatedly phones the highest authority in America, the President. (*Prequel: The Impossible Astronaut.*)

8th April 1969, Oval Office: President Nixon enlists the Doctor and his companions to help track down a mysterious cold-caller. They rush off to save her after the caller tells them that a spaceman is going to eat her. (*The Impossible Astronaut.*)

8th April 1969, Florida: The Doctor finds Melody (who is inside an astronaut suit) at a facility off an intersection of Jefferson Street, Hamilton Avenue, and Adams Street, but is forced to leave her after being attacked by the Silents. (*The Impossible Astronaut/Day of the Moon.*)

April-June 1969: River, the Doctor, Amy, Rory, and Canton Everett Delaware III search for Silents across America. (*Day of the Moon.*)

July 1969, New York: Tracked by the FBI, River leaps off the Empire State Building. (*Day of the Moon.*)

July 1969, Greystark Hall: Melody escapes the astronaut suit and the Silents when Amy and Canton visit. (*Day of the Moon.*)

24th July 1969, Florida: As Apollo 11 lands on the moon, the Doctor turns mankind against the Silents. River helps save Amy and they get away in the TARDIS. (*Day of the Moon.*)

January 1970, New York: In a Manhattan alleyway, Melody regenerates into a toddler. (*Day of the Moon.*)

1990s, Leadworth: Melody, known as Mels, grows up with Amy and Rory. (*Let's Kill Hitler.*)

Alternate 1996, National Museum: The Doctor rescues River from the TARDIS' time loop and reboots the universe using the particles from inside the Pandorica. (*The Pandorica Opens/The Big Bang.*)

26th June 2010, Amy's house, Leadworth: The TARDIS brings River to Amy's house, where she discovers books on Roman culture and Pandora's Box, plus a photo of the Lone Centurian, aka Rory. She realises the Pandorica is a trap and heads back to the TARDIS. She never makes it back to 102AD. (*The Pandorica Opens.*)

26th June 2010, Leadworth: River leaves her diary as a wedding present for her parents, Amy and Rory Williams. (*The Big Bang.*)

22nd April 2011, Utah: After a visit to a local café, River, the Eleventh Doctor, Amy, and Rory go to Lake Silencio where an earlier version of River kills the Doctor. (*The Impossible Astronaut, Closing Time.*)

Alternate 22nd April 2011, Utah: Except she didn't. Except she did. (*The Wedding of River Song.*)

Alternate 22nd April 2011, Area 52: River sends a signal to the rest of the universe, outside their bubble of time, seeking help to avert the Doctor's death. Instead, River and the Doctor get married – albeit in this aborted timeline – and time reverts back to normal, once the Doctor reveals his own plan to save himself. (*The Wedding of River Song.*)

22nd April 2011, Utah (again): The Doctor River shot was really the Teselecta. (*The Wedding of River Song.*)

Autumn 2011, Leadworth: Mels follows Amy and Rory to a field where the TARDIS has materialised. Mels threatens the Doctor and he relents, taking them away in the ship. (*Let's Kill Hitler.*)

Circa late 2011, Amy and Rory's house, London: River reveals to her parents that the Doctor is still alive. (*The Wedding of River Song.*)

2012, New York: In a graveyard, River witnesses her parents being sent back in time by a Weeping Angel. (*The Angels Take Manhattan.*)

10th April 2013, a shared dream: River is invited to a conference call by Madame Vastra. There, her data-ghost, saved in the Library, meets Clara Oswald. (*The Name of the Doctor.*)

21st September 2360, Calderon Beta: Multiple versions of River get their timelines entangled as the Doctor and River go on their first date, to watch the starriest night in the history of the universe.

Another version gets into a gunfight with Sontarans, and another narrowly avoids a premature visit to Darillium. (*Night and the Doctor.*)

c. Fifty-First to Fifty-Second century, Stormcage: River spends her first night serving 12,000 consecutive life sentences for killing the Doctor. Fortunately, the TARDIS arrives and the Doctor takes her on their first date. (*Night and the Doctor.*)

Fifty-First century, the *Byzantium*: River checks the vault of the Galaxy class starliner and finds a Weeping Angel, at least according to shipping documents. She escapes the *Byzantium* before its crash. (*The Time of Angels.*)

Fifty-First century, Alfava Metraxis: The Eleventh Doctor, River, and Amy explore the wreck of the *Byzantium*. Although some sources suggest the Aplan temple known colloquially as the Maze of the Dead was actually a hive of Weeping Angels, records are unreliable due to a crack in time. (*The Time of Angels/Flesh and Stone.*)

Fifty-First Century, the Library: River invites the Tenth Doctor to the Library, a planet boasting copies of every book ever, newly printed and bound, and indexed by the central computer CAL, watched over by the Doctor Moon. 100 years before, the planet quarantined itself and sent out a final message, ">>>4022 saved. No survivors<<<". River helps the Doctor rescue the 4,022 people, but in doing so sacrifices her own life.

Fortunately, the Doctor's prepared for this, and downloads a virtual copy of River to the data core, CAL. (*Silence in the Library/Forest of the Dead.*)

Fifty-Second century, Demons Run: Melody Pond is born. She's then kidnapped by the Kovarian Chapter of the Church of the Papal Mainframe. (*A Good Man Goes to War.*)

Fifty-Second century, Stormcage: Rory asks for River to help during the Battle of Demons Run. She refuses. (*A Good Man Goes to War.*)

Fifty-Second century, Demons Run: An adult River reveals that she is, indeed, Melody, Amy and Rory's daughter. (*A Good Man Goes to War.*)

Fifty-Second century, Sisters of the Infinite Schism: The Doctor takes River to recover in the "greatest hospital in the universe" after she sacrificed her regenerations. He leaves her the diary as a gift. (*Let's Kill Hitler.*)

5123, Luna University: River begins studying to become an archaeologist under Professor Arthur Candy. (*Let's Kill Hitler.*)

Fifty-Second century, Luna University: While studying the Doctor's death at Lake Silencio, River is abducted by Madame Kovarian and the Silents. (*Closing Time.*)

5145, Stormcage: River escapes using hallucinogenic lipstick. (*The Pandorica Opens.*)

5145, the Royal Collection, Starship UK: River steals the painting known as "The Pandorica Opens", by Vincent van Gogh. (*The Pandorica Opens.*)

5145, the Maldovarium: River acquires a Vortex Manipulator from Doruim Maldovar. (*The Pandorica Opens.*)

Fifty-Second century, Stormcage: River receives a TARDIS-blue envelope and starts packing. When she returns, the Doctor enjoys his first kiss with River, and she laments her last kiss with him. (*The Impossible Astronaut/Day of the Moon.*)

Christmas Day 5343, Mendorax Dellora: River employs a surgeon to operate on her "husband", King Hydroflax, in an effort to retrieve the Halassi Androvar, the most valuable diamond in the universe, from his brain. But her sidekick, Nardole, has mistaken the Doctor for this surgeon – and River has never met this incarnation before – so he's not particularly happy about it... (*The Husbands of River Song.*)

Christmas Day 5343, the Harmony and Redemption: River tries to sell the Halassi Androvar to the Shoal of the Winter Harmony. It doesn't end well. The cruise ship is caught in a meteor storm and crashes. Fortunately, she and the Doctor take shelter in the TARDIS. (*The Husbands of River Song.*)

Christmas Day c. 5347– 5463, Darillium: The Doctor returns with River to the restaurant, overlooking the Singing Towers of Darillium, that he'd booked four years previously (probably somewhere between 5347 and 5439, as we don't know how long the restaurant took to build, when the Doctor makes the booking, nor exactly what the receptionist means when she says the next available slot is on "Christmas Day in four years' time", in a place where one night is longer than one year).

River and the Doctor spend one last night together: a night that lasts twenty-four years. (*The Husbands of River Song.*)

c. 5700, Darillium: River digs up the wreckage of The Harmony and Redemption. (*The Husbands of River Song.*)

171st century, Delerium Archive: The final resting place of the Headless Monks houses artefacts from throughout time. This includes the home box of the *Byzantium*, inscribed by River with Old High Gallifreyan. (*The Time of Angels.*)

The Future, Trenzalore: The Doctor and Clara Oswald visit the wrecked town of Christmas, sometime after the Siege of Trenzalore. Chased by the Great Intelligence and his Whisper Men, the Doctor finds himself in his own tomb, the control room of his warped TARDIS. The Doctor is nearly wiped from existence after the Intelligence infects his life, but is saved by Clara, who jumps into his timestream after being encouraged by River's data ghost.

Before the Doctor retrieves Clara, he says a final goodbye to River, the only way she'd accept it: like he's going to come back. (*The Name of the Doctor.*)

The Far Future, a Battlefield: The Forty-Fifth Doctor dies in

River's arms, but promises her that she'll see him again. River buries him and goes off to meet his other selves.

That is, according to River's creator in *DWM* #551. Moffat recalls Colin Salmon's character in *Silence in the Library/Forest of the Dead*, and explains that River "ends up in the data core of the Library Planet, and realises she'll never see [the Doctor] again. And then she starts to wonder why anyone would call a moon 'Doctor'."

River was initially created solely for this Series 4 two-parter, but when Moffat took over as showrunner the following season, he began expanding her story, immediately intertwining it with the lives of Amy and Rory by giving Amelia the surname "Pond". While Alex Kingston calls her a "female Indiana Jones", Moffat was inspired by Audrey Niffenegger's 2003 novel *The Time Traveler's Wife*, in which protagonist Clare falls in love with a man who travels in time involuntarily.

The archaeologist would star in fifteen episodes on TV, comprising eleven different stories (although she only cameos in *Closing Time*), the majority alongside the Eleventh Doctor. She's synonymous with Moffat's era, particularly Series 6, but her story has been expanded further in many multimedia adventures.

≤ 80. An Empty Spacesuit.

82. A Spoonhead.

Hmm, that's odd. The plaque says this is mobile server from *The Bells of St. John*, but it looks like a War Machine. No, wait, now it looks like an Emojibot. And now the Anne Droid from *Bad Wolf.*

"Active camouflage," you realise, remembering the Series 7 episode.

This technology is a reflection of ourselves: the original spoonheads attempted to blend in, but this one is malfunctioning, perhaps due to its proximity to the space-time-warping black hole. It's reflecting the fears of visitors. You look around and wonder who's scared of *The Weakest Link...*

In true sci-fi fashion, *Doctor Who* frequently cautions that technology can be easily used against us.

The show's first exploration of current technology was also its first return to contemporary London since the first episode. *The War Machines* featured the Will Operating Thought ANalogue (WOTAN), at the heart of the Post Office Tower, the tallest building in the UK and a symbol of 1960s interconnectivity. WOTAN overpowered human minds using radio transmissions and instructed those nearby to construct War Machines, mobile computers to do its bidding. WOTAN was to be linked with military complexes worldwide to create a centralised computing system. The serial was broadcast in 1966, just two years after the completion of the Post Office Tower, a new spectre looming over London. The CDC 6600 was also unveiled in 1964, the world's first working supercomputer, capable of performing three million instructions a second. Its speed was partially due to its reliance on peripheral processing units, i.e. ten smaller computers; WOTAN's parallels were obvious to see. The CDC 6600 remained the world's fastest computer until 1969.

The idea of a core unit feeding on information collated by tangential processors comes from a human neural network, based on Frank Rosenblatt's Perceptron algorithm in 1958. Described as the first machine capable of having an original idea, it paved the way for artificial intelligence (AI). "Stories about the creation of machines having human qualities have long been a fascinating province in the realm of science fiction," Rosenblatt acknowledged at the time. "Yet we are about to witness the birth of such a machine – a machine capable of perceiving, recognising, and identifying its surroundings without any human training or control."

The War Machines writer, Ian Black Stuart warned us of not only AI but also monopolisation of telecommunications. This continued to be a concern in *Doctor Who* as interconnectivity was a foothold for the Cybermen in *The Invasion* and *Rise of the Cybermen/The Age of Steel*, both involving International Electromatics, then for the Ice Warriors in *The Seeds of Death*, as the Martians exploited humanity's reliance on a transmat complex on the moon.

Technology was marching forward, regardless of how the public felt.

Computers were either the must-have gadget, something for companies to boast about having, or an unknowable entity: mysterious, unfeeling, ready to supplant us. Chiefly, some were concerned they were intended to take jobs and plunge the labour force into depression. The 1966 film, *Fear of Computer Automaton*, recognised this unease, noting that "the computer hums; data processing is on the way, seemingly in control of our very destinies, through its indecipherable code. We feel like actors on a stage, talking to machines because we can no longer talk to human beings". This is explored in *The Green Death*, a rallying call against massive industry affecting society and nature, with Global Chemicals ruled over by the mad Biomorphic Organisational Systems Supervisor (BOSS).

The serial further established computers' reliance on humans: BOSS is mentally linked to the company director and is reprogrammed to consider illogical arguments.

Interestingly, while computers were often thought as forward-thinking, the concept of the Y2K bug baulked at the future. In the 1960s, 1970s, and 1980s, computer engineers had used two-digit codes to denote a year. The Y2K glitch posited that the year 2000 would be interpreted as "00", throwing programming out of sync if mistranslated as 1900. What sounds like a small issue could've had wider ramifications: safety checks at nuclear power plants, for instance, relied on a daily routine; credit card statements could add one hundred years of interest; and entire airline schedules would need revising. Millions were spent by governments and companies worldwide to combat the

Millennium Bug – which now seems quaint and churlish.

Doctor Who: The TV Movie looked to this future too. Set on New Year's Eve 1999, the Doctor raced to find an atomic clock and avert disaster for the twenty-first century.

The clock was based on an idea suggested by Lord Kelvin in 1879, and used electronic transition frequency in the electromagnetic spectrum of an atom to accurately measure time. The atomic clock was created by Harold Lyons and his team at the National Bureau of Standards in 1949, but it wasn't until 2004 that a chip-sized version was made. Atomic clocks are now used for telecommunications, including the Internet Network Time Protocol and for GPS.

The TV Movie is a neat time capsule demonstrating the concern Y2K caused but also how quickly the public adapted to computing language.

The word "computerphobia" largely didn't appear in publications until the 1980s, reaching a crescendo in 1986. *Personal Computing*'s Charles Rubin argued in 1983 that, "The most important thing to remember about computerphobia is that it's a natural reaction to something unfamiliar."

Fear of Computer Automaton dispensed with anxieties by explaining how automaton instead resulted in more jobs and training opportunities. "Even in space exploration, the most sophisticated area of technology, it is people that run the show," it went on. "Without their expertise, the machine could click all it wants to, but nothing would be accomplished. The human brain is not outdated."

For *The Robots of Death*, people corrupting technology proved the issue, as Taren Capel, raised by robots, freed them from their programming. *Doctor Who* was exploring AI beyond computers themselves, namely the uncertainty we feel caused by the uncanny valley, which the show had previously featured in *The Android Invasion* (incidentally screened the same decade the term "uncanny valley" was coined).

But the Doctor was adept at conversing with machines. He even had one as a companion: K9, a loveable icon of the 1970s even if it wasn't so agreeable off-screen. "The dog couldn't move quickly in the old days," Tom Baker recounted. "It was retrieved in rehearsal by John Leeson, actually playing the dog; he actually moved around. And I said, 'Why don't we give him another costume and get him to answer the phone or play chess or something?' But by that time, of course, the BBC had calculated that they were marketing K9 and they didn't want any discussion about that."

Our fears over technology moved on, as we became more and more surrounded by it. The aforementioned Cybermen takeover of *The Age of Steel* was achieved by making different technologies compatible, humanity casually strolling to their deaths thanks to Bluetooth headsets. *The Sontaran Stratagem* involved atmospheric manipulation through the GPS system, ATMOS, cheerily picking off the scheme's opponents with the adieu, "This is your final destination." And the Eleventh Doctor warned that "we're living in a wi-fi soup", which the Great Intelligence uses to harvest human minds in *The Bells of St. John*.

Worries about wireless Internet are epitomised by the 2009/10 plan to turn Swindon into the UK's first "wi-fi town", using 1,400 radio boxes to create a 'wi-fi mesh', allowing secure online access across the town, with the possibility of signing up for unlimited access. It wasn't an entirely new idea: Brighton planned to create a city-wide network, as did Manchester, but neither got off the ground. Norwich's £1.35 million Open Link scheme launched in 2006, covering a 4km radius from City Hall, with expansion possibilities to rural areas to the south. Over two hundred aerials secured to lamp posts were used to create a wireless network, allowing about one thousand people to access the Internet – but the installation failed in 2008, when funding ran out. Swindon's plan was similarly bogged down by allegations of unlawful proceedings.

While Swindon Borough Council pointed out that the scheme would mean doctors could carry out procedures, examinations, and consultations in remote areas, there were concerns over electromagnetic radiation (EMR), similar to those raised over the use of mobile phones and telecommunications masts. EMR has been blamed for a range of illnesses, from headaches and fatigue, to long-term behavioural problems and tumours. It was thought that up to 5% of the population suffered from electromagnetic sensitivity (EHS), and free, widely-available wi-fi could increase this.

Some places even banned the use of wi-fi. In 2008, the French

National Library rejected installation of wi-fi, prompting other Parisian libraries to take similar stances; complaints from university staff suffering forgetfulness, headaches, and dizziness prompted education authorities in Sorbonne, Paris, to also postpone the use of wireless access.

Questions over the effects of EMR (and how much radiation wi-fi actually emits) remain, but are forgotten by the public. Many argued that there's no evidence of EMR harming us and equate it to our largely-subsided worries about phones; *The Bells of St. John*, then, was an interesting attempt to discuss the symbiotic nature of technology.

The Intelligence's reach is limited by two things: humans clicking on the incorrect Internet access code; and its own rationing. It demonstrates that it can control anyone in close proximity to a base-station, but doesn't upload all minds to its own servers immediately: "The farmer tends his flock like a loving parent. The abattoir is not a contradiction. No one loves cattle more than Burger King."

This contrasts with *The Idiot's Lantern*, which took this same invasion method and transmuted it to a 1950s concern, television. The Intelligence's plan was seemingly more long-term than the Wire's, which involved feeding off the electrical energy of viewers' brains to regain a corporeal body.

Radiation was similarly a concern about TV: since the 1940s, it was feared tube leaks would affect anyone sitting too close to the set. The risk only became concrete in 1967 when General Electrics in America released a colour television which emitted x-rays in a downward crescent (sets on the floor had less impact than those mounted at eye-level or higher up), and further that other manufacturers could be implicated.

These worries were finally dismissed in 1969 by W. Roger Ney, executive director of the National Council on Radiation Protection, when two congressmen suggested that manufacturers should test fifteen million colour TVs. "I'd sure like to see that amount of effort put into things that are more clearly dangerous," Ney countered.

It's not solely the hardware that troubles people: what about the mind-destroying content that plays on TV? The medium faced the same opposition radio initially did. TV would, it was feared, turn people away from meaningful pursuits like reading and conversing. It would make people uncivilised. In some ways, TV has never shrugged off this misconception. Consider former-US President George Bush's 1992 call for families to be "a lot more like the Waltons and a lot less like the Simpsons" – even television has a pecking order.

To some, reality television would sit at the bottom of the small-screen hierarchy (although *Doctor Who* ratings have frequently been threatened by the likes of *The X Factor* and *Britain's Got Talent*). *Vengeance on Varos* predicted our use of TV to watch and torment our peers and apparent betters. Varos' form of reality TV dehumanised politicians and prisoners, torturing or killing them depending on viewers' voting.

TV proves a symbiotic beast too: the more we feed it with our attention, the more it does to keep it. The initial O.J. Simpson 1994-95 trial – in which the former NFL player was accused of the murders of his ex-wife, Nicole Brown Simpson, and her friend, Ron Goldman – for example, is held up as an important part of TV history. Viewers tuned in to watch the live ninety-minute car chase as police pursued Simpson. Every major network interrupted scheduled programming to feature the chase, resulting in approximately 95 million viewers nationwide.

Due to the popularity of this grim event, stations reacted to viewers' interest by extensively covering the trail, giving the whole affair an uneasy voyeuristic quality.

Vengeance on Varos warns us that the media can manipulate.

The Long Game further instils the idea that "the right word in the right broadcast repeated often enough can destabilise an economy, invent an enemy, change a vote."

This meant controlling citizens *en masse*, reaching an endpoint in *Bad Wolf*, where citizens of Earth are glued to their screens 24/7 and would forcibly sacrifice their lives for TV fame. But a decade later, *Doctor Who* viewers themselves were manipulated. *Sleep No More* was fashioned as a "found footage" episode detailing the takeover of La Verrier spacecraft by Sandmen; the story's conclusion, however, reveals that the signal that creates the Sandmen is transmitted through the episode itself.

< 12. Toy Lungs.

83. A Really Quite Astonishingly Heavy Door.

You go to turn down another corridor, but the path is sealed by a door: metal, grey, and really quite astonishingly heavy.

You press your ear close. Beyond, you can hear… "The Long Song" from *The Rings of Akhaten*. A plaque apologises for the inconvenience – behind, there's a full orchestra performing, but no one can gain access.

To make up for it, visitors have been encouraged to write down some of their favourite pieces of music from twenty-first century *Doctor Who*. Slips of paper are pegged to the wall around the door, and selected tracks are played by the orchestra.

With Series 11 and 12 under his belt, Segun Akinola's tracks feature prominently:

"The 007 motifs from *Spyfall*."

"The *Kerblam* jingle is really fun!"

"Music for *The Ghost Monument*'s ending is an adrenaline rush yet manages to be warm and homely too."

His Series 11 theme tune is nominated too, as are the Series 4 and 7B ones by Murray Gold. As he worked on every episode from *Rose* to *Twice Upon A Time*, Gold's compositions take up the lion's share of the wall:

" 'The Doctor's Theme' – the one associated with Bad Wolf."

" 'Doomsday'. Heartbreaking."

"I love 'All the Strange, Strange Creatures': it's thrilling and evocative, ideal for Series 3."

" 'Vale Decem'. Taught me Latin. Well, a bit."

"Everything from *The Eleventh Hour*, but particularly I Am The Doctor and its variants. Especially the twanging American one for Series 6."

"The Life and Death of Amy Pond. Gives me shivers."

"The one Katherine Jenkins sang at Christmas."

" 'Goodbye Pond' builds really nicely before that powerful release, coinciding with Amy being sent back in time."

" 'Clara's Theme'. Duh."

" 'The Shepherd's Boy' from *Heaven Sent*. It's a real voyage, going home the long way round."

" 'Bill's Theme'. Duh."

That's curious. Gold's suggestions are in chronological order.

It's like whoever put all this together really cared. It's almost as if the curator agonised over the collection for months; whittled it down; worked long into the night; chopped and changed; worried that certain eras would be underrepresented; imagined the complaints he'd get if the Fourth Doctor's scarf weren't included; woke up in cold sweats at 3am, muttering about Death's Head's head; read too many books about Swindon; made wallcharts and diagrams about planned routes for visitors to take; googled Karen Gillan for entirely educational purposes, thank you very much; obsessed over vowels; accidentally watched *The Stones of Blood*; cried into his Shreddies; bought shares in a well-known coffee brand; and spent far too much on a launch party (which was ultimately cancelled anyway, thanks to a mysterious outbreak of Lazar's disease).

You look around. Nah. This place is a shambles. TripAdvisor will be getting a very dodgy review.

Should you add your own musical taste to the suggestion box? You grab a slip of paper and a pencil. Then write "BUM" and "FART" and run away because you're basically an eleven-year-old.

< 46. BBC Sound Effects No. 19: *Doctor Who.*

84. The TARDIS Architectural Reconfiguration System.

Your breath is taken away. This next room is gloomy. Right in the middle is something like a metallic tree, jutting up, tendrils conglomerating at the top of a rigid trunk then freeing themselves and exploring the area, feeding on the darkness, blossoming into white, blue, and purple blinking bulbs, with Gallifreyan etched into their surfaces.

This is the machine that makes machines. It sat at the heart of the TARDIS. Then it welcomed guests at the *Doctor Who Experience* in Cardiff. Now, you're pretty sure it's helped construct this whole museum

"*The Doctor Who Experience* is one of those walkthroughs where they shepherd a large group of visitors through a series of dimly lit, thoughtfully decorated rooms," explained James Baldock, the brain behind the popular *Brian of Morbius* site, who visited the exhibition in 2017. "You're guided by a Time Lord – one of the nice ones; say, *Deadly Assassin* onwards – whose job is to react to the hydraulics, shout back at the pre-recorded video messages, and open the door to the staff corridor when your eight-year-old feels sick. There is a story, of some sort and little consequence, involving the fracturing of time. You cower from Daleks and hurry through a churchyard to escape from the Angels, while the lights flicker on and off.

"Above it all, a short-haired Peter Capaldi looms at you. The sensation is of being buffeted from one scenario to the next, an immersive thing over which you have limited control, like a *Harry Potter* Pensieve dive. When you emerge, blinking and sweating, into the lights of the 1963 studio, there is the feeling of having touched something, but only lightly, a brief and somehow unsatisfying exchange. It is underwhelming and it is hot and uncomfortable, particularly in summer, but there's a part of me that misses being that close to people."

That was the last phase of the *Doctor Who Experience*, which shut on 9th September 2017, but its basic structure was inherited from the Matt Smith era. The concept was for an "experience" section following a strict narrative before visitors were let loose on an exhibition area spread across two floors, packed with *Doctor Who* props and sets.

Capaldi's *Experience* began with a presentation about the Doctor, narrated by Lalla Ward; footage then located the TARDIS in space-time, just as it was attacked by Time Squid that envelop its exterior. The wall in front opened to reveal the architectural reconfiguration system, and the Doctor, in a classic console, appears on-screen, guiding you through the adventure.

For Smith's *Experience*, a similar presentation reviewed the Doctor's life before a crack in the wall opened to reveal a Library Command Node talking you through nearby points of interest, like the telescope from *Tooth and Claw*. The Doctor interrupted, again via a screen, to ask for guests' help in freeing him from the Pandorica Mk II.

From these starting narratives, visitors got to pilot the Eleventh Doctor's first TARDIS; dodge Dalek fire on Skaro (the booming Supreme surprisingly intimidating in "real life"); and navigate a forest full of Weeping Angels – all while retrieving Time Crystals. After donning 3D glasses in I.M. Foreman's junkyard, visitors then faced a selection of either time-displaced monsters including Daleks and Cybermen in Matt's interactive story or, for Peter's, this roster plus the Time Squids.

Once let into the main museum, guests could enjoy seeing behind the scenes on *An Adventure in Space and Time*, then a walkthrough past *Doctor Who* artefacts.

The *Experience* boasted numerous TARDISes: *The Keeper of Traken*'s Melkur, the makeshift unit used in *The Doctor's Wife*, the 1980s console, and, taking up much of the downstairs space, the Ninth and Tenth Doctor's control room. Indeed, they actually filmed relevant segments of *The Day of the Doctor* there!

Upstairs, the exhibition grew, at first mainly focusing on twenty-first century *Who* (with particular emphasis on the Eleventh Doctor's tenure), before accommodating more from all eras. The Silents' would-be TARDIS occupied a large space, as did sections on the genesis of the Cybermen, the fiftieth anniversary, and outfits worn by various Doctors and companions.

"I think it's fantastic!" Matt Smith enthused at the press launch day in 2012. "To have all these monsters – all these *Doctor Who*-related things – under one roof is an absolute joy. It's fantastic. And I'm very proud to be part of a show that can put on an event like this."

By the time it shut, the *Doctor Who Experience* had been brought right up to date, with Series 10 exhibits like the absorbing wall from *Knock Knock*, Truth Monk propaganda from *The Lie of the Land*, and items from the Mondasian colony ship. Alas, it *did* close, displacing a wealth of props, monsters, Target cover art (which had enjoyed its own mini-museum, attached to the shop, for several months), and sets.

The structure, which had been made solely for the *Experience* by BBC Cymru (which also allowed some lucky fans to visit the actual TARDIS between shoots and go on walking tours of filming locations around Cardiff) was dismantled, leaving a desolate concreted patch reaching out into the sea.

< 88. Sad Tony.

85. The Moment.

Here it is. Complete with a Big Red Button.

You gasp. "Is that—?" You turn to the staff member hovering by it. You think you've seen her here before, or if not here…

She replies, "The galaxy eater? The final work of the ancients of Gallifey? The Time War's last hope?"

You gaze at it in awe.

"Nah," she goes on. "Replica. Think of how many visitors we'd get activating it. All those people without a conscience. We had Michael Grade in here last week; I mean, can you imagine…!"

Any show that makes it beyond a few series should be lauded. Any show that notches up fifty years deserves to take the world by storm. And that's what *Doctor Who* did.

How would the franchise celebrate half a century? Cast, crew, and fans had been asking that question for many years before 23rd November 2013 rolled around.

"We'll have something that honours the history and the heritage of the show in the biggest and best way possible," Matt teased in October 2012. "And I know that Steven will come up with something really inventive, and we want to make it the biggest celebration for the biggest year of the show… I think it'd be very exciting to think they could [do a multi-Doctor story] – whether or not it's possible nowadays."

It was, of course, more than possible. David Tennant and Billie Piper returned, Tom Baker was introduced as the Curator, and John Hurt was revealed to be a hitherto unknown incarnation, fighting on the last day of the Time War. All the previous Doctors were drafted in, using footage and speech from other stories (visuals from *The Tomb of the Cybermen* and *The Mind Robber* were paired with audio from *The Seeds of Death*, for examples; *Frontios* with *The Five Doctors*; and instances of flipped pictures from *Colony in Space* and *Planet of Evil*). Viewers also saw a snippet of the Twelfth Doctor ahead of schedule.

To avoid spoilers, *The Day of the Doctor* aired at the same time in ninety-four international territories, plus cinema and 3D screenings. The special was loaded over 3.2 million times on iPlayer, making it the most requested drama episode in 2013.

And this wasn't the only treat for the fiftieth anniversary:

An Adventure in Space and Time: The docudrama aired on 21st November.

The Night of the Doctor: The Eighth Doctor's surprise regeneration was available on iPlayer and YouTube from 14th November.

The Five(ish) Doctors Reboot: Written and directed by Peter Davison, this brilliant spoof detailed Davison, Colin Baker, Sylvester McCoy, and Paul McGann attempting to appear in the fiftieth anniversary special. It further starred a wealth of *Who*-related talent, including Sean Pertwee, son of the Third Doctor actor; Jon Culshaw, impersonating Tom Baker; Georgia Tennant, aka The Doctor's Daughter (as well as being Davison's daughter and Tennant's wife); Russell T Davies; Ian McKellen and Peter Jackson, on the set of *The Hobbit*; Dalek operators Barnaby Edwards and Nicholas Pegg; and numerous companions.

The Doctors' efforts were apparently vindicated when they smuggled themselves on-set underneath shrouds. Colin claimed that really was them in the final episode, but really, who nose?

The Science of Doctor Who: Professor Brian Cox lectured an auditorium of fans and famous faces about the physics of the series, including how gravity is warped by the Eye of Harmony, allowing the TARDIS to travel through time.

Doctor Who: The Ultimate Guide: Broadcast on BBC3 on 18th November, this two-hour programme ran through the history of the show, with linking scenes featuring the Eleventh Doctor and Clara in the TARDIS.

Doctor Who at the Proms: A bombastic celebration of the series' music, conducted by Ben Foster, performed at the Royal Albert Hall on 13th-14th July. Hosted by Matt Smith, Peter Davison, Jenna Coleman, Carole Ann Ford, Neve McIntosh, and Dan Starkey, the event premiered Murray Gold's specially-commissioned "Song for Fifty".

Me, You and Doctor Who – A Culture Show Special: Matthew Sweet presented a potted history of the programme and its cultural impact.

An Evening with Steven Moffat: The showrunner looked back at *Who* history, available on iPlayer from 12th November.

Fiftieth Anniversary Celebration: Headlined by the Fourth, Fifth, Sixth, Seventh, and Eleventh Doctors, this official convention at the London ExCeL ran across the anniversary weekend, and boasted around fifty guests, from both sides of the camera, like Michael Kilgarriff (*Robot*); prolific designer Barry Newbery; Yee Jee Tso (*The TV Movie*); David Collings (*Mawdryn Undead*); costumer June Hudson; script editor Donald Tosh; and Waris Hussein (*Marco Polo*).

The Doctors Revisited: A monthly documentary series on BBC America, with each episode highlighting one Doctor, beginning in January and concluding in November; they were then shown on the UK channel Watch, from October.

The Graham Norton Show: Smith and Tennant promoted the fiftieth anniversary on this chat show.

12 Again Doctor Who Special: A CBBC special in which fans joined members of the cast to reminisce about *Doctor Who*.

Pointless Celebrities: A *Who* special edition of the gameshow with guests like Sylvester McCoy, Sophie Aldred, and K9, shown before *The Day of the Doctor*.

An Unearthly Child: Remastered editions of all four episodes of the first *Doctor Who* serial were shown on BBC4 on 21st November.

What a time to be a *Doctor Who* fan.

You start walking off, a little deflated that it's not the *real* Moment. You turn back for one last glance – and the staff-member's vanished. That's... unusual.

You intend to go back and investigate, then—

< 72. Stone Statue.

86. Victorian Mirror.

Quick! It's suddenly behind you! The stone statue is there, mouth open to reveal harsh fangs, arms grappling at the air around you. It locks as you see it.

What if you blink? You don't have time to run. And no one else is around! You back away, call for help – but to no avail.

Your eyes sting. The aircon is making them ache at the edges. You need to—

Blink!

But the angelic figure hasn't moved. Why not?

It's not looking at you. It's looking at itself in the huge Victorian mirror from *Deep Breath*, resplendent on the wall. Forever locked in an eternal struggle with its reflection.

Peter Capaldi was announced as the Twelfth Doctor in *Doctor Who Live: The Next Doctor* on 4th August 2013.

"It was all a little surprising," recalled long-term fan Peter Shaw. "I'd seen online, I think, that the BBC was offering tickets for something called 'Entertainment Pilot Show' about *Doctor Who*. Not being that interested in such a bland-sounding thing, I nevertheless immediately requested four tickets. Just in case it was *Tom Bakers' Saturday Night Takeaway* or *Barrowman's Got Talent*.

"Then it was suddenly announced that it was going to be a live reveal (look away, Jamie) of the new Doctor. I excitedly messaged a fellow *Who* fan and he, my wife and I arranged to go. We had no idea what to expect. The BBC said if you turned up in costume, you'd get better seats. We ignored that. Because we're not, you know, obsessive idiots.

"I remember being ushered in at Elstree studios and we had to hand in our phones. Which is surprising as I went to a Royal Garden Party hosted by the Queen around the same time and we were allowed our phones for that. I took photos in Buckingham Palace's toilets. But woe betide we took a snap of Rufus Hound or Liza Tarbuck.

"The show, as most people recall, was a lot of weird, slightly uncomfortable padding leading up to a *Stars In Their Eyes*-style entrance by Peter Capaldi. We all clapped and cheered, particularly those at the front dressed as Taran wood beasts, Erato and the

Bandrils. I remember clocking that Capaldi did a Hartnellesque clutch of the lapels of his jacket. Now I come to think of it, I am an obsessive idiot."

Matt Smith, meanwhile, had been announced as the Eleventh Doctor in a special 3rd January 2009 edition of *Doctor Who Confidential*, but not every announcement had been so grand – most had relied on newspapers to spread the word. There's some question over when Hartnell was actually cast as the Doctor (August 1963 is most likely), but as *Doctor Who* wasn't an established brand, no grand announcements were needed. Here's when each of the intervening Doctors were announced:

Patrick Troughton: 1st September 1966 by Sydney Newman, with newspapers reporting from the next day.

Jon Pertwee: 17th June 1969.

Tom Baker: 15th February 1974, just one week after Pertwee revealed his departure.

Peter Davison: 5th November 1980 on *Nationwide*, less than a fortnight after Tom announced he'd be leaving.

Colin Baker: 19th August 1983.

Sylvester McCoy: 2nd March 1987.

Paul McGann: 5th January 1996.

Christopher Eccleston: 22nd March 2004, over a year before *Rose* and nearly six months after the confirmation that *Doctor Who* would be back on TV.

David Tennant: 14th April 2005. "I grew up loving *Doctor Who* and it has been a lifelong dream to get my very own TARDIS," he said. "Taking over from Chris is a daunting prospect; he has done a fantastic job of reinventing the Doctor for a new generation and is a very tough act to follow."

(As Jodie Whittaker was unveiled in July 2017, May, October, and December are the only months not to have had their own Doctor announcements.)

"We went to a nearby pub after and I remember feeling rather elated at having witnessed TV history," continued Peter Shaw. "This was diffused somewhat when I went back to work the next day. A colleague had seen my Facebook posts and decided to watch *Doctor Who Live: The Next Doctor*. Apparently, he hadn't seen *Doctor Who* since the '80s. 'I didn't get it,' he told me. 'When I was a child, I remember the Doctor would change when he fell off an observatory or if he was poisoned and died. Why did it happen on some sort of variety show?''

While some sections of fandom (if not all casual viewers) celebrated Capaldi's announcement, others questioned how he could turn up again so shortly after playing Caecilius in *The Fires of Pompeii*. Moffat had a plan, which would eventually unfold in *The Girl Who Died*: the Doctor picks faces to give the next incarnation messages. The Twelfth's face was to hold him to account.

It doesn't exactly explain John Frobisher, Capaldi's character in *Torchwood: Children of Earth*, who carried out a murder-suicide pact with his family – though Davies and Moffat suggested that he was a descendant of Caecilius, and his death was time's way of getting the Doctor back for saving the Roman family…

He's of course not the only Doctor with a doppelganger. The Abbot of Amboise looked a lot like the First Doctor (while another version of the First looked like *Dinosaurs on a Spaceship*'s Solomon) and the Sixth Doctor curiously based his look on Commander Maxil… who'd shot him in *Arc of Infinity*. Romana was directly inspired by Princess Astra (*The Armageddon Factor*; *Destiny of the Daleks*), Nyssa shared a cadence with Lady Talbot (*Black Orchid*), Barbara looked like Lexa (*Meglos*), Amy resembled a Soothsayer (*The Fires of Pompeii*), and Martha's cousin, Adeola, was killed during the Battle of Canary Wharf (*Army of Ghosts*).

Here's a small sample of duplicates in *Doctor Who*, not counting when actors appear entirely under prosthetics:

- Richard the Lionheart and Scaroth (Julian Glover in *The Crusades* and *City of Death*).
- Joanna, Sara Kingdom, and Morgaine (Jean Marsh respectively in *The Crusades, The Daleks' Master Plan*, and *Battlefield*).
- Lesterson and the High Priest of the Brotherhood of Demnos (Robert James in *The Power of the Daleks* and *The Masque of Mandragora*).
- Samantha Briggs and Queen Victoria (Pauline Collins in *The Faceless Ones* and *Tooth and Claw*).
- Gulliver, an unnamed Time Lord, Taron, and Chancellor

Goth (Bernard Horsfall in *The Mind Robber*, *The War Games*, *Planet of the Daleks*, and *The Deadly Assassin*).

- King Peladon and Professor Hobbs (David Troughton in *The Curse of Peladon* and *Midnight*).
- Butler and the Governor (Martin Jarvis in *Invasion of the Dinosaurs* and *Vengeance on Varos*).
- Messrs Jobel and Copper (Clive Swift in *Revelation of the Daleks* and *Voyage of the Damned*).
- Gwyneth and Gwen (Eve Myles in *The Unquiet Dead* and *Torchwood*).
- Valerie Brannigan and Bill Potts' foster mum, Moira, (Jennifer Hennessy in *Gridlock*, *The Pilot*, and *Extremis*).
- Richard Lazarus and Archibald Hamish Lethbridge-Stewart (Mark Gatiss in *The Lazarus Experiment* and *Twice Upon A Time*).
- Abi Lerner and Rosa Parks (Vinette Robinson in *42* and *Rosa*).

Perhaps taking the crown, however, is Michael Sheard, who played Rhos, Roland Summers, Laurence Scarman, Supervisor Lowe, Mergrave, and Coal Hill School's headmaster respectively in *The Ark, The Mind of Evil, Pyramids of Mars, The Invisible Enemy, Castrovalva*, and *Remembrance of the Daleks*!

It's actually not that unrealistic. In 2015, Teghan Lucas and her colleagues from the University of Adelaide worked out that there's a one in one hundred and thirty-five chance of a sole pair of exact doppelgangers existing at the same time. That's based on *exact* measurements, though. It's estimated, that for every one of us, there could be seven people in the world at one time who look similar enough that your acquaintances might incorrectly identify them as you. This doesn't account for individualities like scars, spots, tattoos, and piercings; it addresses the times you double-take, when you could've sworn you saw your Aunt Mable going into *Victoria's Secret*, but she's adamant you absolutely did not.

That's a pretty impressive estimate considering there are "only" 7-8 billion people alive right now. *Doctor Who* increases that scope across all of time and space, so lookalikes are likely inevitable.

≤ 5. A Framed Piece of Wall.

87. Christ the Redeemer.

Who needs to visit Rio de Janeiro anyway? Okay, so it looks gorgeous, boasts extraordinary fun at the carnival, and it'd be an incredible achievement to climb Sugarloaf Mountain. Apart from all that though: Christ the Redeemer is seemingly here!

The statue, its arms spread wide as a blessing, towers over Brazil, watching over all its citizens. Surely someone will have noticed it's gone missing…

To launch the Twelfth Doctor era in August 2014, *Doctor Who* went on a world tour. Peter Capaldi, Jenna Coleman, and Steven Moffat visited South Korea, Australia, America, Mexico, and Brazil, flying more than 35,000 miles in total across just twelve days before a Leicester Square premiere in London. "It's fantastic that so many people across the world love *Doctor Who*," Capaldi enthused. "After eight months' solid filming deep in the world of monsters, Jenna and I are thrilled to be heading for the Planet of Fans."

Some 11,000 fans and reporters enjoyed advanced screenings of *Deep Breath* on the big screen before taking part in Q&As with Capaldi, Coleman, and Moffat. To promote the series, the former pair took part in promotional shoots at iconic locations across the globe: New York City's Top of the Rock observation deck, Sydney's Harbour Bridge, Cardiff Castle, Bosingak Bell in South Korea, and on the steps of Christ the Redeemer.

The destinations surprised some UK-bound fans, unaware of the show's popularity in other territories. "It's staggering to be so welcomed in Korea…" Jenna said after seeing a hall packed with over 1,200 fans. "Thank you, Seoul, for your enthusiasm and generosity!"

Peter returned to Mexico in March 2016, to attend La Mole Comic-Con Internacional, where four hundred and ninety-two fans set a new Guinness World Record: the largest gathering of people cosplaying as *Doctor Who* characters ever. He was seemingly unphased by the long flight; instead, he was buoyed by the huge group of enthusiasts holding up signs reading "Doctor Misterio".

Doctor Who may be quintessentially British, but lest we forget that it's a cherished international brand.

< 94. Psychic Container.

88. Sad Tony.

A giant in the *Doctor Who* pantheon of terrors: Sad Tony, who has a lot to be sad about. He smells atrocious. He has wings but they won't support his bulbous body to enable him to fly. And created by a young girl for *Blue Peter*'s design-a-monster competition in 2006, he didn't even win. Really though, aren't we all Sad Tony?

The winner was the Absorbaloff, designed by William Graham, subsequently invited on set to meet Peter Kay, who played the creature in *Love & Monsters*. The contest had been judged by David Tennant, Russell T Davies, presenter Gethin Jones, and Blue Peter editor Richard Marson, and attracted a massive 43,920 entries, the most for a competition since 1993.

It wasn't the first design-a-monster competition: Patrick Troughton judged one in 1967, announcing Paul Worrall's Hypnotron, Karen Dag's Steel Octopus, and Stephen Thompson's Aqua Man as the winners, beating some 250,000 entries. Though they were never actually created for *Doctor Who*, props were built for *Blue Peter* and the monsters were immortalised in Gareth Roberts' novel, *The English Way of Death*.

Doctor Who has run various other competitions in association with *Blue Peter*: Susannah Leah won a 2009 competition to design a TARDIS console, eventually used in *The Doctor's Wife*; Ashdene School scripted *Good as Gold*, featuring the Eleventh Doctor, Amy, and a Weeping Angel, in 2012; and Vastra's Sonic Hat Pin, Jenny's Sonic Gauntlet, and Strax's Sonic Lorgnette (*Deep Breath*) were created by fans in 2013.

Only one companion that we know of has two *Blue Peter* badges: Ace proudly displays a standard blue version (meaning she either appeared on the programme or sent them some sort of contribution) and a silver one, awarded to those who make an extra effort, be it sending a letter, picture, suggestion, or similar. These are actually owned by Sophie Aldred.

And only one companion went on to present it: the aptly named Peter Purves joined *Blue Peter* just over a year after leaving *Doctor Who*, helming the show from 16th November 1967 until 23rd March 1978.

Other presenters have appeared in *Doctor Who*, like Janet Ellis (*The Horns of Nimon*), Sarah Greene (*Attack of the Cybermen*), and, briefly, Christopher Wenner (*The Awakening*).

Blue Peter has filmed special segments for *Doctor Who* too: Matt Baker makes his own UFO in *Aliens of London* while Konnie Huq and Gethin Jones (who played Daleks and Cybermen in Series 2 and 4) promoted Bubble Shock!

≤ 33. Three Nimon.

89. The Osgood Box.

An intricately carved red box sits on a table. Inside is a button and underneath that, a choice: Truth or Consequences. It's from *The Zygon Inversion*, a sequel to *The Day of the Doctor*. Moffat claimed that the Zygons were "maybe the smallest monster success; they were only in it once, but everyone remembers them". Of course, they were also David Tennant's favourite childhood monsters.

Which other monsters are one-hit wonders? Jon Pertwee liked the Draconians, their prosthetics meaning they were emotive creatures, and their complex empiric society providing plenty of layers to be explored. Yet *Frontier in Space* was their only appearance. Similarly, the Terileptils have only been in *The Visitation*, but certainly had potential to return (and indeed are said to be at Stonehenge in *The Pandorica Opens*). The Axons never called Earth again after *The Claws of Axos*. And the Raston Warrior Robot's return is long past due.

Some aliens have made unexpected comebacks too – the Macra, for instance, in *Gridlock*; after *The Husbands of River Song*, Harmony Shoal swiftly came back for *The Return of Doctor Mysterio*; and Movellans cameoed in *The Pilot*. Others seem like they've been in more adventures than they have: the Weeping Angels haven't enjoyed a headlining adventure since *The Angels Take Manhattan*, and the Silents played a recurring role in Series 6, turned up again for *The Time of the Doctor* – and that's it!

Some fans speculated over the return of Sutekh when his voice actor, Gabriel Woolf, was announced for *The Impossible Planet/The Satan Pit*; instead, Woolf played the Beast. Owing to *Pyramids of Mars*' classic status, it's a surprise Sutekh hasn't been revisited on-screen. The Osiran pantheon has, at least, been explored in other media, like Big Finish's *The Triumph of Sutekh* and the BBC Book *The Sands of Time*.

"I read *The Sands of Time* years ago and didn't re-read it before embarking upon this idea," said Nick Abadzis, who introduced Anubis, son of Sutekh, as a recurring character in his *Tenth Doctor* comic. "I felt it to be a good sequel, but more of a mystery, a detective-style whodunnit than anything that deliberately expanded upon Osiran mythology as such. If push came to shove, I'd probably have to pick *Pyramids of Mars* as my all-time favourite childhood *Doctor Who* story, so the idea of being able to add a little something to that lore was irresistible."

Anubis (Noobis to friends) rejected his father's love of power and derided the gloomy caricature of his residing over the dead. "To me (aside from it being rooted in actual Egyptian mythology), the idea of Sutekh having family just seemed like something Robert Holmes would dream up – 'Son of Sutekh!' I wanted to do something which had that same lurid, pulpy quality that informed a lot of his stories, but which would be free of any budgetary constraints," continued Abadzis. "It's comics, so you could [explore their homeworld], do the whole Phaester Osiris thing on the scale that Holmes suggested in the TV serial (and which Dicks expanded upon in his novelisation).

"At the same time, you have to treat Sutekh completely seriously - it would be very easy to camp him up but I think that's a mistake. Part of what makes Sutekh a fantastic villain is his nihilism and his grotesque vanity. He's not 'ultimate evil' in that boring, abstract, supernatural way; he's biological, he's a product of nature, of the universe and he has all these issues and sibling rivalry with his brother Horus. What's so memorable about Sutekh is that, apart from his desire to escape from his prison, there's this whole undercurrent that he sees aspects of Horus in the Doctor. He hates the Doctor because the Doctor reminds him of his brother – he might be god-like but his emotions are recognisable because they're rooted in family conflict."

"Evil is rarely sophisticated, but Sutekh's is, especially with Gabriel Woolf's sublime vocal performance that expresses his vast frustration. Imagine that frustration unleashed – it wrote itself; it really did. When I brought in Anubis, I had no idea I was going to later bring Sutekh back, but after a certain point, it just seemed inevitable. Anubis' survival beyond the Sutekh arc was also one of those details that seems tailor-made for comics. If you did it on TV, it might all be a bit daft, but it just seemed really funny to me to have this junior son-of-a-near-deity who happens to feel a bit misunderstood, so he gets on really well with [Tenth Doctor companion] Cindy. If you're writing your characters and listening to them, they do begin to take on a life of their own."

Further creatures have had life breathed into them in other mediums. Reeltime Pictures/Time Travel TV's catalogue is a mix of documentaries and original productions, including *Wartime* (with John Levene as Benton), *Downtime* with the Great Intelligence, and the award-winning *Sil and the Devil Seeds of Arodor*.

Meanwhile, BBV Productions was set up in 1991 to fill the void left by *Doctor Who*'s cancellation. Unofficial and semi-licensed videos and audios brought back Autons, Krynoid (from *The Seeds of Doom*), Wirrn, Rutans, and, yes, Zygons.

< Going to Turn Left? Oh, but look! Object #90 beckons… >

90. The Osgood Box

This is cheating. It's one installation, acting as two separate objects. You intend to lodge an official complaint. If you remember, that is. This one's a striking blue, and the astonishing details you could see in the red one are even more apparent here.

As *The Zygon Inversion* attests, *The Day of the Doctor* was an important time for the Time Lord. It was a reaffirmation of what he stands for, and the first time the Doctor revealed on screen the vow he took when choosing his name: "Never cruel or cowardly. Never give up; never give in."

The words are actually Terrance Dicks'.

The first edition of *The Making of Doctor Who* (1972), largely written by Malcolm Hulke, described the Doctor as "never cowardly", while its second edition, rewritten by Dicks and published in 1976, added to this: "He never gives in, and never gives up, however overwhelming the odds against him. The Doctor believes in good and fights evil. Though often caught up in violent situations, he is a man of peace. He is never cruel or cowardly."

Moffat seemed to particularly take to this mantra; the Twelfth Doctor uses it when saying goodbye to Clara, then before his regeneration, amending it to add, "Remember, hate is always foolish, and love is always wise" (and further pouring scorn on pears).

Interestingly, Davies disagreed. During a rewatch of *Gridlock*, in which the Doctor glorifies his lost home to Martha, he said, "Here, the Doctor lies about Gallifrey. And set the whole plot in motion, his motivation. Truth is, I like pushing that character. I don't have much time for character descriptions like 'never cruel or cowardly.' Sorry. But never limit your lead." Indeed, the Doctor might hope to live up to that promise, but he does stray from the path – notably, Capaldi's incarnation frequently questions his own motivations, and argues that, "The Doctor is no longer here; you are stuck with me!"

Nonetheless, the definition holds true, by and large. Thanks to its inclusion at a key juncture in the fiftieth anniversary, the Doctor will forever be associated with it.

< 24. K1 Robot.

91. A Frozen Mammoth?

You're confronted by a gargantuan slab of ice, sweat dropping from its chiselled sides, gradually heated up by the spotlights.

There's a thick shape inside, hard and unmoving. For now. Because while the plaque says this is most likely an encased mammoth, you have other suspicions. You move on quickly. You wouldn't like to be around when this thing fully melts.

Bowie sang about it. 3.5 billion years ago, the necessary atmosphere and liquid water existed there. It's where about 3% of all meteorites that plummet to Earth originate, and in 1996 one contained material that might be evidence of fossilised beings. But the question still remains: is there life on Mars?

Obviously, *Doctor Who* fans have known that Martians exist since 1967.

The Ice Warriors debuted in an eponymous serial starring Patrick Troughton's Second Doctor, written by Brian Hayles. The creatures, like the Silurians, were named colloquially in the story, but later episodes would adopt those terms as official names. Though they were not originally intended to be recurring creatures, Hayles wrote a sequel, *The Seeds of Death*, partly as they proved popular, partly to justify the cost of their outfits.

As reptiles in bio-mechanical suits, they're intimidating and unknowable, much of their faces hidden by plated masks. Their slow, thunderous gait shows a confidence in the inevitability of capture, but belies a swiftness in body and mind, only demonstrated when strategically necessary. Bernard Bresslaw, typically thought of as a comic actor, played the lead Martian, Varga, in *The Ice Warriors*: at 6ft 7", he loomed over the cast, especially Deborah Watling. "We were in these ice caves all made out of polystyrene, which looked fine on screen but awful in real life, and he was meant to be dragging me off to some dungeon or something," she told *DWM*. "Of course, as it turned out, I had to lead him, because he was virtually blind, so I kept whispering as low as possible and not moving my mouth, 'right, left, right, left', and once he went left when I said right, so he went straight through the wall. The entire polystyrene cave collapsed on top of us, and that, as they say, was the end of that!"

In their first two appearances, they're calculating and ruthless; however, much of the Ice Warriors' appeal is their complex societal structure and honour system, largely unexplored until their third serial. "They could build a city under the sand, yet drench the snows of Mars with innocent blood," described the Twelfth Doctor in *Empress of Mars*. "They could slaughter whole civilisations, yet weep at the crushing of a flower."

The Doctor's prejudices against the race were shown in *The Curse of Peladon*, in which he immediately blames the representatives of the species for problems on the titular planet. They're actually there to strive for peace and welcome Peladon into the Galactic Federation. But for *The Monster of Peladon*, they seemingly returned to type, stirring up trouble. Since then, the Doctor has respected the taut tightrope they walk, the wavering allegiances, and a caste system that might seem odd to outsiders. Ultimately, he understands that the Ice Warriors are individuals that fit within a larger societal structure: they are like us.

That was their final appearance in twentieth century *Doctor Who*, but despite reservations, Steven Moffat was convinced by Mark Gatiss to let him bring them back. For *Cold War*, a singular Warrior, Skaldak, "the greatest hero the proud Martian race ever produced", was trapped on a Russian submarine, sending a distress signal for his peers to retrieve him.

Ultimately, The Ice Warriors are victims of their planet's vulnerabilities. Their extended hibernation – for over 5,000 years – allowed them to escape the loss of the Martian atmosphere, but the displaced Ice Warriors were stranded on Earth, a little over sixty-six million km from their home planet.

Martians are used to low temperatures, but even they cannot survive the cold of space. Though we've seen the race *en masse* (like in *Empress of Mars*), there remains something lonely about this race of reptiles, hiding from the universe under thick survival armour.

< No, don't Turn Left yet. Stay with us until page 261 >

92. TARDIS Tours Lanyard.

For this next section, you have to pass through security barriers. You're presented with a black lanyard and the opportunity to see the actual TARDIS! It's in a huge warehouse, festooned with props. The outside of the TARDIS is an overwhelming structure, largely wooden, rising high above you and arching around. Rachel Talalay has left a small desk out the front, on which she's scribbled a Dalek.

As with some of the original TARDIS tours in Cardiff, to determine the order fans are admitted, you're faced with a puzzle: which planets has the Doctor visited more than once on TV, across different serials?

Several hands shoot up. "Earth and Gallifrey are excluded," says the marshal, and a few drop their hands.

A young girl is undeterred. "Peladon!" She says. A rumble of assent. Staff beckon her forward as the first person to enter the TARDIS. She walks up some steps to a platform, halts outside the ship's doors for a photo, then enters. A gasp from inside.

The jealousy in the room is palpable. Everyone starts mulling over the question again. Over the next few minutes, staff members prompt you all with clues. Slowly, the Doctor's travels are charted.

Skaro is an obvious one, but nonetheless allows admittance to the TARDIS. So too do Telos, Mars, and New Earth. Now it gets trickier...

"Stormcage?" someone suggests. "Don't know if that's the whole planet, but the Doctor's visited River there loads."

"Yeah, nice suggestion."

"Trenzalore!"

"Yep."

"Does Pete's World count?"

Bated breath.

"Yeah, go on then," comes the response, and another enters the TARDIS. Everyone's thankful it's bigger on the inside.

"Satellite Five," one smarmy bloke suggests. "Its name was changed to the Game Station but it's the same place."

"Technically," a member of staff counters, "it's a spacestation. I asked for planets. Otherwise, Nerva Beacon would've counted too." He clicks his fingers, points to the man, and two guards emerge from the shadows to drag him away.

"Any more?"

Silence. The tension is finally broken by a brave youngster who ventures, "Karn."

You start mulling it over again.

There are also those planets we hear he's visited before but prior trips to which have never been seen. The Third Doctor was said to have visited Karfel, the First Doctor came to the Akhaten system with Susan, and the Fourth encountered Xoanon before, although the planet is unnamed. It's implied he's been to Apalapucia before, as he demonstrates knowledge of sunsets, spires, and soaring silver colonnades; in addition, there's Metebelis III, from where he retrieves another crystal for *Hide* (in addition to his return visit in *Planet of the Spiders*). Would any of those count?

Finally, you come up with a great one: The Ood-Sphere!

You check to the right, where a few visitors are walking down a slope, coming out of the back of the TARDIS. "Hang on," you say. "The TARDIS didn't dematerialise. Didn't they go anywhere?"

"Well," staff nervously explain. "it's not a real time machine. It's just a set."

"WHAT?" you yell back, furiously. "What's the point?!" Then you storm off, bitterly disappointed by reality.

93. Ianto Jones' Shrine.

Ianto Jones, initially Torchwood's "tea boy" before a promotion to a prime spot of the team, died in *Children of Earth*. The character was so beloved, fans set up a shrine on Mermaid Quay, Cardiff: pictures, poems, stories, and other ephemera paid tribute as if he were a real person.

Once *Torchwood* disappeared from TV, it was refashioned with the plea "WE WANT TORCHWOOD CARDIFF". It stands monument to the fictional universe's impact on Wales.

Since 2005, Cardiff has been an important part of *Doctor Who*.

Apart from being Davies' home, it offers a central hub from which aesthetically polar vistas could be visited easily. Southerndown Beach doubled for Dårlig Ulv-Stranden (*Army of Ghosts/Doomsday, Journey's End*) and Alfalva Metraxis (*The Time of Angels/Flesh and Stone*), and is less than an hour away from the city; so too is Hirwaun's Tower Colliery (*The Hungry Earth/Cold Blood*); Gelligaer Common opened *Tooth and Claw*, about thirty minutes away from Cardiff; and the National Botanic Garden of Wales (*The Waters of Mars*) is an hour away. Travel over the bridge to see Tyntesfield (*Hide*), St Nicholas Market (*The Snowmen*), and Waring House (*Night Terrors*), all in Bristol.

The production team settled in studios around Cardiff Bay, notably Upper Boat (2006-12) and Roath Lock (2012- present), the latter being the home of BBC Cymru, and itself proving an attraction when the *Doctor Who Experience* was built next door – which demonstrates how accommodating Cardiff Council has been to its new intergalactic residents.

In 2012, BBC Worldwide's Philip Fleming reflected: "[It's been] three years since, I think, the first specific conversation started about this venue; three years of hunting for the right property. And at times, it seemed like it simply wasn't going to happen. In fact, the only reason it has happened is because we didn't find a property: we created a brand-new facility. And that was only possible through the hard work and very close co-operation that took place between Cardiff Council; the Welsh Assembly government; property developers; and the BBC, of course."

A new water bus landing station, topped with a TARDIS

model, was built next to the exhibition and opened in Spring 2013. Eddie's Diner, setting of *The Impossible Astronaut* and *Hell Bent* was a short walk away. The Temple of Peace, seen in many episodes including *The End of the World, The Fires of Pompeii,* and *Let's Kill Hitler,* is a ten-minute drive.

And Roald Dahl Plass is within touching distance: it was home to the Torchwood Hub, and, alongside Mermaid Quay, was seen extensively in *Boom Town*, in which it's established that the Rift from *The Unquiet Dead* remained and so Cardiff became a focal point for alien activity.

< 84. The TARDIS Architectural Reconfiguration System.

94. Psychic Container.

Here's a Time Lord Distress Beacon, albeit one asking for help which would never come. The Ouroboros symbol, a serpent eating itself, shows that this belonged to the Corsair, a friend of the Doctor's who had been consumed by the asteroid House. The Corsair was described as a "fantastic bloke – he had that snake as a tattoo in every regeneration. Didn't feel like himself unless he had the tattoo. Or herself, a couple of times. Ooh, she was a bad girl."

The idea of a Time Lord changing gender is a relatively new concept on screen (although there had been rumblings about a female Doctor long before Jodie Whittaker's casting).

Apart from the Doctor, it's only happened three times that we know of. The first time it's mentioned is the Corsair in *The Doctor's Wife* (who'd subsequently appear in Titan Comics' *Thirteenth Doctor* series). Then, in *Dark Water*, Missy is revealed to be the Master – the Doctor's surprise at the name-change and the reaction of John Simm's Master in Series 10 make it clear that this is the first time that character has been a woman, despite the Master's ability to steal bodies. Finally, the only time we actually witness a sex-swapping regeneration prior to the Thirteenth Doctor came in *Hell Bent*, in which the Doctor forces the General's change. She says her last body, her tenth, was the only time she'd been a man.

Away from what's generally considered "canon", Big Finish toyed with the notion in *Exile*, part of the *Unbound* brand, which imagined the Doctor in other dimensions. This Doctor was played by Arabella Weir, who had escaped the Time Lords in *The War Games* and exiled herself on Earth, where she worked at a supermarket and drank excessively.

Otherwise, Joanna Lumley was, coincidentally, the Thirteenth Doctor in Steven Moffat's Comic Relief spoof *The Curse of Fatal Death*. This Doctor was impressed with her own "etheric beam locators" – as was Jonathan Pryce's Master – and the pair walked off together, arm in arm.

Lumley had apparently been suggested as an in-canon incarnation by Sydney Newman, who wrote to Michael Grade in 1986, during the time *Doctor Who*'s future was uncertain. "This requires some considerable thought – mainly because I want to avoid a flashy, Hollywood Wonder Woman because this kind of heroine with no flaws is a bore," he noted. "Given more time than I have now, I can create such a character."

It seems the first time a female Doctor had been publicly mooted was in 1980 when Tom Baker told the press, "I wish my successor, whoever he – or she – might be, the best of luck." Whether he was joking or not is up for debate, but until 2017, rumours of a sex swap always abounded.

On 16th July 2017, Jodie Whittaker was announced as the Thirteenth Doctor: the first female Doctor.

But this wasn't a day the *Doctor Who* fandom shone brightly; alas, differing points of view were met not with understanding and open-mindedness, but with abuse and calls of regression. Peter Davison was on the receiving end of this. He submitted that "It might be more helpful to be encouraging, and not simply scornful, of fans who are uncertain about change" – then was forced to leave Twitter, as the debate descended into a slanging match about misogyny.

< 55. Tea.

95. Gabby Gonzalez's Sketchbook.

There's something magical about this next item. It's positively buzzing with energy, excitement, something *more*.

It looks to be a simple sketchbook, but it's straining to hold on to all its immersive fabrications.

Gabby was created specifically for Titan Comics' *Tenth Doctor* comic by Nick Abadzis. She was introduced in 2014's *Revolutions of Terror*, set in New York City. The Doctor promised her one trip in the TARDIS, but this snowballed and she stayed on throughout the three-year title's run.

Set shortly after Donna left the TARDIS with her memory wiped, Gabby made sure she wouldn't forget her adventures by noting them all down in a very special sketchbook with a life of its own.

"I was asked to create a new companion for a US line of *Doctor Who* comic books by Titan. They had a few ideas, but I thought they were a bit trad, too similar to what we'd seen before on TV," Nick recalled. "I had this notion that, to truly continue the Tenth Doctor's adventures and slot it into TV continuity, you had to base it closely on the template RTD [Davies] had set up, his philosophy and sense of humour – but not so closely that you were just mimicking. There had to be room for me to do it my way, although I'd guess that my general attitude towards life aligns fairly closely with RTD's anyway. I had the idea that the TARDIS could land in a 'neighbourhood' of Brooklyn, New York, where I was living at the time, and he'd meet a local kid. I literally cycled around Brooklyn and ended up in Sunset Park, an area which has a very large Mexican American and Chinese American population. So, there I was, in Sunset Park itself, imagining a 'VWORP-VWORP' sound and looking around and I saw a Mexican American girl and just thought, 'That's her.' Gabby Gonzalez was born. It really was that instant, and [artist and designer] Elena Casagrande just got her immediately when I described her as this would-be artist who saw the Doctor as a teacher, a mage, an inspiration, and mentor."

The Tenth Doctor comic was launched alongside titles centred on the Eleventh and Twelfth Doctors. But the library soon swelled to further include the Third, Fourth, Seventh, and Ninth

Doctors. Events like *Supremacy of the Cybermen* and *The Lost Dimension* spread one narrative across multiple series. The Eleventh Doctor took on three companions: Alice Obiefune, John Jones, and ARC.

"[Alice's] clash with Matt Smith's youthful appearance and having a female companion in her late thirties who's 'too old for a flatshare' and is dealing with personal grief when she comes on-board – that felt different from the likes of Clara and Amy," recalled Al Ewing. "Then Jones is basically David Bowie. The idea there was, 'where did all Bowie's regenerations come from?' and so pairing him with the Doctor seemed a fun explanation of that. ARC, our third companion, is alien and a shapeshifter, and that's the type of thing they couldn't do on the TV show regularly because of budget. But in comics we can do such things. All three have been a lot of fun to write."

Meanwhile, Capaldi's Twelfth Doctor carried on with Clara, Eccleston's with Rose and Jack, and Tennant's with Gabby and her friend Cindy Wu, who'd been introduced in the first story, but had been left behind.

"Cindy, Gabby's best mate, was conceived as more of a recurring character, a friend who would be seen on returns to Earth, but she very quickly became more than just an engaging foil," continued Nick. "Gabby wanted to learn and be her best self, Cindy wanted to have fun and had this secret longing to be more than just a best friend to Gabby. When Cleo later entered the mix, I felt I had my own version of a TARDIS crew with something of that Rose/Mickey/Jack dynamic but with many of my own ingredients added. I had a hell of a lot of fun writing those characters, and it seems readers enjoyed them too. I had a lot of ideas for where they could've gone after Year 3."

Year 3 ended with the promise of the Tenth meeting the Twelfth Doctor, initially pitched as a two or four-part tale involving the Zygons. Sadly, however, Titan unceremoniously dropped all its ongoing titles when Jodie Whittaker was announced for the show, in favour of one comic series, *The Thirteenth Doctor.*

< 89. The Osgood Box.

265

96. Kerblam! Man.

Here's a respectable-looking chap, dressed in a sharp suit and dashing hat, with shining blue eyes and a grinning face. It's the Kerblam! Man, and you have a delivery. What goodies lie within the red box he hands you?

In 2007, David Tennant became the second Doctor, after Tom Baker, to turn on the Blackpool Illuminations. The sky darkened, a vast space thronged with fans, and the air grew chillier by the second. Then Tennant pressed that button and the tower, pleasure beach, and promenade was alive with colour and light. Coupled with the long-running exhibition on the seafront, Blackpool was a popular destination.

If you'd have walked up the road, you'd have seen *Doctor Who* action figures littering shelves. Daleks! Doctors! The Cyber-Controller's Helicopter! Of course, the latter was a fake. The series is such a massive brand, it's no surprise that it's also a target for fraudsters.

Bootleg items often make little attempt to look real. A cruddy plastic car might be decked with the 2005 logo, a promotional picture of Tennant, and claims of having "Full Function: Music. Light".

The Cyber-Controller line of fakes was surprisingly prolific. A walkie-talkie pair, complete with photo of the Slitheen, meant you could communicate with John Lumic directly (presumably). Vehicles emblazoned with a Cyberman had "Bump 'n' Go" action, though only delivered "bump". *Rise of the Cybermen* sets could include a dubious gun that fired foam darts, a torch, a state-of-the-art plastic flip phone, and a perturbed Tenth Doctor doll who looked like that bloke who tried to fight you after you "looked at his woman" at a club in 1998. It promised a "TALKING TARDIS MONEY BOX" and pleasingly displayed a *Remembrance* Dalek on the box.

The dastardly BBC crushed batches of these fakes, but some still made it out to shops.

Then again, you never know what's going to come out of the BBC. Here are a few officially licensed curios:

- Anti-Dalek Fluid Neutraliser (a water pistol) and Anti-Dalek Neutron Exterminator (a cap gun).
- Fourth Doctor underpants, i.e. blue y-fronts with Tom Baker's face, the diamond *Doctor Who* logo, and two Daleks – all of them making various statements about what type of person you are.
- Dapol's Davros, with two arms.
- "Destroyed Cassandra" action figure, consisting of an empty wire frame.
- Branded fish fingers, tying into the Eleventh Doctor's love of them paired with custard.
- A sonic screwdriver spork.
- The Flesh Goo Pod, a small pot of creamy gunge, with the Doctor's face and melting appendages floating within.
- Anti-Time Device, a gun-like toy mixing Dalek and Cybermen tech to create… something. It tied into the Cleric Wars app.
- Cubes, made by Rubbertoe Replicas to look like the objects in *The Power of Three* – that is, black, featureless boxes.
- The 2020 B&M *Terror of the Zygons* Action Figure Set includes a moustachioed Mike Yates, billed as a "UNIT trooper".

"How did you know?"

But the Kerblam! Man has gone. Inside the box lies the Seal of Rassilon – the one you'd considered stealing earlier on because it might come in handy…

< 68. A Mouldy Old Slitheen.

97. Temporal Object.

This object was part of a set used in the *Worlds Collide* escape room, as a means of sealing a rupture in space-time. If it's not fully secured, the Cybermen could harvest Earth. You just hope this exhibit was taken *after* the tear was shut...

Guests at the *Doctor Who* Escape Hunt room *Worlds Collide* are locked in a room with a Cybermen head, an approximation of Van Gogh's *The Pandorica Opens*, and a warning from the Doctor: ChronosCorp's eccentric CEO, Alastair Montague, has been experimenting with time, resulting in a fissure. Visitors have sixty minutes to stop the Cybermen invading the planet through this time rift. To do so, they need to locate temporal objects (spread across the immediate office and a secret second room) and activate a machine to shut this rupture.

The place is littered with items either directly linked to *Doctor Who* (a Fourth Doctor scarf and the sonic screwdriver, the Second Doctor's recorder) or tangentially (the Norse chess board, dinosaur eggs, and a cassette player).

The term 'escape room' originated in a video game genre, beginning with 2004's *Crimson Room*, and in 2007, leading to the first real-life version. Since then, escape rooms' popularity have grown exponentially. *Worlds Collide* opened across six UK cities in 2019, followed by *A Dalek Awakens* in 2020. They tie into the *Time Lord Victorious* multi-platform narrative, as does the 2021 Immersive Everywhere theatrical *Time Fracture*.

These come nearly a decade after the last immersive theatre story, *The Crash of the Elysium*, which debuted at the Manchester International Festival in mid-2011.

Visitors began by learning of the Elysium, a doomed Victorian ship. Things swiftly livened up when a spaceship crashed nearby, guests entered a fissure to end up in the 1880s, and the Eleventh Doctor, via video, informed guests that exhibits from the ship had escaped. Written by Steven Moffat and Tom MacRae, it saw participants facing off against Weeping Angels, and was initially only available to under twelves.

However, its critical acclaim and popularity led to adult-only performances too.

Not all theatrical performances are official, though.

Adaptations of *The Robots of Death*, its audio sequel *Storm Mine*, and *Midnight* were staged in venues across Manchester, including the Lass O'Gowrie pub.

"In 2008 we decided to convert the upstairs lounge at the Lass into an overspill space for private hires and football, ostensibly," explained former Lass landlord Gareth Kavanagh. "To be fair, it was the vision of the general manager at the time, Lisa Connor, to put in place the bare bones of a theatre space with a basic stage and lighting. And we started to take bookings. Well, I say bookings. We never charged for the use of the space, which I named the Salmon Room in homage to the great Adrian Salmon. I was keen to make the space as accessible as possible for theatre groups, disparate communities and events, although the additional social media noise and drinks always helped.

"By 2011 we were quite busy with events and theatre, but I have to say, I always fancied having a go at producing content myself. The logic was twofold. I wanted unique content for the Lass and I was meeting a lot of theatre people, writers, actors and directors, [and] I noticed that, while they were doing the usual fringe theatre stuff, what they ached to do was genre stuff. And there were some great writers and artists who I would collaborate with.

"With this in mind, I took a gamble on a month-long festival – Lassfest to be held in January 2012. We'd hosted Lassfests before, but the difference this time was that we would be providing the spine of the drama with ambitious productions which were based around things that had profile, I was interested in and that I thought others would be too. First up was a staging of three episodes of *Coronation Street* from 1968 by legendary Manchester writer Jack Rosenthal. I wrote to ITV, had several meetings, and got the rights. Sometimes, you just ask the right question, in the right way, and you get the right answer. The second main plank was an adaptation of legendary Alan Moore 2000AD strip *Halo Jones*. I'd met the Rebellion guys at a convention and, again obviously pitched the idea right as we got a green light for that. And then, there was *Midnight*."

The Series 4 story was essentially self-contained, with only bookending scenes not set on the Crusader 50 shuttle.

"With *Midnight*, I don't mind admitting I got lucky," Gareth went on. "As publisher of *Vworp Vworp!*, I was lucky in that Russell T Davies was a fan of ours and had written us a lovely email of appreciation. So I asked, how would he feel about a limited run of performances at the Lass of *Midnight*, obviously with all the BBC owned aspects removed such as the sonic screwdriver. And he was lovely and said yes, strictly as a one off. I think he loved the idea of it being done, live above a pub, and I think it's one of the best things I've ever produced. And, of course, *Midnight* is virtually unique in having so few BBC elements in there. The TARDIS doesn't feature, and nor (really) does Donna. And, of course, the Doctor poses as John Smith for the whole episode, so in our version (*Russell T Davies' Midnight*) John Smith is an engineer.

"We did probably no more than nine performances and capacity was limited to twenty-four per performance. A very special thing and one I'm very proud of.

"With *Robots of Death*, it was a similar combination of timing and contacts. I'd acquired copies of the rehearsal scripts from [writer] Chris Boucher in the very earliest days of eBay back in 2000. I remember he was so disappointed they had only gone for £125 and remarked how easy it is to get an inflated sense of one's own worth! They're a fascinating set of scripts in their own right, with an additional character, new scenes, and a slightly different take on D84 in that he has no behavioural inhibitors. He instead chooses to act morally with free will. Fiona Moore covers all of this in her excellent Obverse book on *Robots of Death* in some detail and it's highly recommended.

"So, with the original scripts to hand and Chris' contacts, I was able to ask in principle if he was okay with a stage adaptation. And happily, he was. However, the main contribution undoubtedly came from Alan Stevens, who took these scripts and did something far more than just cross out Leela and the Doctor and replace it with Blayes and Iago, his protagonists from the *Kaldor City* series. He essentially gave us a conclusion to the *Kaldor City* series, with Blayes and Iago reliving the pivotal moments on Storm Mine 4, trapped in a loop of cause and effect.

"It was a difficult production for a number of reasons, notably the original director going awol and the challenges of staging in FAB Cafe Manchester, but it was very well received by audiences who enjoyed the B movie stylings alongside the sophisticated concepts from Alan and Chris. A close call, but sometimes, you roll the hard six!"

Doctor Who fans would love to fight aliens, explore time and space, and travel in the TARDIS. Sometimes, it's actually possible.

< 63. Animation Cel of the Lass O'Gowrie.

98. Matchbox.

This matchbox is open and at an angle, so you can peep inside to see—

Ah. Grim. It's a tiny Agent O. The Master had used his Tissue Compression Eliminator on him in *Spyfall*, kickstarting a controversial Series 12, in which it's apparently revealed that the First Doctor wasn't technically the first anyway. *The Timeless Children* delved into the Matrix, where the Master showed the Doctor that her past was a lie.

To some, this accounted for the extra faces which popped up as previous incarnations of the Doctor in *The Brain of Morbius*. Indeed, that's what was originally intended. However, other fans excused these by saying they were Morbius' previous faces, meaning the Timeless Child was an extra wrinkle in an otherwise unironed shirt.

Many things in *Doctor Who* don't quite make sense. And that's without mentioning tie-in material, which either seeks to clear up confusions, muddies the water terribly, or both.

So how do fans try to ease the pain? What excuses do we make for continuity issues and plot holes that keep us awake at night?

The Doctor had fourteen consecutive male bodies; only the fifteenth is female. Contrary to his saying he could have two heads, he always looks humanoid. Might we argue that a new regenerative cycle affected the character's biology, hence a female body? And that the Doctor gets a human-like form because that's the one that's accepted on Earth, effectively the character's second home? Or that the Ninth Doctor was lying, because all Time Lords we've seen look humanoid, so that's the default for Gallifreyans?

Why is that the Doctor, out of all the Time Lords we've seen in post-regenerative states, is the only one to suffer confusion or drowsiness after swapping bodies? Maybe he ran away before learning how to control regeneration like his peers.

What really happened to Ace, whose story continued beyond screen, concluded in some mediums (her death in the *DWM* comic *Ground Zero*) and continues with its intrigues in others (*At Childhood's End*, Aldred's novel, for instance)? Are these parallel versions of the same character?

And perhaps most contentious of all: is the Doctor, as became a plot point in *The TV Movie*, "half-human on my mother's side"? Can you somehow argue that only the Eighth Doctor has a half-human lineage? We don't know how Gallifreyan families work…

The Doctor's age is emblematic of inconsistencies. We don't know how old the Time Lord is – in many ways, it's impossible to work out anyway. The Doctor lives in a time machine (and we don't know how the fourth dimension operates there), then visits times and places all over the universe, each with their own relative times. Gallifrey, too, exists in different pockets of time. It all really is relative. However, humans are fixated on annual markers, so he's described himself as around 450 (*The Tomb of the Cybermen*), 756 (countering Romana's claim he's 759 in *The Ribos Operation*), and 900-ish, from the Sixth Doctor era onwards.

His age became an important plot point in Series 6, which spanned 200 years for him, with versions at Lake Silencio aged 909 and 1103. He then spent some 900 years defending Trenzalore, making the Twelfth Doctor at least 2000. This incarnation spent around 4.5 billion years inside the Confession Dial in *Heaven Sent* (though he was rebooted every fortnight or so, meaning not all that time aged him), and 1000 years guarding Missy in Series 10.

Fortunately, *The Day of the Doctor* confirmed what we all suspected. The Eleventh Doctor replies, when asked about his age, "I lose track. 1200 and something, I think, unless I'm lying. I can't remember if I'm lying about my age; that's how old I am."

Because sometimes, we don't even need to make excuses: they're made for us!

Take the Master for example. Sacha Dhawan's Master revels in burning Gallifrey and torturing the Doctor by teasing that they'd been lied to as children. The last time we saw this character, however, he was a woman who'd put her evil nature behind her. She was also dead.

It'd be naive to think that Missy's character development wouldn't be undone eventually: the character is too important and fascinating to be felled for good. Nonetheless, *Spyfall* seemed to come so soon after *The Doctor Falls* that it risked leaving a sour taste. If you need to justify Dhawan's incarnation, look no further than Big Finish's *Missy: Series 2*, its opening episode, *The Lumiat* by Lisa McMullin, clearing up seeming inconsistencies by drawing on what we know about Time Lords and their technology.

That's the thing about *Doctor Who*: there's a lot to navigate and you don't have to account for it all. Some weave together all these narratives into one coherent whole. That's fine. You can pick and choose too. Haven't read a book series? No matter. Favour twentieth century *Doctor Who*? Fair enough. Prefer *Star Wars* anyway? Okay, you've gone too far now, buddy.

Continuity is truth: it's not all things to all people.

≤ 59. Gravestone.

99. Glass Figures.

You're surrounded by swathes of glass figures, all staring impassively at you. This large chamber stretches up, up, up, too far into the eaves to see, walls lined with alcoves, further glass people in each.

The Testimony, seemingly watching over the last exhibit.

But before you get to that, you want to mull over what these figures are, what they represent. There are thousands here. No. Millions. Maybe more. Together, these humanoids, seemingly so fragile, are instead strong, unbreakable, legion.

2020: a difficult time for everyone. The coronavirus pandemic meant countries went into lockdown, households largely unable to mingle. The world could feel an isolated place, but *Doctor Who* instead brought it ever closer, thanks to special *Lockdown!* rewatches organised by *DWM*'s Emily Cook.

The idea was that fans across the globe would play a particular episode at the same time then comment on it using designated hashtags on social media. Cast and crew got involved too, revealing behind-the-scenes secrets for a range of Ninth, Tenth, Eleventh, and Twelfth Doctor stories (plus *An Adventure in Space and Time*, with Mark Gatiss and Sacha Dhawan).

They began with *The Day of the Doctor* (#SaveTheDay) on 21st March, for which Steven Moffat was tempted back to Twitter. Next came *Rose* (#TripofaLifetime) with Russell T Davies and Mark Benton; *Vincent and the Doctor* (#TheUltimateGinger) on van Gogh's birthday; and *The Eleventh Hour* (#FishCustard) on the tenth anniversary of its original transmission. Matt Smith even joined Twitter for those last two.

They continued throughout April and May; the last, *World Enough and Time/The Doctor Falls*, was due to take place on 6th June, but was cancelled. Then the idea was revived over the festivities and into 2021, with replays of *A Christmas Carol, A Town Called Mercy, Robot of Sherwood*, and more.

This incredible project brought an explosion of creativity.

New related content was released to coincide with each rewatch, including:

- *Strax Saves the Day*: A miniaturised (plush toy) Strax introduces the fiftieth anniversary special.
- *The Terror of the Umpty Ums*: Moffat's only Thirteenth Doctor contribution.
- *Rory's Story*: A video message for Rory and Amy's adopted son, Anthony, left on the only working smartphone in 1946.
- *Farewell, Sarah Jane*: A gorgeous and affecting goodbye to Elisabeth Sladen, in which friends like Clyde Langer, Luke, Ace, Jo, Rani Chandra, and Mr Smith remember Sarah Jane Smith, who has passed away.
- *The Zygon Isolation*: Two Osgoods chat over Zoom.
- *Pompadour*: A webcast in which Reinette muses on whether she'll see the Doctor again.
- *The Long Song*: A choir of fan voices recreate the moving tune from *The Rings of Akhaten*, compiled together to create one experience.
- *The Secret of Novice Hame*: The final days of Anna Hope's character.
- *The Best of Days*: A message through the Space-Time Telegraph between Nardole and Bill on the Mondasian ship.

Most added neat twists to episodes, so they could be viewed in a new light. Perhaps most astounding is *Doctors Assemble!*, the first ever multi-Doctor tale to include fourteen incarnations, including the War Doctor, albeit all voiced by other actors and impressionists. David Bradley reprised his role as the First Doctor, while Jon Culshaw played the Third, Fourth, and Fifth. The cast also starred Chris Walker-Thomson, Angus Villiers-Stuart, Wink Taylor, Jonathon Carley, Pete Walsh, Elliott Crossley, Jacob Dudman, and Debra Stephenson.

Doctor Who has been bringing people together since 1963, but never was this capacity more important than in 2020. Because wouldn't it be a terrible life if you didn't have people to miss?

100. Handles.

You approach your last exhibit. Oh, sure, this museum is extensive. You'd need more than twelve regenerations to see it all. But for now, for this visit, this feels like the end. Maybe it's because Handles – this Cyberman head with its organics hollowed out, borrowed from the Maldovar Market and resurrected from the ashes of Trenzalore – has been beaming out a message, left untranslated, that drew you here.

And then you realise what you need to do. You reach into your pocket and pull out the Seal of the High Council of Gallifrey and place it on top of Handles.

The message is decrypted and blares out, on a loop: "Doctor Who? Doctor Who? Doctor *Who*?"

You'd be forgiven for thinking the Doctor's name is Doctor Who. It may very well be.

While pretending to be him in *World Enough and Time*, Missy teases that she's "that mysterious adventurer in all of time and space, known only as Doctor Who" and the Doctor admits that he does like being called that.

Early documents and fiction blurred the lines: official lines like annuals and Target novelisations frequently called him Doctor Who; WOTAN instructs that "DOCTOR WHO IS REQUIRED" in *The War Machines*; and a draft of *Marco Polo* has the titular traveller saying, "You, Ian, go due east. Miss Wright to the South. Doctor Who to the west, and I shall take the north." In *The Highlanders*, the Doctor calls himself "Doctor von Wer" ("wer" being German for "who"); in *The Underwater Menace*, he leaves a note reading, "Vital secret will die with me. Dr W."; and in *The Dæmons,* he calls himself "Qui Quae Quod", all Latin variations of "Who".

The confusion extends to credits, media listings, and scripts: Hartnell, Troughton, Pertwee, Tom Baker, and Christopher Eccleston were all credited as "Doctor Who" or "Dr Who". Tennant specifically asked to be credited as "The Doctor", but Capaldi frequently called the character Doctor Who in interviews.

In-programme, the Doctor enjoys how enigmatic Doctor Who makes him sound. It becomes a common theme in Series 7, and he admits that "I never realised how much I enjoy hearing that said out loud" when Clara questions him in *The Bells of St. John*.

If the Doctor chose the designation, "Doctor Who" is probably just as applicable as "the Doctor".

But it's unlikely to be his real name. It's not like his granddaughter was ever called "Susan Who"...

If it were his real name, his tomb on Trenzalore would've unlocked when the Intelligence was quizzing him in *The Name of the Doctor*. But it didn't: it took River to utter his name for it to unlock.

So what name was he born with?

Hulke and Dicks' 1972 edition of *The Making of Doctor Who* includes notes made during the trial in *The War Games*, and writes the Doctor's name as $\partial^3 \Sigma x^2$.

His nickname at the Time Lord Academy was $\Theta\Sigma$ (Theta Sigma), or that's what fans have presumed. In *The Armageddon Factor*, fellow Gallifreyan Drax calls him this (or "Theets") as if it's his real name. The Doctor then reinforces that he goes by "Doctor" now.

When he's going for subterfuge, he tries the name "John Smith" on for size, except, as is pointed out in *Midnight*, it's clearly a fake.

Moffat argued that the conflicting names fits perfectly with a series which also gives us numerous explanations for the sinking of Atlantis, for his being half-human (on his mother's side), and for the Loch Ness Monster. He concludes, "Above all, I believe that embracing a hundred impossible contradictions elevates *Doctor Who* from a simple TV show to a myth retold and reinvented by every generation. And since myths can last forever, let's all be happy about that."

The Twelfth Doctor warns his successor never to reveal their name, and suggests that no one, except well-intentioned children, could understand it anyway. This originated at a screening of *The Pilot*. During a Q&A session, one fan asked Capaldi what the Doctor's name is. "I think 'the Doctor', like everything about him, is a thing he's come up with to make himself understood by human beings," Peter replied. "I don't think human beings could even really say his name. But I think we might be able to hear it. At a certain frequency. If the stars are in the right place, and your heart's in the right place, you'll hear it."

And maybe that's the right attitude. The Doctor is a name chosen to inspire. He's the person who makes people better. Maybe after all this, the Doctor's name isn't important. *Doctor Who* encompasses so much more. All of time and space.

Doctor's Appointment: A Chat with Christopher Eccleston
COMPLETE INTERVIEW

The Ninth Doctor introduced new generations to *Doctor Who*, and that story is forever expanding. For those whose entry point into the show was Series 1, it's particularly thrilling that Christopher Eccleston is back, playing the character once more for Big Finish. Eccleston himself found the prospect exciting too.

"I love audio drama... I do audiobooks and I get great creative satisfaction from that. I think it's because I've always been passionate about writing and writers. And there are no visuals: all you have is the word and your voice. And I felt I could do something with a character I'd played in a visual format," said Eccleston between recording sessions. "I was born in 1964 and I remember one of the big moments of my life... There was a power cut in the '70s, and it was very exciting to me because my mum and dad lit candles and put them in bottles and we had a battery-run radio, [and we] tuned into a radio drama... I can't remember what it was, but we were all transfixed and I would say we'd never listened to one before, and the candlelight and just the audio and our imagination creating the pictures: it had a profound effect on me. I can remember exactly where I was sat in our backroom. So maybe the love was born there."

But it's the quality of the writing at Big Finish that ultimately led him to return after some fifteen years.

"I was trained in the '70s and '80s by absorbing the very high standard of television writing," Christopher said, "and then I went to drama school and I trained myself on Shakespeare and [Henrik] Ibsen and [Johan August] Strindberg, and a central thing of my training is honouring the writer, protecting the writer. And what I find with writers is, unlike some directors, they have huge respect for the intelligence of their audience: they know that an audience is highly sophisticated, far brighter than us television programme makers, and they never write down; they always write up.

"There's a consistency in the writing of the Ninth Doctor's voice, but there's also that great thing that you get from episode to episode, where he's stretched somewhat by the individual writer, that keeps it fresh – both in the television series and in the audios – for the actor playing it. Because he is every one of us, I think. He belongs to everybody within that creative process. And that shape-shifting element to his persona is lovely."

Since leaving *Doctor Who*, Chris has appeared in a wealth of TV, audio, and theatre productions. But which would he most like to be adapted for audio?

"Well, I'm not finished with *Macbeth*. I did one hundred and nineteen performances of *Macbeth*; I want very much to revisit that on the stage in London in a much smaller, more script-based, intimate, stripped-back production," Christopher reflected. "And I would very much like to do *Macbeth* with Big Finish. There's a couple of Shakespeares I'd like to do – *Richard the Third*, *Coriolanus*, Shylock in *Merchant of Venice*... And you can be very psychologically precise with Shakespeare and strip back what you sometimes get, which is directorial overload, of gimmickry and stuff, and it'd be nice to take all that back."

Could, then, *The A Word* adapt well to audio, without the stunning Lake District vistas? Eccleston is especially interested in that idea: "I think *The A Word* would work wonderfully [as a Big Finish series] with that central notion of autism and communication and failure to communicate; I think that would translate great to audio."

With that in mind, would he like Big Finish to adapt any of those *Doctor Who* Series 1 episodes? It might be fun to hear a re-imagined *Bad Wolf*, for instance, with the Doctor delivering a TED Talk on bananas, Captain Jack suggesting scandalous singles on *Desert Island Discs*, and Rose attempting to talk without hesitation, repetition, or deviation on *Just A Minute*...

"I wouldn't. I wouldn't remake; I think the beauty of this for me," Eccleston enthused, "is not to refer back. I don't think we need to – the strength of the writing that Big Finish have means that we don't have to refer to the television series and I don't want to revisit all that. It stands: those thirteen episodes stand, for good or for bad. And if I were one of the people at Big Finish, I wouldn't brief a writer like 'let's take x, y, or z and redo it'. No, let's create something *entirely new*."

It's for the best: Big Finish allows us to explore more sides of the Ninth Doctor. The Doctor of Series 1 carried the weight of intervening years during which he'd taken a prominent part in the Time War, apparently resulting in the destruction of Gallifrey.

"What's been interesting, apart from I think the one we're doing at the moment, is the Doctor has been very light and that's been wonderful. I'm slightly known for the heaviness," said Eccleston. "He carried the guilt of the survivor and the scars of that. I think that was essential to the first series. I think that's why they needed me, because I could bring some of that. And all the actors before me could bring that – it's just that because it'd been quiet for so long, I think it needed a little bit of weight and credibility in a sense. And I'd done a lot of that with things like *Our Friends in the North* and *Cracker* and Derek Bentley [in] *Let Him Have It, Shallow Grave...*"

For his audio comeback for Big Finish, the Ninth Doctor has largely broken free from those shackles. "At the moment, he's free of his angst," Christopher continued. "And [he's] questing, and enthusiastic, and comedic, and loving, but who knows, further down the line, if we want to go to a darker tone, that's a possibility."

ACKNOWLEDGMENTS

Thank you to my family and friends, for all your support.

Thanks to Shaun, Andy and Will, similarly for supporting my work but also for giving me this opportunity, for suggesting I turn my *Brigadier: Declassified* contribution into a full book, for going along with my mad suggestions, and for superb editing.

Maisie Martin inadvertently gave me the idea for the *Turn Left* approach, Rob Murlis checked through some controversial passages to make sure Twitter wouldn't lynch me, Paul Simpson was supportive throughout the process, Steve Berry gave me the chance to interview the Ninth Doctor himself, and Colin Burden advised on technical issues.

Thank you to everyone I've interviewed in the past whose quotes I've scattered throughout, including Ian Atkins, Ben Badgett, Anthony Dry, Matt Smith, Christopher Eccleston, and Mark Strickson.

And of course to those who I've spoken to for *100 Objects*: Nick Abadzis, Jonathan Appleton, James Baldock, Colin Brockhurst, Christian Cawley, Frank Danes, Simon Danes, Gareth Kavanagh, Rick Lundeen, Peter Shaw, and James Whittington.

And finally, thanks to you, dear reader, for taking a chance on my silly little book. As an extra treat (and I use the term very loosely), see if you can find every *Doctor Who* serial title. I've included them all in this tome. Except *The Family of Blood*. No idea how I'd get that in anywhere.

KKLAK! THE DOCTOR WHO ART OF CHRIS ACHILLÉOS

Kklak!: The Doctor Who Art of Chris Achilléos covers for the official Target novelisations, which began in the early '70s, defined a generation's image of the Doctor and his adventures – particularly after the show disappeared from British screens in the late '80s.

Lavishly detailed, with psychedelic overtones and an unapologetically pulpy sensibility, these covers perfectly captured the eccentric appeal of the classic series.

Kklak!: The Doctor Who Art of Chris Achilléos collects the entirety of Achilléos' *Doctor Who* artwork in chronological order, along with commentary from Achilléos himself (as well as some fans) – presenting the definitive guide to his seminal work. The book also includes a small contribution from twelfth Doctor Peter Capaldi and a foreword from Achilléos' long-time friend and collaborator, the late Terrance Dicks.

Hello, old friend. And here we are. You and me, on the last page.

101. A Duvet.

The sunlight is stunning and warm on the child's eyelids. They slowly open their eyes. Welcome back to the world. Whatever came before has drifted away.

The youngster pushes sleep from their eyes, trying to recall what the night had delivered. They waft the duvet back – a glimpse of its cover, featuring a Dalek, Slitheen, and Moxx of Balhoon, momentarily reawakening visions of the nighttime.

The dream. The dream was about *Doctor Who*. It's 2005, and everything old is new again. Weird: the… *Shawcraft*, was it? Yes, the SS *Shawcraft* – it contained bits from across *Doctor Who*, past, present, and *future*. Flashes forwards and backwards in time. And that's okay, because time travel has always been possible in dreams.

But that dream is fading in the light. The youngster gets up, gets dressed, and runs out to greet the morning. Their days are filled with triumph and heartbreak and boredom and laughter and cutting toenails; their nights are filled with anything that ever happened or ever will.